PRAISE FOR THE NOVELS OF WENDY WAX

"[A] sparkling, deeply satisfying tale."
—*New York Times* bestselling author, Karen White

"Wax offers her trademark form of fiction, the beach read with substance." —*Booklist*

"Wax really knows how to make a cast of characters come alive . . . [She] infuses each chapter with enough drama, laughter, family angst, and friendship to keep readers greedily turning pages until the end." —RT Book Reviews

"This season's perfect beach read!" —Single Titles

"A tribute to the transformative power of female friendship, and reading Wendy Wax is like discovering a witty, wise, and wonderful new friend."
—Claire Cook, *New York Times* bestselling author of *Must Love Dogs* and *Time Flies*

"If you're a sucker for plucky women who rise to the occasion, this is for you." —*USA Today*

"Just the right amount of suspense and drama for a beach read."
—*Publishers Weekly*

"[A] loving tribute to friendship and the power of the female spirit."
—*Las Vegas Review-Journal*

"Beautifully written and constructed by an author who evidently knows what she is doing . . . One fantastic read." —Book Binge

"[A] lovely story that recognizes the power of the female spirit, while being fun, emotional, and a little romantic."
—Fresh Fiction

"Funny, heartbreaking, romantic, and so much more . . . Just delightful!" —The Best Reviews

"Wax's Florida titles . . . are terrific for lovers of women's fiction and family drama, especially if you enjoy a touch of suspense and romance." —*Library Journal Express*

# BEST BEACH EVER

## WENDY WAX

BERKLEY
NEW YORK

BERKLEY
An imprint of Penguin Random House LLC
375 Hudson Street, New York, New York 10014

Library of Congress Cataloging-in-Publication Data

Names: Wax, Wendy, author.
Title: Best beach ever / Wendy Wax.
Description: First Edition. | New York : Berkley, 2018.
Identifiers: LCCN 2017055517| ISBN 9780399584411 (paperback) |
ISBN 9780399584428 (ebook)
Subjects: LCSH: Female friendship—Fiction. | BISAC: FICTION / Contemporary
Women. | FICTION / Romance / Contemporary. | FICTION / Humorous.
Classification: LCC PS3623.A893 B47 2018 | DDC 813/.6—dc23 LC record available at
https://lccn.loc.gov/2017055517

First Edition: May 2018

Printed in the United States of America
1   3   5   7   9   10   8   6   4   2

Cover design by Rita Frangie
*Beach huts* © by Andrew Demic/Getty Images
Book design by Kristin del Rosario

# ACKNOWLEDGMENTS

Each book leads in new directions and presents opportunities to learn and explore new things. The Internet is great, but for me talking to people willing to explain what they do—and why—is even better.

This time out I'd like to say thank you to First Assistant Director Bobby Bastarache, who shared his time, insights, and vast experience in the world of film to help me bring this part of the story to life. Thanks also go to Gary Kaufman, GK Associates for his expertise in forensic accounting and for loaning me his name, to Hugh T. Moody, CIMA for discussing money and its management and to attorney Deborah W. Young, my brother Barry Wax, and Corporal H. Glenn Finley of the Pinellas County Sheriff's Office for their help with the legal aspects of the story. Whitney Manns of WM Wardrobe Consulting "dressed" Maddie and others.

Though I always try to get things "right" this is a work of fiction and sometimes liberties are taken.

I'm overdue in thanking longtime friends Ingrid Jacobus and Justine Fine who are always willing to answer questions about St. Petersburg and Islamorada, respectively. The Ten Beach Road series would not be what it is without them.

As always, huge thanks go to BFFs and critique partners Susan Crandall and Karen White. I'm pretty sure I've said this before, usually after wine, but I hope I never find out what it feels like to write a book without them an email, text, or conference call away.

I also want to thank all of you who've read and shared in my characters' journeys. You're the best.

To my husband John who keeps asking why, after writing so many novels it hasn't gotten any easier, I can only say, I love you, but I'm going to have to get back to you on that.

Many people will walk in and out of your life, but only true friends will leave footprints in your heart.

—ELEANOR ROOSEVELT

# One

Nicole Grant Giraldi stood in front of a far-too-full-length mirror that hung on a wall of the too-small cottage where she, her husband special agent Joe Giraldi, and their twin daughters currently lived. It exposed two primary reasons women were not designed to give birth at forty-seven: lack of elasticity and surplus gravity. She closed one eye and shifted slightly, but the expanse of flesh did not become easier to contemplate.

Despite all of her fears and doubts, the body she was staring at had performed admirably. It had adapted and stretched to accommodate Sofia and Gemma. Against great odds, it had carried them full term, propelled them into the world nine months ago, and then provided sustenance. What it had not done was snap back into anything that resembled its previous shape.

Her eyes slid away. She forced them back. It was time to accept reality. Her breasts hung lower than seemed anatomically possible. Blue veins streaked across them, no doubt to match the ones that now crisscrossed the legs she'd once been proud of. Stretch marks cut across the stomach that jiggled as she turned. Although she knew it was a mistake, she looked at her rear end, which had grown wider and had somehow been injected with cottage cheese. Most likely while she'd been sleeping. Or confined to bed rest.

"Are you ready?" Joe called.

She sighed and turned her back on the mirror as she wriggled into a jogging bra, slipped her arms into a T-shirt, then began to pull the too-tight spandex up over her thighs. "Almost!"

"I'm going to put the girls in the stroller. We'll be outside."

Nikki tied her hair back into a low ponytail, donned a lightweight running jacket, and laced up her shoes. Careful not to look at herself again, she left the bedroom and made it through the tiny cottage in a matter of seconds.

It was the second day of January. On the west coast of central Florida, that meant a vivid blue sky, butter yellow sun, and a cool salt breeze. She breathed in the crisp air as she stepped onto the concrete path that bisected the Sunshine Hotel property and nearly stumbled at the sight of Joe and the girls waiting for her.

*Were they really all hers?*

Tamping down a swell of emotion, she moved toward the stroller taking in the pink and white knit hats neatly tied beneath their chins and the streaks of sunscreen slathered over their cheeks. Sofia had her father's dark hair, sparkling brown-black eyes, and sunny temperament, while Gemma was auburn haired and green eyed like Nikki. Where Gemma's oversize lungs and the will to use them had come from was still under debate.

"All present, recently diapered, and accounted for. Requesting permission to move out." Joe shot her a wink and saluted smartly.

Though he was closing in on fifty, Joe remained broad shouldered and hard bodied with a chiseled face and piercing dark eyes that too often saw right through her, a skill she blamed on his FBI training. They'd met when he'd used her to help him catch her younger brother, Malcolm Dyer, whose three-hundred-million-dollar Ponzi scheme had left Nikki and then-strangers Madeline Singer and Avery Lawford with nothing but shared ownership of Bella Flora, a 1920s Mediterranean Revival–style mansion at the south end of the beach.

She saluted back and fell into step beside him. A few u.. down they passed the two-bedroom cottage that Madeline Singer and her daughter, Kyra, and grandson, Dustin, had just moved into.

"It'll be great having Maddie here, but it's so strange to think of someone else living in Bella Flora," Nikki said, thinking of the house they'd brought back from the brink of ruin and that had done the same for them. After they'd first renovated Bella Flora, Dustin's famous father, mega movie star Daniel Deranian, had bought it for Dustin and Kyra. It had become home to all of them when they'd needed one most, but Kyra had been forced to rent it out.

"Yeah," Joe agreed as they wheeled past Bitsy Baynard's one-bedroom, which the former heiress had taken in lieu of repayment for the money she'd put into their now-defunct TV show. "When is Bitsy coming back?"

"I don't know. She said she was going to stay in Palm Beach until she found someone who knew something about where Bertie is hiding." Nikki grimaced. In her former life as an A-list matchmaker, Nikki had brought Bitsy, heiress to a timber fortune, and her husband together and had counted them as one of her biggest successes. Right up until last January when Bertie disappeared with Bitsy's fortune and an exotic dancer who was pregnant with his child.

When the walkway split they wheeled the stroller toward the low-slung main building, a midcentury gem that they'd renovated for what they'd hoped would be a new season of their TV show, *Do Over.* The sound of voices and the scrape of furniture reached them from the new rooftop deck, where tables and chairs were being set up. The pool area was quiet. The lifeguard would take his place on the retro lifeguard stand at noon when temperatures had risen and the rooftop grill started cranking out hot dogs and hamburgers.

By the time they wheeled through the opening in the low

pink wall and onto the beach, Nikki was feeling slightly winded. Joe was not. Despite the weak morning sun and the breeze off the gulf, he pulled off his T-shirt and tucked one end into the waistband of his running shorts. His chest and abs were hard, his arms and legs muscled. Dark hair smattered with gray dusted his chest and arrowed downward. She considered his body with an unhealthy mixture of admiration and jealousy. And a devout wish that men carried the babies in our species.

"You know we don't have to run," he said when they reached the hard-packed sand near the water's edge. "It's a gorgeous day just to be outside."

"Definitely gorgeous," she agreed, admiring the dip and dance of sunlight on the slightly choppy water's surface. A windsurfer skimmed by as she began to stretch, his brightly colored sail bulging with wind. "But I know you're ready for a run." She had to hold on to his shoulder as she reached back to grab her foot and stretch her quads. "And so am I."

"All right." When she'd finished stretching, he flashed her a smile and opened his arms wide, leaving their direction up to her. "Lead the way."

To their right lay the historic Don CeSar Hotel and the northern half of St. Petersburg Beach. In the other direction . . . she shrugged as if it didn't matter, but she could not deny the tug she felt. Without a word she pivoted left and broke into a slow jog, heading toward the southern tip of Pass-a-Grille. And Bella Flora.

Joe turned the stroller and fell in beside her. For a few heady minutes she simply gave herself up to the fresh air, the wash of water on and off the sand, and the caw of gulls wheeling through the sky. But it wasn't long before her breathing grew uneven and her strides became shorter. She flushed with embarrassment when she realized that he had checked his stride to match hers. Her chin went up and she picked up her pace. She'd recently weaned the girls to formula, and while nursing had helped her drop weight, she was going to have to do more than crawl if she ever hoped to get her body back. "You worry about yourself and the girls," she snapped, careful not to huff or puff. "I'll be fine."

"Okay," he said easily. "You're the boss." His movements remained fluid, but she could still feel him holding back. "There's no shame in taking it easy, Nik. And walking is exercise, too. A walk could be nice."

"Right." Surely that wasn't her breathing that sounded so . . . labored. Or her legs that had turned into lead weights. She pinned a smile on her lips and focused her eyes down the beach. She'd run this distance a thousand times. There was no reason she couldn't do it now. She *would* do it now. And if she felt a little uncomfortable, well, no one had ever died from discomfort. Otherwise she would have expired early in her pregnancy. She picked up her pace another notch and ignored Joe's look of concern. She was not going to whine or complain, and she most definitely wasn't going to walk. Breathing was overrated. And it was nothing compared to pride.

• • •

Shortly before her life imploded, Madeline Singer had decided to refurbish it slightly. Her nest had emptied and she'd hit the big five-oh. The time seemed right to take down a few metaphorical walls. Raise a few ceilings. Open things up.

What she'd envisioned as a minor renovation turned into a total gut job when her husband lost everything in Malcolm Dyer's Ponzi scheme. The life she'd only planned to tweak got demoed, blown to bits before her eyes.

There were casualties. Somehow she managed to drag her family clear of the rubble. Ultimately, those who were still standing constructed a new life, one that bore almost no resemblance to the original. Not exactly a "do over," but a chance to do and be more.

Today was January second. The first usable day of a brand-new year and once again her life was under construction. Yesterday she, her daughter Kyra, her four-year-old grandson Dustin, and Dustin's new puppy Max had moved out of Bella Flora into the newly renovated two-bedroom cottage she stood in now. Soon Kyra and Dustin would go to Orlando so that Dustin could play his father's son in Daniel Deranian's directorial debut. At which point Maddie would be completely on her own. A fact that both excited and terrified her.

In the kitchen, the lack of counter space forced her to work more efficiently, and in less than fifteen minutes she'd assembled an egg soufflé, slid it into the oven, and set the timer. The soufflé was of the never-fail variety, guaranteed to pouf in exactly sixty minutes. Unlike life, which came with no guarantees and often "poufed" when you least expected it.

Soon the scent of melting cheese teased her nostrils and began to fill the air. She pictured it wafting down the short hallway to the second bedroom, slipping under the closed door, and crooking its finger. While she waited she put on a pot of coffee and puttered, unpacking and organizing the exceedingly compact kitchen. The cottage felt like a dollhouse after the castle-like Bella Flora, but Maddie felt oddly content. She lacked space and income and her résumé consisted only of a brief and excruciatingly public stint on their renovation-turned-reality-TV-show. But the cottage belonged to her. And so did the new life that lay ahead.

A text dinged in and the face of William Hightower, the rock icon formerly known as William the Wild, appeared on the screen. A reminder that the life that lay ahead included a relationship with a man whose poster had once hung on her teenaged bedroom wall.

*Mornin' Maddie-fan. Hud and the fish send their regards.*

*Ha.* She had discovered early on that the fish that lived in the Florida Keys had a nasty sense of humor. Despite Will's efforts to teach her how to fly cast, she was no threat to the fish population and they knew it. *Catch anything yet?*

*Nope. But the sun's on the rise and it's so beautiful down here this morning I'm not sure I care.*

*Liar.* Will loved to be out on the flats around Islamorada above all things, but he did not like to be bested by anything covered with scales.

*True. And Hud's making me look bad. He and the fish want to know when you're coming to visit.*

*They're just looking for entertainment.* Hudson Power, Will's longtime friend and fishing guide, had taught her to drive a boat and been very patient with her ineptness at fly casting. But she was fairly certain she'd heard the fish laughing at her on more than one occasion.

*True,* he texted again. *But I miss you madly, Maddie-fan.*

A warm glow formed in her chest and radiated outward. She did not understand why Will, who had finally won his own personal war on drugs and was once again topping the charts, had chosen her when he could have his pick of younger, prettier, and undoubtedly firmer women, but she'd finally stopped asking. Plus, it was hard to argue with his physical reaction to her. Her cheeks flamed at the thought, and despite her two left thumbs, she was very glad they were texting and not FaceTiming.

*When are you coming down to Mermaid Point?* They had met when their former network sent Madeline, Kyra, Avery Lawford, and Nicole Grant down to the Keys with instructions to turn Will's private island into a bed-and-breakfast, an idea he did not appreciate in the least.

*As soon as Kyra and Dustin leave for Orlando.* Kyra, who'd met and fallen for the megastar on her very first film set, was not at all happy about the upcoming film. Or having to spend six weeks on set with Daniel and his equally famous movie star wife, Tonja Kay.

*Can u tell me when?*

*In 2 weeks.*

*That's 2 weeks 2 long.*

She was still smiling when she heard the first sounds of movement from the second bedroom. By the time she'd finished setting the dinette table, pulled the orange juice out of the refrigerator, and cut up a bowl of fruit, there were only a few minutes left on the timer. A woof and the shake of a dog's collar were followed by the creak of a bed frame. Despite the early hour, the soufflé had worked its magic. She poured herself a cup of freshly brewed coffee.

Today was the first day of the rest of her life. Now all she had to do was figure out what to *do* with it.

• • •

In the small second bedroom of her mother's cottage, Kyra woke to the scents of coffee and egg soufflé.

Dustin slept on the railed bunk bed above her. Max, the Great Dane puppy his father had unexpectedly and unaccountably given him for Christmas, stood next to her, whimpering. She did not want to get up, but she definitely didn't want to clean up another accident.

Max nudged her with his wet, cold nose and she threw off her sheets.

Today was not a good day. Today was the day a stranger would move into Bella Flora.

Max began to circle and sniff the floor. Kyra sat up, careful not to hit her head on the upper bunk. She was debating whether she could make a run to the bathroom when Max's whimper turned more urgent. "Got it. Hold on!" She grabbed him and raced for the door, holding him out in front of her.

"Good morning." Maddie moved to throw open the door.

"Um-hmmm." She sniffed appreciatively as they passed the oven that held the soufflé. Madeline Singer was the mother everyone deserved but didn't necessarily get. She'd created a home everywhere they'd landed, from the initially uninhabitable Bella

Flora to Max Golden's neglected Deco home in South Beach to the rickety houseboat tethered to William Hightower's dock.

While Max anointed the grass and the nearest bush, she lifted her cell phone and roused it. The first six months' rent had been released from escrow and deposited into her account, but the sight of all those zeros didn't make her anywhere near as happy as it should have. It meant there was not going to be a last-minute reprieve. The tenant would move in today. For the next six months he, she, or they would have the run of Bella Flora and the option to stay on for six more months after that.

Which meant she and Dustin and Max could be sharing a bedroom in Maddie's cottage for an entire year while a stranger lived in the house they'd poured their hearts and souls into and that was "home" in every way that mattered. She'd been a fool to believe that everything would somehow magically work out when she'd taken the loan to finance the Sunshine Hotel renovation and their own version of *Do Over*.

Max woofed happily as she pulled a plastic bag from her pocket, picked up his "offering," then dropped it in a nearby trashcan. She'd changed Dustin's diapers easily enough but she'd known the day would come when he could toilet on his own. Unless they moved into a rural setting, Max was never going to be able to dispose of his own droppings. She did not want to think about how big Max was going to get, or what size plastic bag he would one day require.

Inside, she found Dustin sitting at the dinette drinking a cup of orange juice and chatting with his favorite person. That person held out a cup of coffee.

"Thanks, Mom." She swallowed a long sip, let the warmth slide down her throat. "The money's in my account."

"That's a good thing, Kyra. That will definitely take some of the pressure off."

"I know. But . . ."

"Come eat." Three plates containing soufflé, buttered toast, and fresh fruit were on their way to the table. Within minutes Kyra was seated. She picked up her fork, but her appetite had fled.

"Kyra, you need to let go of the worry. It's done. Bella Flora's only on loan. She still belongs to Dustin and you. Emotionally she'll always belong to all of us."

"It's just . . ." Kyra took a bite of soufflé, but her usual bliss over the cheesy wonderfulness was missing. She needed to see the tenant for herself. Needed to make sure he wasn't some Attila the Hun of tenants, bent on destruction. Or someone fronting for Daniel Deranian and Tonja Kay for some nefarious reason she'd yet to figure out. She took another bite of soufflé then washed it down with another long pull of coffee.

John Franklin, the Realtor, was meeting the tenant at eleven to hand over the key. She stole a glance at her phone. It was early. There would be plenty of time after a leisurely breakfast to shower and dress and discover that she'd left something at Bella Flora that they couldn't possibly be expected to live without.

. . .

Avery Lawford did not want to get out of bed. Not now. Not ever. She clutched the pillow more tightly to her chest and kept her eyes shut. It would take a crowbar to pry them open. A tow truck to move her.

Something warm passed under her nose. It smelled dark and steamy before it moved just out of range then back again. The lovely fog of sleep that had enveloped her began to dissipate. She closed her eyes tighter and wished she could shut her nostrils, but Avery braked for coffee. She drank it for the protection of others and had the T-shirt to prove it. She burrowed deeper into the cocoon of blankets but her nose betrayed her.

*No.* She would not be ruled by coffee. She was stronger than coffee. The smell retreated. She'd begun to relax back into sleep when the crinkle of paper sounded near her ear. There was movement. A new scent joined the first. She sniffed, a reflex, nothing more. She was only human. *Sugar.*

"Avery?" Chase Hardin's voice was warm and seductive.

"There's nothing you could say or do that would make me get out of this bed right now."

"Nothing?" The mattress dipped as he sat on its edge. "You mean you don't want this Dunkin' Donuts coffee or glazed donuts?" He waved each item as he mentioned it. His voice grew muffled as he took a bite of donut and chewed appreciatively. "Ummm, that's good." He bent over and kissed her with warm lips sticky with sugar. This was what came of sleeping with a man who knew your weaknesses.

She opened her eyes. A large foam cup of coffee sat on the nightstand.

Chase finished off the donut, licked his fingers, and grinned. "I don't remember the last time I spent almost two days in bed." His blue eyes glittered. Dark stubble covered his cheeks, and his hair stuck up in a variety of directions. "I thought we needed sustenance." When she didn't make a move, he drew a donut out of the bag and placed it on a napkin next to the cup of coffee.

She'd known Chase since childhood, much of which she'd spent crushing on him. They'd grown up on their fathers' construction sites, but had gone their separate ways. She'd become an architect. He'd taken over Hardin Morgan Construction. He'd been a royal pain in the ass the whole time he was helping them renovate Bella Flora. And then one day he wasn't.

"Your cupboards are bare," he said. "A man cannot live on sex and Cheez Doodles alone."

"This woman can," she replied, stung that he would disparage the snack that in the darkest of times could help make life worth living.

"I give that donut and coffee about fifteen seconds." He looked at her knowingly.

She wanted to argue. And she really, really wanted to be asleep. She could resist if she wanted to. She could. But what would be gained by rejecting a warm, gooey glazed donut and a steaming cup of coffee?

"If you were looking at me like you're looking at that donut right now, we could spend another two days in bed." He stretched and scratched his chest. "I owe my sister big-time for having Dad and the boys up for the week." His blue eyes turned dark and steamy. They were a magnetic force. The siren call of coffee and donuts grew softer as a shiver of anticipation snaked up her spine. They'd been in bed since New Year's Eve and to-day was . . . "Oh, no!" She sat up.

"What?"

"What day is it?" She ran her hands under the covers but her phone wasn't there.

"It's Monday."

"Are you sure?"

He nodded without hesitation.

"But that means it's . . ."

"January second," they said simultaneously. But it was just a date on the calendar to him. She began scooting out of bed.

"What time is it?"

He glanced down at his watch. "It's . . . ten forty."

She took one bite of donut, swallowed it whole, and grabbed the cup of coffee. "How far away did you park?" She moved to-ward the bathroom, very glad the cottage was so tiny.

"Hmmm?"

"You didn't park here at the Sunshine, right? I told you I didn't want anyone to know that we're . . . you know . . ." She nodded toward the bed, which looked like it had been struck by a hurricane. Or lifted by a tornado and tossed around for a night or two.

"Everybody knows, Avery. There's no reason to keep it a se-cret that we're back together."

"But we're not back together." She raced into the bathroom, turned on the shower, raced back to retrieve the donut. "Having sex doesn't mean we're back together. It just means we're still attracted to each other and spent a couple of days in bed to celebrate the New Year."

Their relationship had foundered during his youngest son Jason's meltdown and rebellion. Jason was doing better now and repeating his senior year of high school, but Avery could still remember exactly how it felt to be pushed away when things got rough. Other than Maddie, Nikki, and Kyra, the Hardins were the closest thing to family she had, yet Chase had completely shut her out when Jason went off the rails. Out of the family and out of Hardin Morgan Construction.

That they were dating again was due to his abject apologies and powers of persuasion. She enjoyed his company and the sex was spectacular, but she didn't intend to open herself up to that kind of hurt again any time in this millennium. And she was not prepared to tie her career to his.

She devoured the donut in a few hungry bites then stepped into the now-hot shower. Ten minutes later she was running a comb through her short blond hair and pulling on a pair of jeans and a *Do Over* T-shirt. She could almost hear her mother's ghost hovering above her and sighing over her lack of makeup, but she was a wash-and-wear kind of girl. And though she no longer hid the Dolly Parton–size bust that was too large for her height in oversize clothes, she had not yet reconciled to the big blue eyes and Kewpie doll features that caused strangers to deduct IQ points before she even opened her mouth. "Are you staying here or coming with me?"

"Where are we going?" He grabbed the bag of donuts.

"Out."

"Out where?"

She grabbed the keys to the Mini Cooper and headed for the front door.

· · ·

Nikki and Joe sat at their favorite picnic table at the Paradise Grille overlooking the white sand beach and the gulf that it bounded. A stream of beachgoers passed in both directions. A jovial game of corn hole played out in the soft sand nearby.

Sofia and Gemma snoozed happily in the stroller, their faces smeared with the remnants of a scrambled egg breakfast. Seagulls eyed the crumbs left on their plates but so far no dive-bombing had occurred.

"God, they're adorable when they're asleep," Nikki said, looking at the girls' angelic faces. "Not that they aren't adorable when they're awake, but . . ."

". . . you're too busy trying to keep them happy to notice."

Nikki looked at Joe. "You don't even bat an eyelash when Gemma goes on a screaming jag. Or one of them projectile vomits all over you."

"I may have ended up in the financial crimes unit, but I do have hostage negotiation training," he said wryly. "I know how to look like I'm not panicking even when I'm scared shit-less."

"So when do you think you'll be able to actually start nego-tiating with them?"

"Well, we know from personal experience that it doesn't work on pregnant women," he said. "I can't remember convinc-ing you of a single thing while you were carrying them. So while I don't know that there's a lower age limit, it's clear ratio-nal thought is necessary. And probably the ability to speak or at least understand and process language are, too."

"Great." Nikki slumped. Every morning she vowed this would be the day that she'd become competent and unharried. The kind of mother who loved her children so much that she never resented the endless demands that created the near-constant state of exhaustion.

"I've got another ten days or so and then I'm going to have to start traveling again."

Her heart sank further. "Oh?"

"Yeah. Which is why I really think we ought to hire someone to help you."

"No. I'm their mother. Taking care of them is my job." Not a job she'd ever imagined for herself. But it wasn't one you could resign from.

"Nik, they're too much for the two of us a lot of the time. I can't leave you alone."

"I won't be alone," she said, trying to keep the panic out of her eyes and her voice. "Maddie will help. And . . . Avery and Bitsy will be nearby." Neither of them mentioned that Bitsy had fallen down on the job the night Nikki went into labor.

"Kyra and Dustin will be leaving for Orlando in two weeks. And Maddie won't have a reason to stay here. She'll be free to travel. Or spend time with Will. Or whatever she feels like. And Avery and Bitsy have no experience with children and aren't looking to acquire it. Plus, they'll both be working."

"I can do it," she said. "End of conversation."

"But, Nikki. I . . ." His face smoothed out. She saw him relax his features, his shoulders. Hostage negotiation training, her ass. "Ready to head back?"

She'd barely made it this far. In fact, about halfway there she'd been doing more of a brisk walk than a slow jog.

"I was thinking maybe I could run back to the cottage and come pick you all up in the car." He looked at her face. "You know, in case you'd like to just chill here for a while."

"Don't think I can make it back?" she challenged though she wasn't totally sure she could. She only knew she was not going to appear too tired or too overwhelmed or too anything in front of him.

"No, of course not. I just thought you might want to get back more quickly. It's getting close to eleven."

"Eleven?" She sat up.

"Yes."

"I wouldn't mind walking a little farther. There's really no rush to get back, is there?"

"No."

"The girls love the jetty. And the fishermen on the dock."

He gave her a long look. "Sure. Why not?" He busied himself gathering the paper plates and cups and was gentleman enough not to say anything when she took her time getting to her feet.

• • •

"That was one of your best egg soufflés ever, Mom. Right, Dustin?" Freshly showered and dressed, Kyra strode back into the living room/kitchen, where Dustin stood on a stool "helping" his grandmother wash the dishes.

"D'licious," he agreed, waving his hands, which were encased in a pair of too-large rubber gloves. Max was under the table licking up the bits of egg that surrounded Dustin's chair.

"What do we say to Grandma?" Kyra asked Dustin as she stole a glance at the clock on the wall then turned her gaze to the coffee table, where the car keys typically ended up.

"Thank you, Geema!" Dustin crowed.

"You're both very welcome," Maddie said, hiding her smile at the speed with which Kyra located and pocketed the car keys.

"If you don't mind keeping an eye on Dustin, I . . . I have a couple of things I need to take care of." Kyra didn't quite meet her eye as she laid a kiss on Dustin's head and moved toward the door.

"Things?" Maddie asked.

"Umm-hmmm."

"Dustin wanna do things, too!" Dustin clambered down from the step and held out his arms. Maddie peeled the large yellow gloves from beneath his armpits and down his arms.

Kyra checked the clock again.

"It's ten fifty," Maddie said. "Where exactly are you going?"

"Oh, you know. Here and there. Not far," Kyra babbled. "I won't be gone long."

"Kyra . . ."

Her daughter looked up as if she'd been caught with her hand in the cookie jar.

"I really don't think this is a good idea."

"I . . . don't know what you're talking about," Kyra protested.

"It would be better to just stay away," Maddie said gently.

"Stay away from what?" Kyra adopted an expression of surprised confusion, but any mother worth her salt could read a daughter's face like a road map. It would take more than feigned indignation to make Maddie believe she was headed out to run errands.

"Kyra."

"Fine." Kyra sighed. "It's not like there's any chance of keeping a secret when we're living on top of each other like this anyway."

"If you're going, we're going with you." She picked up the leash and attached it to Max's collar then handed Dustin his sweatshirt.

"Where we going, Geema?" Dustin asked as his mother pulled open the cottage door.

"If I'm not mistaken, I think we're going to Bella Flora to get a look at the person who's going to live there."

# Two

Kyra breathed deeply as she drove south on the narrow two-lane road, but each breath carried its own little dart of panic that sent fear of who and what she'd find at Bella Flora shooting through her. She turned onto Gulf Way, her thoughts jumbled and her gaze slightly unfocused. The familiar scenery rippled and shimmered before her eyes, giving the mom-and-pop hotels and expensive new homes on her left and the low wall and crossovers that bordered the beach on her right a fun-house vibe.

The blocks were short and the avenues that stretched from the bay to the gulf were even shorter. At the Hurricane restaurant her foot eased further off the gas pedal so that the minivan passed Eighth Avenue, Pass-a-Grille's main street, at what could only be called a crawl. The closer they got to Bella Flora the slower she drove and the sharper and more pointed the panic became. *What if the tenant was Daniel Deranian or Tonja Kay or one of their emissaries? What if he/she/they were trust fund babies with no respect for other people's property? What if they looked unstable or had a herd of children who would abuse Dustin's mini–Bella Flora playhouse?* The number of things the new tenant would be free to do in and/or to their home bombarded her. *How could she let some stranger sleep in her bed? Hang their clothes in her closet? Lie on their couch? Mix drinks in the Casbah Lounge?* How on earth could she have let this happen?

"We can still turn around," Maddie said. "It's not too late." She hesitated. "No one will ever know we even thought about doing this."

But though Kyra was driving as slowly as any newly arrived retiree, Bella Flora's gravitational pull was simply too strong to resist. So was Kyra's urge to protect her even though it was far too late for that.

They passed a couple pushing a jogging stroller. That couple was Nikki and Joe. So much for a lack of witnesses.

And then she came face-to-face with Bella Flora. Rising out of the low-walled garden. A pale pink wedding cake of a house with banks of windows framed in white icing trim and bell towers that topped a multi-angled barrel-tile roof and jutted up into the brilliant blue sky.

"Are we going home?" Dustin asked uncertainly.

God, she wished they were only coming home from a trip to the grocery store or some other mundane errand and not about to watch some stranger move in. Eyes blurred with tears, Kyra pulled into a parking space. The blue Mini Cooper in the next spot belonged to Avery Lawford.

Max gave a happy woof as they joined Avery and Chase on the sidewalk. A minute later Nikki and Joe arrived, the twins sound asleep in the stroller. Kyra was trying to decide who looked the most embarrassed when a lone figure walked up the path from the jetty. His Gatsby-style pants fluttering lightly in the breeze, and wearing a mint green vest buttoned over an oxford shirt, Ray Flamingo, former designer to the stars, walked up to them. "Beautiful day, isn't it?"

"Don't even try to pretend you were just out for a stroll," Avery said.

"Who me?" Hands in pockets, Ray turned to face Bella Flora. "I didn't realize a house could send a distress signal until today."

"You know that whoever is renting Bella Flora has spent a

lot of money to live in her," Joe said gently. "There's every reason to expect that person will treat her well."

John Franklin's Cadillac pulled up in front of Bella Flora at exactly eleven A.M. The car was a classic, like its octogenarian owner and driver. Kyra's father, Steve, who now worked at Franklin Realty and had been responsible for finding Bella Flora's mystery tenant, was with him.

With Max straining against his leash they trundled over to meet them.

"You all look a little more like a lynch mob than a welcoming committee." John Franklin had a ruff of white hair around an otherwise bald scalp and a long face dominated by the droopy brown eyes of a basset hound. Those eyes looked worried as his hands tightened on the handle of his cane. "Is there a problem?"

"That depends," Kyra said.

"On what?" her father asked.

"On whether the tenants look as if they can fully appreciate their luck in getting to walk through Bella Flora's front doors. If they don't, I might need help stringing them up from the reclinata palm out back."

Chase and Joe laughed. Maddie, Avery, and Nikki exchanged worried glances.

"We don't necessarily have to deliver a welcome basket," Ray said in a conciliatory tone. "But I don't think we need to be contemplating violence, either."

"Neither do I," Maddie said. "In fact, I'm not altogether sure we should be here." As usual her mother seemed intent on keeping the peace. And preventing Kyra from committing a stupid act. If only that had happened before Kyra took the loan out against Bella Flora. "But clearly we're all curious to see who's moving in. So I think we should at least *act* like a welcoming committee. We can also let them know that we're nearby if they have any questions about the workings or idiosyncrasies of the house."

They milled relatively quietly until a car turned off of Pass-a-Grille Way onto Beach Road, passed the Cottage Inn, and pulled into Bella Flora's brick driveway. The car was low, sleek, and silver with tinted windows that revealed little.

They inched closer, stopping just short of the garden wall as John and her father walked up the driveway. Kyra wasn't the only one holding her breath as the driver got out of the car. Through the palms and tall bushes she could see only slices at a time; a lone male head of blond hair atop a body that seemed tall and well formed. There was a flash of blue denim and some kind of dark jacket or blazer. He moved with a confident stride that Kyra chalked up to arrogance. Did that mean he would be careless with other people's possessions? Or did it mean that he was used to nice things and would take care of theirs?

She moved in an attempt to get a better look, but everyone was jockeying for position. Between the bushes and trees, John and her father's backs were the only things clearly visible. Her father froze briefly. John Franklin's normally hunched shoulders went stiff. Murmurs of what sounded like surprise reached them.

Heart pounding, knees pressed against the concrete, she leaned over the garden wall in an attempt to see more. The tenant cocked his head, and she sensed him peering between John and her father as if looking for something or someone. Dustin dropped her hand and moved toward the driveway. A prickle of unease raised the hair on the back of her neck, but she knew from the blond head and build that it wasn't Daniel Deranian. Was it another movie star? A famous athlete or musician?

"Lookit, Mommy. Lookit who's here!" Dustin shouted as he ran up the driveway.

Kyra detached herself from the wall and the group to race after him. The breath caught in her throat as the tenant stepped around the two Realtors and reached down to pick up Dustin. She blinked rapidly, trying to make sense of what she was seeing.

Troy Matthews, network cameraman, personal nemesis, and perpetual pain in the ass, stared down at her. A satisfied smile spread across his smug, freshly shaven face.

"What are you doing here?" she asked through gritted teeth as the rest of the group moved up behind her.

"Moving in," he said easily.

"You?" She didn't understand. She'd never seen him in anything but scruffy jeans and T-shirts. His hair had always been shaggy and his annoyingly handsome face had generally been covered in stubble. When she'd not so politely asked him to take a hike almost a year ago, he'd left in a beat-up car. If he weren't currently holding the key to Bella Flora, she would have bet money that he'd stolen the Porsche he'd arrived in. "You paid two hundred and fifty thousand dollars up front to rent Bella Flora?"

"Yep."

She could barely breathe. Her brain could not seem to process what was happening. Apparently the group behind her was having the same problem, because they remained silent. "But why?"

"I really like this stretch of beach, and I needed somewhere quiet to work on a new . . . project." He shrugged as if shelling out a quarter of a million dollars in rental money was nothing more than a hotel night.

Her gaze narrowed as she studied him. In all the years she'd known him, he'd dressed and acted like any other cameraman. Now everything about him shouted money. She sniffed suspiciously, wondering if she'd be able to smell it, but only an agreeably woodsy citrus scent tickled her nostrils. She swallowed. Told herself to remain calm. But it was as if someone had reached up while she wasn't looking and realigned the stars in the sky. "Is this some kind of sick joke?" she demanded. "And what's with the whole stupid cloak-and-dagger thing? Why didn't you tell me?"

He shrugged again but didn't snap back at her. "We didn't

part on the best terms. Would you have said yes if you'd known it was me?"

She glared at him but said nothing.

"Yeah, that's what I thought."

"You need any help with your things?" her father asked, his surprise already giving way to an infuriatingly amiable tone.

"No thanks, I didn't bring much. As I recall Bella Flora's pretty well equipped." He shot her a wink as he set Dustin on his feet and patted Max on the head, which was when she realized that instead of staying out in the pool house as he had before, he'd be taking over the master bedroom. *Her* master bedroom. "Which is a good thing in case I need to exercise the option for the second six months."

"I don't understand," she sputtered in anger, her heart palpitating wildly. "Where did you get the money to do this? How on earth can you afford it?" The last time she'd seen him, he'd been working for room and board and acting as if he didn't have two nickels to rub together.

He shrugged and flashed the shit-eating grin that had always accompanied the taunting eyes. "You can't always judge a book by its cover, Kyra. Not everybody's into flash and trash. Some of us would rather be judged by our actions, not our possessions."

Kyra pulled herself to her full height as heat and adrenaline rushed through her. She felt as if her head might explode at any moment. "There is absolutely nothing in your past behavior that has ever made me see you as anything but a gigantic pimple on the face of humanity." She bit out the words, her anger making her blood begin to boil. "And I don't care how many banks you've robbed or illicit drugs you've sold to get enough money to shove us out of our house. You could be the richest man in the world and you'd still just be a goiter on its butt as far as I'm concerned."

"Kyra, honey. I know this is a surprise to all of us." Maddie turned to Kyra's father. "This *is* a surprise to all of us, isn't it?"

Steve Singer and John Franklin nodded.

"But at least we know Troy loves Bella Flora and will take good care of her." Her mother's tone held a warning note, but Kyra was beyond caring.

"Maddie's right," Avery said. "Troy is way better than a stranger."

"It's true," Nikki added almost apologetically.

Her father and John Franklin stayed mercifully silent.

Troy stayed silent, too, but there was nothing merciful about it. He studied her through narrowed eyes as if she were a bug under a microscope. The fact that his sun-streaked blond hair appeared freshly cut and layered stoked her anger even further.

She was still trying to get herself under control when Chase stepped forward to shake Troy's hand. Joe did the same. Her mother made Troy promise to be sure to let them know if he needed anything.

Their ready acceptance of the man who had always been so judgmental, so quick to expose her every flaw or misstep, sliced through her. With a huff of disgust, Kyra turned on her heel and pushed her way back through the traitorous crowd. She strode toward the minivan not wanting to see Troy fitting the key into the lock and disappearing into Bella Flora.

For the first time, getting away from here and going on location seemed the lesser of evils. Troy Matthews had never been one for quiet solitude and reflection. If she were lucky, he'd get bored hanging out playing lord of the manor before they even got back. There was no way he could want to live there by himself for even six months, let alone a year.

"Oh, Kyra?"

She whirled at the sound of his voice and grimaced at the white-toothed smile he flashed at her.

"Feel free to stop by anytime. After all, *mi casa es su casa.*"

# Three

The year was in its infancy and it already sucked. The suckage had begun on New Year's Eve when Bitsy slipped into her lone remaining evening gown and accompanied her former next-door neighbors, current hosts, and sole remaining friends from her former life, Eleanor and John Wyndham, to a rash of New Year's Eve parties. She'd subjected herself to the possibility of spending the evening as a pariah stranded alone in corners in hopes of learning something about Bertie's whereabouts. Yet in Palm Beach, where gossip was practically an art form, no one seemed to have the smallest scrap of new information about her absent husband. In the end she'd been showered with a deluge of faux sympathy and grilled for intimate details to share with others.

"God," Bitsy groaned when they'd gotten back to the Wyndhams' and John had gone up to bed. "I feel like a bone that's just been gnawed by a whole pack of dogs. And I have absolutely nothing to show for it." Sherlock, the French bulldog that Bertie had also left behind, padded into the foyer and nudged her in greeting.

"This is the first time you've been back since Bertie's vanishing act. You know how things work here when a potential tasty morsel presents itself." Eleanor smiled sadly.

Sherlock snuffled at the sound of his former master's name. Bitsy wasn't sure if it was a snuffle of despair or dismissal.

"At least we didn't run into Alex Binder," Eleanor continued. "He's constantly telling everyone what a perfect fit your home is for him and his new wife. Who is absolutely gorgeous. And young enough to be his granddaughter."

Bitsy sighed with a weariness that had nothing to do with the lateness of the hour, and stroked Sherlock's head. "I'd say it serves Bertie right that the house he lavished so much love and money on belongs to a man he detested. Except I loved that house, too." Bitsy's eyes filled with tears. *Almost as much as she'd loved Bertie.*

"I'm so sorry for everything that's happened, really I am." Eleanor slid her arm around Bitsy's shoulders and led her up the grand staircase. Sherlock followed at their heels. "I think you're brave and marvelous. John and I'll keep our ears open for any mention of Bertie. I promise I'll let you know if either of us hears even a scrap of anything." Her smile was sad but warm. "I hope you know you're welcome here anytime."

"Thanks." Bitsy swiped at the tears that blurred her vision. "That means a lot."

Bitsy hugged Eleanor good night and slipped into the lavish guest bedroom that was double the size of her entire cottage at the Sunshine Hotel. As she slid between the Porthault sheets and closed her eyes, she told herself that her upcoming meeting with her former money manager could provide a clue to Bertrand's whereabouts and maybe even help her regain her fortune. She drifted off to sleep clinging to this possibility and dreamed of Bertie being yanked out of his girlfriend's arms in whichever country they'd been hiding. As he was dragged back in handcuffs, he proclaimed his love for Bitsy and swore that he'd only fled with her assets in order to protect them for her.

She woke feeling hopeful as if her dream portended a silver lining to the dark cloud of her situation. That notion began to dissolve in the early morning light. It evaporated completely in Gene Houghton's office two days later.

"I'm very sorry, Bitsy," her former money manager said in a genuinely apologetic tone. "It's a horrible thing. I'd love to see Bertie caught and punished. No one would blame you for shooting him on sight should you find him."

She'd vowed to find him. Shooting was too good for him. But even if she found him, how would she get the money back?

"We did try to protect you." He looked at her. "But you took Bertie's advice over ours in almost every instance."

This time she didn't point out how well Bertie had handled her money before he stole it. Or how he'd protected her assets from Malcolm Dyer's Ponzi scheme and sidestepped any number of other losses and downturns that other managers, including the man sitting in front of her, had not.

"You refused to ask him to sign a prenup. You insisted that all your accounts be joint. Then you allowed him free rein over a trust with assets exceeding thirty-five million dollars when you made him sole trustee."

Shame heated her skin. She had actually petitioned a judge to do this.

"When the remaining assets were liquidated and the funds wired offshore, we assumed it was with your approval."

"But you didn't check with me. You used to check with me."

"Yes. And in virtually every case you told me that you had complete confidence in your husband's actions on your behalf." He sighed. "If I'd been in town, I have no doubt I would have called you. But he chose the perfect time. He waited until I was out of the country—cell reception is a bit spotty when you're climbing Kilimanjaro—and he demanded that everything be liquidated and the funds be transferred to a Cayman account that had been set up for some time. In fact, he bullied the young woman who handled the actual liquidation orders and transfers. Rained down all over her. The employees in that position sit in a windowless closet-size room and move money around as directed. We are required by law to respond immediately and make the money available within three days." He steepled his hands, rested his chin on them, in half prayer, half condemnation. "We've been over this before."

That had been days after she'd discovered that Bertie and her money were gone. When she'd been in shock, too bruised, too beaten, too panicked to absorb it.

"Is she here now?"

"No. She's no longer with us." His look of discomfort was brief. "She had a bit of a breakdown afterward." He sighed. "If I'd been her and in that situation, I'd probably be in a padded cell myself right now."

Yet here he was nattily dressed and going about his business. Bitsy closed her eyes against the press of tears. She could no longer remember why she'd thought coming back to Palm Beach was a good idea or what she thought she'd achieve. A year had passed and Bertie and her fortune were still gone. Her losses were still her fault. Because she had not protected herself and her fortune as she should have.

She felt Gene's eyes on her and for the millionth time asked herself what others had been asking from the beginning: Had Bertie been working a long con? Had he simply taken his time, building her trust in him over their fifteen-year marriage the same way he built the holdings he planned to steal from her? Had he ever really loved her?

"We provided copies of all the liquidation and transfer orders the moment we were notified that Bertie was not acting on your behalf." And no doubt to protect their asses.

Bitsy nodded numbly. She vaguely remembered large cardboard boxes coming from the firm. But she'd been a basket case, having to get out of her home, handing everything she owned over to the auction house in an attempt to try to pay off some of her massive debt. She'd put the boxes in the Land Rover with her remaining belongings. But she had not had the internal fortitude to open them.

She barely felt Gene's hand on her elbow as he escorted her to the elevator. Nor did she remember crossing the parking lot to her car. She only knew that her heart was too heavy for her chest and her thoughts were weighted with self-doubt and re-criminations as she drove back to the Wyndhams'. She slowed in front of her former home, which up until today she'd been careful not to even look at. Without planning to, she pulled onto the side of the road and stopped just before the gate.

Now she sat and stared at the entrance to the Palm Beach estate that Bertie had fallen in love with on sight and had spent close to five years restoring. Anger and hate coiled tightly inside her as she contemplated the wrought iron Bertie had agonized over and that now kept her out, but so did the ache of loss and the memory of his smile. He'd made her feel cherished, had convinced her that he was in love with her and not her bank account. And she had believed him. Right up until the moment last January when he'd fled, taking her fortune and his pregnant exotic-dancer girlfriend with him.

Her heart thudded as she pictured the child that had most certainly been born. A child that might have been hers if Bertie had ever seemed the least bit interested in fatherhood.

The Land Rover's engine idled roughly, emitting sporadic puffs of exhaust into the crisp morning air. An army of palm trees rose behind the gates and ran along the driveway that curled through the lushly landscaped property to the Palladian villa that both Maddie and Kyra Singer had described as Bella Flora on steroids. Bitsy had taken their home's size and grandeur for granted just as she had the millions of dollars that had been poured into it, never for a second imagining her flow of money from the Fletcher family timber fortune could ever end.

Now the home she'd last seen in her rearview mirror as she'd slunk out of town belonged to Alex Binder, a preening peacock of a man that Bertie had hated. For a moment she pictured the peacock and his shiny new wife traipsing through the marble hallways and entertaining guests in the massive formal dining room, and renewed her vow to hunt Bertrand down and drag him back so that she could divorce him, regain her fortune, and put him in jail for being so crushingly disappointing.

Her head dropped as the first tear fell. A second followed it. She was attempting to stem the flow when a knock sounded on the car window. Startled, she looked up. A young, sandy-haired Palm Beach policeman peered in at her.

He tapped again and motioned for her to lower the window. Her eyes met his. She saw him register her tears and her undoubtedly blotchy face. She pushed the button and the window began to lower. It got stuck halfway and refused to go farther.

"Is everything all right, ma'am?"

She nodded numbly.

"Then I'll have to ask you to move your car."

His eyes traveled over the Land Rover with its faded paint and dented bumper. Their cook and housekeeper had used the vehicle for errands. Bitsy had driven it out these very gates when the house and all its contents had been repossessed. It and the things she'd managed to fit inside it were all she had left.

"We had a call from the owner and one of the neighbors. They said there was a, um, lone woman"—he said this in the same tone one might say "lone gunman"—"sitting outside the gate with the car running."

"And they were right."

"Yes, ma'am." God, he was young. And almost ridiculously good-looking.

"I'm pretty sure I'm on public property, Officer." Actually, she knew this for a fact. "I don't think I'm doing anything illegal."

"Not technically, no," he agreed politely. "But you are making the owner uncomfortable."

*Uncomfortable?* Clearly the perimeter cameras weren't properly aimed. If Alex or the latest Mrs. Binder had seen who was sitting in the driver's seat staring longingly at their property, they'd be the opposite of uncomfortable. They'd be rolling on the floor laughing or patting each other on the back.

A car slowed as it drove by, and she felt the burn of embarrassment. "I promise I'm not here to case the joint. I used to live here." She held up her hands. "I'm just going to reach in my purse so I can show you my driver's license, okay?"

At his nod she attempted to lower the window. This time it inched up before it stuck. She tried to reverse it. Nada. "Here, let me show you." Bitsy fumbled with her purse, pulled out her wallet, and retrieved her license. Her hand shook slightly as she passed it through the partially open window.

He looked at the license then back at her.

"I used to live here, Officer," Bitsy said. "My husband and I remodeled the entire estate. I moved a year ago. I haven't had a chance to change my driver's license. I'm in town visiting and I just thought I'd take a look. You know, for old times' sake."

His expression was more dubious than suspicious. They both looked up at the sound of the gate opening. A white stretch limo emerged. The rear passenger window slid down. Alex Binder's ferret face appeared. He took in the policeman currently holding her driver's license, the dented and dusty Land Rover with its temperamental window, and grinned. She had no doubt he had already rolled on the floor laughing at her. And was probably only leaving the estate at this particular moment in order to enjoy her humiliation up close and personal.

"Well, hello there, Bitsy!" he crowed happily as a breathtakingly beautiful and very young face appeared beside his. Extremely lush lips tipped into a smile. Perfectly arched brows rose almost to the matching cap of shiny blond hair. A peal of merriment escaped her mouth as Alex whispered something in her undoubtedly lovely ear. "I heard you were in town. I can't tell you what a treat it is to see you again!"

Bitsy smiled tightly, trying to keep the flush of heat from

staining her cheeks and telegraphing her humiliation. She and her car might have seen better days, but she was still Bitsy Fletcher Baynard. Heiress to the Fletcher Timber fortune, former pillar of Palm Beach society. Bitsy straightened her shoulders, raised her chin. "Alex."

"Be sure to give my best to Bertie *if* you ever hear from him!" Malicious satisfaction rang in Alex Binder's voice. "Don't worry about her, Officer. She's no threat at all." There was another burst of laughter as the window slid up effortlessly and the limo pulled away.

Bitsy turned to face the officer. It took every ounce of self-control she possessed to keep her chin up and her voice from quivering. "I know when I lived here I was very impressed with the efficiency and responsiveness of the local police department." She managed a smile. "I can understand that my little stroll down memory lane might have looked a bit odd, but as you just saw, I know the new owner, and I didn't come to do anyone bodily harm."

He watched her face for a long moment and she saw what could only be pity flash briefly across it. "My mistake, ma'am. I'm sorry to have bothered you. You be sure and have a nice day."

"Thank you, Officer. You too." She put the car in gear and drove with extreme care past the high plaster wall topped with sharply pointed wrought iron to the next property.

He stood beside his police cruiser until she'd punched in the Wyndhams' code and driven through their gate. As if he were memorizing every detail of what had just taken place for future retelling. Or in case she decided to make a break for it and come back to ram the gates she had built to keep other people out.

# Four

The breeze off the water was cool and the temperature in the low sixties as Avery carried an industrial-size bowl of Cheez Doodles and her beach chair through the Sunshine Hotel property. She found Maddie, Kyra, and Nikki setting up on a patch of sand that afforded an unobstructed view of the Gulf of Mexico and the sky above it. Paper plates of Bagel Bites and crackers smeared with Ted Peters smoked fish spread sat on a makeshift table of coolers.

"I come bearing offerings of puffed cheesiness." Avery set down the Cheez Doodles, opened up her beach chair, and accepted an insulated glass from Kyra. Nikki filled it from a pitcher of margaritas. Glasses in hand they sat and turned toward the sky where the show would soon play out, and set about getting comfortable.

"It's weird to be doing our sunset toasts in such a public place," Kyra said, motioning down the beach, where other sunset watchers were settling into position. Up on the rooftop bar and grill behind them there was the tinkle of glassware and conversation.

"I think it's kind of nice," Avery said, reaching for a Cheez Doodle. "I mean, it allows us to have our feet in the sand. And we are close to the water and theoretically the sunset." She took another long sip of the margarita, enjoying the crisp tartness that slid down her throat. "Hey, I think that could be my one good thing. Does that qualify?"

"I am not the arbiter of one good things," Maddie said, though it had been she who started the tradition of finding something good to toast at sunset back when they were first desperately renovating Bella Flora. At the time, coming up with anything good had been a challenge. "But I'm glad to see you finding a silver lining in Bella Flora being rented. It could have been worse."

Kyra snorted. "Worse than Troy? He pretended to be poor. He drove a beat-up car and acted like he had no job and no-where to live. He refused to leave. And now he just shows up like some Rockefeller or something. What kind of project could he possibly be working on?"

"Maybe you should ask him instead of giving him shit," Avery said, reaching for another Cheez Doodle. Kyra and Troy had always sparred with each other. Kind of like she and Chase had in the beginning. Oops. She nipped the comparison off before it could take hold. She had vowed not to think about Chase tonight. Or the things he'd said. Or how hard he'd begun lobbying to get her to move back in with him.

"What do you think, Nikki?" Maddie asked.

"Sorry, Kyra," Nikki said. "But I think Troy being the ten-ant is a lucky break."

"Seriously?" Kyra shook hot sauce onto the smoked fish spread and popped the cracker into her mouth.

"Yes," Nikki said. "Because he isn't a stranger. And he loves Bella Flora, too. And if we needed to pick up something or bor-row something, we could." She took a long sip of her margarita. "I don't know. Now that he's not working for the network and his job isn't trying to catch us on video in the most humiliating way possible, he's not really a problem."

"He clearly didn't need that job humiliating us," Kyra coun-tered. "Plus he's a guy. Which means he won't clean up after himself. Ever."

"But he can afford a cleaning service," Avery pointed out, shocking herself with her own positivity. "Can *that* be my good thing?"

"No," Nikki said. "I think we're still waiting for Kyra to come up with a positive."

"All right then, my good thing is that I haven't killed Troy Matthews," Kyra said. "Yet."

There was laughter.

"At the risk of actually sounding like the 'good enough' police, I have to tell you I really don't think *not* killing someone qualifies," Maddie said.

"Fine. How about, it's a good thing I'm not in prison for killing Troy Matthews," Kyra said. "That puts the emphasis on not being in prison and not what I would have been put in prison for."

"Kyra." Maddie's tone was suitably disapproving, but Avery could see her fighting off a smile.

"Sorry, Mom. That's the best I can do. I mean, did you see that shit-eating grin on his face? All I could think about was wiping it off. Preferably in the most painful way possible."

Nikki laughed and poured them all another round. "I think someone better come up with an actual, intentional good thing before we run out of alcohol to toast with. We've done a lot of debating, but not a lot of accepting."

"You could always go back to the cottage and whip up another batch," Avery pointed out.

"No, I could not," Nikki said. "Because if the girls are still awake and they catch sight of me, I won't be able to get out again. I am so not going back until they're in bed. I told Joe to text me when they were asleep and the coast is clear. When that happens I will not be running a blender."

"I don't blame you," Maddie said. "Steve and I used to go out on Saturday nights when Kyra and Andrew were little. One time we sat through the same movie twice, so the babysitter would have enough time to get them to sleep. I think both of us fell asleep during the second showing." She smiled. "Get your glasses ready. I have a good thing."

"Thank God," Avery teased, enjoying the warm glow provided by the margaritas and the women around her.

"Okay. Steve seems to be happy selling real estate, and Kyra and Dustin will be away on location," Maddie said. "So I think I'm going to go down to Mermaid Point to visit Will and then go on tour with him."

There was applause. Avery held up her glass. "To Maddie getting to say, 'I'm with the band.' And to being whisked all over the place in limos."

They clinked glasses and drank. Avery stared up at the sky and watched the red ball of sun slip smoothly toward the water.

"You're the girlfriend of a rock star, Maddie. That's like every woman's secret fantasy." Nikki's smile dimmed. "And you'll have enough energy for sex. And go places without a double diaper bag stuffed to the max. And wear clothes that aren't stained with formula or baby food. And . . ." Nikki's voice trailed off.

"Nikki?" Maddie said quietly.

"Hmmm?"

"Are you okay?"

"Yeah. Sure."

"The tour is only for a month," Maddie said. "Then I'm going to come back and . . . well, I need to find something I'm good at and passionate about. A purpose."

"God, that sounds lovely," Nikki said.

"You have a purpose, Nikki," Maddie said. "Raising children is one of the most important jobs on earth."

"I'll drink to that." Kyra raised her glass and they clinked and drank.

"I know. I'm ashamed of myself for not understanding before now how hard full-time mothers work," Nikki said. "I'm not that great at it, but I'm trying. It's just that I can actually feel my brain getting mushy. I love the girls, but they take up every waking second and a lot of the sleeping ones, too. It would be nice to have something besides sleep schedules and the introduction of the right solid foods to think about." She downed the remainder of her drink as the sun sank closer to the water.

"How about you, Avery?" Maddie asked. "You've been in an unusually good mood the last few days. What's going on?"

Avery finished her Cheez Doodle and licked the last of the cheese residue from her fingers. She didn't bother to hold back the smile she could feel stealing over her face.

"I'm in a good mood because I have my first non-Sunshine-cottage tiny house client." Just saying it made her feel good.

"That's so great," Kyra said. "Who are you designing it for?"

"I was approached by a couple named Wyatt. They want their mother to move in with them. She's been resisting because she doesn't want to be a burden or give up her privacy. They've got this great spot in their backyard with a water view right over on Vina del Mar. I'm going to design and build a custom tiny house for her."

"Cool," Kyra said.

"A lot of tiny houses are built elsewhere and moved into position or are built to be mobile, but in this case I think I can build it on-site. Vina's not even a mile from here."

"Is Chase going to work with you?" Maddie asked.

"No," Avery said a little faster than was necessary.

"But you're obviously back together and you guys worked really well together when you were designing homes for Hardin Morgan," Kyra said.

"Well, I'm not just an architect anymore. I have a contractor's license, so I'm doing this on my own." She hesitated. "And we're not back together. We're just dating."

"He was here for three days," Nikki said. "We never saw either of your faces. We just assumed . . ."

Avery blushed, but she was a consenting adult. "Well, don't. I'm not getting in that deep again. Not now." *Possibly not ever.* "There's nothing wrong with just dating and spending time together. And having mind-blowing sex."

"Mind-blowing, huh?" Nikki teased. "I'm going to put my jealousy of your sex life aside for the moment because I do believe you've come up with another incredibly good thing. And because it's practically un-American not to drink to truly great sex."

Avery grinned and raised her glass as the sun puddled into the gulf sending smudges of light across the surface. They clinked and drained their glasses, their eyes on the display Mother Nature had laid out before them.

"You know, Avery," Nikki said in the gathering darkness. "You can call your relationship with Chase whatever you want. But you look pretty 'together' to me. In my experience if it looks like a duck and walks like a duck, it is a duck."

Maddie smiled enigmatically.

Kyra laughed and added a final "quack."

# Five

"I assume you're ready to concede that this is a complete waste of time." Nikki blew a bang out of her eye and repositioned Sofia in her lap. The stream of potential nanny candidates Joe had insisted on interviewing over the last three days had been long and disappointing. Or would have been if she'd actually wanted or needed a nanny.

"Nothing is a complete waste of time," Joe said despite the list of crossed-out contenders that proved otherwise. Gemma was curled against his chest, sucking her thumb quietly as if she hadn't just screamed so loudly through the last two interviews that one candidate had held up her cross as if warding off the devil, and another had fled without saying good-bye.

"Well, Dorinda seemed competent," Nikki said. "And she did have a nice smile. But I assume the fact that she felt she could fit both of the girls on her Harley is a deal breaker."

Joe shuddered, nodded.

Nikki looked down at the notes she'd made, mostly to hide her smile. It wasn't often she got to see Joe squirm. "Now, Mandy was interesting. I thought the whole Goth thing was over. But maybe black lipstick never goes out of style?"

Joe sat very still.

"But then we're looking for a caregiver not a fashionista, right?"

"Right." His smile was more of a grimace.

"I didn't feel at all good about Pandora's insistence that keeping the girls on a schedule might stifle their future creativity, but she was the only one who wasn't at all fazed by the fact that there are two of them." Nikki looked down at her notes. "Maybe there'd be a better pool of candidates if we pretended we only had one child. I could take Gemma out for a while and let you talk to the next candidate with Sofia."

"And when she shows up for work? What then?"

"I can act like I just discovered a second child we didn't know we had. Or opened the door and found her in a basket on the front porch. Or . . ."

"We're not going to pull a bait and switch with our daughters. And I still cannot understand why you're so resistant to having help." Joe repositioned Gemma in the crook of his arm. "I would think you'd be glad to have some time off. And honestly I think it would be best for all three of you while I'm traveling."

Gemma put her thumb in her mouth and sucked quietly. She was always happiest in her father's embrace. But then weren't they all? "We'll be fine. And when I need a break or help, I'll get a babysitter for a few hours. Or ask Avery or Bitsy to come by and lend a hand. And it's not like Maddie won't ever be in town."

Joe looked at her steadily, his X-ray vision attempting to peel away her defenses.

"I'm their mother. They're my responsibility." Nikki banished any trace of uncertainty from her voice. Mothering might not come naturally to her like it did to Maddie and Kyra, but she would not lean on a stranger to do her job.

"You know this is not an indictment of your mothering abilities. I love them with all my heart, but there are two of them and only one of you. I have it on good authority that most women would be glad of the help." He flashed the smile that sometimes made her forget what they were arguing about. "Not that you're most women."

"Surely you have to admit that there hasn't been a single acceptable candidate yet," Nikki countered.

"True," he conceded. "But we still have one more interview. Who knows? Maybe she'll be the one."

Nikki snorted. "If the last eight candidates are any indication, I doubt it, but I guess you never know." She looked her husband in the eye, shocked as she always was that he and the girls were hers. "But I want you to agree that if this next one isn't Mary Poppins or her equivalent, we table the search."

Joe flashed his smile again. "I'll agree to that if you agree to keep an open mind and that if this last candidate is strong, we hire her."

Given the people they'd seen so far, the likelihood of this seemed remote. "All right," she said finally. "If Mary Poppins, or her equivalent, walks through the door today and wants the position, we'll give it to her. Does that work for you?"

"It does." His smile grew and something she couldn't identify flickered in his eyes.

The doorbell rang. The noise set Gemma to shrieking. Sofia popped awake and joined in. With a now-squalling Sofia in her arms Nikki went to answer it, wondering if the candidate was already beating a hasty retreat.

The woman who stood at the opened door did not look like someone who would ever retreat, hastily or otherwise. She was built a bit like a Mack truck. Or a sausage packed too tightly into its casing. Her face was extremely white, as if it rarely saw sunlight. But her eyes were a brilliant emerald green and her hair, which had been pulled back into a tight, serviceable bun, was a very deep red.

"Hullo," she said in a cheery British accent. "I'm Luvie. Just the one name. Like Madonna." Without asking she reached out and took Sofia, settling her on one broad hip. Sofia closed her mouth. The crying ceased. "Now then, where's the other little dumpling?" She marched past Nikki, nodded at Joe, and scooped Gemma out of his arms, something Gemma normally protested at full volume. Gemma barely blinked as the stranger propped her on the other hip. Both girls laid their heads against the prow of her ample bosom. "Now then, why don't you show me around and tell me what sort of shed-ule you'd like me to keep the girls on."

Nicole's mouth gaped open. Her surprise turned to shock as Gemma reached out a hand to cup the woman's apple-shaped cheek. Her twin cupped the other.

Luvie's cheeks creased with pleasure. "Now then, aren't you the clever girls?"

Nikki looked at Joe. He was grinning madly.

"James Marley sends his thanks and good wishes," Luvie said to Joe. "Now, why don't you take yourself off and let us women get acquainted?"

"Gladly." He stood and practically saluted. She could see he was trying not to laugh.

"You!" Nikki pointed a finger at him. "You set me up."

Joe laughed out loud while the girls patted Luvie's cheeks. "No, I just asked a friend for a referral." He shrugged. "I saved his life once. He wanted to help. Luvie is apparently known in certain London circles, but moved to St. Petersburg a few years ago to look after a family member."

"That's right, dear," Luvie said. "I stayed on after me mum died. Absolutely love the weather, but have to slather on buckets of sunscreen to keep from crisping like a rasher of bacon."

Joe ducked his head to hide his smile but there was no missing his air of satisfaction.

"You should be ashamed of yourself," Nikki whispered as he prepared to take himself off.

Joe only shrugged. "All's fair in love and childcare. And in case you're worried, I think you should know that James insists Luvie makes Mary Poppins look like a slacker."

• • •

"Yes?" The sound of Troy Matthews's voice on the other end of the line turned Kyra's response monosyllabic, some might say curt.

"You really shouldn't grit your teeth like that. You could end up with TMJ or lockjaw or something." Troy Matthews tsked. He sounded far too happy for her liking. Especially since he was being happy in their house.

"I'm afraid that's what the mere thought of your existence does to me." Her teeth weren't the only things that clenched whenever she pictured him living in Bella Flora. Eating in her kitchen. Sleeping in her bed. Like some twisted version of the Three Bears.

"Is there something you need?" she asked. "Because I'm pretty sure Franklin Realty is supposed to be handling any problems."

"No," he replied airily. "I was just calling to see if you and Dustin would like to go out on the boat this afternoon."

"You have a boat?"

"Of course I have a boat. I am living on the water. It would be kind of odd not to bring my boat."

"Oh, so you already had a boat. Where do you normally keep it?" She really wanted to tell him where to shove that boat, but managed to keep the suggestion to herself.

"At my house on the other coast."

Kyra swore under her breath. She'd already shown more interest than she wanted to. She would not ask whether he meant the east coast of Florida or the west coast of the United States. She did not care how many homes he owned or what kind of toys he kept in them. The only question that mattered was why he'd needed to take hers. But she was not going to give him the satisfaction of asking.

"You really should consider having a dock put in here. I had to rent a boat slip at the yacht club. You're talking to a brand-new member of the St. Petersburg Yacht Club at Pass-a-Grille."

"That's great. But we're busy."

"How about tomorrow?"

"Also busy."

"Seriously? I didn't even say what time."

"Doesn't matter. I'm completely busy getting ready for the shoot in Orlando."

She smiled at the silence that followed. She treated herself to a mental picture of Troy Matthews gritting or possibly even gnashing his pearly whites.

"Then how about I just take Dustin?"

Silence.

"I've taken care of Dustin before. I can come pick him up if you don't want to drop him at the house or the yacht club. I can even pick him up in the boat. He'd probably love that."

She closed her eyes and attempted to count to ten.

"You can think of it as babysitting. Maybe you and Maddie can go shopping or to a movie or a museum or something."

"I don't need a babysitter."

"Why don't you ask Dustin if he'd like to come out on the boat with me?"

"I am not asking Dustin that question or any question that concerns you. We're . . ."

"Ask me what, Mommy?"

She hadn't heard him come back in from walking Max with her mother. She looked over her shoulder and saw Maddie standing behind Dustin in the bedroom doorway. Max stopped slurping water from his bowl and came to poke his head around Dustin. All three of them looked at her expectantly.

"Why don't you put Dustin on so I can invite him personally?" Troy asked cheerfully.

"No."

"So you would deprive your son of an afternoon on the boat because . . . ?"

"Who is it, Mommy?"

"No one important." Kyra closed her eyes and took what was meant to be a calming breath. It was bad enough knowing Troy was living in their home. She would not let him insinuate himself into their lives, too.

"I thought you were working on a project."

"Oh, I am. But you know what they say about all work and no play."

"Who is it, Mommy?" Dustin was standing at her side now and reaching up for the phone. "Is it my Dandiel?"

"No." She hesitated briefly but refused to allow Troy to cause her to lie to her son. "It's just Troy."

"Broy!" Dustin's face lit up. "Can I talk to him?" He reached out a hand.

Kyra sighed. She had no problem refusing Troy. She could tell him no until the earth stood still. But Dustin's big brown pleading eyes were another thing altogether.

. . .

Avery took the Twenty-first Street bridge off Pass-a-Grille Way onto Vina del Mar. According to Realtor John Franklin, who had lived on Pass-a-Grille since God was a boy, the lovely island neighborhood had begun life as a submerged coral reef covered in mangroves and been dredged up into its current shape in the early fifties. Somewhere along the way the pedestrian "Mud Key" had evolved into the far more elegant "Vineyard of the Sea," and development had flourished.

The home that now belonged to Jonathan and Sandra Wyatt was a sixties ranch that had been enlarged and no doubt updated over the last decades. Architecturally it was unremarkable. Its view over the bay and Bird Key was not.

She followed the couple around the house to the backyard,

where Jonathan's mother, Martha, waited. She stood beneath a stand of palm trees that swayed lazily in the breeze. Sun glinted off the water. Birds soared with wings outstretched like a squadron on maneuvers.

"What a gorgeous spot," Avery said as the introductions were made.

"Yes. The sun rises right over there." Martha Wyatt raised an age-spotted hand and pointed a gnarled finger due east. "And if we build here, it won't block the view from the main house."

"I keep telling her we're not worried about any of that." Like his mother, Jonathan Wyatt was tall and lean with even features. His wife, Sandra, was smaller and rounder with the no-nonsense manner of the emergency room nurse she was.

"We've begged her to stay in the house with us," Sandra said. "She raised Jonathan and his sister in it—but she turned us down."

"We all need our privacy," Martha interjected. "Plus I'm the one who gets a brand-new custom-built house." She cocked her head of short white curls in Avery's direction. "What do you think of this spot?"

Avery considered the main house, the placement of the home's windows, and the hedge that ran up the property line. "Honestly, I think it's perfect. There's plenty of shade but there will be sunlight, too, it commands a million-dollar view, and if we add a row of mature hibiscus right here, both homes will have almost complete privacy."

"That's exactly what I thought." Martha smiled. "Renée Franklin told me you were a smart girl." Her face was heavily lined and her skin was leathered from the years in the sun, but her dark eyes were sharp. "What happens next?"

"Don't you want to look at some of Avery's work? Maybe speak to some of her former clients?" her son asked.

"Renée and John Franklin's recommendation is good enough for me." Martha's tone indicated that was the end of the conversation. "You're hired," she said to Avery. I'm eighty-five. I don't have any time to waste. What do we do first?"

"First you both sit." Jonathan pulled two Adirondack chairs into the shade and held one steady while his mother lowered herself into it. By the time Avery had taken the other chair and opened her notebook, Sandra had returned with two tall glasses of iced tea. She placed a cell phone on the other arm of her mother-in-law's chair. "We'll leave you two to it. Just call if you need anything."

For a moment Avery and her new client sipped their iced teas and stared out over the water.

"I never thought I'd have a new home at this age," Martha said quietly. "But I'm glad for the adventure. And I'll be grateful if I can see the sunrise from here every day until the end."

Avery sketched and made notes as they talked square footage and window height and room for the great-grandchildren to come out and spend the night. Their conversation was punctuated by a refill of tea, the offering of a sweater, as Martha Wyatt's family demonstrated their concern and love in a hundred tiny ways that made Avery long for the father who had raised her and the mother who'd come back twenty years after she'd abandoned them only to die soon after they'd reconciled. And then there was Chase and his father and sons, whom she loved but was afraid to let all the way back into her life.

She had vowed to focus on rebuilding her architectural career post–*Do Over* by designing and building tiny homes for others, but now as Martha Wyatt's home began to take shape in her mind, her own life suddenly felt unbearably small.

Avery hugged her new client good-bye, but her smile felt false and her heart rang hollow. As she drove the Mini Cooper back over the Vina del Mar Bridge, she was relieved that they wouldn't be toasting the sunset that night. She, who had been feeling so positive all week, would have been hard-pressed to come up with even the tiniest good thing.

# Six

"I've started going through the boxes of financial records." Bitsy sat across from attorney June Steding, former social worker and sole remaining partner in the Tampa law firm still known as Steding & Steding. Unlike the lawyers that had stopped returning Bitsy's phone calls when her fortune disappeared, June Steding had not attended an Ivy League law school and preferred costume jewelry to bespoke suits. She was not the cool, unemotional shark that Bitsy had originally thought she needed. But she took what happened to her clients personally and could be relentless in her pursuit of cads and deadbeat dads. Bitsy worked at Steding & Steding three afternoons a week in exchange for legal help and advice.

"So they finally coughed up the records," June observed. "You could take them to court over the ridiculous delay."

"Um, yeah." It was Bitsy who coughed and shifted uneasily in her seat. There was no way she could bring herself to admit that it was not her money managers dragging their feet that had kept her from mining the paperwork for clues, but her own inability to face reality. She'd found the boxes exactly where she'd left them, buried under a mound of suitcases in the back of one of the unfinished Sunshine cottages. With a strength born of shame and embarrassment, she'd dragged them back to her cottage one at a time then begun the painful and laborious process of getting them in order. Land sold. Houses and apartment buildings purchased. Steel in India. Reams and reams of purchases and sales and transactions. Bertie had claimed that he was diversifying her portfolio and increasing her liquidity to protect her just as he'd protected her from downturns in the market and Malcolm Dyer's Ponzi scheme. She had questioned nothing.

She'd left the papers strewn across the dinette for the last ten days as a stark reminder of her folly. Her naïveté. Her stupidity. Her loss. She who had been given everything including an education that should have helped her protect the fortune that had been left to her, had ceased all critical thinking simply because she'd fallen in love and believed that love would never be betrayed.

"I can't believe your financial advisors didn't warn you about making him a trustee." June Steding shook her head, sending her long turquoise earrings swinging. "And sole trustee?"

Bitsy winced. "They did warn me. Repeatedly. I . . . I just refused to listen." She had committed the financial equivalent of putting her hands over her ears and shouting gibberish in order not to hear.

Then after Bertie had disappeared and the truth became apparent, what had she done? Hidden the proof away where she wouldn't have to see it and wallowed in self-pity. She'd given him an entire year to hide the money and cover his tracks. "I didn't even let him sign a prenup when he offered."

"Well, very few prenups would have still been in effect fifteen years later," June said. "They're typically designed for shorter-term defections. So I wouldn't beat myself up about that."

"Right. Not when there are so many other things to beat myself up over." Bitsy grimaced again as she remembered how disinterested she'd been in the details. It was time to fully face up to what she'd tried so hard not to see. Her losses were the result of her believing that Bertie had ever been in love with anything but her money.

June leaned forward and folded her hands on the desk, turquoise and silver rings encasing her plump fingers. "Now that you have the records, it's time to bring in an expert. As a trustee he's clearly guilty of not upholding his fiduciary responsibility to his client, but having a forensic accountant find and document the fraud in detail will give us a much firmer legal leg to stand on." She smiled. "He can also follow the money trail."

"Is that even possible at this point?" Bitsy asked. "I want him found and punished more than anything—and I definitely need to divorce him—but is there any chance at all that we'll ever find the money? That final transfer to the Cayman bank took place a year ago."

"Offshore banks aren't as secretive as people think, especially in today's world of terrorism and digital access." Her face was kind, her tone firm. "If anyone can figure this out and trace your money, it's Gary Kaufman." She handed Bitsy a business card with a New York address and phone number. "He's licensed in New York and Florida and I have complete faith in him. I told him you'd be sending him a copy of all the records."

"But . . . I can't afford to . . ."

June Steding placed a hand on Bitsy's. "He's a very old friend. We go way back. He's prepared to work on a contingency basis and he'll get started right away."

. . .

Kyra spent the next morning praying for rain. At noon, when those prayers had not been answered, she and Dustin walked down to the beach, where they waited at the water's edge under a beautiful blue sky filled with white puffy clouds.

"Lookit Broy's boat!" Dustin dropped her hand and pointed at the brightly painted speedboat making its way toward them. "It's got blue stripes!"

Troy waved jauntily, and cut the engine and tilted the motor so that the boat glided silently into shore.

Dustin jumped up and down with excitement as the bow

gently nudged onto the sand and Troy vaulted out of the boat, a child-size neon orange life vest in his free hand.

"Broy!" Dustin held still just long enough for Troy to slip the vest on him. As soon as it was buckled he leapt happily into Troy's arms.

Kyra did not. Begrudgingly she noticed how low his swim trunks hung on his hips, how surprisingly ripped his tanned torso was, how many shades of blond his hair appeared in the sun. His eyes remained hidden behind a pair of reflective sunglasses, but she could feel them trained on her.

"Glad you could join us," he said, easily settling Dustin on one hip.

"I don't really remember being given much of a choice," she said, still waiting for his trademark smirk, but he was smiling with what appeared to be complete sincerity.

He turned to place Dustin in the boat then took a step toward her. "May I?"

Before she could respond, he leaned over, placed his hands around her waist, and lifted her onto the bow as if she weighed no more than Dustin. Biting back a gasp of surprise, she swung her legs into the boat and watched him from beneath her lashes. He might possess more money and better manners than he'd ever let on, but he was still Troy Matthews. Wasn't he?

He pushed the boat off the sand and into deeper water then vaulted into the boat with animal grace. "I thought we might ride up to John's Pass and have lunch at Gators." He smiled politely. "If that's all right with you."

Her eyes narrowed. In the years she'd known him, the cameraman had taken great pleasure in catching her at her worst, wrestled with her for control of *Do Over*, and made no effort to hide his disdain for her relationship with Daniel Deranian. Even his occasional acts of kindness had been carried out with a certain level of snarkiness. This mask of smiling civility was no doubt meant to hide some self-serving ulterior motive.

"Are we really gonna eat alligators?" Dustin asked.

"You never know." With one hand on the steering wheel Troy turned the key in the ignition. The engine growled to life. "We might."

"Can I help park the boat when we get there?" Dustin asked.

"I might have to handle the docking until you get a little taller," Troy said, taking his seat. "But you can definitely help steer us there."

"Oh, boy!" Dustin clambered into Troy's lap and fit his hands on the wheel between Troy's. "I'm a good driver! My Dandiel tole me so!"

Kyra smiled grimly to herself. Troy was not a Daniel Deranian fan and was no doubt already formulating a snide comment or jab. But once again he remained silent, only nudging the boat into gear. Another nudge and the bow rose. Kyra plopped into the passenger seat and braced her bare feet against the dash as the boat planed and picked up speed.

Dustin laughed happily. His dark curls tossed in the wind just beneath Troy's chin. Troy smiled while Dustin chattered about everything from what he'd had for breakfast to the dolphin he spotted off a nearby buoy. She'd come prepared to defend herself from Troy's cutting comments and observations, but he didn't seem to feel the need to comment on anything. In fact, he said almost nothing at all as he helped Dustin steer the boat. When a full five minutes went by without a comment, snide or otherwise, her jaw loosened.

She breathed in the salt air, tilted up her chin. The sun and wind buffeted her cheeks. The hum of the engine and its gentle vibration beneath her soothed and calmed. Kyra's eyelids grew heavy. Her shoulders began to relax. A splash, a caw, a low male murmur. Sounds mingled and became distant. Dustin's giggle was the last thing she heard.

She roused when the boat stopped moving and the engine

went quiet. She heard conversation, the slap of water against wood.

"Kyra?"

"Hmmm?"

Her eyes blinked open. Troy's face hovered just above hers. She'd never really noticed how expressive his eyes were. Normally she would have been focused on whatever annoying thing he was saying or doing. Irritation might turn into attraction in certain kinds of movies and books, but in reality it was just irritating. A silent, noncombative Troy was not.

"We're here. At Gators." It was as if some alien life-form had shown up and sucked all the antagonism and swagger out of him and left this surprisingly attractive shell. She dropped her feet and sat up.

"What?" A smile hovered on his lips.

"Why are you acting like this?"

"Like what?" He straightened.

"Like a normal, *friendly* person." Her eyes narrowed. "I can't figure out what you're up to, but whatever it is I'm not falling for it."

A series of emotions and reactions flitted across Troy's face. She had the sense he was trying to decide which one to go with. Finally, he shrugged. "It's just a boat ride and lunch. I wouldn't go trying to turn it into some Machiavellian plot."

She stared at his face. It was possible that her jaw dropped. "Did you just say 'Machiavellian'?" Who was this man and what had he done with the real Troy Matthews?

"Even lowly cameramen are entitled to a vocabulary," he said coolly. "But if it's confusing for you, I'll try to stick to single syllables during lunch." For a brief moment she glimpsed her former nemesis and all-around smartass.

"Come on, Mommy." Dustin took her hand and tugged. "I wanna have bites of gators."

"Me, too." She let Dustin pull her to her feet. "As long as we don't have to wrestle them into submission."

"Wrestle them like this?" Troy scooped Dustin up, tossed him over his shoulder, and made a show of hauling him off the boat. Kyra followed, trying to make sense of the kinder, gentler Troy Matthews and wondering how long he planned to play the genial Dr. Jekyll before he turned back into his more familiar Mr. Hyde.

• • •

"You go first." Nikki motioned Joe toward the door of the cottage. "I'll hang back and distract them." It was their last night together before Joe left town, and he'd insisted they go out for a nice dinner and alone time. The only problem was that the twins did not like to be left behind. Leaving them without causing a double meltdown required the strategic planning of a clandestine operation.

"You're a brave woman. Your sacrifice will not be forgotten." Joe kissed her on the forehead, moved quietly to the cottage door, and slipped outside just as only someone trained at Quantico could. The twins didn't even glance up from the tower of blocks Luvie was helping them build.

Nikki cleared her throat and squared her shoulders. They'd discovered the hard way that an official good-bye was necessary. But once it was given, there could be no hesitation or dillydallying on the way out the door.

"You all have fun!" she called out gaily even as she hunched her shoulders, covered her ears with her hands, and took a first step.

But there was no crying. No screaming for her not to leave. No sounds of frantic crawling as they rushed to grab onto her. She turned.

"That's it, dear." Luvie reached out a hand to guide Sofia's. "How high do you think it can go before it 'all falls down'?" Her accent and hand gestures made both girls squeal with laughter.

"Brish!" Gemma directed.

"Fah don!" Sofia added. They both clapped their hands. Nikki prepared to sprint if necessary, but their eyes were locked on Luvie. The nanny had stayed with the twins twice, and already they could follow her every word and would stop whatever they were doing for a chance to play peekaboo or hear her sing "London Bridge."

Luvie looked up. Her brilliant green eyes were merry. "It's quite all right, Mrs. Giraldi," she said. "I'm going to sing 'London Bridge Is Falling Down' as many times as they like. And then we are going to have a lovely bath, put on our pajamas, and read all about Sleeping Beauty."

Gemma and Sofia smiled happily. Their eyes remained pinned to Luvie's face. In this moment their mother was, in fact, chopped liver.

"Brish," Gemma cooed.

"Booty," Sofia added in perfect accord. When they were older a high five would no doubt follow.

Nikki knew she should be grateful. Knew that Joe would be absolutely thrilled, and not at all threatened, that the girls were so infatuated with their Mary Poppins. He could leave town knowing that she had backup and enough free time to run errands and shop and maybe even take a nap without two extra appendages.

"Wave bye-bye to your mummy," Luvie said. "And tell her 'cheerio'!"

The girls did as they were instructed. Then they turned their backs on Nikki. She was only halfway out the door when Luvie began to sing "London Bridge Is Falling Down." At nine and a half months, her daughters only echoed the occasional word. But unless she was mistaken they already seemed to be developing British accents of their own.

# Seven

Kyra zipped up her suitcase and set it next to the one she'd packed for Dustin. Then she scanned the tiny bedroom they shared, looking for forgotten items. Dustin's bag of carefully chosen toys and Max's paraphernalia were already loaded in the rental car she'd picked up that morning.

She pushed some hair off her forehead and plopped down on a chair. Her mother had taken Dustin out for a day filled with all his favorite things including breakfast at Paradise Grille, a sandcastle build on the beach, a swim in the pool, and a shopping trip to the Dollar Store.

Tomorrow they would head not for Orlando as she'd originally been told, but to an address in a place called Winter Haven about forty-five minutes south of it.

Maddie stuck her head in the open doorway. "Are you ready for sunset toasts?"

"Almost." Kyra reached for the sweatshirt she'd left on the bed and began to slip it over her head. "Has Dad picked up Dustin?"

"Yes, and they took Max." She hesitated. "They're going to cook out with Troy."

Kyra stopped and turned. "At Bella Flora?"

"Yes."

"So he's going to be entertaining my son in his own house." Kyra felt her blood begin to heat.

"I promise you Dustin isn't seeing it that way. He's just excited to be grilling with the guys."

"Grilling with the *guys*? I thought he was going to have dinner with Dad while we did our sunset toasts."

"He is having dinner with his grandfather."

"And Troy. Troy is not one of the guys. Troy is a schemer. A squatter . . . a . . ."

". . . godsend. Whatever you think of Troy he paid a boatload of money to rent Bella Flora. Money that allowed you to hold on to the house for Dustin and gave you the freedom to choose whether to let Dustin do the movie or not."

Kyra snorted. "Troy as a tenant is not a godsend. In baseball terms, Troy is a sac bunt when you were swinging for the fences."

"Kyra, things were set in motion that can't be taken back. The only thing you can do now is make the best of the situation."

Kyra jammed her feet into her sneakers. She might not be able to argue with her mother's logic, but she didn't have to like it. "Fine. Let's go." She stomped out of the cottage and huffed onto the concrete walk.

"Someone has her panties in a twist." Nikki was waiting for them outside her cottage.

"Who's with the girls?" Maddie asked.

"Luvie. Who else?" Nikki said. "According to my parenting books, they're supposed to have a problem separating from their mother at this age. But they didn't even notice I left. Again."

"Honestly, I'm pretty sure that's a sign that they're secure," Maddie said. "In my book that's a good thing."

"You heard that, right?" Nikki said to Kyra. "I am now in possession of an officially sanctioned good thing for tonight."

"Well, if you're handing them out, I'll take one," Kyra said as they reached the main building and walked past the pool. The sound of conversation floated down from the rooftop deck, always a popular location for watching the sunset. So far, it and the dining room were just about breaking even and beach club memberships were growing. Cottage sales continued to languish. Even the two that had been purchased after last spring's Sandcastle Showdown had not yet been finished out.

Maddie gave her a look. "Coming up with one good thing is an exercise in positivity. All things considered, I think it would do you good to take the time to come up with something of your own."

Kyra flushed at the unusual sharpness of her mother's words and focused her gaze on the weakening sun.

They joined Avery and Bitsy just beyond the low concrete wall that separated the pool deck from the beach. Folding chairs had been arranged around a low cooler on which an assortment of snacks had been placed. The breeze off the gulf was brisk. The palm trees swayed and rustled.

"It felt too cold for blender drinks, so I brought wine." Bitsy wore sweatpants and a mink jacket that had seen better days. Avery's blond hair was hidden beneath a flannel hoodie.

"I see Avery was in charge of snacks." Nikki observed with a nod to the array of cheese products arranged around a bowl of her beloved Cheez Doodles.

"Hey. Don't dis the Cheez Doodles," Avery protested. "They're one of the few things that a woman can always count on."

"Hmmm." Kyra dropped into a seat and reached for a Cheez Doodle. "So this"—she held up the C of puffy cheese—"is more enjoyable than, say, Chase Hardin?"

"Well, it's a lot less demanding." Avery popped a Doodle into her mouth. "It's designed to give you pleasure and it doesn't expect a major commitment in return."

Kyra wasn't the only one watching Avery's face, but it was Maddie who asked, "What's going on?"

"Nothing's going on," Avery said. "Absolutely nothing. I haven't heard from him since I told him I just wanted to date and, you know, have a good time." She took a long, somewhat desperate sip of her wine. "If you're looking for a good thing from me tonight, I'm going with the snack that never lets you down." She consumed a handful of Cheez Doodles for emphasis and turned to the person next to her. "How about you, Bitsy? I've hardly seen you since you got back from Palm Beach. How'd it go?"

Bitsy pulled the fur coat tighter, but Kyra didn't think her shiver was due to the cold. "In terms of humiliation-to-achievement ratio? It sucked." Bitsy, who could and had drunk them all under the table on more than one occasion, finished her glass of wine and poured another. "But if you're looking for a 'good thing' from me, it finally forced me to face reality. I mean, I've spent a whole year hoping he'd come back with some sort of acceptable explanation."

"You mean other than lust and greed?" Nikki asked.

Bitsy nodded. "But I've finally let go of the fantasy and I've sent all the financial records to a forensic accountant June recommended. It's a first step in tracing the money and documenting fraud that could get the authorities involved." She refilled all of their glasses and raised hers. "My good thing is facing reality. Ugly though it may be."

"To facing reality." Kyra joined in the toast, trying hard not to think about her own reality and all that tomorrow would bring.

From her seat next to Bitsy, Nikki raised her glass. "Tonight my good thing is that my daughters are apparently secure enough to ignore me." She sighed and drank without waiting for a formal toast.

"Really?" Avery asked. "We're drinking to that?"

"Hey, we didn't call you on using Cheez Doodles for the umpteenth time," Nikki snapped. "Maddie told me it qualified, and I don't have anything more positive to offer at the moment since I've been replaced by Mary Frickin' Poppins." Nikki's gaze narrowed. "Besides, we're not supposed to judge whether a good thing is good enough. We're just supposed to come up with one."

As tension prickled around her, Kyra looked up at the sky, surprised by how low the sun hung over the water. They'd wasted most of the "show" trying to spin their problems into positives. Although she wouldn't have thought it possible, she felt worse than when she'd gotten there.

"Sorry," Nikki said. "Sofia and Gemma may not be experiencing separation anxiety, but I guess I am." She drew a deep breath. "Let's face it, Maddie. You and Kyra are off for new adventures tomorrow. The rest of us are being left behind."

"Yeah, well, Mom's the only one going somewhere she actually wants to go," Kyra said.

"She's going to go on tour with the rock icon formerly known as William the Wild," Avery added. "*And* she gets to sleep with him."

"And he's in love with her," Bitsy said.

Kyra looked at her mother, watched her rein in her excitement, the care she took to keep her smile in check. "And we are total bitches for making her feel like she has to hide her happiness."

"We are." Nikki held out her plastic goblet. "Fill'er up so we can drink a toast to Maddie. Who deserves every good thing that happens."

"To Maddie!" They clinked plastic rims and drank as the sun sank beneath the water. They drank another in the fading light.

"You don't want to drive with a hangover tomorrow, honey." Maddie reached for Kyra's empty goblet and removed it gently from her hand.

"I don't want to drive tomorrow at all."

"Isn't changing location for an entire major motion picture at the last minute kind of unusual?" Nikki asked.

"Well, I'd say so, but the only big-budget film I ever worked on was *Halfway Home* and I wasn't exactly privy to those kinds of decisions." Tears pricked the back of her eyelids as she remembered her brief and turbulent time on her first and only feature film, an unwelcome addition to the knot of worry that tightened in the pit of her stomach every time she thought about what lay ahead.

"So, you don't think it's a negative? Or a sign of problems?" Avery asked.

"I really don't know," Kyra said, grateful for the gathering darkness as she struggled to hold back the tears that threatened. "I mean, I don't see how it could be a positive, but it might just be a matter of logistics." Their faces blurred in the fading light. Or maybe it was the sheen of tears that she couldn't seem to blink away. "Honestly?" Her voice broke on the word. "It wouldn't matter if we were shooting around the corner. I'm afraid I'm not strong enough for this. How will I handle watching Daniel with his wife and family? How will I bear everyone knowing that I was a stupid girl who believed a movie star when he told me that he loved me?" She meant to stop there, but the alcohol and—no doubt, her fear—had loosened her tongue. "How will I protect Dustin from being hurt? He's never really questioned why his father isn't with him all that much or the way he pops in and out of his life, but . . ." She swiped at the tears, willing them to stop. She'd already said far too much.

The rooftop deck was emptying and there were sounds of the staff cleaning up. Here, in their small circle of beach, it was too dark to see, yet she could feel everyone's eyes on her.

"Daniel loves him, Kyra," Maddie said softly. "Despite the original legalese, he's acknowledged Dustin as his son and made sure he's had far more than the basics. And he has even more reason now to make sure he's comfortable on location and on set." Her mother's arm went around her shoulders, warm and sure. "You've committed to this and now I think you have to show up hoping for the best but prepared for the worst."

The others murmured their agreement.

"And you can come back some weekends, right?" Avery said. "I'll be here. And so will Nikki and Bitsy."

"And your dad," Maddie said. "And you know I'll come back if you need me."

"And let's not forget Luvie," Nikki added. "I have no doubt she could handle the girls and Dustin with one hand tied behind her back. Your village will be here waiting if you need it."

Kyra's cheeks were damp. She nodded and sniffed.

"And if Daniel Deranian or Tonja Kay or anyone else on that movie set gives you trouble, you just call us," Bitsy said.

"And we'll come drop a whole lot of whoop ass on them and bring you home. They won't know what hit them." This threat came from Avery.

"Whoop ass?" Nikki said. "Seriously?"

"Hey, sometimes you just have to tap into your inner redneck," Avery said.

There was laughter. Maddie squeezed Kyra's arm and helped her to her feet. They began to gather things up in the dark.

"Thanks," Kyra said as they parted. "I'll sleep a whole lot better knowing you guys and your whoop ass are on call."

She didn't, though. In fact, she barely slept at all. And as she'd discovered on more than one occasion, there was no holding back the dawn.

# Eight

The minivan was packed and ready for the trip down to the Keys when Maddie walked Kyra, Dustin, and Max to the rental Jeep the next morning. Dustin and Max raced for the car. Kyra moved slowly, her eyes wary, the skin beneath them hollow and dark from lack of sleep.

Maddie wrapped her arms around her daughter. "Just breathe deeply and remember that your entire purpose for being there is to make sure Dustin's comfortable. That's it. You have nothing to prove or defend. Not to anyone."

"Right." She stepped back, her smile tremulous, but there, as she turned to Dustin. "Are you ready to hit the road?"

Dustin threw his arms around Maddie's waist and hugged her tightly, vibrating with excitement. "I'm going to hact with Dandiel."

"I know, sweetheart." She hugged him back, his small, sturdy body solid and warm against hers. "I can't wait to see you up there on the big screen."

Dustin climbed into his booster seat. Max bounded into the backseat and settled beside him as Maddie clicked the seat belt into place. "Have fun. And you be sure to tell Mommy if anything bothers you."

"Have a great time, Mom." Kyra hugged her almost as tightly as Dustin had. "And don't worry about us. We'll be fine."

"I know you will." She cupped Kyra's face in one hand. "But keep me posted."

"G'bye, Geema!" Dustin threw her a kiss through the window. Max woofed beside him.

Maddie threw a kiss back then stood waving, the smile affixed to her face, until they disappeared from view. Then it was her turn to breathe deeply, grateful as she got in the van that she was on her way to Will and a new adventure, doing something just for herself. Just because she wanted to.

On the high-arched span of the Skyway Bridge she hit "play" on Hightower's latest album and looked over her shoulder at Pass-a-Grille, a sliver of sand floating on an aquamarine sea.

• • •

Based on the billboards Kyra passed as she headed east on Interstate 4 toward the center of the state, Winter Haven's chief claim to fame was its chain of fifty lakes. This was followed by citrus groves that you could tour and then pick your own fruit. Its only serious attraction appeared to be Legoland, which was aimed at the two-to-twelve-year-old set. Although Dustin would undoubtedly enjoy the theme park, she doubted that brightly colored bits of plastic could compete with Mickey Mouse. Which begged the question, why had filming been moved here?

The GPS directed her off I-4 and wound her through what could only be called a very small town. It was a pretty place with pockets of historic homes, several lakefront parks, and a certain quaint charm. Their final destination was not a fancy hotel in an upscale resort area but a winding dirt road that ended abruptly at a guard gate.

"I'm Kyra Singer. I . . ."

"Yes, of course, Ms. Singer. We've been expecting you." The guard was a slight, white-haired woman with a friendly smile and a face that had once been beautiful.

"Your cottage is on Lantana Lane; it'll be the third small street on your left. There's only one guest cottage per street." She handed Kyra a small map with an X marked on it. "This is more of a compound than a neighborhood. There are a total of eight homes, all of them lakefront. There's only one road and it makes a complete circle around the lake. The gate is always manned if you have a problem or need anything. It's the only way in and out. We do take security here very seriously." She smiled pleasantly and raised the barrier.

Kyra drove slowly. Heavily wooded lots curved around the lake. Stands of trees lined the opposite edge of the paved two-lane road providing shade and privacy. They passed two signs and the turnoffs that followed before coming to Lantana Lane. Their cottage was a lovely Craftsman-style bungalow with a broad wooden front porch, squared fieldstone columns, and a shingled roof nestled under a stand of pine trees. Dustin climbed out of the Jeep with Max, who headed for the nearest tree. Spotting the lake at the rear of the property, she and Dustin walked toward it, Max sniffing his way and winding between their feet. At the edge of the lake a private dock stretched before them; an upturned canoe sat on the shore.

"Lookit! A boat!"

The only other home visible from where they stood was a sprawling multilevel log home on the opposite side of the lake with walls of glass fronting the water. The other cottages were apparently hidden by the trees, but each had a long, narrow dock like theirs that stuck out into the lake like the spokes of a wheel.

"Kin we go out on the boat?"

"Let's get our things and see the cottage first." She took Dustin's hand.

Max's head went up. His ears pricked back and forth. At his first bark Kyra looked up and saw Daniel coming down the back porch steps and walking toward them.

"My Dandiel!" Dustin made a beeline for his father, who

picked him up and swung him around. Max woofed and nosed his way into the father-son reunion. "Is that my boat?"

"It's yours to use," Daniel said. "But only with your mother or another adult." He set Dustin down then ruffled his curls. "Let me help you bring your luggage in."

Dustin skipped happily ahead with Max at his heels. Daniel fell in beside Kyra.

"So you're producer, director, and bellman on this film?" she asked in the friendliest voice she could muster. She was not, after all, here by choice.

"I am a man of many hats at the moment." His smile was decidedly less dazzling than usual. It was the first time she'd seen him less than immaculately groomed, if you didn't count some of the less flattering disguises he'd donned to visit them.

"And assuming you were the person who decided to shoot here instead of Orlando, that would make you what, the location scout?"

Daniel sighed. The hand that had caressed Dustin's hair ran absently through his own dark curls. "We didn't really have a choice."

"What happened?"

His jaw tightened.

"What?"

"We had an agreement with Disney to shoot in the park and around it. We never hid the fact that the screenplay was based on *The Exchange*. Hell, Grant Fowler, the author, adapted his book for us. It was in all the media."

"And?"

"And I guess no one at Disney had read the book. Or the CliffsNotes. Or watched him or Tonja or me on a morning talk show."

"And then?" she prompted.

"And then someone in management got a copy of it for Christmas."

She stifled a smile at the outrage in his voice. She could still hear his too-hearty *Ho! Ho! Ho!* when he'd arrived at Bella Flora dressed as Santa to deliver the Great Dane puppy, now known as Max, without warning on Christmas Eve.

He removed his sunglasses and pinched the bridge of his nose as if fighting off a headache. She was shocked by the dark circles beneath the warm brown eyes that had always been so hard to resist. "On December twenty-sixth we got a call asking why we hadn't told them that the story revolved around a child abduction at the Magic Kingdom."

"I take it they didn't feel good about that."

"No, they did not feel good. In fact, they freaked out completely. Said there was no way they could ever allow something like that to be shot in the park or sanctioned by them in any way. Not good for the brand, you know." He turned and looked out over the lake, his expression bleak. "Never mind that we already had a contract and that a good part of our production budget was going to them. Never mind that they'd been begging us to shoot there, desperate to have us in the park, staying in their hotels, eating in their restaurants. We'd already spent a month there prepping, completing casting, hiring crew, building sets for the in-studio work. We were a bigger draw than It's a Small World." He snorted. "I'm not sure I'll ever get that song out of my head."

"And it never seemed odd to you that they weren't worried about being tied to this subject matter?" she asked, remembering her own surprise when she'd first learned of the location.

"They'd never said a word." He shook his head again. "Even when they freaked out about the subject matter I didn't think they'd go back on our agreement."

She watched his face as he drew a deep breath then expelled it.

"Then two weeks ago they told us that we couldn't shoot a single frame anywhere on the property. That we couldn't use the words 'Disney World' or 'Magic Kingdom' or anything else that belonged to them. Our lawyers are trying to get some of that money back, but in the meantime we had to find another location to replace Disney, which puts us behind and significantly over budget before we shoot a single scene."

"I wouldn't think there are a lot of places that could offer what Disney could."

"You would be right about that."

"We're not shooting at Legoland are we?" Kyra asked. It was the only theme park she'd seen signs for in the area.

"No. Even if it could be made to work for the script, they apparently have a brand to protect from us, too." Anger and puzzlement flickered across his too-handsome face, battling for dominance.

For a brief shining moment Kyra thought they were about to be set free. That her worry and trepidation had been for nothing. That she and Dustin could simply turn around and go home. Or at least go to the Sunshine. It would be tough living in the cottage while Troy made himself at home in Bella Flora, but even that would be preferable to what lay ahead here. "So, you're . . . rethinking the film? And you don't need us here?" she asked hopefully.

His brown eyes lost their warmth, turning decidedly unbedroom-like. "I knew you didn't want Dustin to do this film. And you've made it clear you don't want to be here with him. But I didn't realize how happy you'd be to see us smacked around this way." His features hardened. "If I'd given up every time someone said no to me, I'd still be working in my family's rug business." Which was, incredibly, where he'd first been discovered.

Kyra seriously doubted that he or Tonja had heard the word "no" even a handful of times in recent memory, but she refrained from saying so. "We're shooting here in Winter Haven then?"

"Yes. It turns out that when Legoland took over what used

to be Cypress Gardens, they only used a portion of the old attraction's acreage. They've leased us everything that's left including the old rides and props and signage. The construction
crew has been working twenty-four-seven to turn it into the
theme park the screenplay calls for. And we're repurposing an
old fruit processing plant into a soundstage for the interiors."

"Sounds expensive."

"It is, but we'll have enough done to start shooting by the
end of the week. And there's a lot we can do in the meantime.
Including getting Dustin acclimated and comfortable with
everyone."

She did not ask who "everyone" was, but the knot in her
stomach tightened.

"The crew is all set and ready to go. We're just waiting on a
few more cast members to arrive this afternoon."

She watched his face as he spoke, noting the signs of stress
and the barely leashed tension that emanated from him. It was
a far cry from his usual easygoing personality, but then he'd
always had others pampering him and the most he'd been responsible for was his own performance.

"You'll have the rest of the day to get settled in." Daniel
lifted the back of the Jeep and pulled out their suitcases. Kyra
retrieved her video gear and called Dustin over to carry the bag
of toys he'd packed. Daniel led them up the front steps and
inside. When he delivered her bag to the master bedroom and
Dustin's to the smaller bedroom beside it, he pointed out each
feature and amenity.

"This is lovely," she conceded, taking in the main living area
with its cozy chenille sectional, the club chairs with ottomans
that faced the fieldstone fireplace. Near the open kitchen, which
was beautifully appointed and stuffed with high-end appliances
her mother would have recognized and appreciated, a maple
dining table sat beneath the bank of windows that overlooked
the lake.

"The refrigerator is fully stocked and there's a concierge on call twenty-four-seven in case you'd like anything delivered. The guard gate is also manned around the clock and the guards are highly trained. No one who isn't authorized will be setting foot inside this compound while we're here."

Her smile was unintentional.

"What's funny?" he asked.

"Nothing. The grounds are beautiful, and if the whole cast is staying here, security will be important." Dustin went back into his new bedroom to play with toys. Her lips tipped up again.

"And?"

"And . . . I'm just picturing the tiny, white-haired woman who let us in holding off a determined group of paparazzi or a stalker of some kind, though those are sort of the same thing," Kyra said. "I mean, she couldn't have been lovelier or more efficient, but she wasn't particularly intimidating."

Daniel tsk-tsked. Which wasn't something you heard every day. "First of all, there's a panic button and other technical devices in the guard gate that automatically summon backup in an emergency situation. In fact, there are several in each cottage that I'll show you. So size and youth aren't really necessary attributes."

"Right. Of course. I know that. It's just . . ."

"And although your feminism is now in question, you should know that that guard's name is Joan McCreary and she is one of the most revered stuntwomen of all time. She did more than thirty films, stunt doubled for virtually every female megastar for decades, and performed stunts well into her seventies. Hell, she was the first woman inducted into the Stuntmen's Hall of Fame." He wagged a finger at Kyra as he continued. "She's also an expert marksman and has a third-degree black belt in karate. Frankly, I'm a little afraid of her." He flashed a smile and suddenly there was the Daniel Deranian she'd first fallen for, gor-

geous yet human with a wicked and often self-deprecating sense
of humor. "She doesn't take an ounce of shit from anyone."

"Good to hear," Kyra replied. "I'll definitely rest easier knowing that Nigel and his cohorts won't be talking their way past
her. Although I'd like to be somewhere nearby with my video
camera if they try."

His smile dimmed. "The only time you'll encounter a pa-
parazzo or a stranger of any kind is if we decide you're going to.
You realize that is going to happen."

She nodded, no longer remotely tempted to smile.

"Also, this will be a closed set so there will be no unauthor-
ized video shot."

"You're telling me I can't shoot video of my own child?" Kyra
asked.

"Yep."

She wasn't sure which hat he was wearing when he said this,
but she had a very strong urge to try to knock it off.

"Right. So . . . ," he continued. "There's a rehearsal and
shooting schedule in that envelope on the counter. A revised
script will be delivered to you shortly."

She nodded, unwilling to tell him just how much Dustin
had been looking forward to being in the film. "He really wants
to please you, you know."

"I know. I'll be careful with him, Kyra. I hope you believe
that." For the first time since they'd arrived he looked at her
as he so often had, with a mixture of sincerity and apprecia-
tion that had always cut through her defenses. No longer the
producer/director under duress who was juggling too many
hats and had too much riding on the film they were about to
shoot. A flicker of what she recognized as sexual interest lit
his eyes, and she felt an automatic and unwelcome tingle of
awareness. An awareness she thought she'd finally managed to
stamp out.

"Tonight at six thirty the whole cast is invited to a cookout at our place. It's the one on the other side of the lake."

Kyra was shaking her head before he'd finished speaking. She'd expected to at least have the rest of the day before she had to confront Tonja Kay and the rest of their family. "I thought we'd just take it easy and have an early night. I think it would be best for Dustin to get a good night's sleep before his first call tomorrow."

"The cookout isn't optional," Daniel said. "It's important for everyone to get acquainted and begin to get comfortable with one another before we start shooting. It won't be a late night."

"But . . ."

"It'll be okay, Kyra. I promise." He was standing too close and his tone felt far too intimate. "Everyone's going to be on their best behavior. And if anyone's not, I'll take care of them."

Dustin raced back into the living room already looking completely at ease. "I have a big boy bed all myself. And there's a bed for Max right next to it! And a cage! What goes in that?"

"I wasn't sure if you were crate training Max or not," Daniel said. "There's a dog walker available and other services, too."

"You really thought of everything didn't you?" she said, taking a step back.

"Our goal is to make everyone comfortable," he replied, lifting Dustin and hugging him good-bye.

His easy use of "our" and "we" conjured unwelcome images of Daniel and Tonja sitting around discussing which cottage to give them and even what amenities it should include, right down to the crate for Max. A reminder not to be a fool.

"Just try to relax," he said as he prepared to leave. "Everything will be fine." As he let himself out the front door, she couldn't help wondering whether he was trying to reassure her or himself.

# Nine

As she drove across the state, Maddie bellowed out the lyrics to Will's songs as if she were in the shower. Her heart sped up when she hit Florida City. On the two-lane eighteen-mile ribbon of asphalt that locals called the stretch, the mountains of debris Hurricane Irma had left in her wake were gone. Fences and billboards were back up. Here, the real world began to dissolve. Residents claimed that heart rates slowed and stress levels dropped during this drive, but the closer she got to Mermaid Point, the faster her heart beat and the more heightened her senses became.

At the top of the Jewfish Creek Bridge, sun glinted off the impossibly turquoise water that flanked her on both sides, the Atlantic Ocean on her left, Florida Bay on her right. A cool salt breeze rifled Maddie's hair, and her pulse kicked up another notch as she wound south toward Upper Matecumbe, the third of Islamorada's four keys. She thought of all the family car trips she and Steve had taken with the kids over the years and their eagerness to get where they were going, and felt that same sweet, impatient anticipation. *Are we there yet?*

There were homes and businesses and even landmarks that hadn't survived Irma, but the residents of the Keys were a hearty bunch. Those with the resources to had hung on. Many were still rebuilding. She whizzed by Whale Harbor Marina and the

Lorelei, and the landmarks became personal, forever tied to William. At mile marker 79 she slowed to turn into the parking lot of Bud n' Mary's Marina, remembering the trepidation of their arrival two years ago when they'd had no idea which "high-profile individual's" home they'd been sent to renovate or how much that individual wouldn't want them there. And even less an idea of just how much that individual would affect her personally.

She spotted Will at the same moment he looked up, and her heart lifted. She waved as he detached himself from the group of anglers and guides he'd been talking with. Moments later she was out of the van and in Will's arms.

"I've missed you, Maddie-fan," he murmured after the first bone-melting kiss. "Nothing's quite the same without you."

"I know the feeling." She breathed in his heady scent of sun and salt water and looked up into the chiseled face that attested to the hard living he'd done and the excesses he'd known. "But I was just thinking how much nicer this arrival feels than the first one did."

He chuckled. "I might have been a little pissed off that Thomas had brought in the cast and crew of a reality TV show to turn the island I was planning to hide out on into a B and B."

"A little pissed off?" She stepped back. He'd been fresh out of rehab the day they'd arrived, his once meteoric career in shambles, emotionally unable to make music, his island recording studio padlocked. "You were an ogre!"

"I notice you're not stammering this time," he teased, retrieving her suitcase and backpack and slinging the soft-sided cooler over one shoulder.

"Yeah, well, I wasn't expecting to meet the rock god whose poster used to hang on my bedroom wall. Or have a camera crew recording it," she said as she locked the van. "Now I only stammer on the inside." Which was where she entertained the doubts and fears that arose whenever she thought about just how many younger, firmer, more beautiful women Will could have, especially now that he was once again topping the charts.

He nodded easily to the denizens of the docks as they passed, lowered her luggage into the open skiff, then handed her in. Across a slice of sparkling blue ocean, Mermaid Point beckoned.

Within minutes they were rounding the northern mangrove-shrouded side of the island. A line of tall, skinny palms arrowed toward a half-moon of white sand beach bisected by a sphere-shaped tidal pool where seagulls and other small birds chased after food on matchstick legs. From here she could see bits and pieces of the main house's pyramid-shaped roof, glints of glass decking that hung off the ocean side of the building. An open-air pavilion overlooked the beach and pool where Will swam the laps that were often a substitute for the alcohol and other substances to which he'd once been addicted.

As they rounded the southeastern edge of the island, Will nodded to the empty hammock stretched between two palms, and his lips tipped up into a smile. "It's about time we got to watch another sunset wrapped up together and swaying in the breeze."

"Sounds good to me," she said, remembering the first week-end they'd found themselves alone on Mermaid Point and all the sunsets that had followed.

A cock-a-doodle-do rent the air, and a rooster strutted out into the clearing. A gaggle of chickens clucked along behind him. "Oh, my gosh, there's Romeo! He's clearly still time challenged, but his harem's gotten even bigger since the last time I was here."

"Yes, and it looks like he's brought every one of them out to greet you."

Romeo and his throng of admirers had greeted them the day they arrived, descendants of early birds brought to the Keys for illegal cockfights and passed off as pets when the feds showed up to investigate.

Will cut the engine so that the skiff glided up to the long dock that fronted the boathouse and its upstairs guest suites, all of them freshly painted a bright tropical green with white trim. Seconds later he was out of the boat and cleating it. She looked up and saw her wild-haired smiling self reflected in his mirrored sunglasses as he offered her a hand up. The warmth in his answering smile sent a tingle of awareness up her spine. When he leaned down to kiss her, she felt an internal tug that had her melting into him again.

"Hey, get a room!" Hudson Power's voice floated down from the balcony of the closest guest suite.

"That's exactly what I had in mind," Will whispered against her ear before turning and looking up at his longtime friend and fishing guide. "Keep your shirt on!"

"I will if you will!" Hud shouted back. "Welcome back, Maddie! I don't know what you see in that guy, but it's good to have you back."

"Yeah, yeah." Will retrieved her bags and pulled Maddie close. "It's time to stop crushing on my girl, Hud, and find one of your own!" It was Hud who had retrieved them from Bud n' Mary's that first fateful day and Hud who'd taught her how to handle a boat.

Maddie laughed and waved. "I'm making egg soufflés in the morning! One of them has your name on it!"

Will led her onto a shaded path and toward the main house where they'd quit *Do Over* and where Will had managed to thwart the network's plans to turn his newly renovated private refuge into a B and B, turning it instead into a sober living facility, one he'd named for the younger brother and bandmate who'd lost his life to the excesses that had almost claimed William.

Near the house they passed a group of men sitting under the shade of a palm tree. Not far away a tai chi class was under way. "Looks like you're full up," she said to Will as they waved and called greetings.

"Yeah. We were able to fit two more living spaces into the garage-turned-guest-house while it was being repaired after the hurricane and we added an open mic night. I kind of hate to be gone on tour for so long."

She wrapped her arm around his waist and laid her head briefly on his broad shoulder. He had come so far and achieved so much. It was his records and sold-out tours that allowed him to keep the facility running and had enabled him to bring a construction crew and building materials from outside Florida post-Irma.

After months of work, the house once again welcomed and soothed just as it had been designed to. Plank floors and acid-washed pecky cypress walls and ceilings lightened the space. The accordion glass doors that stretched across the ocean side of the great room with its communal kitchen and living and dining room had been folded open to let the sunlight and ocean breeze inside.

That sense of peace evaporated when Will's assistant Lori Blair raced out of the downstairs office like a very young and very blond animal shot out of its cage. "Hello, Maddie!" She offered a quick but sincere hug then turned to Will. "Thank goodness you're here. Aaron called," she said. Aaron Mann was Will's producer at Aquarian Records. "There's some problem with the last track on the album that he needs to talk to you about. He wants you to go into the studio and recut it. And the tour operator wants to add another concert in Houston, the first one sold out in like fifteen minutes, and . . ." She raised a phone to her ear. "I'll get him on the line right now and . . ."

Will reached for the phone. She tried to tuck it out of reach, but he took it gently like a parent taking a dangerous toy from a toddler, and turned it off. "No. We're not going to talk to Aaron now."

"But . . . ," Lori began.

"No, no buts," Will said quietly. "And no more work today."

"Oh, no!" She shook her head of short spiky hair, her wide, mobile mouth already forming another protest.

Maddie winced at the panic that filled the girl's huge hazel eyes.

"I promised Aaron that as soon as you got back I'd . . ."

Will slipped the phone in his pocket. "I'm giving you the rest of the day off. I promise you all those things can wait until tomorrow."

"Oh, no," Lori said. "You can't do this. I . . ."

"Maddie just drove all the way down here and she's, well, she was just telling me how beat she is. So, we're going to take a . . . a nap."

A nap? She and Lori looked at him with similarly surprised expressions.

He looked down at Maddie and raised one dark eyebrow. Then he nuzzled her head with his chin.

"Ah," she said. "That's right." She feigned a yawn. "I'm really tired from that drive." She did not meet Lori's eyes.

"After we rest we'll probably head over to the Lorelei for sunset," Will added. "So we'll see you tomorrow. I hear we're having egg soufflés for breakfast if you want to get an early start."

"But there's so much that we have to do. Aaron specifically asked that you go back into the studio ASAP."

"And I will. Tomorrow."

"But this is my job. This is what I get paid to do. I can't just go take the whole afternoon off. Aaron will . . ."

"For God's sake, Lori. You're a millennial. It's time you start acting like one."

Lori opened her mouth.

"That's an order," Will said.

Lori closed her mouth, nodded.

"We'll see you in the morning." He swept Maddie up the stairs without a backward glance.

"We could have at least waited until she left," Maddie whispered on the upstairs landing.

"No," he said. "We couldn't." He opened the door and pulled her into his bedroom. She felt a wicked flush of lust as he closed the door behind them and dropped her suitcase on the floor. "I haven't seen you in weeks. I'm not sure how in the hell I even waited this long."

. . .

Kyra would have given anything to be sharing the sunset that night with her mother and the others at the Sunshine. Would have happily come up with a whole slew of good things if she were still back on Pass-a-Grille with people who cared about her and Dustin, and not about to knock on the front door of the Deranian-Kay lake house.

She knew she'd been standing there too long when Dustin, whose hand she clutched, looked up at her expectantly. "Kin I do the doorbell?"

"Absolutely." She lifted him up so that he could reach. Not wanting to be caught cowering behind him, she settled him on one hip and attempted to rearrange her lips into something approximating a smile.

Dogs barked. She may have uttered a small prayer as footsteps sounded on the foyer floor. That prayer was answered when Daniel, and not Tonja, opened the door. "There you are! Everybody's been waiting for you!" he said jovially, reaching for Dustin then flashing her a smile. "I'm assuming you didn't get lost?"

She flushed slightly at even the inference that she might have been unable to find her way on a single circular road. But letting him think her geographically challenged felt preferable to admitting that she'd wasted a good deal of time pretending she just might not go at all and then agonizing over what to wear. Ultimately, she'd driven as slowly as mechanically possible, resenting each rotation of the tires.

"Is this your house?" Dustin asked.

"It is while we shoot the movie," he answered easily.

"It's big!" Dustin said as his father led them into a high-ceilinged great room dominated by a soaring stacked stone fire-place.

"It is," Daniel agreed, striding across the room and out through the open glass accordion doors to an immense pool deck cantilevered over the lake.

A crowd of adults mingled around the pool, drinks in hand, while children of various ages jumped in and out of it. Hamburgers and hot dogs sizzled on the grill. Iced coolers of soft drinks were arranged so that no one would have to take more than a couple of steps to reach one. The ring of horseshoes hitting their mark echoed from beneath the trees. Through the scrim of leaves she saw what looked like a game of corn hole in progress.

"Corn pole!" Dustin pointed and shouted, his face lighting up. He wiggled to get down.

"Okay, little man. Go get 'em!" Daniel set Dustin on his feet without asking or warning her.

"But . . ."

Daniel turned to her. "He'll be fine."

"There's a pool here and a lake, and I don't see any fences," she said. "Plus he doesn't know anyone." Okay, maybe that was her fear and not Dustin's. "You can't just let him go off on his own."

"Kyra, there are close to thirty adults here. And almost as many staff between the servers and babysitters and bodyguards. I promise you nothing's going to happen to him. And I think he'll have a better time meeting people on his own rather than being taken around and introduced person to person."

He looked at her closely. "But I'm happy to introduce you around if you're up for it." He nodded toward the pool deck where costars Derek Hanson and Christian Sommersby stood talking. His gaze shifted to the shallow end of the pool. "That's Rodney . . ."

". . . Stanfield," Kyra gushed as Daniel pointed to the iconic Director of Photography, whom Kyra had worshipped as a film student and would have given anything to meet. If she'd been here as a working member of the crew and not as the mother of Daniel Deranian's illegitimate son. "No, not right now."

"Kyra." He stepped closer, put a hand on her shoulder. The warm musk of his cologne teased her senses.

"Well, look who's here."

The voice was instantly recognizable. Its tone was far more pleasant than it had ever been when directed at Kyra. She looked up to see Tonja Kay moving toward them. Her blond hair gleamed in the last shards of sunlight; her skin shone like polished alabaster in the halter-topped floral sheath that clung to her curves and made Kyra's sundress look like it was designed for an Amish schoolgirl.

Daniel took his hand off Kyra's shoulder. Kyra resisted the urge to fall back when Tonja stopped and placed one slim white hand where Daniel's had been. Her left hand fell on Kyra's other shoulder as she leaned forward and kissed each of Kyra's cheeks, looking right into her eyes as she did so. The actress's long fingers were cool, her lips cold. Her eyes were even icier, putting a lie to her warm smile.

"Now then, that wasn't so horrible was it?" she murmured in a teasing tone so at odds with the disdain of her gaze it made Kyra's flesh crawl. "I've promised to make you comfortable and I will." She turned to Daniel. "Will you bring me a drink, darling? Oh, and one for Kyra, too. You would like something, wouldn't you?" She said this as if to a child. "Jared makes lovely wine spritzers and a grapefruit and vodka that's incredibly refreshing."

"Um, yes. Thanks. Either one would be fine."

Tonja shooed Daniel off to do her bidding like a queen sending off a page.

"I think I should go make sure Dustin's okay." Kyra turned, intending to step out from Tonja's grasp. Tonja's grip loosened but instead of letting go, she turned along with Kyra and slipped one arm through hers. As if they were best girlfriends.

"Don't be silly. Dustin's fine. *We're* the ones who have an audience."

It was only then that Kyra noticed the silence that had fallen. The expectant looks. "They're waiting for some sort of catfight," she said.

"Yes, of course." Tonja continued to smile.

Kyra's heart pounded. She wanted to slap away Tonja's arm, find her son, and take him as far away from this place and these people as possible. She straightened. "I didn't come here to be the entertainment. Maybe Dustin and I should go now."

"No. No running." Tonja spoke without moving her lips or altering her smile. Apparently she was not just an actress, but a ventriloquist as well. Kyra tensed, preparing to move.

"No. Please." Tonja forced the words out around the frozen smile. "We can't afford any hint of animosity. Here's Daniel. We'll have a drink together, all three of us. Then I'm going to walk you around and introduce you."

This time Daniel kept a professional distance while Kyra sucked down the drink he'd brought. When he left to circulate, she accepted another from a passing waiter. The alcoholic cushion kept the smile on her face and lubricated her conversations, but it wasn't long before her jaw throbbed from smiling, her head ached from making small talk, and her neck hurt from imitating a bobblehead.

Somehow she survived the scrutiny, met and held the eyes that noted the irony of the situation in ways their words never would, and held her chin high. She sagged in relief when the grill master banged the hanging triangle as if summoning ranch hands and bellowed, "Come and get it!"

"I think we've managed to talk to pretty much everyone,"

Tonja said, finally letting go of Kyra. "Why don't you sit and have something to eat?" It was more an order than a suggestion.

"Of course," Kyra said in the faux friendly tone they'd adopted. "Let me just go find Dustin. I haven't even caught a glimpse of him." Though not for lack of trying. "I'm sure he'll be hungry."

"Oh, I left instructions for him to be fed with the other children," she said airily. "I'm sure they're having a much better time together than they would have with us. They have their own ice cream sundae bar for dessert. After we eat we'll make sure he meets Rodney and Chris and Derek as well as the First Assistant Director and Costume Coordinator."

"You did what?" She'd done what had to be done, completed what appeared to be her part of tonight's bargain, but she'd had more than enough of pretending.

"If he weren't okay, we'd know about it," Tonja said. "I promise you no one is holding him against his will."

Kyra wanted to storm off to find Dustin, wanted to scoop him up and take him back to their cottage and away from the knowing eyes and, no doubt, wagging tongues. Instead she took the seat she was motioned to, accepted a plate that held a cheeseburger, warm German potato salad, and a lettuce leaf topped by large slices of onion and tomato. She'd managed to choke down half of the burger when Daniel stood and clanged a knife against a glass. His wife stepped into place beside him, a gracious smile on her face. "Tonja and I want you to know how happy we are that you are a part of *The Exchange*. We both loved the book and are very excited about Grant's screenplay." He motioned to the author and screenwriter, who nodded his leonine head and raised a hand in acknowledgment. "I look forward to working with all of you both as an actor and, for the first time, a director. I imagine I'm about to find out it's not as easy as so many of the people who've directed me over the years made it look."

There were smiles and murmurs. As always, Daniel had

managed to strike just the right tone. Tonja smiled and raised her glass. Everyone followed suit. "To my husband, Daniel. The love of my life." She looked directly at Kyra. "Partner in all things. And one of the most talented men I've ever known."

There was a roar of approval. More toasts followed, but all Kyra could think about was escape. When the staff began to clear, she stood, intent on finding Dustin. She'd taken only a few steps when a group of children materialized at the edge of the pool deck. She thought she recognized Daniel and Tonja's four from the tabloids. Two were dark haired, two blond; although they'd been adopted, they vaguely resembled their famous parents. They stood not far from Dustin, who started running toward her the moment he spotted her.

He was missing one shoe and looked as if he'd been crying. As she swept him up he buried his face in her neck and said, "How come those childrens told me Dandiel is their daddy?"

*Oh, God.* With barely a nod of good-bye she carried Dustin to the car and buckled him into the car seat. His thumb stole into his mouth, his shoulders drooped. And she knew as she watched him in the rearview mirror that the misery etched on his face was her fault. Because she'd wasted so much time dithering over whether to let him do the film that she'd failed to prepare him in any way.

"I don't understand how that happens. I tole them that Dandiel is *my* daddy!"

"Of course he is," she said, trying to gather her thoughts, wondering far too belatedly how best to explain. "Let's get you in the bath. We can talk about it then."

They found Max lying on the living room floor surrounded by goose down, his nose buried inside the sofa pillow from which that down had been liberated. A favorite sneaker lay nearby, riddled with teeth marks. She closed her eyes briefly. Max's mess was nothing compared to the misery in Dustin's eyes. Misery she could have prevented.

"So," she said gently once she'd helped Dustin into the tub and begun to soap up a washcloth. "Tell me what happened."

"I was playing corn pole with Marcus—he's five. And when I won he told me I wasn't so special. That there was lots of basards like me." He looked up into her eyes and she thought her heart might break. "I don know what a basards is, but it's bad, isn't it?"

Kyra could hardly force the words out around the lump in her throat. "No one should ever call someone that." But clearly someone in his household had, and Kyra's money was on Tonja.

"Then his big brother told me I'm immegitimate." Once again it was clear he knew only that this was not a good thing. "He said him and Marksis and Tawny and Sapina are Dandiel's real childrens. He's even gots Dandiel's same name."

"What else did he say?" She squeezed the washrag tightly in both hands but made no move to use it.

"He told me that their mommy is married to Dandiel and you're not."

Kyra's heart thudded dully in her chest.

He cocked his head and pinned his huge brown eyes on her face. "How come *you* didn't marry him?"

This was a good question. Another one she clearly should have been ready for. She ran the washcloth across his shoulders and down his arms as she tried to come up with an explanation. If only there was a washcloth capable of cleaning away his hurt.

"Because daddies can only be married to one person at a time." She swallowed. "And it's . . . it's not my turn." *Had she really just said that?*

"When it's your turn will Dandiel come live with us?"

Her mind raced, searching for the right words as she took the washcloth and soaped it up again. "So, the thing is . . ." Still stalling, she squeezed the washcloth. It was only as she dunked it in the cooling water that she realized that while the whole truth might crush him, *a* truth might do the opposite. "No matter where we live or how many other children Daniel has, you will always be his son. And he will always love you."

She watched him take in her words, consider them. He drew an unsteady breath. "But what if he loves them more? Because he lives with them?"

"That's not the way it works," she said with a certainty she didn't feel. "Mommies and daddies love all their children no matter where they live. Just like Geema loves Andrew and me whether we live in the same house with her or not. And don't forget that he asked you to play his son in his movie." She closed her eyes briefly, appalled that she'd used the thing she hated as proof.

But even as she silently berated herself, his brow unfurrowed and his eyes brightened. "He did. He aksed me! Dustin Deranium."

By the time she helped him out of the bath and into his pajamas, he'd been all out of questions and ready to go to sleep. She, on the other hand, had tossed and turned as all the things she should have said and done to protect her son darted through her head. When she'd finally climbed out of bed in the weak morning light, she'd vowed that from this moment forth she would have her son in her line of sight every moment on set, as the Screen Actors Guild rules stipulated for a child his age, and off. She had committed one of the worst sins a mother could; she had ignored her gut. Then she'd compounded that sin by failing to prepare and protect her son. Then she'd allowed Tonja Kay to take control of the situation. Her son had paid the price. The only way that would ever happen again would be over her dead body.

# Ten

Maddie pulled the egg soufflés out of the oven early the next morning, grateful that their renovation of Mermaid Point's kitchen had included the commercial-grade Wolf stove that she'd come to love.

She'd gotten up early to mix enough soufflés to feed everyone who was on the island including the ten men currently transitioning in the Tommy Hightower Sober Living Facility, their two counselors, as well as Will, herself, Hudson Power, and Lori Blair, who would no doubt spend the day chasing after Will trying to convince him to do whatever Aquarian Records thought he should.

"Mmm, God, I love that smell." Will walked in through the back door, put an arm around her, and nuzzled her neck. He was still damp from his morning laps and smelled faintly of salt water, which was a smell she'd come to love and which was, if she were honest, its own brand of aphrodisiac. No doubt due to how often they'd had sex following his stints in the pool. His dark, gray-peppered hair was slicked off his forehead, and his dark eyes glinted with mischief. "I don't suppose we're going to be eating egg soufflés on the road."

"Well, if we end up anyplace that has a kitchen and you ask real nicely, *anything's* possible," she said. After all, as far as she could tell, her sole function on tour appeared to be to keep Will happy, which was a blush-worthy job description if ever there was one.

"What do you hear from Kyra?" he asked, pinching a grape from a nearby bunch.

"Nothing," she said as she cut each soufflé into eighths then slid a piece onto each plate that Will held up. A helping of hash brown casserole and a serving of fruit completed the plates.

"Just a text yesterday telling me they made it to Winter Haven. I know they're supposed to report to the set today, but I have no idea what's scheduled. Every time I think about them there alone trying to navigate through all the potential minefields it makes me crazy." Not to mention guilty. As if she'd somehow shirked her duty to her daughter and grandson.

"Well, if she's anything like her mother, she can handle whatever's thrown at her."

She smiled at the compliment. It was only when things had fallen apart that she'd discovered just how much she could handle. But what if Kyra couldn't handle the movie and all it entailed? What if Kyra and Dustin fell apart and she wasn't there to help put them back together?

With a personal comment to each man in line, Will handed out the plates of food. Maddie poured coffee and juice then did her best to join in the conversation around the table. After the men headed out to morning activities, she lingered with Will. But no matter how many times she reminded herself that Kyra was an adult and that there was no reason to waste this gift of a day, she couldn't stop imagining worst-case scenarios.

"Maddie?" Will was no longer sitting across from her. He stood next to the table, Lori Blair beside him. "Are you okay?"

She nodded and smiled. Pulling her thoughts back where they belonged, she stood.

"Lori needs me to look at the additions Aquarian wants to make to the tour schedule."

"I'm good." Maddie got up and began to clear the table. "I'm just going to put the dishes in the dishwasher and tidy up a bit."

"You know one of the guys has KP duty." He was watching her closely. "You don't have to do that."

"But I'm glad to. I've got most of the day free."

Maddie cleaned up then wandered outside. The sky was a clear blue, the ocean a layered turquoise. Seagulls skimmed low, diving when something caught their eye beneath the surface. With nowhere she had to be and nothing she had to do, she wandered past the pool and across a small slice of beach. The hammock that she'd been sleeping in that long-ago holiday weekend when Will first approached her—the one she'd considered her "lucky" hammock ever since—swayed gently as she climbed into it. She lay quietly for a time while she debated whether to text Kyra. Who was a grown-up. And a mother. And was undoubtedly fine.

There was activity around her—yoga in the pavilion, a discussion about addiction on the front porch, Romeo the rooster and his harem pecked at the ground in a nearby clearing, but none of it required her attention.

Finally, she texted, *R U okay?*

For a time she held the cell phone tightly in one hand waiting for a response. Then she stopped looking at the screen and instead focused on the jagged green palm fronds above her in stark counterpoint to the cloudless blue sky. The breeze off the ocean picked up, stirring the palms, a moving scrim of shade and light. The drone of insects grew louder. Her thoughts slowed and scattered, breaking the dark mass of worry into smaller bits.

Cocooned, she swayed gently. Her limbs began to loosen. Her head lolled to one side. She couldn't remember the last time she'd felt this relaxed. She was just shy of sleep when a text dinged in. Raising her cell phone and rousing the screen, she peered at the message from Kyra.

Depends on what you mean by okay. And what you're supposed to
say when your child asks how his father got other children.

• • •

Nikki followed the flower-lined path to the Sunshine's main
building and stepped into the lobby they'd remodeled in an
unsuccessful attempt to turn *Do Over* back into the renovation
program they'd originally envisioned. The result was a beautiful
mix of new materials and vintage charm that had given the
midcentury hotel and beach club new life.

Her gaze ran over the refurbished sand-colored terrazzo floor
with the blue and black bits that stood out in the sunlight that
now streamed through new south- and west-facing glass walls.
The sagging roof had not only been replaced but raised and a
rooftop bar and grill added above it. The long, light-filled space
held card and game tables as well as vintage pinball machines.
Seating areas composed of clean-lined sofas, love seats, and Arne
Jacobsen–style Egg chairs surrounded reproduction free-form
Noguchi tables. All of it upholstered in brightly colored fabrics
designed to hold up under damp bathing suits and tracked-in
sand.

She paused in front of the wall of photographs that interior
designer Ray Flamingo had framed and hung. Shot between the
hotel's opening in the forties until its closing in the early eight-
ies, the photos featured the Handlemans, who'd owned and run
it, as well as the regular guests and beach club members, who'd
been treated like extended family.

At the soda fountain that duplicated the original down to
the vintage cooler from which ice cream sandwiches could be
taken on the honor system just as they had been when Renée
Franklin and her sister Annelise Handleman were children,
Nikki eyed the glass-dome-covered dish that held a tantalizing
assortment of homemade brownies. Her mouth watered, but
memories of her attempts to squeeze into pre-pregnancy cloth-

ing sent her into the glass-walled dining room in search of coffee instead.

There she found the waitstaff clearing the last of breakfast
and setting up for lunch.

"There's half a pretty fresh pot in the kitchen," Randy, whose
company operated the dining room and rooftop grill, offered.
"And a couple of cinnamon buns."

"Thanks." Coffee in hand and willpower still in place, she
headed back out to what they generously called the gift shop
but was actually a series of small displays that had been worked
in around the hotel's original front desk.

An assortment of Sunshine Hotel and Beach Club T-shirts
and sweatshirts hung on a curving wrought iron display rack
framed in a slice of window. A shelf affixed to the wall held a
variety of postcards. Visors and neon-colored flip-flops filled
some of the wooden cubbies that hung on the wall next to the
sun-shaped clock. Original forties-era cottage keys with dangling nameplates filled the others.

She straightened the merchandise and greeted a foursome of
beach club members who'd reserved a card table for bridge. She
considered calling Joe, to whom she'd blubbered pathetically
last night when she'd been unable to fit her current body into
her former clothing, but she was reluctant to bother him while
he was working. Because, really, what did she have to share?

Next she rearranged and refolded all the T-shirts while
sneaking peeks at the brownies on the soda fountain counter.
When she imagined she heard them calling her name, she
turned her back and caught a glimpse of Luvie wheeling the
double stroller from the beach through the low pink wall.

A deep flush of shame and guilt heated her face as she realized that she was standing here doing pretty much nothing
while someone else took care of her children. At Luvie's cheery
wave, Nikki stepped outside.

"Goodness, but we've had ourselves a lovely walk." Luvie

tightened the strings of the large floppy straw hat without which she did not venture outside.

"That's great, isn't it, sweeties?" Nikki smiled and bent to kiss her daughters' cheeks, which was when she noticed that Sofia and Gemma's sun hats were identical to Luvie's.

"Gwak!" Sofia repeated happily. Gemma reached her hands out in an attempt to touch her bare toes. When she couldn't reach them, her face scrunched up. Nikki braced for a shriek of displeasure, but before Gemma could emit a squeak let alone one of her bloodcurdling wails, the supernanny handed her a squeaky toy shaped like a puppy. Gemma chortled happily and said, "Oof! Dokkie!!" Neither of them said "Mommy" or tried to get out of the stroller to reach for her.

"Nice hats," Nikki said.

"Oh, I do hope you don't mind. They seemed to love how mine flopped about, and I felt they offered a bit more protection from the sun than those adorable baseball caps they'd been wearing."

"Of course."

Luvie waited. When nothing else was said, she smiled brightly. "Well then, I'll get the girls back to the cottage and start preparing their lunch, shall I?"

"Lunch!" The girls said in unison and quite clearly. Nikki knew she was just imagining the British accent. But as the nanny wheeled the girls away, Nikki was the one who felt like the odd one out. She wanted a do over.

• • •

"Please go to the bathroom," Kyra begged Max. "The car is already waiting." She offered an apologetic wave to the driver who sat behind the steering wheel of the SUV that would deliver them to the production offices.

But Max was not stupid. He'd figured out that once he finished he was going back inside, and so he took his time squatting for a small piddle here, another over there. This was followed by sniffing and circling as if something important was about to happen.

During lunch Kyra had done her best to try to prepare Dustin for what he might expect on set and at today's wardrobe fittings. She'd also prepared a few "talking points" for Tonja should the opportunity or need arise, and had vowed to never again allow Dustin to be alone with the Deranian-Kay children. What she hadn't figured out was how to get Max to do his business on command.

"You've got five more minutes," she said. Because after that she'd need another five to ten to get him into the crate. Not that the crate had proven overly effective or particularly Max-proof.

At precisely one P.M., Kyra and Dustin were delivered to the film's base camp. As its name implied, the area surrounding a film location looked a lot like a military installation. In this case the camp was arranged around the former fruit processing plant that now housed the film's production offices and a massive soundstage.

The production assistant, Mary, who greeted them with a toss of her dark hair, was young, pretty, and enthusiastic. She was also close to the age Kyra had been when she reported to work on her first and only movie set, and Kyra wondered if the girl would fare better, be smarter.

It was hard to avoid the comparisons or the memories as Mary led them through the maze of temporary outbuildings, tent-covered areas, and trailers, whose arrangement, Kyra knew, was far from random. Big stars had big trailers. Supporting actors had smaller trailers farther from the center of action. Bit and day players were even farther away and were lucky to be assigned to multi "hole" units referred to as three bangers and five bangers, each banger typically consisting of a bed, television, and toilet.

Mary pointed out the honey wagon comprising multiple potties, which existed for those without trailers. A food tent stretched along the opposite perimeter.

"First stop is wardrobe and makeup," Mary said as they passed the main production office then walked through the soundstage where hotel interiors were under construction. Her friendly chatter and Kyra's walk down memory lane came to a screeching halt at the sight of Tonja Kay waiting for them in the wardrobe department. The PA blinked nervously in the movie star's presence. Kyra dropped her hands to Dustin's shoulders and pulled him up against her protectively.

Tonja looked the part of the working producer, comfortable on set, her blond hair in a French braid, her makeup flawless but subdued, her clothes casual but perfectly put together. The PA had not yet recovered the use of her vocal cords when Tonja introduced them to Margaret Mills, a smiling, fiftysomething woman with short salt-and-pepper hair who sized up Dustin expertly then pulled a collection of shorts, T-shirts, pajamas, and bathing suits from a hanging rack with his name on it.

"Let's slip these on. When you're dressed, I'll take a few pictures to show the director and to make sure I remember which outfits we'll use for which scenes. Then you can be on your way."

The wardrobe session moved quickly with Margaret, as she asked to be called, helping Dustin in and out of each outfit.

The visit to the makeup department was even briefer.

"Four-year-old children are never perfectly groomed or coiffed, are they?" Tonja smiled at Kyra in a mother-to-mother kind of way that set Kyra's teeth on edge. Then she bent down to brush Dustin's bang out of the way as the makeup artist scribbled notes.

"Children aren't perfectly groomed or coiffed," Kyra agreed. "And sometimes they repeat the truly nasty things they've heard their parents say in order to hurt another child."

Tonja's smile puckered slightly.

"If that were to happen again, the hurt child's mother would have to remove her child from the situation." She held Tonja's gaze as she delivered the threat. "Do you understand?"

"I do." With a crisp nod, Tonja led them outside and escorted them to one of the largest trailers closest to the soundstage. A numeral three had been taped to its side. "This is Dustin's."

"This is for Dustin?" Kyra asked, certain she'd misunderstood. Daniel and Tonja would be numbers one and two on the call sheet. She'd assumed that Derek Hanson and Christian Sommersby would be three and four and that Dustin would share a small trailer with some other young supporting actor.

"Yes."

They stepped inside the long, beautifully appointed space with its plush built-in sofa and seating area. A big-screen television took up most of the opposite wall. A bedroom and bathroom filled the remainder of the space. It was almost identical to the trailer in which Daniel had first seduced her, the place she'd naively thought of as "theirs."

"This will be your home away from home while you're on set. It will come along with us when we're on location." The explanation was aimed at Dustin, but Tonja's eyes never really settled on him. She was looking at Kyra.

Kyra shook her head. "We don't need anything this lavish. We'll be fine in something smaller and more utilitarian." It was a refuge for an adult, not a four-year-old child.

"Daniel insisted," Tonja replied.

There was a quick rap on the trailer door and Daniel bounded inside, filling the large space with his astounding looks and oversize personality. A small whimper escaped Mary's lips. Kyra almost felt sorry for the Production Assistant but even now, knowing him as well as she did and with his wife standing right there, she had to fight off a similar reaction.

"How do you like your trailer, little man?" Daniel went down on one knee so that he could look Dustin in the eye.

"Is awesome in here!" Dustin pointed to the video game console that sat beneath the television. "Wanna play a video game, Dandiel?"

He reached over and ruffled Dustin's curls. "I have some work I have to take care of right now. But a little later we thought we'd take you to Legoland." Daniel remained on one knee making direct eye contact. "Would you like to do that?"

"Legoland?" Dustin's voice trilled with excitement. "I love Legoland!"

"Did you really just do that without even running it by me?" It was Christmas and Santa arriving with a Great Dane puppy all over again. "And I've already explained to Tonja that I didn't appreciate some of the words that were thrown around last night." She would not repeat those words in front of Dustin. "He won't be going on an outing with your family."

Tonja remained silent, her face expressionless.

"I'm sorry to hear there was a problem." Daniel managed to sound both surprised and contrite, though he didn't ask for details. "But we weren't planning to take the whole family."

He sent her the smile that had always turned her legs to rubber. "We need to build a relationship between 'Tyler' here"—he clapped a hand on Dustin's shoulder—"and his on-screen parents that feels convincingly familial before we start shooting. And the park's right there." He motioned toward the theme park they'd driven past earlier.

Kyra felt Tonja and Daniel's eyes on her. It was a reasonable request, one that could help Dustin get comfortable with being a part of the fictional Roberts family and help prepare him for what lay ahead. "All right," she said. "I guess we could do that. What time were you thinking?"

Daniel and Tonja exchanged glances.

"I should be able to break away by four o'clock," Daniel said.

"But you do understand that it'll just be Dustin, Tonja, and me. You know, so we can establish rapport and start looking and feeling like a real family."

"No," she said once again feeling blindsided. "I didn't understand." And she didn't like the idea one bit.

# Eleven

It was six P.M. on Tuesday and Bitsy was in the process of locking the front door of Steding & Steding when a young woman, holding a little girl by the hand and a baby cradled in a sling across her chest, rushed up to it. "I know I'm late," she said, gasping for breath. "I'm Erin Clayton. My appointment was at four, but I had to take two buses to get here. And one of them broke down and . . . Lucy's been cutting teeth." She looked down at the baby sleeping against her chest. "And . . ." She swallowed. "Please let us come in so I can talk to the lawyer. I . . ." She stopped talking and looked up at Bitsy beseechingly, her blue eyes flooded with unshed tears. "I . . . online it said that the first appointment was free." Bitsy remembered how afraid she was when she'd arrived that the free half hour was just some sort of come-on. "I really need to talk to somebody."

Bitsy stepped back and ushered them in. "Ms. Steding is on the phone right now," she said, showing them to seats in the waiting room. "But you're absolutely right. The first consultation is free."

Erin's shoulders slumped in obvious relief.

"Why don't you fill out this form while I let her know you're here."

"Thank you." There was a quiver in Erin's voice. "Thank you so much."

The little girl climbed up onto the chair next to her mother then scooted against its back. Only her feet reached past the edge. Her lank brown hair hung in messy braids on either side of her pale, pinched face. Her white tights were stained, the Mary Janes scuffed. Bitsy assumed she was no more than five or six. Until she looked into her eyes, which were way older than they should have been.

"Would you like something to drink?" Bitsy asked.

"I'm fine," Erin said. "But maybe a glass of water or juice for Susanna if you have it?" Erin's eyes shimmered with tears that she somehow managed not to shed. As if she'd learned it was safer to keep them in. The little girl looked straight at Bitsy.

"Susanna's a pretty name."

"It's from the song 'Oh! Susanna,'" she said.

"I've always loved that song," Bitsy replied. "My name's Bitsy."

"Like the itsy spider?" Susanna asked skeptically.

"Yes, just like that. Funny that we both have songs that go with our names, but of course mine has hand gestures, too." Bitsy twisted her fingers in the way she'd learned when she was about Susanna's age. The girl's small smile felt like a major victory.

"Let me go see what's in the refrigerator. I'll be right back."

On her way to the kitchen, Bitsy poked her head into June's office and explained the situation. "I'm sorry. I know it's after six, but I just couldn't turn them away. They looked so . . ."

"No problem." With her steady gaze, kind smile, and wash-and-wear red-gold hair, June Steding looked like a cross between June Cleaver and Margaret Thatcher, not at all the pit bull that Bitsy had originally been looking for. But the sole practitioner's tenacity often allowed her to triumph over stronger, louder, more pedigreed firms. Her passion for protecting those who needed it most made her an extremely effective advocate.

Bitsy brought Susanna a juice box and a bag of Goldfish crackers, which were received as if they were a great gift. "How would you like to sit here and color while you have your snack?" Bitsy asked, presenting a coloring book and small box of crayons that were kept on hand for just these kinds of situations. "We'll leave the office door open in case you need anything."

Susanna nodded and was already opening the crayons as her mother mouthed a silent thank-you and followed Bitsy in to meet June Steding.

"Would you mind taking notes while Mrs. Clayton tells us why she's here?" June asked Bitsy.

Bitsy pulled a bottled water out of her jacket pocket and handed it to Erin then took a seat and pulled out a notepad as the young mother opened the bottle and nodded her thanks.

"Mrs. Clayton?" June prompted.

"Please call me Erin."

"All right, Erin," June said gently. "Why don't you tell me what happened."

Erin downed a long swig of water as if it were whiskey. "I don't understand what happened. I mean, everything seemed fine. I . . . I thought we were happy. And then one day my husband got up and went to work and . . ." She swallowed as if the words had gotten stuck in her throat. "And he just never came home."

Bitsy's hand stilled. Except for the going to work part, this was exactly what had happened to her. She waited to see if Erin's husband had left with all her money and a stripper that he had impregnated, like Bertie had.

"He emptied out our checking and savings accounts."

Bitsy sighed as June pulled the details from Erin. Just outside the office Susanna munched the Goldfish. Bitsy was glad she couldn't hear her mother's words.

"Do you suspect foul play?" June asked gently.

Erin shook her head dully, and Bitsy remembered being asked this same question when Bertie first disappeared and how much she had wished she could say yes. How desperately she wanted to believe that Bertie had not *chosen* to leave her and steal from her. The tears Erin had been holding began to spill.

"I tried his cell phone, but it was disconnected. I tried his friends but nobody answered. Then I called his mother and she said . . ." The tears were coming faster now. June set a box of tissues in front of the crying woman. In this office tissues were a necessary and important budget item.

"She'd tried to talk him into coming back and doing the right thing. But he wouldn't listen to her." She pressed a balled-up tissue to her eyes. "He ran away. Like he was the only one it got to be too much for."

In the waiting room, Susanna colored intently. Bitsy wished she had something that might drown out the horror of this too-familiar story.

"I'm two months behind on the rent. I don't have childcare and I can't . . . well, I can't work because . . . I can't leave them home alone." There was something in Erin's voice that indicated she'd considered this option and only recently let go of it.

Bitsy kept her head down and kept scribbling, taking down June's suggestions, the referrals to city, county, and charitable programs, her explanations of what kinds of help each might provide.

"But can't you just find him and make him come back?" Erin asked.

Bitsy's heart ached at the question. She couldn't bear to look at the young mother or the child bent over the coloring book in the waiting room as June told Erin what Bitsy already knew, that finding a deadbeat husband was one thing. Finding one with wages that could be garnished was another. And neither of those things was likely to happen before Erin and her daughters lost their home.

June spent way more time than the thirty free minutes Erin had come for. It was seven thirty when she ended the conversation.

"I'm so sorry for your trouble," the attorney said, clasping Erin's hand. "I promise to do everything I can to find your husband. I'll also speak to your landlord."

Bitsy knew the two hundred and fifty dollars in cash that was kept for emergencies had been transferred in the handshake.

"Thank you so much for your time and for offering to help." Erin's gratitude shone in her eyes as she released June's hand.

"Thank you for the snack," Susanna added. Her eyes were still far too old but there was no bitterness in them. She did not allude to or ask about her missing father. "I been thinking that my song needs hand gestures, too."

Bitsy smiled. "Maybe you can show them to me next time."

Bitsy stood beside June as the Claytons departed. As she watched them go, Bitsy began to relive her own abandonment. Felt that chasm of panic at losing everything.

And then, possibly for the first time, she chastised herself for making the comparison when she had a roof over her head and friends at her back, and Erin Clayton and her poor daughters did not.

. . .

"Shh . . ." Nikki held a finger to her lips as she opened the door and motioned Bitsy into the cottage. "Hold on a sec," she said before turning and tiptoeing toward the nursery like a thief in the night. There she held her breath as she pulled the nursery door gently closed. As if waking and/or dealing with her daughters was something to be avoided at all costs. As if she, and not Luvie, had fed, bathed, and put them down to sleep in the first place.

"Tough day?" Bitsy asked.

"Not really," Nikki said. Because despite all her protests about not needing or wanting help, she had been very careful not to come home this evening until she was sure Sofia and Gemma would be asleep. And while killing that kind of time when one did not have a job, a husband in town, or a home that needed cleaning or decorating took a good bit of energy, it simply didn't qualify as "tough." "But I don't think that rules out drinking, do you?"

"Hell, no," Bitsy said as Nikki opened a bottle of red, poured two generous glasses, then clinked her rim against Bitsy's. "*Salute!*" She downed almost half of it.

"*Salute.*" Bitsy took a long sip.

It was only after she picked up the bottle and led Bitsy toward the sofa that she noticed the large cardboard box that now sat on the coffee table. "What's that?"

"I brought a few of your things back from Palm Beach."

"Things of mine?" Nikki asked, confused.

"Yours," Bitsy said, motioning her to open it.

Nikki ran a fingernail under the tape and pulled open the lid. Reaching in, her hands pressed down on what felt like folded clothing wrapped in tissue paper. She leaned closer to open the top layer. The scent of Chanel No. 5 wafted upward as she pulled out a pair of paisley silk lounging pajamas.

"Oh, my God. Where did you get these?" Nikki held the flowing fuchsia pieces designed by Coco Chanel up to the light. "They were one of my first splurges." In fact, she'd bought them the day she opened the West Coast office of Heart, Inc., the A-list dating and matchmaking service she'd created long before the Millionaire Matchmaker had copied, coarsened, then commercialized her concept.

"I bought them back when you were first selling off your vintage clothing," Bitsy said.

Bitsy had been one of her only matchmaking clients who had not deserted her when it became known that Malcolm Dyer, whose Ponzi scheme decimated much of Palm Beach, was Nikki's brother. For a decade and a half Bitsy's marriage had appeared to be founded on love, not avarice.

Nikki reached back into the box and found a vintage Emilio Pucci jumpsuit. A pale blue linen Givenchy suit lay beneath it.

"I thought the dress I married Joe in was the only thing you'd saved."

Bitsy smiled. "I bought quite a few of your things. I meant to give them all back to you when the time was right." Her smile faltered. "When everything fell apart, I forgot all about them. Eleanor Wyndham, the neighbor friend I visited over New Year's, had bought them at auction to return to me. She thought they were mine." Bitsy topped off their glasses.

"They are yours, you know. You're free to sell or keep them." Nikki reached back into the box and pulled out a Prada sundress with spaghetti straps and a flounce around the bottom. "I seriously doubt I could fit into this dress." She glanced down at her still-bulky stomach and the breasts that had apparently not gotten the message that they no longer needed to provide nourishment.

"You will," Bitsy said. "But I wouldn't mind borrowing something now and again."

A cry rose from the nursery. Nikki froze, waiting for an answering cry from twin number two. She didn't start breathing again until there'd been a full minute of silence.

"Are you all right?" Bitsy asked, her eyes on Nikki's face.

"Of course." She was the luckiest woman alive, what with a husband who loved her, more help than she needed, and two beautiful, healthy babies. "Couldn't be better." Whatever would she have to complain about? "How about you?"

Bitsy didn't answer immediately.

"Did something happen?" Nikki sat up.

"Well, I did have a bit of a wake-up call today," Bitsy said. "It finally hit me that witnessing other people's misery can be harder than living your own."

Nikki lifted her glass to her lips and waited for Bitsy to go on, glad to have something other than her own unwarranted sense of misery to contemplate.

"A lot of the women who come through June Steding's office

are completely alone with no means of support at all. Plus, they have children they need to take care of. And debts that need to be paid. They're completely underwater and don't have anyone else to turn to." Bitsy lifted her glass again. "I never thought I'd feel lucky to be poor. Well, actually, I never thought I'd be poor at all. But it's becoming pretty clear that things could be worse." Her smile was crooked. "I find myself wondering if Maddie would accept that as my one good thing."

Nikki shook her head. "Unlikely. But since we're not watching a sunset and I don't think either of us are planning to call and ask her . . ." Nikki raised her glass. "Here's to knowing that things can always be worse." They drank. "And to not being the most pitiful people we know."

"You, my friend, are not in a pitiful position." Bitsy looked around the small living room/dining room/kitchen. Baby paraphernalia was piled in one corner. "A somewhat cramped position, maybe, but not pitiful."

A knock sounded on the door. Nikki got up to open it.

Avery stood on the welcome mat with a large pizza box in her hands. "Anybody hungry?"

"I am! Come on in." She stepped back so Avery could enter.

"Pizza!" Bitsy, whose former life had included a personal chef and a staff to wait on her, looked as excited as Nikki, though that might have had more to do with the change in topic than the arrival of dinner. "What kind is it?"

"Given that Avery did the ordering I'm guessing it's topped with cheese, cheese, and . . ." Nikki sniffed theatrically. "Cheese."

"Very funny." Avery set the pizza box on the dinette table and opened the lid. "There's no such thing as a pizza with too much cheese on it. But I did get half with mushroom and pepperoni. You know, for the picky people in the group."

"Perfect!" Bitsy grinned and moved to the table while Nikki pulled paper plates and napkins out of the cupboard then found and opened a second bottle of wine.

There was a brief silence as they chewed appreciatively.

"When's Joe due back?" Bitsy asked as she dabbed politely at the corners of her mouth.

"He's not sure," Nikki replied, not understanding why each day he was gone seemed longer than the last. Small and packed as the cottage was, it often felt empty without him. Despite Bitsy's earlier ban on the word, at the moment she was *pitifully* grateful not to be alone.

She could have been at Joe's Miami house. *Their* Miami house. Which was far more spacious and closer to Mermaid Point. But she couldn't follow Maddie around like some frightened child. At least the Sunshine was home base to Maddie and Kyra. They'd be back. Not to mention, Avery and Bitsy and the Franklins were here. And, of course, there was Luvie . . .

"How's the tiny house coming?" Bitsy asked.

"Good," Avery replied around a mouthful of cheese. "Everything's been ordered and I've got a three-man crew. The space is too small for a lot of bodies. It's going to be a quick build. I think we can have the shell complete by the end of the day tomorrow and start framing on Thursday."

"That's good," Nikki offered.

"Yes, very good," Bitsy added. "I'm pretty sure if Maddie were here it would count."

They paused almost reverentially at the mention of Maddie. Who had always been their center.

"Has anyone heard from her or Kyra?" Avery asked.

"They haven't even been gone three full days . . ." Nikki said, though it felt a helluva lot longer.

"Right." Avery lowered her head and reached for a second slice of pizza. "I guess it just feels longer. Because they left first thing Sunday morning."

"It does feel longer." Bitsy dabbed her mouth then reached for another piece. "And quieter."

Nikki managed not to add anything that might sound, well, pitiful. She had the girls. And Joe would be back soon.

"Yeah," Avery said almost wistfully. "I wonder what they're doing right now."

"Well, I certainly hope Maddie is enjoying carnal knowledge of William Hightower," Bitsy said with a wicked smile. "And that Kyra is busy getting to know Derek Hanson and Christian Sommersby. They were both in Daniel's last film and they are completely and totally hot."

They finished the second bottle and, whether it was the company or the alcohol, Nikki's mood had begun to lift.

"Nik?"

"Hmmm?" She looked up to see Bitsy looking at her expectantly.

"I was wondering if you might be able to take a few of my shifts at the Sunshine?" Bitsy asked. She helped out as needed in the hotel office and manning the small gift shop that had been added to the lobby. "June's trial date got moved up and she asked me to work more hours."

"Um, sure," Nikki said. "I'd be glad to help out." She stood and began to clear the table. She did not add how nice it would be to have something to do other than killing time and feeling guilty for allowing someone else to mother her children. Doing something productive would go a long way to making her feel less pathetic.

# Twelve

Avery took the Gandy Bridge to Tampa the next evening then followed Gandy Boulevard to Bayshore, where she could catch glimpses of Tampa Bay through the keyholes in the concrete balustrade. It wasn't the fastest route to the Hardins' but was, in her mind, the most scenic. At the moment, she wasn't looking for fast. She was in no hurry to find out whether Chase would be there for the dinner his father, Jeff, had invited her to, and had no idea whether he'd be happy to see her if he was.

When she arrived the garage door was closed, so she had no idea whether Chase's truck was inside. She sat in her car for a few moments, waffling, but she'd accepted Jeff's invitation and she was here. She was a grown-up. It was time to act like one.

She parked and walked slowly up the driveway to ring the bell. It was Chase who opened the door. The surprise that washed across his face made it clear he was not expecting her. "I'm guessing you're not here selling magazine subscriptions."

"Jeff invited me for dinner."

"Oh." He stepped aside to let her in. "That explains the sneaky smile on his face, the casserole in the oven, and the chocolate fudge cake he had me bring home from Alessi's."

"Sorry." She attempted a casual shrug, but the accompanying smile felt wobbly. So did her knees. "I . . . he . . ." She cleared her throat. "I hope you don't mind."

"Come on in."

Her heart was actually thundering in her chest and she was having a hard time catching her breath. So what if she'd forgotten how blue his eyes were? The way a smile could light up his whole face. This was Chase. The man who would only accept all or nothing.

"Is that our guest?" Jeff's voice reached her from the kitchen. "Bring her on in, boy. Where are your manners?"

Chase stepped back and motioned her to go ahead. She was aware of his solid presence behind her all the way into the kitchen.

"Wow, that smells fabulous." She bent over to place a kiss on Jeff's cheek, remembering how once she'd been unable to reach his face without going up on tiptoe. He'd been her father's closest friend and business partner, the only parental figure she had left. "In fact, it smells a lot like your famous cheeseburger casserole."

"That it is." Jeff wheeled his chair backward. "I was just thinking about how nice the kitchen used to smell when Deirdre was taking those cooking lessons we gave her."

"A completely self-serving gift as I recall," Chase observed.

"It was," Avery said. "But it was the first time I ever saw her enjoy being in a kitchen." It had also been the last.

"Why don't you come have a seat, Avery?" Jeff said in a tone that acknowledged the unexpected hole her mother's absence had left. "Chase, can you open that bottle of wine?"

Chase pulled a corkscrew from a kitchen drawer while Avery took the seat Jeff pulled out for her. She watched Chase's broad back and the slight ripple of muscle as he pulled the cork from the bottle and poured two glasses of wine, which he carried to the table. He set one in front of his father's place and one in front of her.

"Can you pull the cheese plate out of the fridge? The crackers are there on the counter."

"Quite a feast you've got planned here," Chase said as he did everything his father asked. But he didn't make eye contact, pour himself a glass of wine, or sit down. He just leaned against the counter while Jeff checked the timer on the oven and plied her with questions about the Wyatt project and how far along she'd gotten on her first official tiny house build.

"Well, we started framing this morning," she said. "I'm aiming for three to four weeks. It's a tight schedule, but I've got a great crew working full-time and a fabulous client who has no problem making and sticking to decisions."

"Why, that sounds great," Jeff enthused. "Doesn't it, Chase?"

"It does." Chase nodded. But he stayed where he was and his smile looked more like a wince.

"Chase is just finishing up a new spec house in Palma Ceia," Jeff said, mentioning a nearby Tampa neighborhood.

"That's great," Avery said, careful not to look directly at Chase. He'd spoken only when prompted and didn't move from his position against the counter except when his father asked him to do something.

When the timer buzzed, Jeff managed to remove the casserole from the oven and place it on a waiting trivet on the table then wheeled to the vacant spot across from Avery. He looked up at his son. "Aren't you going to come sit down?" He motioned to the third place at the table.

"No," he said.

Jeff looked at him more closely. Avery busied herself unfolding her napkin and smoothing it over her lap. If she could have, she would have covered her ears with her hands.

"That's the problem with springing something on someone. Sometimes that person has somewhere else they need to be."

Jeff looked at Chase in disbelief. Avery just felt sick to her stomach.

"Well, I know Jason's occupied tonight. What could be more important than having dinner with us?" Jeff demanded.

One of Chase's dark eyebrows sketched upward. An odd, yet

unapologetic, smile played around his lips. "I'm afraid I already have plans for dinner tonight." He detached himself from the counter. "I've got a date with someone who's interested in more from me than 'just a good time.'"

. . .

Bitsy sat in June Steding's office feeling almost as miserable as the clients who'd come in that day in search of the lawyer's help. "I don't understand how you do this every day," she said, her grip tight on the bottled water she'd been nursing. "It seems like everything is a finger in the dike with no real hope of holding back the rising water."

The attorney nodded. "It's true. Mostly you do a little bit for a lot of people. In baseball, I think they call it 'small ball.' Lots of singles to move the runners around the bases instead of relying on a home run."

"What about Gary Kaufman?" Bitsy asked, thinking about the forensic accountant who even now must be working through her financial records. "Is he a home-run hitter?"

"I've seen him hit more than a few." June smiled and tilted back in her chair. "Knowledge is power. And if anyone can follow the money and figure out what crimes Bertie's committed, it's him."

Bitsy lifted the water bottle to her lips. "I never thought I'd be eager to prove my husband committed crimes. Especially crimes against me."

"Well, documenting fraud is key and can point us in new directions. In the meantime there is a way to divorce Bertie even if we don't find him and can't serve him with papers."

"Really?" Bitsy sat up. "I mean, I want to see him locked up and I really, really hope we can find where the money's stashed. But I also want to be free." She studied the woman across from her. "Is it very complicated?"

"Not really. It's a matter of filling out a form that documents your efforts to locate him. At the same time, we prepare a Notice of Action for Dissolution of Marriage for publication in a newspaper that specializes in classified legal advertisements. If the missing spouse doesn't respond in twenty-eight days, we file a motion for a default divorce. From start to finish you're looking at about ninety days."

"You never mentioned this before." She considered the attorney, hoping it wasn't a sign that June thought the odds of finding Bertie were slim.

"No, I didn't." June folded her hands on her desk. "Because I really want to see him dragged back and locked up. And the money returned. But it's always good to have a backup plan in case you need it."

When Bitsy got home, Sherlock met her at the door with what she was pretty certain was a sympathetic expression on his face. She lingered outside, drawing in great gulps of fresh air while he visited and anointed his favorite bushes and trees, only heading back inside in the gathering dusk.

She was eyeing the Lean Cuisine she'd nuked and had no interest in eating when a knock sounded on the cottage door. Sherlock sat up, cocked his head, and woofed. Bitsy looked through the peephole then opened the door.

Bits of sawdust clung to Avery's short blond curls. Dirt and grime streaked her cheeks. Her cargo pants were filthy and the logo on her T-shirt was no longer recognizable.

"What happened?" Bitsy asked. "Are you all right? Do you need to use my shower?"

"No. I couldn't find my corkscrew." Avery held up a bottle of red wine. "I need you to open this bottle. And then I need you to help me drink it."

"It's a little late for sunset toasts."

"I didn't really come here to toast. You can toast to anything you want. I'm mostly interested in the drinking part." Avery pulled a second bottle out of an oversize pant pocket. "I really don't have a single good thing to share. I meant to bring Cheez Doodles. But the wine seemed more important."

"No Cheez Doodles? Now I know it's serious." Bitsy stepped back so that Avery could enter. "But I loaned my corkscrew to Nikki." She poked her head out and glanced down the walkway. Seeing that the Giraldis' porch and living room lights were on, she sent Nikki a text. Two minutes later Nikki arrived carrying the corkscrew, a bottle of wine, and a baby monitor.

Bitsy pulled three wineglasses out of the cupboard while Nikki opened the first bottle. Avery paced, which took real skill considering the minimal square footage. "Come sit down. You're making me nervous."

Avery sat. Nikki settled on the love seat beside her. Bitsy took the lone chair and raised her glass. "To?"

"Do we have to drink *to* something?" Avery asked.

"Well, we would if Maddie were here," Bitsy said. "But I'm not sure I have the strength to come up with anything, either." She was pretty sure finding out you could divorce your thieving husband of fifteen years by publishing it in the paper would not qualify as a good thing.

They clinked glasses and drank.

"You're just lucky the 'good enough' police aren't listening in. But just in case they are, let's drink to sleeping children," Nikki said with a glance at the monitor. "And to the whole eight ounces I've lost over the last three days."

"Eight ounces, huh?" Bitsy asked. "I think I can see it in, uh, your cheekbones."

Nikki snorted. "Yeah, I think that four ounces on each side is making a pretty significant difference."

Avery rolled her eyes. It was an automatic gesture, but a small smile followed. "Good thing I didn't bring those Cheez Doodles. I know how hard a time you have resisting them."

It was Bitsy's turn to snort. She took a healthy sip of her wine, glad not to be drinking alone.

Nikki looked Avery up and down. "So, I can't help noticing that you're wearing a lot of building materials. Were there any left on-site?"

Avery took a long pull of wine. "Very funny. I'm working on a tiny house. That means close quarters. It's not like staying clean is a primary construction goal."

Nikki was still eyeing Avery. "Didn't you have dinner at the Hardins' last night?"

"Yep."

"How was it?" Bitsy asked, noting Avery's squirm and the quick gulp of wine that followed.

"Dinner was fine," Avery said. "It was great to see Jeff. And Jason's doing way better since he came back from the Outward Bound program. He's been filling out college applications."

"And Chase?" Nikki asked. "How's he doing?"

Avery reached for her wineglass. "Oh, he seems to be doing fine, too. We caught up a little bit. Of course, that was before he had to leave to go pick up his date."

"Ouch." Bitsy winced.

"Yeah, well, to be fair, I don't think he was intentionally flaunting it. He didn't know I was coming to dinner. And I'm the one who didn't want a serious relationship. He is free to date anyone he wants to."

Nikki sat back and closed her eyes briefly. "This is that moment when Maddie would have said the perfect thing."

"Yeah," Avery agreed. "I almost called her to ask for advice. But then I thought she's finally free to relax and not worry about anyone else. And I didn't want to interrupt her time with Will." She paused. "I guess doing a conference call or getting her on speakerphone right now is out of the question?"

There was a brief but hopeful silence. Bitsy knew it would only take one of them to cave and hit speed dial. This was what happened when your glass-is-half-full person was missing.

"We can't do that. She deserves a break from being there for all of us," Nikki finally said. "Me included. But, God, I miss her."

Bitsy topped off their drinks as they stared stupidly at each other.

"But we all know Maddie pretty well. Sometimes I can even hear her voice in the back of my head," Nikki continued. "Maybe all we really have to do is ask ourselves WWMD—what would Maddie do."

# Thirteen

Maddie had no earthly idea what to do. It was eight A.M. on Friday. Will had eased out of bed before sunrise, leaving her a note that he was headed into the studio to work on the new song. One he'd been working on all week and was determined to finish before they left on tour.

Lori was in the office happily checking things off her count-down-to-tour list. Hudson Power had been out on the flats for hours guiding two longtime anglers to favored fishing spots. Every other person on Mermaid Point was busily engaged in either helping others or working on themselves.

Back before their lives had been decimated by Malcolm Dyer's Ponzi scheme, Maddie had contemplated her recently emptied nest and believed that a shiny new life was about to begin. She had imagined the freedom to do whatever appealed to her; to be anything she chose. She had dreamed of doing absolutely nothing for a really long time.

Those dreams had been put on hold while she did what had to be done to ensure her family's survival. In the process she'd grown stronger than she'd ever imagined. She had learned how to leap tall buildings in a single bound. How to face and conquer whatever life threw at her. Except, it appeared, free time.

She'd been on Mermaid Point for four and a half days now. Four and a half days spent reminding herself how lucky she was to be there, how great it was to have no responsibilities and nothing she had to do. Four and a half aimless, endless days of waiting for everyone else to finish what they were doing so that she wouldn't be alone with nothing to do.

Who knew that doing nothing could be so hard? Or that she might be so incredibly bad at it.

She got up and wandered through the great room, admiring the plank floors that she'd help refinish, trailing a finger over the tobacco leather furniture that surrounded the fireplace feature wall of pressed shell, rock, and barnacle, tilting her head back to take in the acid-washed pecky cypress walls that rose to the vaulted beamed ceiling. All of it imagined by Deirdre Morgan, made a reality by her daughter Avery Lawford with the lot of them serving as slave labor while the network recorded their misery. The work had been brutal and she'd hated the network's mean-spirited reality TV version of the renovation show they'd envisioned. But *Do Over*, stressful as it was, had given shape and purpose to their days.

She wandered past the pool table and large pine farm table to the eastern end of the room. The accordion glass wall had been folded open and she stepped out onto the balcony. The ocean breeze that set Mermaid Point's palms swaying rifled her hair and caressed her cheeks as she stared out over the pavilion and pool to the turquoise-streaked ocean that stretched out into infinity. Morning sun sent shards of reflected light bouncing off the steel frame of the Alligator Reef Lighthouse in the distance. Boats passed in the far channels, their frothy white wakes unfolding behind them.

She leaned over the balcony railing to watch seagulls and other small birds chase after food in the sphere-shaped tidal pool.

In the clearing Romeo threw back his head, puffed out his chest, and crowed. Even the time-challenged rooster had a reason for being and a gaggle of admirers to witness him doing it.

Did standing around worrying about doing nothing qualify as doing nothing?

*Stop it,* she chastised herself. *Take the boat to the mainland and go shopping. Go out for lunch. Take a dip in the pool. Lie in the hammock and read the novel you haven't even opened.*

She could practically see Kyra rolling her eyes at what she liked to call "first-world problems." Kyra, whom she'd left alone to navigate a hostile environment, so that she could be with Will.

Maddie pulled her phone from her pocket and hit speed dial.

Kyra answered on the first ring. "Mom?" Her voice trembled slightly.

"Are you all right?"

"Of course." The assurance was automatic, but the tremble remained. "They're lighting Dustin's first scene right now. We're just leaving the trailer to head over to the food tent for breakfast." She paused. When she continued the tremble was gone. "I know he'll do great. And I've explained to him that if it takes a few tries to get the scene down, it's no big deal."

"Should I wish him luck? Or do people still say 'break a leg'?"

"We've got to get going. But I'll tell him for you. Maybe we could call you after?"

"That would be great." Maddie knew she should simply hang up, but every single maternal instinct she possessed was jangling. "Are you sure you're okay?"

"Of course." Once again, Kyra's response was automatic, her tone cheerful. But to her mother's ear her daughter sounded like a child trying her hardest to sound like an adult. It sounded like a cry for help. "Why wouldn't we be?"

Maddie stood stock-still, staring out over the ocean after Kyra hung up, replaying the conversation. The tremble in her daughter's voice, her fear and uncertainty, had been unmistakable. But she'd also heard the bravado, the will to see things through, the can-do attitude in the face of adversity; the very combination that had gotten Maddie through so many tough times. Kyra was an adult. A mother. She would handle whatever was thrown at her. Intellectually, Maddie knew this. And yet the urge to race to her daughter's side, to help smooth the way for her and Dustin, was a visceral thing.

It was that primitive instinct to protect her offspring that made her rouse her phone, Google distances, figure out logistics. It was 302 miles from Mermaid Point to Winter Haven. If she got in the car right now and took the Florida turnpike, she could be there in five hours, too late to watch Dustin's first scene, but in time for the aftermath. Maybe they'd even spend the weekend at the Sunshine. Where she could check on Nikki and the twins and Bitsy and Avery.

She turned and headed back through the great room with a heretofore missing sense of purpose, her thoughts full of what she'd need to take with her, how quickly she could pack. Whether she should come back to Mermaid Point next week or just meet Will in Dallas for his first concert and then travel on with him.

Her step faltered. *Will.* Whom she loved and who was under a ton of pressure of his own. How could she leave Will?

She left the house, hurried down the path, and slipped through the opening in the massive run of palm trees and tropical foliage to his studio. All the way telling herself that he would understand. That he had Hud and Lori and the entire staff at Aquarian, while Kyra and Dustin were alone.

The squat one-story building was built of tapioca-colored blocks and topped by a simple gabled tin roof. It sat on a small rise that overlooked the ocean. Will claimed the small porch commanded the best sunrise view on the island and often watched it from there, guitar in hand.

Maddie paused on the front porch remembering the first time she'd seen the studio padlocked and abandoned, remembering Will's rage when he'd found her pressure washing the building he'd forbidden them to touch, and was unable to set foot in.

How would he feel if she left after only four and a half days?

There were lights on inside, but the red light that signaled a recording in session wasn't lit. Before she could change her mind or lose her nerve, she knocked. When there was no answer, she knocked louder then kept knocking until the door whipped open.

"What is it?" Will's hair was askew, his clothes were rumpled, and his eyes were unfocused. If she hadn't seen him in the middle of building a song before, she might have thought he'd slipped back into drugs. This was Will high on music. "Is something wrong?"

"Not exactly," she hedged. "You didn't hear me knocking?"

He massaged his forehead as if trying to loosen something inside. "Sorry. I've been trying to get that second verse right but I can't seem to find the way." He was looking right at her but his mind was still inside the song.

"I'm sorry to interrupt, I just . . ." Nervous now, she motioned to the two rockers on the porch. "Can you sit for a minute?"

He nodded and she could see him reeling himself in. Slowly he lowered himself into a chair. She did the same. He looked at her, clearly waiting for her to begin.

"Right." She glanced out over the ocean, but there was no explanation there. "So, I just spoke with Kyra. They're shooting Dustin's first scene this morning. And I'm worried about them. I'd like to, I mean, I feel like I need to go to Winter Haven. To be there for them."

His eyes were totally focused on her now, dark and probing. "'Be there' as in . . . ?"

"Be there to offer moral support, to make sure they're okay with the huge thing they're in the middle of. You know . . ."

"I do. I believe that's what you've been doing for me."

"Well, yeah. It's just that they're all by themselves in what sounds like hostile territory."

He remained silent.

"Then I thought I'd go by the Sunshine and visit for a few days. But I'd be back in plenty of time to fly to Dallas with you. Or I could even meet you there." Even to her ears it sounded like a treat being offered to a child.

"Wow." He sat back in the chair, scrubbed a large hand over his face. "I know I've been kind of wrapped up in the new song and tour prep. And I know that I've left you on your own a lot, but I thought that was part of the plan." There was hurt and disappointment in his voice and eyes. With the whole record company machine revolving around him and his rocket return to celebrity, even she sometimes forgot Will's vulnerability and the dragons he had to slay on a daily basis.

"Well, I don't seem to be particularly good at hanging out, but it's not that." At least she hoped it wasn't. "I won't go if it's a problem for you, Will. I love you. I love being with you. And I'm looking forward to going on tour with you. It's just that I'm really worried about Kyra and Dustin."

"So she asked you to come."

"Well, not exactly." In fact, there was every chance Kyra would be angry that she had ignored her insistence that she could handle things on her own. "But this is my daughter and grandson we're talking about." She forced herself to look him in the eye. "Will you hate it if I leave?"

He was silent again, and it wasn't the comfortable kind of silence they often shared.

"Of course I'll hate it," he finally said. "But I'm a big boy. I expect I'll get over it." His jaw set. "Only I can't help wondering when, or if, you'll ever be ready to put our relationship first. I'm getting kind of tired of always coming in second."

"Oh, but I . . ."

He stood, cutting her off. "You go do what you have to do, Maddie. If you intend to come with me on tour, you'll need to be back by Thursday night. We fly out early Friday morning."

"I will. And I hope you understand that this is not about you. Not at all. It's . . ."

Will put out a hand. "You need to stop right there. Don't even think about adding the 'it's me' part of that sentence." A grim but rueful smile lifted his lips. "Hell, 'it's not you, it's me' always used to be my line."

. . .

Kyra was not a skilled liar. She didn't think she'd done a particularly good job of fooling her mother on the phone and could only hope she did a better job of hiding her nerves over breakfast in the food tent.

All week she'd watched Dustin for signs of stress and unease, but while she'd felt both stressed and uneasy and sensed the tension building in Daniel, Dustin had remained even-keeled. He enjoyed the outing at Legoland and looked forward to the time he spent each day with his father and Tonja, time that was carefully blocked out and choreographed for his enjoyment and that she tried not to be jealous of.

The week had been filled with new experiences and ever-increasing expectations, but so far Dustin's smile remained sunny, his eagerness to please undiminished. Today, of course, could change all that. Today Dustin was scheduled to shoot his first scene, the one in which he and his parents checked into the hotel at the theme park from which he would ultimately be abducted.

As they moved through the breakfast line, Kyra's dread was a lead weight in her stomach. Dustin's biggest concern seemed to be whether there would be chocolate milk to go with his egg sandwich. He chattered happily to his stand-in, Jonathan, a twentysomething little person who resembled Dustin in everything except for the size of his Adam's apple and the telltale razor burn.

"Dustin's a credit to you." Christian Sommersby's voice behind her startled her. "Even if he did get my trailer."

Kyra colored slightly. "I told them he didn't need anything like that. I mean, he's just a child." She'd also been careful to make sure that they took meals with the rest of the cast and crew rather than having them delivered to the trailer and that Dustin always said please and thank you. She remembered all too well how a movie crew reacted to those singled out for what they saw as unearned special treatment. Nor did she want all the attention going to his head.

"That was meant to be a joke," the actor said. "I don't actually buy into the whole numerical hierarchy thing. We'll all ultimately be judged on our performances."

"Yes." Her leaden stomach grew heavier as she placed Dustin's coveted chocolate milk on their tray and thought about all the things that could go wrong during filming. What if Dustin got stage fright? What if he flat out froze when the time came to act on cue, or forgot his lines?

When they reached the end of the buffet, she looked out toward the dining tables with a trepidation that did nothing to lighten her discomfort. While everyone had been very careful with Dustin, she had not missed the conversations that ended abruptly when she entered a room or the speculative glances that followed her as she walked by. Two tables over, Brandon Holloway—the First Assistant Director who served as the Director's right hand and was responsible for scheduling, safety, and the smooth running of the shoot—waved them over and then made sure there was room for all four of them to sit. While the female crew members fluttered around Christian, Brandon focused on Dustin. "You ready for your first scene?" he asked with a friendly smile.

"Absolutely!" Dustin said, repeating Brandon's most often heard response.

"Give me five then." Brandon grinned, raising his hand high then moving it down low for a second slap. Dustin turned and repeated the high five/low five with Jonathan.

Dustin happily ate his egg sandwich and slurped his chocolate milk through a neon-colored straw while the others at the table talked around her. Kyra pushed her food around her plate unable to summon any appetite at all.

"He'll be fine," Christian said to her. "He's what, four years old? No one's expecting him to get his first scene down in one take. Hell, I'd be happy to do that myself."

Brandon nodded. "Chris is right. The last thing anyone wants to do is apply too much pressure on day one. There'll be plenty of time ahead for that."

. . .

Now, just an hour later, Kyra stood where she'd been placed, just out of camera range but within eye contact of Dustin as he rehearsed his scene with Tonja. After that Daniel stepped in so that the three of them could rehearse for the camera.

"He'll be fine." Once again Sommersby materialized beside her. "He looks pretty comfortable to me."

And then Daniel nodded to the First AD, who stepped into position next to the monitor.

Kyra drew a shaky breath as Dustin, Daniel, and Tonja moved into position one, just outside the glass double doors. The expression on Dustin's face was one she'd seen while he played corn hole—focused yet relaxed. As if he were enjoying himself.

"Quiet on the set!"

"Rolling."

"Scene one, take one." The slate clacked in front of the camera lens.

Brandon yelled, "Action!"

Five seconds later the trio entered the lobby, maintaining a predetermined distance from the camera, which was being pulled backward on a dolly ahead of them. They ignored the camera, talking as they walked. An assistant pulled the lens so that as the camera moved, the shot widened. Kyra held her breath through the entire forty-five-second move, listening to the dialogue as the three of them approached the front desk discussing which rides "Tyler" wanted to go on and how fast he could get ready. She was shocked by how completely and stunningly believable Dustin was. How easily he played a child on vacation with his parents. As if there was no camera. No crew. No pressure. If she hadn't been present and in a world of pain during his birth, she might have believed that Tonja Kay was actually Dustin's mother.

"Cut!"

There was a moment of stunned silence while everyone present registered the perfection of the first take. Then Daniel whooped, lifted Dustin in his arms, and twirled him around in a flash of identical smiles. Tonja threw her arms around both of them. The studio erupted in spontaneous applause.

The lead weight in Kyra's stomach lightened. Laughter and relief bubbled upward as she moved through the press of bodies toward her gleeful son. She was almost to him when the first digital flashes went off. She turned to see Nigel Bracken and a handful of paparazzi pressing forward.

"Well done, Dustin!" Nigel Bracken shouted.

"The kid's a natural!" another shouted.

Daniel and Tonja smiled triumphantly, holding Dustin aloft like a child-size trophy. The laughter had already died in Kyra's throat at the sight of the three of them wrapped so tightly together, when Brandon placed a hand on her shoulder. "Do you mind giving them just a few minutes for the photo op?" It was gently put but it wasn't a question.

The crew members were busy slapping each other on the back. A couple of people even shot her a congratulatory smile or a quick thumbs-up.

Dustin was soaking up the congratulations and attention and had not yet begun to look for her. Tonja and Daniel were euphoric. This was the cinematic version of the Red Sox finally overcoming the Curse of the Bambino. The *Titanic* sidestepping the iceberg.

Kyra didn't have to ask who had invited the paparazzi. Who had spirited them on set to get shots of scene one, take one of *The Exchange*.

She had no control and could not demand that anyone tell her what they would have done with the paparazzi if Dustin hadn't done so well. If he'd dissolved in tears because he couldn't remember his lines or missed his mark, would they have confiscated cameras? Paid people off? Or would they have allowed Dustin to look bad on *Entertainment Tonight* and on the cover of *People*, just to feed the publicity machine?

When the flashes slowed and the paparazzi were no longer shouting questions, Brandon gave her a nod and a smile then cleared a path for her through the crush of bodies to where Tonja was still looking at Dustin as if he were the dearest gift she'd ever been given. Daniel was smiling like a man who'd just won the lottery.

"Clear the set. We're back to position one in five. The director wants a couple of safeties before we move to the next setup." Brandon set about getting his crew back to work.

"Mommy!" Dustin wiggled out of his father's arms and raced to her, his arms outstretched. "Did you see me? I was acting just like Dandiel told me!"

Daniel shot her a private wink and gave her a thumbs-up. An acknowledgment of his pride in *their* son. She winked back. For once she cared nothing at all for Nigel and his gang as she lifted Dustin up. "You were absolutely fabulous," she said, hugging him tight against her. "But just remember, every take doesn't have to be perfect. And you know what else? I got a text from Grandma. She's on her way to visit so that the three of us can celebrate."

# Fourteen

"Geema!" Dustin greeted her at the door and pretty much leapt into Maddie's arms. "I had my first scene today. And I nailed it!"

"He did. He handled it like a total professional. The crew was still talking about it when we left." Kyra didn't exactly leap into her arms but her hug was a long, crushing thing that made Maddie's decision to flee—make that *leave*—Mermaid Point feel like a solid parental decision and not the semi-desperate act it had been.

Max's happy tail wagged in high gear, thwacking into everything and everyone in its path as he nosed his way close. If her daughter had had a tail, it would be wagging, too. Or possibly drooping with relief. After almost five days of Maddie feeling like an afterthought in other people's lives, Kyra's, Dustin's, and even Max's excitement at her mere presence was a balm to her soul.

"Did you have any trouble finding the place?" Kyra closed the front door, pulled Max's nose away from Maddie's crotch, and led the way into the living room. Which was strewn with an assortment of unrelated, shredded things.

"No, my GPS seems to know its stuff. I . . . what happened here?"

"Max. Max happened here." The puppy lifted his head expectantly at the sound of his name. The tail picked up speed.

"That was not a compliment," Kyra said to the dog as she began to pick up what turned out to be a shredded sock, a partially chewed sneaker, and . . . toilet paper in pieces the size of confetti. She sent Dustin into the kitchen to do the same. "We've been trying to crate train Max—apparently all the other Deranian-Kay dogs responded to the method. But this baby appears to be part Great Dane and part Houdini."

"Cute place," Maddie observed as Kyra and Dustin finished picking up the items Max had liberated, tasted, and redistributed; then Kyra led the way outside and out to the dock that overlooked the lake.

"I'm so glad you could get away. Did Will mind? When do you need to get back?" Kyra threw out the questions so rapid-fire that Maddie didn't have to answer. Which was just as well because she still felt slightly queasy at the speed of her departure.

At the end of the dock Kyra pointed across the glassy basin of water to the big house on the opposite shore. "We've apparently taken over the whole compound. That's Daniel and Tonja's place."

"Dandiel's other childrens live there. They're my brothers and sisters," Dustin piped in. "Pretty soon it's gonna be my mommy's turn to live with him."

Maddie's eyes went to Kyra's face, which had turned a bright red.

"I wasn't ready for the question." She lowered her voice to a whisper. "And I didn't do as good a job explaining things on a four-year level as I would have liked."

"All we can do is the best we can do." Maddie was having far too hard a time figuring out her own life to criticize her daughter's, yet she couldn't help wondering how Kyra would explain things when Dustin realized his father was not planning a duly-scheduled wife swap.

Dustin followed Max off the dock to explore the edge of the

lake. Kyra's gaze fixed on the distant house. "So. How's everything going? Does it feel better or worse than you expected?"

"I hardly know." Kyra folded her arms tight across her chest. "I spent most of the week worrying about how Dustin would do today. Not so much for Daniel or the film, you know. But for how he'd feel about himself." She shrugged, but her arms remained crossed, her gaze fixed. "Of course, most of my focus was on the possible worst-case scenarios, of which there were many. I did realize he might do well, but I never expected that perfect first take or all the really good ones that came after it." Kyra shook her head. "It was crazy, Mom. All that pressure and tension didn't even seem to faze him. There's so much riding on this film and on Daniel's shoulders. And they've put Dustin right in the middle of it. Today was unbelievable. But what are the chances that he's going to breeze through this whole thing without it taking its toll? I mean, he's only four." The eyes that met Maddie's were clouded with worry.

Maddie slid her arm around her daughter's shoulders. Together they walked back to the yard. "In my experience there's no point borrowing trouble. You need to count today's performance as a very good thing and try to relax. Maybe everything will go better than expected, and in the meantime all you can really do is protect him to the best of your ability and help him remain the truly wonderful child he is."

Inside, Kyra poured them both iced teas and they settled on the screened-in porch to watch Dustin and Max romp. "God, I can't tell you how glad I am to have the weekend off," Kyra finally said. "And even gladder to have you here. Is there anything special you'd like to do?"

Maddie sipped the tea and looked out over the smooth surface of the lake. It was so much smaller and calmer than the Atlantic that surrounded Mermaid Point and the Gulf of Mexico that edged up to Bella Flora and the Sunshine. "My main goal in coming was to spend time with you and Dustin. And to make sure you were okay."

"Which we mostly are." Kyra grimaced. "I mean, I'd give a whole lot to be able to leave on today's high note and not come back. But running away isn't an option."

"No, definitely not an option." Odd that she could say this with such certainty when she herself had bolted just that morning.

"How long can you stay?" Kyra asked.

"Well, I thought I'd spend the weekend and then go on to the Sunshine."

"When is Will expecting you back?"

"Thursday," Maddie said. "He's really busy working on new material and getting ready for the tour. I just need to be back in time to fly out with him Friday morning like we planned."

"What happened?"

"What do you mean?" Kyra's look was pointed and Maddie almost missed the teenaged years when Kyra had barely noticed her mother let alone expressed interest in her life. "Clearly something happened."

"No, not really. I just . . ." Excuses leapt to her tongue. But she had always tried to be honest with her children. "I was worried about you and Dustin, and I wanted to see for myself that you were all right. But, it just seemed like everyone else had so much to do and I had no sense of direction. I was just kind of killing time." God, she sounded so pathetic.

"That's called relaxing, Mom. Recharging. Doing that on a private island in the Keys? With a rock star? Some people might even go out on a limb and call it a vacation."

"Yes, well, I didn't do as good a job at it as I would have liked." She offered Kyra's words back to her hoping she'd let go of the topic Maddie seemed unable to come to terms with. She was fifty-three years old, a grandmother, and she still didn't know what she wanted to be when she grew up. "Anyway, I'd like to have a couple days back in my own space to prepare for going on the road with Will." As if anything could prepare one for going on tour with a rock band.

"Me too. Or at least a couple days in a space owned by someone who loves me and isn't trying to turn my son into his on-screen Mini-Me."

"Are you allowed to leave?" Maddie asked, sitting up and pushing away the tea.

"Yep. Monday call is seven A.M. And I'm definitely not planning on partying over at the director and producer's lake house. Or giving them any more bonding time with Dustin before then." She was already on her feet.

Maddie looked around for her cell phone. "I haven't GPSed the drive from here to Pass-a-Grille. But . . ."

"One hour, twenty-eight minutes," Kyra replied before Maddie had located her phone. She picked up their iced teas. "It's four P.M. I can have Dustin, Max, and me in the Jeep in fifteen minutes. Even if we hit rush-hour traffic through Tampa, we could make it home in time for sunset."

· · ·

Nikki sprinted the final mile back to the Sunshine telling herself that she was not really light-headed, that one thousand calories a day was more than enough for any woman, at least any woman who had been crazy enough to have babies at the age of forty-seven when her metabolism had already slowed to a crawl and clung to each ounce of excess fat like a drowning man might cling to any bit of flotsam.

The cooling air had turned her sweaty skin clammy, her running clothes were plastered to her body, and her hair hung limp around her face. She was tired and her calf muscles were currently screaming in protest, but she wasn't in any real hurry to go home, where Luvie would be making everything Nikki sucked at (and child rearing in particular) look like child's play.

Just outside the low pink wall that separated the Sunshine's pool deck from the beach, she bent, put her hands on her knees, and breathed until those breaths stopped impersonating an asthma attack. Then she took her time walking to their cottage. It was possible she held the doorknob in her hand longer than necessary before pushing the door open.

Luvie was sitting on the couch with the girls, holding the phone up to Gemma and Sofia's ears. Nikki could tell the voice they were listening to was Joe's because they were wearing identical smiles and chanting "da-da-da-da-da!" while happily waving their arms.

She dropped a kiss on each girl's head and smiled her thanks at Luvie because really, how could she not? The cottage was immaculate, the girls' dinner already served and cleaned up. The only messy, disorganized thing in sight was Nikki.

Luvie stood and greeted her warmly. "Mr. Giraldi is on the line. I'll go along and give the children a bath and pop them into their pajamas so you two can talk."

"Thank you." She took the phone and watched as Luvie, Gemma, and Sofia disappeared into the nursery.

"Greetings," she said, walking to the refrigerator to count out the six leaves of lettuce, four baby carrots, three grape tomatoes, and two tablespoons of fat-free dressing that would, with her four ounces of chicken breast, serve as tonight's dinner. "How did everything go today? Are you almost finished tracking down financial slimeballs and saving democracy?"

With that she sat at the dinette, put the phone on speaker, and listened as she consumed her meal. Letting the sound of his voice do all the warm, wonderful, fuzzy things it did for Sofia and Gemma.

. . .

Just down the beach Avery stood inside Martha Wyatt's tiny house looking out the opening where the double-hung kitchen window would go. Happily, she inhaled the scent of sawdust. A smell that had always clung to her father's clothes and been the smell of his love, and of security and safety. Especially in the wake of her mother's desertion.

Over the last years the scent had become associated with Chase, turning heady and intimate. A scent with aphrodisiac properties they might one day bottle and sell to DIYers.

"I couldn't really see it before." Martha held tightly to the temporary railing as she climbed the two boxy plywood steps where the porch would go. "But now that the spaces are becoming defined . . ." The woman's smile deepened the lines that radiated from the corner of her eyes, confirming what Avery had suspected; her wrinkles had come from smiling rather than disappointment. "The kitchen's larger than I expected. And so are my bedroom and bath," she continued once they were inside. Martha turned to look up at the area that would become the children's sleeping loft and playroom. "The great-grandkids are already arguing about who gets to sleep over first. I can't wait until they see the bunkhouse bunk beds Ray sketched out. I'm going to be the most popular great-grandmother ever."

Avery smiled at the woman's pleasure. "I'm guessing you're already pretty near the top of that list, but I'm so happy that you like the layout and feel good about the space."

"Like it? I love it!" She reached a gnarled, age-spotted hand out to take Avery's. "I did torture them a bit, but I'm so glad Jonathan and Sandra found you. This is such a perfect solution. I've been bragging about you to all my friends at book club." Her soft brown eyes shimmered with tears. "The only thing that would make it better would be if Henry were here. He always did love a new adventure."

With Martha's praise still ringing in her ears, Avery drove over the Vina del Mar Bridge and took a right on Pass-a-Grille Way in no hurry to go back to her own tiny home. Just because it was small didn't mean there was no room for emptiness. She did not need to fill it with regret or even her own foolish loneliness. Spending a weekend alone with no obligations was not something to dread. Still, she couldn't stop her thoughts from turning to Chase. She couldn't believe how much she missed him. How much she wanted to walk him through the tiny house on Vina and see it through his eyes.

The sun had not yet started to set as she turned onto Thirty-first, and pulled the Mini Cooper into a parking spot. She could take a walk on the beach. Or maybe even have a drink up at the rooftop grill. She was still working on her pep talk when she noticed the beigy gold minivan parked at the curb. A minivan she wasn't expecting but was beyond relieved—no, make that thrilled—to see.

...

Bitsy ate her TV dinner in front of the television since that seemed what they'd been designed for. As she ate her way through the Salisbury "steak," Tater Tots, and green beans, she did her best not to think about the fact that she was home alone in her 450-square-foot cottage on a Friday night eating food out of a compartmentalized container that she'd microwaved, with only Sherlock for company.

The entertainment "news" flew by. Miley Cyrus wearing something inappropriate, Caitlyn Jenner offering beauty tips, Kanye West behaving badly, a host of celebrities that she had never heard of spotted in places she would never choose to go.

As it so often did, her mind lingered on the fact that she was living in limbo—not fully committed to the life that was now hers even as her former life became less and less real. At the moment, her hopes were pinned on Gary Kaufman and the information the forensic accountant had promised to share in the coming week. Information she prayed would enable her to bring Bertie to justice and reclaim the life he'd stolen.

She stabbed at her final Tater Tot trying to visualize, and

savor, the look of fear on Bertie's face when he discovered that he'd been found. She was imagining herself aiming a pistol at his black heart while he begged her not to shoot him, when an image of Dustin Deranian gazing up at his father in what looked like a hotel lobby snagged her attention. The next words out of the reporter's mouth were, "Today on a film set in Florida, Daniel Deranian's son films perfect first take! Right after this!" Quick shots of him in the middle of a pack of paparazzi filled the screen then dissolved into a commercial.

The report that followed focused primarily on Tonja Kay, Daniel Deranian, and their on-screen son, Dustin, along with a recap of the particulars of his conception and birth. Several brief and unflattering cutaways of Kyra standing off to the side and watching the perfect take had been inserted.

"Jeez." Bitsy did not understand how they were able to make a naturally beautiful twenty-seven-year-old woman look so bad, but it didn't bode well for the rest of them. She was still picking at the alleged dessert in the final tiny square of the microwaved meal—a dessert Sherlock had turned his nose up at—when a knock sounded on her door. She opened it to Avery.

"Maddie and Kyra and Dustin are here. We're going to do sunset!" She sounded like a child about to open presents on Christmas morning.

The words made Bitsy feel equally giddy. "Are you sure?"

"Yes, it's been almost a week, but I'm pretty sure I still recognize them." This was accompanied by an eye roll.

"Not arguing. But I just saw Dustin and Kyra on *Hollywood Tonight* and the film was shot this afternoon."

"Well, they're definitely here." Avery's smile grew larger. "Just think of me as your personal Paul Revere. Dustin's going to spend a couple of hours with Steve, and Luvie volunteered to stay on with the twins. Bring whatever you have to drink. I'm going to go grab some Cheez Doodles." She paused. "Is it pathetic that I'm so desperately happy to see them?"

"Yes," Bitsy said even as a smile spread across her face. "But I feel exactly the same way."

A few doors down Nikki, too, was pathetically happy. Ten minutes after Avery stopped to share the news of the Singers' arrival, she was showered and dressed.

"I fixed a plate of Ted Peters smoked fish spread on crackers for you if you'd like to take it," Luvie said. "It's there on the counter."

"Thank you. I know everyone will appreciate it." Nikki retrieved a half bottle of white wine from the refrigerator and tucked it under one arm, then scooped up the Saran-wrapped paper plate. "But, you don't have to stay. I mean, I appreciate the offer but Sofia and Gemma are asleep. And if I take the monitor with me, I can hear them if they wake up and be here in thirty seconds." She knew this because she'd tested it. Now that she was running again she could probably make it in twenty-five.

"I have nowhere I need to rush off to," Luvie said. "You go enjoy yourself. There's nothing like friends to perk a body up."

There was no arguing with this statement. Nikki had felt calmer after her conversation with Joe. He'd be back in exactly a week so the countdown had begun, but having Maddie and Kyra here for a full-fledged sunset? That was definitely a good thing. She smiled as she imagined beating Avery and Bitsy to toasting this, which meant she'd have to volunteer to be the first to share a good thing. *Ha.* She picked up her pace, her step far lighter than it had been after her run. As if arriving first would have anything to do with it.

By the time they'd assembled on the beach with their folding chairs and snacks and drinks, the sun was close to setting. None of them cared. As far as Maddie was concerned the hugs and easy chatter were enough to make up for the shortened "show" they'd ostensibly come to watch and toast. And pretty much everything else.

As she breathed in the evening air with its hint of salt, her heart stopped racing. Her pulse slowed. Her thoughts began to solidify. Much, she imagined, like a drug addict finally getting their fix.

Mermaid Point had stunning sunrises and sunsets, an ocean of salty water, its own beach, *and* Will. Yet sitting in this small circle of women muffled the roar of panic that had shot her here like an iron ball out of a cannon.

They raised their glasses and clinked. Nikki passed around the plate of snacks she'd brought. "Courtesy of Luvie."

Avery passed the bag of Cheez Doodles. "Courtesy of Wise and the Dollar Store. I think I may have cornered the market." She popped a Doodle into her mouth.

"Oh, joy," Nikki said.

Under the layer of sarcasm, Maddie thought Nikki sounded pretty joyous. "Are you sure you don't want something to eat?" She'd passed on the snacks and sipped her glass of wine.

"I've already eaten."

Avery snorted. But only after licking the cheese residue from her fingers. "Yeah, probably five or six lettuce leaves. A feast."

Nikki shot her a look. "Just because your metabolism is fully functional and your taste still runs to artificial cheese products, doesn't mean everyone else can or should eat like a teenager. It's only two more months until the girls turn one, and I'd like to lose this baby weight. If I don't do it now, it might never happen."

Avery opened her mouth to protest or, possibly, to consume another Cheez Doodle. Maddie wasn't sure which. Before she could do either, Nikki turned to Maddie and said, "By the way, my one good thing tonight is having you and Kyra back, so that we can do sunset together. I feel like you've been gone forever." She raised her glass.

"Thanks." Maddie raised her own glass. "I can't tell you how glad I am to be here."

"Me too!" Kyra raised her glass. "When Mom showed up, I

realized how much I needed to get back even if it was just for the weekend."

"Ditto!" Bitsy chimed in, glass up.

As one, they looked at Maddie.

"I am so not the 'good enough' police," she said as she so often had. But she could have laughed for joy herself as she said it.

"Figures the first time I volunteer to go first everyone co-opts my good thing," Nikki complained, but she, too, was smiling as she raised her glass a bit higher. "To all of us being together again."

"And feeling good about it."

"To us!" They clinked and drank and munched as the sun oozed into the water like a Dalí painting.

Maddie thought the stars in the sky were glorious, the sand between her toes spectacular. But it was the people around her that were priceless. She pinched a Cheez Doodle and chewed it thoughtfully. Perhaps they should do a Mastercard commercial.

There was a contented silence as the sky darkened.

"I'm beyond glad to see you both." It was Bitsy who broke the silence. "But what are you doing here? I was just watching Dustin's miraculous first scene on *Hollywood Tonight*—his very first take was perfect. And the next minute you were here."

"Wow, a perfect take?" Nikki asked.

"Cool!" Avery added.

"Yeah," Kyra said. "Hit his mark, said his lines, acted convincingly. It was unbelievable." There was pride but no happiness in the telling.

"Is everything okay?" Nikki asked.

"Yes," Kyra said quietly. "But it feels a lot more okay now that we're home. I swear I think even Max sighed with relief when we got here. But that could be because there actually isn't room for his crate here."

"Max has a crate?" Avery said.

"Yes. Apparently all Deranian-Kay family dogs are crate trained. But Max isn't exactly enthusiastic about the experience. And I haven't found a crate yet that can hold him." Kyra's voice didn't encourage more questions. She turned to stare out over the water.

"How about you, Maddie?" Avery asked. "Is everything all right?"

"Yes. I just . . . felt like I was at loose ends," Maddie said. "Once we're on tour I'm sure there will be plenty for me to do." *What? Find a way to make egg soufflé? Make sure Will goes to bed happy?*

Her voice trailed off as she replayed that morning's conversation. Will's hurt that she was leaving. His assertion that he was tired of coming in second. The way he'd said "if you intend to come on tour" as if he doubted she'd be back.

"When is Joe due back?" Maddie asked Nikki, eager to turn the conversation.

"Next Friday. Thank goodness." Nikki took a very tiny sip of her wine.

"You're so lucky to have Luvie," Bitsy said.

"Yes, very lucky." The response was somewhat wooden, but it was far too dark now to read Nikki's expression.

"She's perfect, isn't she?" Kyra asked. "Like a nanny sent over from central casting."

"She's pretty perfect all right," Nikki agreed.

Conversation slowed to a halt as the sky grew darker and stars began to appear. Nearby on the Sunshine's rooftop deck, chairs scraped back from tables. Murmurs of good-bye and the clatter and clang of clearing and closing up floated down on the evening breeze.

Maddie yawned. Glad as she was to be back, it had been a long day. "Are there any plans for tomorrow?"

There was silence as they stood and began to gather their things. In the dim glow of a distant pool light, she saw Bitsy and Avery look at each other then at Kyra.

It was Nikki who finally spoke. "Troy invited us all over to Bella Flora for a cookout tomorrow."

Kyra went still, but only for a moment. "Is that right?"

"Um, yeah. It's at noon," Avery added. "Steve is coming."

"And I think the Franklins are going to be there," Bitsy said.

"Yeah," Nikki said. "He told me I should bring the girls."

There was a harsh rasp of laughter from Kyra. "Troy Matthews is entertaining *my* father and *my* friends. In *my* home."

"I'm sure he'd love for you and Dustin to be there," Avery said.

Maddie knew for a fact he would, but Kyra gnashed her teeth.

"Maybe I'll just give him a call," Bitsy offered. "To let him know that you're in town. And, um, find out if there's anything he'd like you to bring."

# Fifteen

As far as Kyra was concerned, "weird" wasn't a strong enough word to describe what it felt like to go to her own house as a guest for a cookout. Being welcomed by a smiling, noncombative Troy Matthews was even weirder.

"Hey, really glad you could make it," he said with an almost blinding smile. He looked freshly shaved. His hair was still sun streaked a million shades of blond, layered and shiny. He still looked like a surfer, not the shaggy, "follow the wave in my beat-up VW van" type but the upscale, glossy kind you might see in a Ralph Lauren ad.

Her son gave a shouted "Broy!" and launched himself into Troy's arms. Her mother handed Kyra the macaroni and four-cheese casserole she'd insisted on making and gave him the kind of hug she normally reserved for family. Max wagged his tail with such happiness that he knocked over the umbrella stand.

*Traitors.* Kyra managed to lift the corners of her mouth into a smile. Instead of pushing Troy outside and locking the door behind him like she wanted to, she handed him her mother's casserole and fell in behind him, checking out each room they passed for signs of mistreatment. But Bella Flora had not been abused or turned into a bachelor pad. In fact, she looked pretty much as they had left her. And, although she tried her hardest not to notice, Bella Flora felt and smelled like home.

In the kitchen, Troy motioned to open bottles of wine on the counter and the full pitcher of something red and frothy in the blender. "Strawberry margaritas. There's another batch in the freezer. There's beer, soft drinks, and juice boxes outside in the cooler.

"Oh, and there's fresh sand in the sandbox. Picked it up this morning. And the playhouse has been looking kind of lonely." He smiled down at Dustin. "Your grandfather's out there firing up the grill."

"Oh, boy!" Without a backward glance he raced outside to the loggia with Max on his heels.

"And, um, maybe I should have mentioned that Steve's date is out there helping him?"

He looked relieved when the doorbell rang again. "Be right back." He winked at Kyra. "Make yourselves at home."

"I think I'm going to need this." Kyra picked up a large plastic cup from the counter and poured herself a margarita. "Mom?"

"Thanks." They clicked plastic rims. "Don't get me wrong. I'm glad your dad has someone to spend time with." Maddie took a rather large gulp of her margarita. "I just didn't realize I was going to meet her today." Craning her neck, she checked her reflection in a glass-fronted cabinet. "Am I wearing lipstick?"

"You look great. And remember, you're the one having a relationship with a rock star."

The sounds of laughter and Troy's voice drew closer.

"Thanks. I'll try to keep that in mind," Maddie said. "And I don't think any of us should forget that Troy paid good money to live here. He has every right to treat Bella Flora like his home. And . . ."

Kyra gulped her drink so quickly she could barely taste it; her greatest hope was that it would kick in just as quickly so that she could survive watching Troy play lord of the manor. *Their* manor.

The "lord" entered the kitchen with John and Renée Franklin and her sister, Annelise. Happy hugs were exchanged.

"We heard you were back!"

"How are things going on the film?"

"How long are you here for?"

John headed outside to help supervise the grill action. Renée found a vase and arranged the flowers she'd brought from her garden. Annelise set a home-baked apple strudel on the counter.

Another ring of the doorbell brought Bitsy, Avery, and Nikki. Bitsy and Avery each held one of the twins. Nikki carried a huge diaper bag stuffed to the brim.

"You look like you're moving back in," Maddie teased.

"If only it were so simple." Nikki's smile turned rueful. "This is what it takes to survive out in the world for more than fifteen minutes. If you're lucky, it's preventive—you know, kind of how carrying an umbrella can prevent rain or getting your car washed can cause it." She shoved the bulging bag into a corner. "Oh, my gosh. Are those margaritas?"

Troy bustled in and out with a huge smile on his face that annoyed the crap out of Kyra. Avery poured the bags of Cheez Doodles she'd brought into large plastic bowls. Her mother chopped and tossed the salad ingredients Nikki and Bitsy had brought. Then she walked over to Kyra and slipped an arm through hers. "Shall we go meet your father's date?"

Kyra nodded, because her mother was already propelling her outside, only stopping when they stood directly in front of Dorene Fletcher. Who turned out to be attractive, age appropriate, and far more nervous about meeting them than they were about meeting her.

"There, that wasn't so bad was it?" her mother asked when Dorene had excused herself to retrieve more hamburger buns from the kitchen. "And you only brought up Will and the tour two or three times." She grinned. "In the first sentence."

Kyra grinned back. "I couldn't help it. But better safe than sorry, right?"

"Absolutely, I just think you could have waited until after the introductions." Maddie laughed. "She handled it pretty well. He could have done worse."

"He has." Kyra thought about the Realtor her father had already been dating the Christmas she'd found out her parents were getting divorced. Then she thought about Troy Matthews, who seemed to be taking his job as jovial host quite seriously.

"Why is he so hard to avoid?" she hissed to her mother when she noticed him just behind her, refreshing John Franklin's drink. "Everywhere I go, there he is. Underfoot. Just like Max."

Her mother's look turned enigmatic as they headed back to the kitchen, where they found Avery munching Cheez Doodles while Nikki blended another batch of margaritas. Troy entered just behind them and went over to help. The whole lot of them were smiling. It seemed Kyra was the only person present who had a problem with Troy and his good mood. Until Chase Hardin arrived with his father, a large bowl of baked beans, and a date. Who was nowhere near as nonthreatening as Dorene Fletcher had proven to be.

Avery's blue eyes got so big they seemed to take over her face. Her Cupid's bow mouth, lightly coated with cheese residue, pursed. Her chest, which she'd always hated because of the way it dwarfed the rest of her, heaved as the introductions were made.

Riley Hancock was a younger, taller, and, at least at the moment, less angry version of Avery and apparently had no idea there was a problem. Chase also looked remarkably unperturbed as they helped themselves to margaritas then wheeled Jeff outside. Which Kyra took as proof that he had a heretofore undisclosed death wish.

Kyra handed Avery a margarita. "Drink this."

"I don't want another margarita."

"Trust me. It'll help you ignore just how big an asshole

Chase is for bringing that girl with him. I've had two and a half and I don't want to punch Troy's face in anywhere near as much as I did when I first got here."

Avery took the glass and chugged it. Then she fortified herself with a large handful of Cheez Doodles.

By the time Troy rang the dinner gong, an accessory that had not come with the house, Avery's anger had been muted enough to allow her to do an impressive job of ignoring Chase and the Dewy-Clingy Barbie he'd brought with him.

Pleasantly full from what had turned out to be a truly stellar meal on top of three and a quarter margaritas, Kyra lay on a chaise watching Troy toss Dustin around the pool. Each splash down produced shrieks of pleasure followed by her son's cries for more.

Surrounded by her family and her "village" and with a whole twenty-four hours left before she and Dustin had to return to Winter Haven, she drowsed lightly, only waking when droplets of water landed on her bare legs.

"It's nice to see you looking so relaxed." Troy's voice was warm and friendly without the slightest edge.

The same could not be said of Troy's body, which was, she noted as her eyes opened, all hard-cut edges, planes, and angles wrapped in smooth, tan skin. Her head tilted back to take in the broad shoulders and chest that tapered down to extremely well-defined abs that did, in fact, resemble a washboard. A light dusting of blond hair covered his chest. It arrowed downward, ultimately disappearing beneath the waistband of low-slung black bathing trunks.

She sighed as a droplet of water slid down the hard slope of his body, then grimaced in an effort to pretend that she hadn't just checked him out. His grin told her she'd failed.

"Do you mind?" He motioned to the chaise, but sat before she responded.

His trunks were damp, his bare legs oddly warm against

hers. She inched away and made a show of shivering, beyond glad it had been too cold to put on anything skimpier than shorts. *Has he always been this hot?*

"Sorry." His grin said he didn't mean it.

He watched her face for several long minutes. Until she was no longer remotely relaxed.

"I saw Dustin on *Hollywood Tonight*," he said finally. "It's incredibly rare to see a child that age appear to perform so effortlessly. Using an actual four-year-old instead of an older child who could play four was a huge risk. Just like so much about that film. Daniel must have been pissing himself with relief."

"Ah, there's the Troy Mathews I've been waiting for." She sat up. "You just can't bear for Daniel to do well, can you?"

Troy's jaw tightened. His blue eyes were pinned to hers. "I don't really give a rat's ass about Daniel Deranian," he said quietly. "Or any personal risks he might take." Once again he hesitated and she prepared to jump up and walk away. "It's Dustin I care about. There's nothing effortless about what it took to pull off that first take. And I don't think there's much Dustin wouldn't do to try to impress and please his father."

Her heart thudded at the mention of the thing she feared most. Not what they asked of Dustin, but what he so wanted to give. Just that morning he'd insisted on working on his lines for Monday before they came to the cookout.

"I understand why they'd celebrate and share that perfect take," Troy continued. "It's hard to blame them when they have so much riding on this film. What with pledging every penny they have and then some."

Her head jerked up in surprise. She'd known that Daniel and Tonja had put in money, but everything they had? "You don't know that."

"Unfortunately, I do." Troy's voice, still quiet, carried real regret. "I have contacts in the business, and people like to talk." He sighed. "I also know what it feels like to want to please your father. And what it feels like when you can't." He continued to watch her. "You're going to have to be careful not to let Dustin turn himself inside out trying to do a perfect take every time."

She scooted as far from him as she could get. "I'm his mother. I don't need you to tell me what to do or how to take care of my son. Why are you forever inserting yourself into my life?" She wanted to get away from him, but she couldn't seem to find her feet. "You've taken over this house like it was always meant to be yours. I don't know who the hell you think you are!"

He had no trouble getting to his feet. By the time she'd rolled to the side and swung her legs over to stand, he was already towering over her. Vaguely, she was aware of others watching, but she'd had it with his interfering. She was sick and tired of holding her tongue.

"I know who I am," he said quietly. "I haven't always liked it and for a lot of years, I ran away from it. You, however, don't know a thing about me."

"Is that right?" All she wanted was to turn and run, but she wouldn't give him the satisfaction. "Then maybe you need to just go ahead and tell me what you think I need to know."

He looked away. She saw him glance at her mother, who had just picked up Dustin to carry him inside. Soon they were the only two left on the deck.

"First of all, I did not steal Bella Flora from you. You put it at risk and could have lost it. I am, in fact, grossly overpaying you for the privilege of renting it and saving your ass."

"This is you saving my ass?" She wanted to slug him. "Well, feel free to stop. In fact, if you don't want to live in Bella Flora, which by the way is way too good for you no matter how much money you have, you can leave right now."

"Kyra, I am not insulting Bella Flora. All I'm trying to say is that I didn't rent her to rub your nose in it. It was the only way I could think of to help. Because I want . . ."

His voice trailed off. Suddenly, he looked uncertain. He

turned, his eyes wild, like an animal caught in a fire trying to find an escape route.

"Yes, I see how much you're helping. Living in our house, hanging out with my friends and family. I don't understand what's going on here. You've got everything I care about in the palm of your hand. What else could you possibly want?"

He looked at her. "Is it possible you really don't know?"

"Know what?"

His shoulders and his chin lifted. Resolve and, possibly, resignation filled his eyes. "I've pretty much had a . . . thing . . . for you from the moment we met in South Beach on Max Golden's front yard."

He winced at the admission.

"A thing?" She was fairly certain her mouth had gaped open as she stood there waiting for the guffaw. The wink. For the hidden cameras to pop out. "You mean when you came there representing the network? When your job was making us look bad and helping them turn our renovation program into that mean-spirited reality TV show. You already had a . . . thing . . . for me?"

He shrugged. But he didn't apologize or hang his head or pretend he'd only been joking. "Okay, that may have been a bad choice of words. But . . . I could be good for you and Dustin. I know I could. And I think we could be good together. If you could just let go of your crush on that pretty-boy movie star and see him for what he is."

"You're crazy." She looked around wildly. But everyone was gone. Except for the noses that might be pressed against the salon windows. "You are making this up to . . . I can't even come up with a good reason why you would say these things."

His voice got so quiet she had to strain to hear. "I'm saying these things because they're true. And because I should have said them a long time ago."

She shook her head as if that might keep the words out. Or make the look in his eyes disappear.

"You asked me what I want?" Troy said. "It's simple. I want you. And I want you to give me a chance to show you why you want me, too."

# Sixteen

Maddie was already awake early Sunday morning when Dustin and Max appeared in the living room. Max whimpered and wagged his tail. Dustin yawned and rubbed at his eyes. "Max needs to go outside and I'm hungry."

"That's a lucky thing," Maddie said, leaning down, lifting him into her arms, and kissing his cheek. "Because there's an egg soufflé in the oven right now and it looks like a beautiful morning." She set him back on his feet and motioned to the wall near the door. "Your sweatshirt's hanging on your hook." She pulled on her own sweatshirt then clipped Max's leash onto his collar.

Dustin shook his head. "I need to memberize." He climbed onto the couch and wiggled back against the cushion. His feet barely reached the edge. "Will you quids me when you come back?"

"Wouldn't you rather come out with us and then have juice and help me make cinnamon toast after?"

"No!" He scooted forward so that he could retrieve the script pages off the coffee table. "Wanna practice my lines!" he said in a tone she'd never heard from him. "Now!"

"Dustin. You know that's no way to talk to anyone."

He dropped his eyes to the pages as if he intended to read them, but he didn't apologize. "I halfta get them right."

Max shook his collar and whined more urgently. With a last

look at her grandson she took Max outside, where he sniffed and squatted and circled. When they returned, Dustin was still staring down at the papers in his lap. He looked up at her, his forehead creased, a frightened look on his face. "I thought I knewed them." His voice broke on the last words.

"Only . . . I can't memember the first thing I say."

"You will," Maddie said. "But you only just woke up. Let's have a juice break and then I can run through them with you. Okay?"

He nodded, blinking rapidly, clearly trying to hold back tears while she went to pour the juice.

"Here you go." Maddie took the papers out of his lap, handed him the sippy cup, then sat down beside him. "Let's just take a little time to wake up."

At his nod she pulled him gently into her lap, his back flush against her chest, her hands clasped around his tummy. Max inserted himself between the sofa and table and rested his muzzle in Dustin's lap. "There we are," Maddie whispered. "Everything's okay. We're just going to sit here and drink juice and give ourselves plenty of time to wake up." She rested her chin lightly on top of his soft cap of curls and waited for him to raise the cup to his lips. He took a long, shuddering sip.

"That's right," she soothed. "Everything's all right. Everything's okay." Finally, he settled back against her. His small shoulders drooped. He took another sip.

"That's right," she said softly. "We have all day. There's no hurry at all."

He sucked thirstily and she felt herself begin to sway, humming lightly, instinctively. Max stayed right where he was, but raised his eyes to her face as if wanting to assure himself she knew what she was doing. *Hush little baby don't say a word . . .* The words to the song she'd been humming echoed softly in her mind, a song she'd sung his mother and uncle to sleep with a thousand times . . . *Papa's gonna buy you a mockingbird.*

Dustin's breathing evened out as she hummed and swayed in a rhythm as old as time.

And she was grateful that she had come.

With a final look in her direction, Max lay down at her feet. Dustin's free hand found a loose curl of hair and he began to twirl it around his finger. It went round and round as she hummed and swayed. His hand loosened on the sippy cup. Carefully she removed it and set it on the table. She was still swaying and humming when the last tendrils of tension let go of their hold on his body and he slept.

• • •

Sunlight slanted through the bedroom blinds hours later when Kyra awoke. The night had been long, filled with fragments of dreams that were both stark and menacing. She sat up in panic, hitting her head on the bottom of the upper bunk. The bedroom was empty. Dustin and Max were gone.

She threw off the tangle of covers and drew in a sharp breath, inhaling the mingled scents of coffee and egg soufflé, familiar and comforting. Her mother's cottage. Dustin was not only safe, but most likely fed. Her heartbeat slowed and she roused her phone. When was the last time she'd slept until ten?

She was considering staying right where she was when last night at Bella Flora came flooding back. Troy Matthews playing host in her home, acting like an adult. Suddenly so different in so many ways that it was almost impossible to take in. And then there were the things he'd said, the feelings he'd shared. She closed her eyes trying to blot it out, but she could still hear the words he'd spoken, the earnest ring in his voice. She had been stunned by his declarations of affection. Her mother had not.

All thought of going back to sleep vanished, she washed her face, brushed her teeth, and pulled on jeans and a T-shirt. Max's head shot up, one ear twitching in her direction when she stomped into the living area.

"Sorry." She gave him an apologetic scratch behind the ear then walked over to the coffeepot, which was, like so many things in her mother's life, half full. A clean mug sat on the counter. The note propped against it read, *Soufflé in fridge. We're on the beach. Come on down.*

Irritation flickered at what she interpreted as her mother's commanding tone. She didn't bother with soufflé and would have rejected the coffee completely if she hadn't needed the caffeine so badly. Filling a large insulated travel mug to the brim, she carried it outside into the postcard-perfect day. Which she took as a personal insult.

On the beach her mother sat on the hard-packed sand at the water's edge. Dustin, Avery, Nikki, the twins, and Bitsy sat with her. Every one of them looked far happier than Kyra felt.

"Good morning." She threw out a general greeting. Eschewing the empty spot on her mother's beach towel, she dropped down on a patch of sand and drew her knees to her chest.

"I'm building a katsle," Dustin said with a sandy-faced smile.

"I see that." Kyra managed to smile back.

"Abery is helping me."

"Yes, it's always good to have a professional on the job." She attempted to mask the tightness of her smile by taking a sip of coffee.

"Did you have something to eat?" her mother asked.

"I wasn't hungry. But thanks for the coffee." She raised her mug in a salute that wasn't as sincere as it should have been. "And for letting me sleep in."

On the gulf, a windsurfer skimmed by. Out past the sandbar a parasailer dangled high up in the bright blue sky. The group gathered on the beach seemed to be having a lovely time. She was the Grinch just waiting to steal someone's Christmas.

"Is there something on your mind?" her mother asked.

Kyra reminded herself that she, too, was a mother. And an adult. She did not want to upset Dustin and she had no right to rain her dissatisfaction with her current life down on these women. Avery appeared intent on the castle wall she was skimming. Nikki seemed occupied wiping wet sand off Sofia's face and out of Gemma's mouth. Bitsy leaned back on her hands and turned her face up to the sun.

Kyra was not fooled. She could practically see their antennae quivering. Homing in on the waves of annoyance she could not seem to hold back. If this had been a honky-tonk, she would be the inebriated good ole boy spoiling for a fight. The best thing she could possibly do right now was keep her mouth closed. Instead she said, "Truthfully, I can't help wondering how you could let *you know who* ambush me like that last night."

"Who's whos know you?" Dustin looked up briefly.

"No one important." She attempted another smile and hoped it looked more reassuring than it felt. "Just someone who's always been a big pain in the . . . rear end . . . and who said some ridiculous things that he should have kept to himself."

With his question answered, if not understood, Dustin went back to work on his creation.

"So, he finally declared himself?" Nikki dove in first. "My matchmaking days may be behind me, but he might be a better choice than the *player* you can't seem to see for who he is."

"It's about time," Avery added.

"Said the woman who told the man who loves her that she's only interested in having a good time. And then had to watch him having a good time with someone else," Kyra pounced.

"You aren't saying you really had no idea?" Bitsy asked.

"Said the woman whose husband stole everything she had and disappeared with another woman," Kyra shot back.

"Kyra. That's enough."

Kyra flushed at her mother's admonition. Madeline Singer did not reprimand lightly. "None of us have any control over what *you know who* feels. And even less control over when and how he chose to reveal it. But the only reason you were surprised is because you've refused to see what's been right in front of you all this time."

"So the fact that he's pretended to be someone and something he wasn't until now doesn't bother any of you?" Kyra asked.

"None of us are exactly how we present ourselves. God knows I learned that the hard way," Bitsy said.

"Maybe instead of analyzing me, we should be asking my mother why she left Mermaid Point after a whole four and a half days when she was supposed to stay two weeks before going on tour with Will." Kyra drew her knees tighter to her chest.

"Don't worry, we'll get to that," Nikki said, pulling a crying child into her lap. "Right now we're talking about you."

"Unbelievable," Kyra shot back. "After everything he's said and done to make our lives miserable? You can't believe he's serious. Or that his having a *thing* for me—that was the word he used, by the way—could possibly be a *good* thing."

"He's serious," her mother said. "For some reason he's been reluctant to share his feelings with you."

"I can't imagine why," Nikki said drily.

"Said the woman who hid her own feelings about the man she loved until after she'd given birth to his children." Kyra shook her head in frustration. "God, so many pots calling the kettle black!"

"Did she just call us pots?" Avery looked up from the castle moat she'd been carving.

"Kyra," Nikki said, gathering a second crying child into her lap. "We all care about you. That's the only reason this conversation is happening. We get that you weren't prepared last night. But maybe you need to consider what was said."

"Oh. My. God." She looked around at the group of them. "This is like some bizarre intervention. I am not a cult member or a drug addict. I am not interested in *you know who*. And I'm not stupid enough to fall for *you know who the first*, ever again." Or at least that's what she kept telling herself. Right up until he stood too close or gifted her with that smile that made her feel like the most important person in his world. At least in that moment.

Kyra was on her feet before she realized she was going to stand. A quick look from Dustin made her careful to keep her voice down and her face pleasant. "If you'll excuse me, I think I'll go up to the cottage and run a load of wash so that I can get our things organized. Then we probably should go ahead and get on the road."

With that she turned and strode back up the beach to the Sunshine. Which was when it hit her that she was about to rush back to the one place she most didn't want to go.

. . .

Hours before they needed to go back to Winter Haven, the Jeep was loaded and Dustin was buckled into his car seat.

Maddie handed Kyra the container of cookies she and Dustin had baked while Kyra did unnecessary laundry, packed it, then cleaned the second bathroom to within an inch of its life.

"I didn't mean to upset you," Maddie said. "Neither did the others. However it felt, it wasn't a planned attack. We all just care about you and want you to be happy."

"I get it," Kyra replied. "I apologize for my behavior."

The words were the right ones, but the tone was all wrong. Kyra held herself so stiffly, Maddie was afraid she might break.

"I hate to see you leave like this. I . . ." Maddie wasn't sure why she was apologizing. She had not orchestrated Troy's confession, or set her daughter up for it, though in truth she thought they were far better suited than Kyra seemed willing to consider. "If we can just let go of the whole Troy thing for a minute, there's something else, something more important that I think you should know about."

For the first time that day Kyra looked something other than angry. "What is it?"

"Dustin had a bit of a meltdown this morning."

"A meltdown?"

"Yes. When he came out to the living room, the first thing he wanted to do was work on his lines."

"And?" Kyra asked carefully.

"He does seem to know them, you know, if you feed him the lines that come before. But he was so afraid that he wouldn't get them right that he cried." Maddie swallowed. "He's wound so tightly right now." She was careful not to add that his mother was, too. "It's so important to him to do a good job."

"I know." Kyra's brown eyes were bleak. "I just don't know what to do about it."

Maddie wished she could hand her daughter a sippy cup of juice and pull her into her lap. "That's why I organized the playtime on the beach. And why I think it's important to try to build in as much 'kid time' as possible."

"I will. God, I hate having to take him back there. I don't seem to be any more immune to meltdowns than Dustin."

Maddie recognized the admission for the apology it was and nodded her agreement. There was no such thing as too old for a meltdown as she herself had demonstrated when she'd bolted from Mermaid Point.

She stood on the curb long after the Jeep had disappeared from view. Then she pulled her phone out of her pocket and speed-dialed Will's number.

The recording said only, "It's Will. If I'm not answering, I'm either making music or out on the flats. Leave a message. I'll get back to you."

Her message was longer. It included a rambling, stammering apology that she wished she could erase even before she'd finished leaving it.

# Seventeen

Eyes closed, Nikki offered a silent prayer to the Diet Gods and prepared to step onto the scale. *I need a loss here—just enough to keep me going. Give me that and I'll do better. I'll eat even less. Exercise more.* She thought thin thoughts. Attempted to visualize her body the way it used to be. Apologized for not appreciating it sufficiently. *Make it a significant loss and I'll never overeat again. I'll become a better person.*

The girls were on the bedroom floor just beyond the bathroom. Sofia treated crawling as if it were an Olympic sport. Gemma preferred to scoot on her behind and had begun to grab onto anything she could use to pull herself up to her feet. A knee, a table leg, her sister's head.

Their babbling drifted through the open door. "Daa daaa daaa daaa daaa! Luff Luff . . . Luffeeee . . ." Nikki waited, afraid that was it, then heard, "Maa . . . maaa . . ." At least they hadn't left her out completely. Why was it that Joe could be gone for weeks at a time and they still called his name first? And Luvie second? Where was the justice in that? How long until they thought Luffie *was* their mother?

*Stop stalling. Any loss is acceptable. One, two . . .* She dropped her robe, held her breath, and stepped onto the scale. *Three.* She forced her eyes open. Double-checked the number. Did the math. She had lost another whole—wait for it—eight ounces?

*Unbelievable!* Even if she "did a McDonald's" and spun that eight ounces into half a pound, it was still only the equivalent of two quarter-pound patties.

She stepped off the instrument of torture with an angry exhale and began to yank on her running clothes. She was sick to death of lettuce and its trendy cousin kale. Without dressing and the other things that gave them some semblance of flavor, she might as well go outside and eat a patch of grass. *Ha!* she thought as she laced up her stupid running shoes. How many calories would that add up to?

She entered the bedroom in time to see Gemma plop down on her bottom. Her chin wobbled with indignation. A sharp cry of frustration followed.

"I feel your pain, Gem." Nikki scooped up her crying daughter then reached down for the other. "Here we go, Sof." Sofia let out a wail. She did not like to be picked up mid-crawl.

"Sorry, guys, but if we don't go now, I won't go at all." After all, if she ran off eight more ounces today, she could be down a whole pound and a half tomorrow.

At the front door she tightened her upper arms and elbows around the girls so that she could get one hand on the doorknob. After a bit of a struggle and realigning her body a couple of times, she managed to turn it and wrestle the door open.

"Hold on!" One small sticky hand grabbed on to her hair. Another wrapped around her neck as she maneuvered them into the double jogging stroller. She was breathing heavily by the time she strapped them in and got their seat belts buckled. Sunscreen came next. Then the sunhats.

She ran back inside to grab the backpack with its emergency snacks, toys, diapers, and changes of clothes. After locking the front door, she hung the backpack on the stroller handle then went back in twice; once for juice boxes, the second time for her cell phone.

For about ten seconds she considered skipping the run. Better yet, she could stretch out on the grass right here and contemplate its caloric content. But the day was crisp and beautiful, the girls were eyeing her expectantly, and she still had all those ounces to lose. "All right then." She dragged air into her lungs, set her shoulders, and began to push the stroller down the walkway toward the beach. "Here we go!"

She made it back to the Sunshine a little over an hour later, out of breath and on jellied legs. The girls were dozing peacefully. Renée Franklin waved her down as she approached the main building. Luvie stood nearby talking with Renée's sister, Annelise.

"There are my darlings." Luvie smiled as the stroller came to a stop. "Did you have a nice run?"

Careful not to look as winded as she felt, Nikki smiled. "Yes. It's beautiful out. But I wasn't expecting you until later this afternoon." Not that she really needed her even then.

"I had nothing going on and I thought you might like to have the whole afternoon," the nanny said. "But I can come back later if you like."

Sofia roused at the sound of Luvie's voice. "Luffeee," she cooed, reaching out her arms. Gemma woke next, her face automatically crumpling in preparation for tears. Until she spotted Luvie. A smile spread across her face.

"Ahhh, such sweet girls. Glad to see your Luvie, are you?" She threw the twins kisses. They giggled happily and sent some back. The nanny turned to Renée and Annelise. "I can't tell you how wonderful it is to get to care for Sofia and Gemma now that me mum is gone and no longer needs me. It really fills the void."

Luvie's voice rang with gratitude and sincerity. She refused to take money for all the extra hours she spent. And Nikki was supposed to tell her to go away and come back later? "Shall I go ahead and take them back and feed them lunch, then?" Luvie asked. "I believe Renée and Annelise have something they want to show you."

"Yes," Renée said. "Do you have a few minutes?"

"Of course." Nikki surrendered as gracefully as she could. She did not point out that there was no reason Sofia and Gemma couldn't have stayed while she did so. Resistance was futile. Luvie was already wheeling them back toward the cottage.

Inside, she grabbed a bottled water from the drinks cooler, careful not to look at even the photos of the ice cream sundaes and banana splits that decorated the soda fountain. Renée and Annelise motioned her back behind the gift shop counter, where an assortment of battered cardboard boxes dotted the terrazzo floor.

"You ordered more items for the gift shop?" she asked, confused by the sisters' air of excitement. And the fact that the gift shop, such as it was, was already full to overflowing.

"No, but we think we may have found some." Renée reached into an open box and pulled out a black and pink one-piece bathing suit, which she handed to Nikki. The label identified the maker as Catalina. The original price tag was still attached.

"Oh, my God," Nikki said, turning it reverently in her hands to look at its back detail. "This is vintage 1950s pinup-style. The straps are removable." The second suit was a draped sheath covered in teal, navy, and white circles with a back zipper and neck tie. "This is a Rose Marie Reid with a snap-in shaper." The last Renée handed her was a gold lamé number that appeared identical to one she'd seen Marilyn Monroe wearing in a long-ago movie. Bathing caps with large bright rubber flowers and turbans piled high with artificial fruit à la Carmen Miranda. "Where on earth did you find these?"

"In our attic," Renée said with a laugh. "John was looking through some of the boxes that had come from the Sunshine and he found these."

"And these." Annelise opened a large manila envelope and withdrew a stack of 8x10 black-and-white photos. The first was a wide shot of the Sunshine Hotel pool back in what Nikki knew had been its heyday. A petite woman with white skin, delicate features, and a halo of blond hair had been captured stepping out from the shaded patio that surrounded the main building. She wore a sleek one-piece black bathing suit, its halter top tied behind her neck, and high-heeled sandals. The pinup-style suit and cat-eye sunglasses screamed 1950s.

"Isn't that . . ."

"My mother," Annelise said.

"And this is me." Renée pulled out another photo that showed a tall, dark-haired teenager in a gingham-checked two-piece bathing suit that showed off long legs, a few inches of midriff, and a budding, coltish figure. The girl carried a flower-covered straw beach bag and wore a broad-brimmed straw hat.

"And here's a shot of me." Annelise presented another glossy black-and-white photo. Though she couldn't have been more than three or four, Annelise was wearing kitten heels with fluffs of fur and a one-piece bathing suit that had been designed to look like a drum. "It was red, white, and blue. I wore it every Memorial Day and Fourth of July until I couldn't squeeze into it anymore."

"As I remember it, you wore it every day for years until it finally fell apart," Renée said. "There's Nana." She pointed to their grandmother, who had been the heart of the hotel and beach club and who, with their grandfather, had raised Renée and Annelise after their father died and Annelise's mother disappeared. A tragic mystery that had finally been put to rest during the hotel's recent renovation. In the picture, Lillian Handleman stood in front of an ancient stand-up microphone with a sheaf of papers in one hand.

"Nana used to put on fashion shows. Friends, family, and hotel guests modeled clothes from local women's shops. She always did the commentary," Annelise added. "I think it started out as entertainment for the guests, but at some point she started carrying and selling beachwear."

She pulled out another photo of their grandmother standing at the podium.

"These are really special," Nikki said, oddly energized by the simple fact of their existence. "There are a lot of companies that produce retro imitations, but these are originals, and having these photos and knowing the history behind them only increases their value."

"How valuable are they?" Renée asked.

"I really don't know. That would require some research." The last time she'd thought about vintage clothing in dollar terms was when she'd been forced to sell most of what she'd acquired after her brother's Ponzi scheme left her broke and unable to save Heart, Inc.

"Do you think we could sell these here in the gift shop?" Annelise motioned to the boxes.

"That's something else that would have to be looked into. You'd have to find a way to market to vintage enthusiasts. That might work better online or in another type of location," she said, thinking now of the pieces that Bitsy had brought her that she still couldn't fit into.

The sisters looked at each other. Renée nodded slightly then turned to Nikki. "Do you think you might have time to do some of that research?"

Nikki's mind began formulating excuses. Her lips were poised and ready to form the word "no" when she realized just how much time and effort she'd been putting into doing absolutely nothing (if you didn't count counting lettuce leaves and calories). This, at least, would be doing something.

"I'd be glad to do a little homework," Nikki finally said. With Mary Poppins constantly on call, Nikki had nothing if not time.

· · ·

Maddie answered her cell phone on the first ring. Which was something you could do when you'd spent the last six hours clutching it in one hand as if it were an appendage. She was so sure that it was Will returning her call from last night that she didn't even glance at the caller ID. It took her a moment to recognize the voice on the other end.

"Maddie? Are you there?" There was the clearing of a masculine throat that did not belong to William Hightower. "It's Troy."

"Oh." She tried to mask her disappointment.

"I wondered if you might be available for lunch." She still hadn't responded when he added, "I'm at the Don. Out near the pool."

There could be little doubt whom and what he would want to discuss. Or that Kyra would consider any conversation with Troy a betrayal. But she had some idea what it might have cost Troy to reach out, and it wasn't in her to reject his invitation. Nor could she spend another minute doing nothing but waiting for Will to return her call.

She walked the short distance to the Don CeSar and found him at a prime table with a view of the pool and the gulf. He stood to greet her then pulled out her chair. When she glanced at the half-empty glass in front of him, he said, "Margarita on the rocks. Will you have one?"

Before she'd finished nodding he'd waved the waiter over with a friendly finesse that made her wonder how he'd hidden the polished manners that now seemed such an inherent part of him.

"Thanks for coming."

"My pleasure."

"So." One eyebrow arched upward. "I'm not sure if you noticed, but the whole confession thing didn't exactly go the way I hoped."

"Yes, we noticed." She squelched the laugh that threatened.

"No, it's all right. I'd be laughing right now myself if that had happened to anyone else." He shook his head ruefully. "What's really funny is that I've been waiting so long to be outed.

"My family knew Bitsy's. I think she and my aunt went to the same boarding school. My family's in timber, too, sawmills. But I guess Matthews is a common enough name." He drained the last of his drink and handed it to the waiter when he arrived with two more. "You'd think that someone who was waiting to be exposed might have been better prepared. But . . ." He shrugged. "Your daughter does not like me one little bit."

"As you pointed out yourself, Kyra doesn't know you at all. And that's not exactly her fault." Maddie took a sip of her drink. It was cold and tart, and it was quite a relief to be thinking about something other than why she was here instead of Mermaid Point and her own general lack of direction. "Why have you been pretending to be a cameraman?"

"I am a cameraman. A good one."

"But you're not the uneducated, lacking-in-financial-resources, clinging-to-a-network-job individual you presented yourself as."

"Not exactly," he conceded with a small smile. "But close enough."

"And you chose that over the family business because?"

"Because I didn't like all the strings that were attached. My brothers and sister think I'm crazy. They're all in the business or living off it. Everyone considers me the 'black sheep.'" He air quoted.

The waiter returned to take their lunch order, and Maddie watched Troy's face and manner. He seemed so comfortable in his own skin, not at all the hostile nemesis that Kyra had been at war with.

"So, not to be too personal," Maddie said, her curiosity mounting. "But you refused to go into the family business, they cut you off, you had to support yourself, and now you don't?"

He ran a hand through his thick blond hair. He'd removed his sunglasses, and his blue eyes were bright and earnest. "I did refuse to go into the family business, but I was never actually cut off. I inherited money from both sides of the family, some of it in trust, some not."

Maddie watched his face. "I just never wanted to live the way my family did. I wanted to earn my own way. Freedom was always more important to me than comfort."

The food arrived, but though he busied himself assembling the parts of the hamburger and putting ketchup on his fries, he seemed in no hurry to eat. Maddie took a bite of her BLT sandwich as gulls wheeled in the sky above them. On a nearby dune a stand of sea oats swayed lightly in the breeze.

"I went to the Salvador Dalí Museum on the waterfront downtown yesterday," Troy continued. "It's a gorgeous building. And apparently houses the largest collection of his work outside of Europe." He cut his burger, set down the knife on the edge of his plate. "But the thing is I'm just as happy seeing a Dalí in a museum. I don't have a need to own one."

"You make it sound so simple," Maddie said after a couple more bites of her sandwich. "But I don't think there are many people who would ignore that kind of money."

He pinched a few fries from his plate and chewed thoughtfully. "I earned enough to drive the car I wanted, buy a boat, live decently—but I chose to be judged by the work I did. And so I left my tux and prep school manners behind and presented myself the way most cameramen would. I didn't need all that money. I didn't plan to ever touch it. Until . . ." He hesitated and she had the impression he would have backtracked if he could.

She folded her hands in her lap and waited.

"Until I realized how much Kyra and Dustin needed it. How much saving Bella Flora meant to her, to all of you." He looked aghast at the admission. She saw a hint of the old Troy's impatience flicker over his face. That impatience seemed to be aimed inward. "God, that sounds so sappy." He exhaled a large breath of air.

"No. I think that was incredibly generous of you, Troy. I'm

grateful that you did what you did for my daughter and grandson. But surely you can see that at least from Kyra's perspective, it all just sort of came out of left field. Deception is a slippery slope. She was deceived by Daniel and look where that's led."

"I get that I should have said something sooner. But how exactly do you tell someone you're not really the overly competitive, jealous, impoverished asshole you've shown yourself to be? Well, I am a little competitive and I can be an asshole on occasion, but I don't understand why she can't see Daniel Deranian for what he is." He took a pull on his drink and picked up another fry.

"Men who are larger than life can be hard to resist." She knew this firsthand. "And, of course, we want to believe the best about the people we're drawn to." Though she had done just the opposite with Will, hadn't she? Instead of sharing her feelings and uncertainties so that he could understand them, she had simply fled.

"So what do I do now?" Troy asked simply. "Seeing as how I've mucked this up so spectacularly."

"Truthfully, most men would look elsewhere," Maddie said. "But then it seems pretty clear that you're not most men."

"My family would agree with you. But I don't think it would be a compliment."

"I think being your own man is a good thing," Maddie said. "Now that you're actually being yourself, you have to find a way to reveal that self to Kyra."

"And how am I supposed to do that?" Troy appeared genuinely perplexed. "I've already tried to explain once and all I did was make things worse."

Maddie finished as much of the BLT as she had room for and drained the last dregs of her second margarita. She felt markedly clearer than when she'd arrived, and hoped it wasn't just because of the alcohol. She hadn't yet figured out her own life or her relationship, but listening to Troy had clarified one thing.

"You can't build a relationship on words or excuses or explanations," she said. "The time has come to do what even writers, who deal in words all the time, struggle to learn: show don't tell."

"And that means?"

"Don't waste another breath trying to tell Kyra how you feel. Figure out how to show her your real self and your true feelings. In the end, I don't think it's the grand gestures that will win her heart. She doesn't need a showboat like Daniel; she needs a man who loves her enough to put her first in all of the little everyday ways."

# Eighteen

*So far so good.* As mantras went, the phrase felt wishy-washy. Underachieving. Nowhere near as motivational as *I can and I will*, as powerful as *be strong, be brave*, or as philosophically biblical as *this too shall pass.*

Despite its lack of affirmational properties, *"so far so good"* was the phrase Kyra lived by. The phrase that sounded in her mind after every good take and anytime a potential meltdown was averted. She'd repeated those four words out loud when each three hours of Screen Actors Guild–allowed daily work were complete, and again when they slid into the back of the black SUV for the drive to the cottage at the end of the 4.5 hours Dustin was allowed to spend each day on set.

*So far so good* had gotten her through the drive back to Winter Haven and the last two days of filming. Which had been a little less perfect than last Friday's first take of the first scene.

At the moment, she sat where she'd been placed an hour ago, out of camera range but close enough to Dustin that they could see and hear each other. So far, one take had been completed. It had been followed by what turned into a half-hour discussion between Daniel and his Lighting Director, the Director of Photography, and the Dolly Grip. This was followed by a fifteen-minute debate with wardrobe and continuity over whether one of Dustin's sneakers should or should not be untied during the scene.

"Okay, everyone, we're back in!" Brandon shouted.

Kyra held her breath as take two commenced. Takes three and four followed. So far Dustin had gotten his lines and his moves right on each take, but Kyra could see his attention and his energy level beginning to flag. Daniel had blown his lines in the first two takes, slightly mangled them in the third, and made it all the way through the fourth. Tonja, playing his wife, Jenna, had nailed each word, each look, each nuance, delivering her lines with a flawless believability in each and every take that was impossible not to admire.

A hush fell as she and Daniel viewed the previous take, not once but twice. A brief but emphatic conversation ensued. It was ultimately Tonja who addressed the crew. "I've asked if we can try that one more time. Dustin was spot on. But I think I could have handled that exchange a little more brightly." She turned back to Daniel. "And I believe your line is actually . . ." She looked to Maureen, the veteran Script Supervisor, who read the line aloud.

"Right," Daniel muttered to himself as makeup dabbed at his face and the key lights were once again adjusted. "All right, here we go for take . . ." Daniel looked to his First AD.

"Five." Brandon raised his hand with all five fingers extended. "Going for five! Stand by!"

The actors moved into position. Tonja placed her arms around Dustin as she had the previous four times. Christian Sommersby stood on his mark just visible through the hotel's glass front door. Daniel stepped back into the shot between Dustin and Tonja, and gave a nod.

"All right!" Brandon called out. "Lock it up. Quiet on the set! Roll sound . . ."

Kyra held her breath as the scene played out. *So far so good. So far so good?* Once again Dustin got his lines and his bit of action right, but she could see the tightening of his shoulders, the too-careful way he held himself as he prepared for the next take, and the take after that. Saw the flicker of fear in his eyes as they flew to Tonja's face afterward to see what she thought. If Daniel hadn't yet realized he wasn't the only one calling the shots, his son was beginning to. And so were the more experienced members of the crew. No matter how politely Tonja attempted to frame it.

When they broke after take seven so that the crew could set up for the next scene, Kyra took Dustin back to the trailer for a potty break and a few moments to decompress. He sat now on the couch, sipping a cup of white grape juice. "Wanna run my lines again," he said with a determined set of his chin that she'd learned to dread.

"You're fine," Kyra said. "You know them. You've been doing so great today."

"Wanna practice!"

She closed her eyes. *So far so* . . . Her mantra was interrupted by a quiet knock on the trailer door. When it opened, Daniel stepped in. He looked tired, frayed around the edges. Far more vulnerable than she'd ever seen him. She'd never realized how attractive that kind of softness could be.

"Dandiel!" Dustin smiled. "Did you come to practice our lines for the next scene?"

"I've told him that he's already got them down, but he doesn't seem to believe me." She sent Daniel a pleading look. "There is such a thing as overpreparing, right?"

For a moment she thought she hadn't been clear enough, but Daniel nodded as he walked toward them. "Your mom's right. You've been on the money every single take today, unlike your old man. You want to keep it fresh. Too much practicing can make the lines feel stale when the time comes to deliver them. What do you say we run them one time? For me. I'm sure Tonja will appreciate it."

Daniel sighed. His eyes met hers. "I knew there would be a

lot more to deal with, but I think I may have underestimated just how much it could affect my performance." He picked up the sides that had been delivered that morning and handed them to Kyra. "Will you read the part of Jenna?"

Kyra had read Tonja's lines with Dustin without thinking much of it, but reading them with Daniel felt decidedly different. "All right," she said. "But only once. Because your father needs help. Are we clear?"

Father and son smiled in agreement, their expressions achingly similar.

"Okay." Daniel laid out the upcoming scene. "Tyler, his mother, Jenna, and his father, Martin, are in the lobby, just back from dinner. Tyler is sleepy but he doesn't want to go to bed. His mommy and daddy promise that if he goes to sleep as soon as they get to the room, they'll go on the rides first thing the next morning."

Daniel hefted Dustin up in his arms the way the script called for Martin to lift Tyler.

As Kyra read Jenna's line, Daniel put his arm around her and pulled her close, per the stage direction, as he recited his line. His lean strength enveloped her; his musky scent filled her nostrils.

Dustin's lines followed. As he would in the scene, he laid his head on his father's shoulder, closed his eyes, and stuck his thumb in his mouth.

"Ahhh . . . alone at last." Daniel's eyes darkened. The way they promised and asked things at the same time pulled at something deep inside her. He drew her closer.

Kyra's eyes dropped to the script and she recognized Martin's line. The scene was part of the story's setup, designed to illustrate Martin and Jenna's love for and attraction to each other. Dustin had no further lines. There was no reason to continue. Yet Daniel continued to hold her against him.

She knew she should step away right now. But the warmth

in Daniel's eyes stopped her. So did the lowering of his face to hers. His lips brushed seductively across hers as he murmured things that made her shiver with anticipation. When he deepened the kiss, her lips fell open. The next thing she knew she was kissing him back with enthusiasm.

Her last semiconscious thought was, *So far, not so good.*

. . .

"Are you ready?" June Steding asked, looking across her desk at Bitsy.

Bitsy wasn't actually sure. She'd been so eager to hear from Gary Kaufman, but now that the forensic accountant was on the line, she realized she was about to hear things she could never unhear. She nodded slowly.

June answered the phone. "Hi, Gary. Bitsy and I are both here and on speaker."

"Thanks so much for going through the records," Bitsy said after greetings were exchanged. "I really appreciate your help."

"My pleasure."

"So what have you got for us?" June asked, giving her a steadying look.

"Well, if it's any consolation, your husband didn't start out crooked. In the beginning he invested your funds in legitimate businesses and deals. And he did manage to keep you out of Dyer's Ponzi scheme. But truthfully? The guy didn't do so well."

"How so?" June asked. She picked up a pen and straightened the legal pad in front of her.

"First off he fell for a number of scams—bought steel in India that the owners had resold ten, twenty times while it was sitting in port. I'm pretty sure it's still sitting there today." Kaufman's delivery was briskly efficient, his accent vaguely northeastern. "He also bought land that didn't exist. And, of course, the worse he did, the more he tried to cover the losses and the riskier his choices became."

Bitsy listened dully, trying to remember what Bertie had said about the deals he'd looked at or the businesses he'd wanted to invest in. But had she ever really listened to the details?

"Things took a steep nosedive when he became sole trustee. He was already in the hole, but he got more aggressive." There was the sound of papers being flipped. "From what I can see, once he'd managed to hide the losses from you, he got more brazen. Watching the progression, it becomes clear that he realized he could do whatever he wanted."

He paused for a moment and she heard him cover the mouthpiece to speak with someone. "Sorry. Where were we?"

Bitsy did not answer. But she knew exactly why she had ignored those records for a whole year. Validation of one's own stupidity sucked.

"Oh, here we are." He cleared his throat. "He did leave enough in your accounts to fund living expenses in the style to which you were accustomed. But he was skimming on both ends and stashing money in accounts in his name in the Caymans. Then he set up a dummy Cayman company, which he then bought for ten million dollars of your money." He paused to let that one sink in.

"The company's only asset was him?" June stopped note-taking to ask quietly.

"Yes. Ultimately the company bought a yacht, a villa, and an office park. All of which were in his name. So basically, he used money from your joint accounts to fund a new life for himself in the Caymans."

Bitsy's face flushed hotly. She peeled off her sweater and reached for the bottle of water that sat unopened on the desk.

"Bottom line?" June asked.

"Bottom line, we definitely have more than enough outright fraud to get the authorities interested." He said this as if it demanded applause.

"And it looks like he had help."

"Help?" Once again the attorney asked what Bitsy couldn't.

"Yeah, from what I can tell, that young woman at Houghton Whitfield that he allegedly bullied into wiring that last chunk?" Kaufman snorted in disgust. "Based on his purchases, which he'd stopped trying to hide some years before, and the pattern of transfers over time, they were clearly involved." He cleared his throat. "In every possible way. And if they didn't know it at the time, I have no doubt her bosses at the firm know it now."

June scribbled harder. Bitsy simply sat and listened. Her head hurt from the blows as the forensic accountant hammered the final nails into the coffin of her faith in humanity and confirmed her inability to determine a good person from a self-centered, self-serving thief. She had chosen Bertie Baynard and she had married him. Then she'd given him a license to steal. She dropped her head into her hands.

"Any questions?"

June asked quite a few, all of them no doubt good ones. Bitsy was already reeling from what she knew now.

"All right then. I've sent a report over. Call if there's anything else. I know a couple of good international process servers. And my money's on Bertie still being in the Caymans; he'd want to stay close to his money."

Then it was just Bitsy and June. Bitsy wanted to curl up and die. Or at least go somewhere dark where she could hide.

"Oh, no, you don't," June said. "You are not going to roll over and give up now. Not if I have anything to say about it."

Bitsy couldn't decide whether to cry or shout, so she did both. "I see all those notes you took, but I don't think you were paying attention. I screwed everything up. This is all my fault!" She took a shuddering breath. "I had an obscene amount of money. An Ivy League education. I could have done or been anything. My background and resources couldn't be more different than the women who come through here. I didn't have to depend on a man. I didn't need one to lift me out of poverty. Or help me go to school. But what did I do? The minute I had one, I abdicated. I turned into a helpless ninny. I deserve what happened!"

June came over and sat next to her. She wore the no-nonsense look she used when delivering the kind of truth most people didn't want to hear. "No one deserves this, Bitsy. No one. We all start with what we're given, who we are, and the hand we're dealt. But you did not deserve this. And you are not going to give up and let him get away with what he's done."

Bitsy looked up in some surprise.

"What?" the attorney asked. "You think I've never seen the look that's on your face? Hell, I've seen it in the mirror. And I've felt all the things you're feeling right now. One day I'll share my story with you, but I can tell you that it's not only uneducated, poverty-stricken women who find themselves in this situation. Anyone can be taken advantage of.

"I went to law school because of a man like Bertie. And I've been doing my best to help the victims of men like him ever since. I love putting men like that in jail. And that's what we're going to do to your husband."

"And how are we going to do that?" Bitsy reached for the bottle of water with a shaking hand.

"I haven't worked out the details yet," June said, sitting back, her arms crossing over her chest. "But the game has changed. Now we have ammunition. We have Gary Kaufman's report that confirms there's been fraud. And we have a paper trail that shows that your husband, a client of Houghton Whitfield, was having an affair with one of its employees."

"But she doesn't work there anymore. She . . ."

"The last thing a firm with a roster of high-net-worth clients can afford is a scandal. Your husband running off with your money is one thing. One of their employees having an affair with him and helping him do it? That is something else entirely. Something the Palm Beach state attorney's office would be interested in." June leaned across her desk, her eyes gleaming. "They didn't just fire her and send her on her way. Though they might have paid her to keep quiet.

"Didn't you tell me you knew someone in the financial crimes area of the FBI?"

"Well, yes, but . . ."

"Do you think he'd sit down with us?"

"Well, he's due back this weekend," Bitsy replied, trying to gather her wits. "I think so but . . ."

"Good." The attorney smiled. "I'd like to talk this through with him, hear his thoughts, see if he can offer some advice. And I really, really want to find and talk to this woman."

# Nineteen

Wednesday passed in a frenzy of waffling that Maddie was grateful no one was present to witness. To call Will or not to call. To assume he had a good reason for not calling her back. Or assume it meant he hadn't forgiven her for leaving so abruptly and for putting him in second place yet again.

The weather couldn't seem to make up its mind, either. One minute, thunder rumbled. The next, pinpricks of sunlight pierced the mountainous dark clouds only to be quashed by heavy sheets of rain that blotted out the horizon. Temperatures hovered in the low fifties, dipped into the forties, came back up. The Weather Channel claimed there'd be an overnight low in the thirties, which meant locals were already breaking out the winter coats and UGG boots that saw action approximately once a year.

By late afternoon the sky had settled on dull iron gray, the air was wet and cold, and the downpour had diminished to an exhausted drizzle. Maddie gazed out the cottage window at the sodden flower beds and puddled walkways. The beach would be equally soggy. There would be no final walk or sunset toasts.

Her suitcase lay open on the bed still half filled with the things she'd thrown in it when she left Mermaid Point. Her toiletries lined the bathroom counter. But she didn't have the will to pack them. She sighed. Blew a bang off her forehead. Stood for a good ten minutes staring out the bedroom window then headed back to the kitchen to stare into the refrigerator. She missed Will and couldn't wait to see him, but what kind of reception would she get? Had he been too busy to miss her? Or had she given him reason to doubt her feelings? Or to reconsider his own?

The knock on the door sounded as sweet as a last-minute reprieve from the governor. Maddie threw it open, the first move she'd made that day without dithering.

Bitsy and Nikki stood on the doorstep. Both had clothing draped over their arms. The roof of the twins' stroller was similarly draped. A rain-splattered sheet of plastic protected the clothing and the twins. Avery hunched under an umbrella behind them.

"Since it's too wet for sunset toasts, we thought we'd have a going-away party," Nikki said as she began to unbuckle the girls. "And we cherry-picked our closets to help you add a few . . . enhancements . . . to your tour wardrobe." Leaving the stroller near the door, Nikki carried the girls inside and set them on the area rug. "Gemma and Sofia napped all afternoon, so I figured they could stay up a little later than usual."

"You're never too young to learn how to tweak a wardrobe," Bitsy said.

"What makes you think my tour wardrobe needs tweaking or enhancing?" Maddie stood aside so they could enter. "I've got plenty of things that won't wrinkle or show stains."

"Tell me none of those things are polyester 'travelers' or mom jeans," Bitsy said.

Maddie watched them carry in the clothing, glad her travelers' three-piece pantsuit with matching skirt wasn't on the premises. "That doesn't sound like a party to me."

"It'll be a party, because we'll be drinking and eating while we do it." Bitsy held up a container of Ted Peters famous smoked fish spread and a cloth carrier that held bottles of wine. "I am in serious need of a party tonight."

"And I hope you won't take this the wrong way, but your wardrobe, while lovely and largely no-iron, doesn't have any 'hey, look at me' things in it," Nikki added.

"That's because my body has asked me not to shout or draw attention to it," Maddie replied. Closing the door behind them, she busied herself pulling wineglasses out of the cabinet and setting out small plates.

"Do you remember when we dressed you that time in Durham for Will's concert? And we had hair and makeup?" Bitsy asked. "Weren't you glad you made the effort?"

"Well, yes." She remembered Bitsy's delight in playing fairy godmother and how shocked she'd been by her reflection in the hotel mirror. Her reflection in Will's eyes was something she'd never forget.

"As I recall, Will was pretty wild about how you looked," Nikki said.

Maddie blushed. Will had loved her in the outfit they'd insisted she wear almost as much as he'd enjoyed taking it off her. It had been the most incredible night and had led to her first and only "walk of shame" the next morning.

"I rest my case," Nikki said. "I'm just going to put these things in your room. After we toast a bit we can coordinate some outfits."

Maddie handed Avery a bowl for the Cheez Doodles and opened the first bottle of wine, but she couldn't imagine any piece or combination of clothing that would make up for the way she'd practically cut and run.

"Wow. I am in serious need of a drink," Bitsy said as she set out the fish spread and poured the wine.

"Me too," Avery said.

"Ditto," Maddie added.

"I'm in!" Nikki said as she returned. "I believe that makes it unanimous."

Rain splattered the windows and drummed a tattoo on the

cottage roof as they arranged the food and drink on the cocktail table and settled themselves around it. On the floor at their feet Sofia began her exploration on all fours while Gemma placed both hands on the side of her mother's chair and grunted loudly as she strained to haul herself to her feet.

They sipped and drank for a few minutes. The others looked at her expectantly. "Okay then," she said. "Anybody have a toast or a good thing to share?"

Bitsy raised her glass. "I can't quite believe I'm saying this, but here's to fraud."

Except for the twins' babbling, the room fell silent. All eyes settled on Bitsy.

"In what universe does that qualify as a 'good thing'? Avery asked.

"That would be my universe," Bitsy said. "Documenting the fraud is the first step in getting criminal charges brought against Bertie." She downed her drink and poured a second. "Oh. I almost forgot. I have another toast." Her glass went up. "To adultery."

"I'm afraid you're going to have to explain that one, too," Avery said while the rest of them gaped.

"Well, it looks like Bertie had an ongoing affair with the woman at Houghton Whitfield that handled wire transfers."

"Seriously?" Avery asked.

"As a heart attack," Bitsy replied. "So it wasn't just Delilah the stripper that he cheated with."

"Oh, Bitsy." The pain and anger etched across Bitsy's face made Maddie's worries about how Will would receive her tomorrow seem small. "I'm so sorry for what you're dealing with."

"Yeah, that definitely sucks," Avery said. "Are you sure you want to drink to that?"

"I have to drink to that!" Bitsy took a long, desperate swallow of wine. "The good part is that June thinks the firm might be paying her to keep quiet. Which could also give the authorities reason to be interested." She set down her empty glass. "She asked if Joe would be willing to talk through our next steps with us."

"Of course he will," Nikki said. "He's home on Friday. Why don't we give him a day to decompress? Maybe Sunday afternoon?"

"Thanks." Bitsy sighed. "So what do you guys think? Good enough? Because frankly that's all I've got. And at the moment it feels like the hurts just keep on coming."

"I am not the 'good enough' police," Maddie said as she had so many times before. "But can anyone rephrase that?"

"Working on it." Nikki got up, walked into the hallway, and came back with Sofia, whom she set back down on her hands and knees. "Why don't we drink to . . . having new evidence that will help bring Bertie to justice."

"Wow, that was good," Avery said.

"Definitely good." Bitsy refilled her glass. "And it can't happen soon enough."

Nikki stood and took a mock bow. "Why, thank you. I am honored to accept the first ever One Good Thing quick-thinking award. And while I'm at it, Joe coming home on Friday *is* my one good thing. I'm so ready for him to get back."

They clinked and drank. Maddie felt the warmth of their friendship wrap around her.

"And." Nikki eyed the girls, and lowered her voice. "I'm also ready for a little less Luvie."

The twins stopped what they were doing to crow, "Luffeee!" Gemma opened her arms as if reaching for a hug and fell on her bottom. A sharp cry of what sounded like indignation split the air.

"Sorry, but the woman is too perfect. And she's always there," Nikki said.

"I would have given anything for that kind of help when Kyra and Andrew were little," Maddie said.

"Yeah, well, there's help and then there's feeling completely superfluous," Nikki said. "But enough about me." She turned to Avery. "How's the project over on Vina del Mar coming?"

"Good. It's good." Avery sat up straighter. "I like figuring out how to make the most of every inch of space. Customizing and making it personal is really satisfying." She munched a Cheez Doodle. "In fact, building tiny is definitely my one good thing." She raised her glass and they clinked and drank. "Plus the timeline is shorter. So there's more immediate gratification for everyone involved."

"Do I sense a 'but'?" Bitsy asked.

"No," Avery said. "No 'buts.'"

"Are you sure?" Nikki asked. "Because I could have sworn I heard a 'but' in there, too."

"Nope." Avery sipped her wine, slathered fish spread on a cracker, added a drop of Tabasco. "I thought we were going to work on Maddie's wardrobe."

"Said the person who cares less about clothes than anyone else in this room. Including Sofia and Gemma," Nikki observed drily.

Avery continued to eat. "I just thought that was what was supposed to be happening."

"So there's no problem?" Bitsy asked.

Avery shook her head no, but her face said yes.

An expectant silence fell. Maddie went to retrieve more napkins. Nikki lifted Gemma, who'd been using her mother's thigh as a balancing board, into her lap.

Bitsy busied herself opening the second bottle of wine.

"Fine! Okay! So there's a problem." Avery threw her hands up. "There's a problem with me!"

They waited.

"Fine," she said again. "The problem is that when I'm on a job, the first person I want to call or tell or show it to is . . ." She stopped.

"Chase?" Maddie asked softly.

"Yes. Chase." Irritation infused each word. "I mean nothing personal, but you guys aren't exactly dying to discuss whether it's worth it to spend the extra money on a composting toilet."

"True. I don't give a shit about a composting toilet," Nikki quipped.

There was laughter.

Maddie reached for a cracker and began to coat it with fish spread. "So you just miss talking shop with Chase."

"Right," Avery said, not quite meeting her eye.

Maddie covered more crackers with fish spread then offered them around. It was actually a relief to watch someone else struggle over a relationship. So much easier than trying to untangle her own.

"And I miss getting his opinion on the custom built-ins at Martha Wyatt's. I know he'd really appreciate the storage I'm building into the stairs that lead up to the loft." Avery stopped talking abruptly.

"I understand what you're saying," Nikki added. "So what you're really missing are the professional aspects of the relationship you shared."

Maddie kept her head down and her smile to herself.

"Well, there are other things I miss about him." Avery's tone softened, but only for a moment. "But I don't really see why he thought he needed more. I mean, what could he possibly be sharing with that Riley Hancock? I bet you that girl doesn't even know which end of the hammer is the business end. And I guarantee she couldn't drive in a nail if her life depended on it."

There was a snort that no one owned up to.

"I hope to hell you aren't laughing at me. Because this is not funny."

"No one's laughing," Maddie said, though it seemed Nikki was. "There's nothing wrong with wanting what makes us the most comfortable. But sometimes we have to listen to what the other person wants. And sometimes if it isn't a complete negation of who we are or what we want, we do it. It's called compromise."

The word "compromise" reverberated in Maddie's brain, making her flush with shame. How much compromising had she done? She'd barely considered Will's feelings. She'd just bailed and expected him to be understanding without thinking about how her actions might affect him or his songwriting.

"So you think I should commit to Chase after he pushed me away the way he did when Jason was having problems? He shut me out completely!" Her voice rang with hurt and indignation.

"But he apologized and said he wanted you back and that he wanted to prove to you that you could trust him. But you didn't really give him a chance," Nikki pointed out.

"That's because he moved too fast. He thought just because we were spending time together again and that we're good in bed meant we would automatically go back where we used to be. And now he's dating that Riley. Even if he weren't, I'm just not ready. I'm . . . I'm scared."

Avery's fear was palpable, the admission nothing short of stunning. Maddie's hands clasped around her wineglass. Was it fear that had sent her fleeing from Mermaid Point? Fear of being insignificant? Fear that Will would finally notice how lacking in drive and ambition she was? Fear that once she was on tour with him and her whole world revolved around his schedule, his needs, that she'd truly cease to exist? She had given herself wholly to her family and claimed that she wanted something more for herself, but still had no idea what. If not Will, then what was it she wanted?

"We're all afraid, Avery," Maddie said, reaching for her friend's hand. "No matter how much we try to push our fears aside or pretend they don't exist." She swallowed, thinking just how much she'd been trying to outrun. "Somehow we have to find a way to do what we want and be with whomever we choose in spite of that fear." Her hand shook slightly as she raised her glass. "To pushing through the fear."

They finished their wine, the silence spooling out around them, the twins' babbles and movements the only sounds.

Nikki stood. "All right. I say it's time for fashion!" She and Bitsy headed for the bedroom.

Avery ate a Cheez Doodle and poured them both another glass of wine. "Thanks, Maddie," she said quietly. "I still don't know what the hell I'm going to do, but I feel a little better. It helps to know I'm not the only one trying to figure it out."

When Bitsy and Nikki returned and spread the clothing out on the sofa, Maddie turned her attention in an effort to be polite. But as coordinating pieces were laid together, she began to realize just how perfect they were and what a great addition they might make.

First up was a pair of nude lace-up block-heeled shoes and an Alice and Olivia lace-accented blouse to go with a pair of boyfriend jeans they'd pulled from her suitcase.

"Nice, right?" Nikki said. "You're welcome to keep the shoes—my feet went up half a size while I was pregnant and they don't seem to be going back. Just have to be sure to roll up the jeans to keep them looking current. And I think this nude bucket bag will go with everything."

Next, Bitsy laid out a pair of skinny black jeans with leather on the front panel. "These are Helmut Lang. They're a classic and they have the added benefit of actually being comfortable— lots of stretch but great sucking-in properties." The top she set above it was a blousy silk floral by Joie. The heels were pointy and black.

"You can also pair these pants or your rolled-up boyfriend jeans with this black V-neck tee and heels. Then you just finish it off with this Alexander McQueen signature scarf. I figured the skull motif would be very rock 'n' roll." The next was a black-and-white T-shirt dress. "I thought this Stella McCartney might be an easy thing to throw on. It's got a great abstract pattern, plus the three-quarter sleeve and a split-layer hem. You can wear it with the nude or black shoes."

The rest of their offerings were equally well chosen. A multi-angled and patterned boatneck top, and a short, sleeveless shell and knee-length sweater in a brilliant blue. Bitsy arranged long pendant necklaces in gold and silver and big hoops and smaller sharp-edged earrings near the clothes. "And I've added these two cold-shoulder tunics for travel because they're comfortable and they'll go with everything. And because, let's face it, our shoulders are often the last body parts to go."

Maddie studied the outfits. Everything was age appropriate, yet current. They would make a statement without shouting. She turned to her friends, who'd gone to such trouble to make sure she wouldn't fade into the woodwork. "These are absolutely perfect! Are you sure you're okay loaning them out?"

"Absolutely," Nikki said.

"God, yes," Bitsy added. "At least our clothes will be traveling and having a good time."

"I hope I'll remember what goes with what," Maddie said, eyeing the pieces arranged on the couch.

"You won't have to," Bitsy said, pulling out her phone. "I'm going to take pictures of the outfits and all the pieces that can go together. My stylist always used to do that. It's awesome having a reference at your fingertips." She smiled as she began to shoot photos.

At a nudge from Nikki, Avery retrieved a simple white box from behind the sofa and handed it to Maddie. "This is from all tree of us." She swayed slightly and corrected, "That's the *three* of us."

"It's for you *and* Will," Nikki said as Maddie opened the box and carefully pulled apart the tissue paper.

A satin peignoir with a simple lace bodice and trim, in the

same brilliant blue as the sweater set, lay folded inside. "Oh, my gosh." Maddie ran a hand over the silky satin. "It's so beautiful. Thank you."

"We thought Will might find this a little more tempting than your plaid Christmas pajamas," Nikki teased.

"Or the ones with the puppy dogs," Avery added.

Maddie joined in the laughter even as her eyes blurred with tears. "As much as I didn't think I needed the tweaking, I'm so glad you put these outfits together. I guess I was more nervous than I realized about what it's going to be like on the road with Will and the band."

The clothes were put away in her bedroom. The twins fell asleep on the carpet as Maddie, Nikki, Bitsy, and Avery finished the wine and snacks. She hugged them close as they said good night, then stood in the doorway watching them walk to their cottages in the moonlight. As she closed the door she thought of all the advice she'd dispensed since she'd arrived, about handling fear and making and keeping commitments. And most of all what she'd said to Troy about showing rather than telling. It seemed the time had come to follow her own advice.

# Twenty

"You don't have to walk me home. I just live over there." Avery pointed toward her cottage.

"Actually, you live that way." Bitsy took hold of Avery's shoulders and turned her in the opposite direction.

"You sure?" Avery squinted but it all looked like a dark, damp blur.

"Positive. Come on, I'll walk you to the door. Otherwise I'm afraid we're going to find you lying underneath a palm tree in the morning. The good news is you're not going to be hurting anyone but yourself. But still, friends don't let friends walk home drunk."

"How'd you get to be such a good drinker?" Avery had to search for the words through the mental fog that seemed to have descended.

"I don't know. Just born that way, I guess. Too bad you can't make a living from the ability to consume large quantities of alcohol without losing your faculties."

"I always thought I felt alcohol so easy cuz I'm so . . . small."

"No, I think this may be one of the few areas where size really doesn't matter." Bitsy laughed. "Bertie was close to six two and after one drink he'd be on his ass. Alcohol was a big part of our social scene, so he finally learned to just carry a drink around with him all night. I actually used to think that was kind of endearing."

"Chase used to be enduring. Or did you say engineering?" She blinked. "Are we there yet? Cuz I'm pretty sure I need to pee."

Bitsy's arm linked through hers and they started walking faster.

"I hate that men can just pee anywhere and we have to find a bathroom. It's so unfair."

"Yeah, I think about that all the time," Bitsy said. "When I'm not busy thinking about how to make a living or how to find Bertie. Or whether there's even any money left to be found."

"Do ya miss him?" Avery stopped and swayed, making Bitsy stop with her. A cottage materialized, no longer a part of the hedge. She was pretty sure it was hers.

"When I'm not furious with him? Yes. Sometimes I wake up during the night and reach for him. It's so beautiful because I've forgotten every awful thing that happened. And I want him." Bitsy expelled a breath of air. "Now I can't even tell myself that the exotic dancer was the first indiscretion. He was just a lying cheater. And I was too stupid to see it."

"I miss Chase. I want him."

"You could actually do something about that, you know." Bitsy brought them to a stop in front of a small porch that looked a lot like hers. "But I'd wait until you're sober. Do you have a key?"

Avery patted her pockets. "No." She patted them again. "Oh, wait." She squatted down and reached under the welcome mat.

"Seriously?" Bitsy took the key and inserted it in the lock for her.

"It worked, didn' it?"

"Yes. But that is the first place a criminal would look."

Avery swayed.

"Okay. I suggest two aspirin and a large glass of water before you go to sleep."

"S' good idea. Thanks for the ride." Avery pushed the door open and stepped inside.

"I'm not moving until I hear the door lock behind you."

Avery slammed the door.

"Don't forget to . . ."

"Okay!" Avery fumbled the lock closed. Her one-bedroom, one-bath "castle" was small, just the way she liked it. She'd like it even more if it would stop spinning. She made it to the bathroom and then to the bedroom, where she plopped down on the bed and struggled out of her clothes. Something clattered to the floor and she bent over to feel for it, which sent the room whirling more wildly. Her fingers closed around her cell phone and she held on to it as she fell back on the bed. The sheets were cool on her naked skin and she closed her eyes, luxuriating in the sensation. The spinning slowed. She sighed with the pleasure of being home and in her own bed. Alone. And naked. Her thoughts drifted, soft as a cloud. Chase. Kneeling over her. His lips skimming down her body, across her navel, his hair tickling her breasts.

Her hand moved toward her body, followed the imaginary path of Chase's fingers and mouth, languid with memory. Her fingers wrapped around something small and hard wedged against her thigh. She lifted it and her cell phone came to life, lighting the darkness. She stared at the screen and before she'd known she was going to do it, she'd hit speed dial. She lay listening to the ringtone.

"Avery?" Chase's voice brought a smile to her lips along with a heady tug of desire.

"Hmmm?" The word felt like a purr leaving her mouth.

"Are you all right?" His voice and the concern in it slid over her like the warm caress she'd been imagining, making her back arch in a totally feline way. "Do you need something?"

"Yes." Her thoughts were thick with memory. Her skin felt so hot it might have been on fire. "Yes," she said. "I'm pretty sure I do." But as she drifted off with the phone clutched to her chest, she wasn't sure whether she'd said the words aloud.

She awoke to the sound of birds chirping outside. Sunlight slanted in through the blinds. Her phone sat on the nightstand. There was a man lying next to her and he was as naked as she was. She knew this because she was pressed up against rock-hard flesh and locked in a muscled forearm. A familiar hand rested on her breast. As if it belonged to him.

She scrambled out from underneath the arm, pulling the rumpled sheet up over her as she sat up against the headboard. Blue eyes opened and took her in. A pair of much-too-familiar lips lifted into a smile.

"Good morning." Chase sat up, not bothering with a sheet. He scratched his chest lazily with one hand. His cheeks were covered in dark stubble. His dark hair stood up every which way.

"What are you doing here?"

"You called and I came."

She shook her head and pain sliced through it. She stilled and poked more gingerly through the pulsing, throbbing mass of cotton wool that was her brain, searching for a memory of the night before. Fragments emerged. She bit back a groan.

"Ah, I see it's coming back to you." Chase grinned cheerfully, scratched his chest again. "You probably need coffee." Definitely naked, he got out of bed and padded—no, make that swaggered, into the kitchen. When he returned she'd splashed water on her face, brushed her teeth, and pulled on her robe. But she hadn't been able to find the . . .

"Looking for these?" He handed her the bottle of Tylenol and a glass of water. "I managed to get some down your throat last night," he said. "But I'm guessing your head is pounding like a bass drum about now."

Furious that he was right, she washed the pills down with a

long drink of water. He went into the bathroom and came out with a towel knotted at his hip.

"Coffee'll be ready in a minute. We can go out for breakfast if you'd like. Or . . ." He waggled his eyebrows. "We can go back to bed. I don't have to be on-site until ten. Or maybe you could take me by and show me the Wyatt build. I'd love to see it."

She looked at her phone then back up at his shit-eating grin. It was almost eight. "I really don't understand what happened here," she said, though it was becoming way too clear.

"Well, I could draw you a picture but . . ."

"I mean why you're here. And why we . . ." She couldn't bring herself to say it and she definitely didn't want to see any pictures of it. The satisfied thrum of her body indicated there was no chance of denying it.

"What can I say? You called and invited me over. In fact, the invitation was so graphic I'm pretty sure it made me blush. But as booty calls go it was damned persuasive."

"Booty call." She repeated the words dully. "You came over here for the specific purpose of having sex with me even though it was obvious I'd been drinking and might not be in my right mind."

"Well, if memory serves, that's how booty calls generally work."

"We had sex because I called you while I was drunk. And asked for it?" She was going to have to have a talk with Bitsy. What was the point of walking an inebriated friend home and not confiscating a weapon as potentially dangerous as a cell phone? Friends shouldn't let friends dial drunk.

Chase nodded. "I'm too much of a gentleman to use the word 'beg,' but I did my best to resist. You were pretty insistent."

"Oh, God." She pulled the sheet higher and wished she could simply disappear beneath it.

"Be right back."

He went to the kitchen to pour coffee while Avery tried to remember making the call, but the only images she came up with were of the sexual gymnastics that had ensued. When he returned she took the coffee he offered, but only because she needed it so desperately. He looked way too comfortable for her liking.

"I'm surprised you were willing to come serve as my plaything," she said tersely. "Given that you've taken such an all-or-nothing position."

He searched her face. The smile she'd found so annoying flickered out. "Look, Avery. I came because I was worried about you. I figured I'd make sure you were okay and tuck you into bed." He shrugged. "But you weren't having it. You're a hard woman to say no to. Then you admitted you missed me and wanted me back in your life."

"I said that?"

"Well, only after you called Riley Hancock a number of names that I don't think bear repeating. But then you told me that you loved me, that you always had and always would. I assumed that meant you were ready to take the next step."

Now that the smile was gone she wished she could put it back, but the words that would do that stuck in her throat. "I do love you, Chase. That's not in question. And I'm sorry if you think I called under false pretenses. I hated seeing you with someone else. And I miss you more than I can say." She swallowed. "But it's taken me all this time to get used to being alone again. I didn't just lose you, I lost your dad and the boys. You were my family. I don't think I could survive that again. That's why I feel like we need to move more slowly. To be safe."

Chase sighed, shook his head. "Safe? In my experience, love isn't safe or predictable. Neither is life. There are no guarantees." He stood, his hands on his hips. "We've known each other since we were kids. We've lived together. We love each other. I'm sorry as hell that I shut you out. But I don't know how to prove future behavior to you. And I don't see how a couple weeks or months of dating are going to make a difference. There's a leap of faith required here, Avery. You either trust me and believe in us. Or you don't."

Her heart thudded dully in her chest. She understood his words, could even see the truth in them. But the fear she felt was real, the leap required too great.

"Right." He took a step away from the bed. "Got it." He gave her one last look. "I'm going to take a quick shower and then I'll get out of your way."

He came out of the bathroom wearing jeans and a T-shirt, his hair still damp from the shower. He barely paused as he strode through the bedroom. "You take care."

When she went into the living room to microwave the coffee that had grown cold in the cup, the key she'd given him was sitting on the dinette. She sat down on the sofa and stared numbly out the window. But she was in no mood for sunshine.

• • •

When Maddie arrived at Bud n' Mary's Marina that afternoon, Hudson Power was waiting for her. She smiled as he walked over to give her a hug and take her suitcase, but she was unable to stop herself from looking around him.

"Will's back at Mermaid Point making himself presentable."

"Presentable?"

"Yeah. We went out to Cape Sable early Monday morning for an impromptu camping and fishing trip. We just got back about thirty minutes ago." Hud handed her into the boat he'd taught her to drive, stowed her suitcase, and started up the engine.

"Did you have a good time?"

"It wasn't the most fun I've ever had, no," he said as he backed the boat out of the slip then putted out of the marina. "He couldn't finish the damned song he was working on. Got all grumpy-assed. He was lucky I didn't leave him out there."

With the marina behind them Hud increased their speed. Within minutes they were skimming across the turquoise water, the wind whipping Maddie's hair. She smiled as she inhaled the salt air. The lack of cell service on and around the isolated beach they'd camped on explained why Will hadn't returned her call. What it didn't explain was if he'd be glad to see her.

As they rounded the mangrove-shrouded island and approached the Mermaid Point dock, the nerves she'd been shoving aside during the drive down from Pass-a-Grille reasserted themselves. She'd turned tail and run like some deer startled out of the bush without thinking why she was running, where she was headed, or what consequences she might face when she returned. And now she was about to find out what kind of damage she'd done.

Hud walked her into the foyer of the main house and set her suitcase beside her feet. There was a sound at the top of the stairs and she looked up to see Will. As always, her heart swelled at the sight of him. His dark hair hung damp to his broad shoulders, which were encased in a plain white T-shirt. The sharp planes and angles of his face stretched beneath newly bronzed skin. His dark eyes gave nothing away as he came down to join them.

"So, a fishing trip, huh?" Maddie hoped her smile didn't look as uncertain as she felt. "How was the catch?"

Will's smile was friendly enough as he greeted her, but his eyes remained guarded and his hug was nothing like the one he'd bestowed the last time she'd arrived. Nor did he seem inclined to drag her upstairs for a "nap."

"It would have been better if Hud had ever stopped talking," he said. "I keep waiting for him to realize that fishing guides are men of few words. But Hud here feels compelled to spout all kinds of nonsense. Scared away most of the fish. The ones we caught threw themselves on the hook just to get him to shut up."

"Ha!" Hud replied. "I wouldn't have had to talk so much if you would've stopped moping."

"I wasn't moping, I was thinking. There's a difference." Will glared at his old friend.

Lori appeared from the first-floor office. "You came back!" She threw her arms around Maddie. "Thank God," she said as she let go. "We were all afraid that . . ."

"You can go now," Will said, expanding the glare to include the young woman. He made a shooing motion at the two of them. When they took off, he gestured toward the open glass at the rear of the great room. "I think the pavilion's empty. Feel like sitting outside?"

She tried not to notice how formally he'd made the request. As if she were a guest and he the courteous host. She followed him outside and into the shade of the open-air building that he'd had rebuilt after Irma. It was an almost exact replica of the original where Dustin had first shared a smooshed PB&J with the rock star who had so intimidated her. He pulled two cans of lemonade out of the refrigerator of the updated version of the outdoor kitchen where they'd once cooked together on camera. This place, this whole island, was filled with the memories of their meeting and what became their relationship. Her horror at what she'd done rose up in a tidal wave of regret that threatened to swamp her.

"I'm so sorry I left the way I did," she said without thought or plan. "I really don't know what came over me. I mean part of it was worry about Kyra and Dustin and I am glad I was there for them but . . ." She paused for breath, but nothing could halt the words that flew out of wherever she'd stuffed them. "I don't know. For some reason I . . . I guess I just kind of panicked." She winced. "And then when you didn't return my call I thought maybe you were so mad you didn't even want to talk to me."

He studied her face then scrubbed a large hand over his own.

"Yeah, well, I didn't even take my cell phone with me. I just picked up the message when we got back." He stared out over the crescent-shaped beach, but she doubted he was watching the small seabirds running around on their matchstick legs.

"I'm not going to lie," he finally said. "I didn't like it when you ran off and left me that way."

"I didn't mean to," she said honestly. "It took me half the week to realize I was running. And the other half to even understand a little bit of what made me do it."

"Well, I hope to hell you're planning to enlighten me," he said gruffly. "Because I tried swimming, fishing, and camping. And you know those three things have gotten me through a lot of shit. But you? I never expected you to mess with my head like that."

"I know." She could barely swallow around the emotion clogging her throat. But she owed it to both of them to try to explain. "I've never been into drama myself. And I never expected to fall in love a second time in my life. And you're not exactly the sort of man a woman like me expects to find herself involved with."

"This is sounding way too much like the kind of 'it's not you, it's me' that ends in good-bye." His tone was dry, but she could see him bracing.

"No," she said quickly, reaching for his hand. "That's not the way I mean it. But I, well, it's one thing when we're alone together and we're just us, you know? But I think I'm afraid of what it's going to feel like on tour. What other people will think. How you'll see me compared to all the women you could have instead of me." His hand was large and warm, his gaze steady. He deserved total honesty even if it revealed the mess of insecurity that had been bubbling inside her. "And I sucked at hanging out doing nothing here. I'm not at all sure how I'll handle that when we're in a different city practically every day and I have no defined role or responsibilities. I'm even worried about whether I'll still be me."

When she finished, he reached a hand out to cup her cheek. "Personally, I don't care what the rest of the world thinks. I've been through enough to recognize the real thing when I find it. And you're it. I don't want to get over you, Maddie. I don't." He looked her in the eye, looked all the way inside her. "I hope like hell you don't want me to, either. But I will if I have to."

He gave her hand a final squeeze and trailed the fingers of his other hand down her cheek. What came next would be up to her.

She drew a deep breath of salt-tinged air into her lungs and continued to meet his eyes. Her heart felt too big for her chest. "Well, as you unfortunately just heard, I seem to have a high degree of uncertainty about who I am, what I want, and even, oddly, whether I might somehow cease to be me." She smiled with trembling lips. "But one thing I have no question or qualms about is you. I love you, Will. Truly and deeply. And no matter what happens, I suspect I always will." She felt the prickle of tears. Saw his face through their sheen. "I'm so sorry that I hurt you. You seem so strong, you've survived so much that sometimes I think I forget that you can still be hurt. I hope you can forgive me." She swallowed, but there was no holding back the tears. "If you still want me to come with you tomorrow, and I hope that you do, I'm in. If there's a problem or a question, we'll talk about it. I'm in it for the long haul." Her smile grew and as full as it was, her heart felt so light, she thought it might sprout wings. Tears slipped down her cheeks and she swiped at them with the back of her hand. "In fact, I'm going to be just like Tom Cruise in *Top Gun*. No matter what happens, I'll be there. I will not leave my wingman."

# Twenty-one

"You go relax and get pampered. Treat yourself to that mani-pedi, and let them blow out your hair. Maybe even have a massage so you'll feel at your best when Mr. Giraldi returns this evening," Luvie said to Nikki.

"Yes, well, I have all that scheduled but not until . . ."

Luvie didn't wait for Nikki to point out that she had several hours before those appointments, but escorted her to the door of the cottage and ushered her out of her own home. Without a squeak of protest from Sofia or Gemma.

She stood on the porch, the closed door at her back, wondering how she had ended up outside and where, exactly, she was supposed to go now.

She'd already taken the girls in the stroller for a run that morning. She'd also already eaten the two-egg-white omelet with a quarter cup of spinach and a pinch of feta, so when she entered the Sunshine's main building she was careful not to breathe in the intoxicating scents of French toast or chocolate chip pancakes, both of which were apparently being served with warm maple syrup.

Bitsy stood in the gift shop. An iced cinnamon bun sat on the counter next to a whipped-cream-covered cappuccino. Nikki's stomach grumbled with longing.

"Where are Sofia and Gemma?" Bitsy asked, taking a bite of

the warm flaky pastry then licking icing off her fingers. Nikki's mouth watered.

"Luvie came in early and my hair appointment isn't until one. I know she means well, at least I assume she does, but . . . do you think the Bankses would have figured things out themselves if Mary Poppins hadn't come along?"

"Mary Poppins and the Banks family are fictional. You and Luvie are flesh and blood. Personally, I think you should enjoy the help and find something worthwhile to do with your free time. But then I've never had children and grew up spending more time with servants than family members, so my thinking may be slightly skewed."

"Right." Nikki turned her back so that she wouldn't have to watch Bitsy take another bite of the cinnamon bun. "I love the way the vintage bathing suits look there."

"Yeah. One of the ladies over in the mah-jongg game asked about the price of the teal Rose Marie Reid. She said she used to have one like it and thought it might make a fun gift for her daughter."

Nikki winced at the reminder of her promise to research prices. It seemed the less she did the less she was inclined to do. "Sorry. I totally forgot. I promise to have pricing by Monday." In no hurry to go out and kill time or add on to her grooming appointments, she studied the space. A pyramid of aqua-colored luggage had been piled in a corner. "Where did those come from?"

"Avery brought them in—Martha Wyatt is downsizing and she found the set in the attic. I'm not sure what we should do with them, but I think they're really cool."

Nikki lifted the smallest piece, a lightweight train case with rounded corners, and set it on the counter. It was covered in some sort of stain-resistant material. The clasp and trim were brass. "It's Lady Baltimore." She pointed to the delicately scripted brass letters. "It was really popular in the sixties." She released the clasp and lifted the top. The past wafted out as she leaned closer to examine the aqua silk lining with its faint floral pattern. "I'll figure out what we might sell them for when I research pricing. And you know, I think we could use them to display more of the vintage bathing suits. They might look interesting mounted on the wall over there." She motioned to an open expanse of wall between the floor-to-ceiling glass and the double front doors.

"Sounds great," Bitsy said. "And since we're throwing out ideas, what do you think about doing a poolside fashion show like Renée and Annelise's Nana used to do? We could ask beach club members to model some of the vintage beachwear. And maybe bring in some of the current retro designs so we have plenty of different price points to sell. We could treat it like we did the Sandcastle Showdown—you know, to draw people in and sell beach club memberships and the cottages. Do you think something like that would be promotable?"

"I do," Nikki said, already imagining the fifties-era food and drink that could be served and the local women's groups they might tap into. "The more visible we can make the Sunshine the better. The rest of the cottages need to be sold and finished out. And this might help."

She left Bitsy to run important errands like picking up dry cleaning and filling the car with gas. She used up another thirty minutes having it washed. The manicure and pedicure ate up another hour. Her hair, including color and cut, took two. Each hour killed felt like ten as her anticipation and impatience grew.

An eternity later she parked the newly washed Land Rover on Thirty-first and hurried to the cottage. When she opened the door she found Joe already there, both girls in his arms and theirs looped around his neck. There was laughter and little-girl giggles. She breathed in the sight of them and ran to join in the family hug, barely caring in that moment that Luvie was still there bustling about the tiny kitchen, very much a part of the laughter.

"How long have you been here? When did you get back?" Her heart flooded with happiness.

"About fifteen minutes ago. My flight got in early. But you won't believe what just happened." Joe's dark eyes sparked with excitement. "When I walked in Gemma was on her feet kind of teetering, you know. But when she saw me she walked. She made it all the way to me—four or five whole steps without falling down!"

"That's right, mum," Luvie said, beaming with pride. "And look at this." She held up her cell phone as if it were a trophy. "I was standing right here and I got the whole thing on video for you!"

. . .

It should have been hard to stay angry when everyone else seemed so happy, but somehow Nikki managed. Even after Luvie excused herself and went home, anger coursed through her. While she and Joe bathed and put the girls to bed together and while they were sitting at the dinette with glasses of wine and Luvie's shepherd's pie, she felt the dregs of an impotent fury.

She pushed the minced meat and potato around her plate, unwilling to fork so much as a bite of Luvie's offering into her mouth while Joe talked about the FBI sting that had caught a ring of doctors and medical labs that had been defrauding Medicare patients and funneling a large part of their illegal gains to terrorist groups.

Her eyes were pinned on Joe's face as he described what he could of his next assignment, but what she saw was the scene she'd walked in on, a scene in which Luvie played the part that belonged to her.

"Nikki?" Joe looked up from refilling her wineglass, whose calories she was too upset to count. "Nik?"

"Hmmm?"

"What's going on? What's wrong?"

She was tempted to deny there was a problem or at least change the subject, but the man read faces for a living. "I can't believe I missed Gemma taking her first real steps. I hate that I missed it." Hated that she'd abdicated her parenting responsibilities without a fight. "I really think it's time to cut back on Luvie's hours."

"But she's so good with the girls," he said reasonably. "And it's not as if you can know when something like that is going to happen. It was a total fluke that I happened to be here to witness it. It's just the luck of the draw."

"But the less I'm here the greater the chance I'm going to miss things." Her fingers tightened around the stem of her wineglass. And it's not like I'm doing anything necessary—I mean, if we needed me to earn a paycheck or I was contributing to the world in any way, that would be different."

"I think you underestimate the impact your love and attention have on Sofia and Gemma. I don't think that's a function of hours spent," Joe said quietly. "But no one's stopping you from doing whatever feels right. If you want to cut back on Luvie that's up to you, although I do think part of why she's putting in so many hours is that she's lonely. You know, now that her mother's gone and she's not in her home country."

Nikki flushed in embarrassment. She had so much and yet she was jealous of an older woman who seemed to have no one. How small of her. And how like Joe to be able to see all sides.

"You're right. I just, I don't know, I guess I feel at loose ends, and I did talk with Bitsy today about working on some things here at the Sunshine."

"It's your call, Nik. But I'd be careful not to cut back too far. There *are* two of them and if Gemma's walking, Sofia can't be far behind. I'm going to be traveling even more given the new assignment. It's easy to underestimate how much you need help when you've got so much of it."

She nodded but her thoughts stayed on Luvie. With the girls

getting more active, surely she and the nanny could at least share the responsibility and care instead of Luvie taking it all on.

The conversation turned. As they caught up, the anger seeped out of her system and she wondered for the thousandth time how she had gotten so lucky. How she, who had struggled for so long alone, had ended up with two healthy children, enough money to be able to choose whether to work or not, and friends she could count on. And at the center this man. Who was so loving. So unflappable. And so incredibly hot.

They dawdled over the meal, their glances growing more intimate, their hands clasping across the table, the atmosphere increasingly electric. When he stood and walked around the small table to draw her to her feet, she was already alight with anticipation.

"I missed you." His lips brushed over hers, warm and provocative. "Missed us." His hands slid down to cup her bottom and pull her more tightly against him. There was no mistaking his intent or his body's reaction to hers.

"You've lost weight, haven't you?" He murmured this into her ear, and the words were like flame to a match; the fact that he had noticed was the ultimate aphrodisiac, *if* she had needed one.

Their kiss was long and deep. Without discussion they moved to the bedroom, where he took his time removing her clothing then waited with barely leashed impatience for her to do the same to him. When he reached out to touch her breast, run a thumb across her nipple, she shuddered and reached for him. The look in his eyes left no doubt of the heat he felt or how much he desired her.

Together they tumbled onto the bed. She knelt above him, teasing his body with hers as his hands moved over her heated skin, urging her on.

Finally, when she thought she might go mad with wanting him, he wrapped his hands around her waist and slowly settled her on top of him. Their bodies melded and grew slick as their rhythm built toward a place where there was no room for worry or doubt. A place where they could only go together.

. . .

"Cut!" Brandon called. "We're clear! That's a wrap for you, little man." The First AD gave Dustin a high five followed by another one down low. "Good job!"

"Absolutely first rate!" Daniel gave Dustin a thumbs-up, but the words were automatic, as was the way he ruffled Dustin's hair.

"But . . . I can do better. Can I try again?" Dustin pleaded as his father moved toward the monitor.

"No can do, amigo," Brandon said. "You are officially off the clock."

Dustin's chin stuck out. His eyes remained on his father and Tonja, whose heads were bent together to watch a replay. The Director of Photography joined them.

"Wanna say good-bye to Dandiel!"

"We need to go now." Kyra took Dustin's hand and tried to lead him away, but his feet seemed to have taken root. The meltdowns were infrequent, but seemed to be growing in intensity.

Tonja looked up at the raised voices, her lovely blond brow lowering. When she saw Dustin's expression she leaned over and whispered something to Daniel. Daniel walked over.

"Did I forget to say good-bye again?" Daniel asked, giving Dustin a big smile that didn't quite reach his eyes. "You did a great job today. All week, really. You're an ace. Everyone's very impressed." He bent and lifted Dustin. "We were just checking to make sure we had everything we needed."

"I can do some more takes."

"Not according to the Screen Actors Guild you can't." There was regret in Daniel's voice, and Kyra knew that if he'd been able to get away with it, he would have let his son work more than the maximum three hours per day and kept him on set longer than the hours allowed.

"Come on, I'll walk you guys to the car," Brandon cut in so smoothly that Kyra could have kissed him. It was the First Assistant Director who created the shooting schedule and who had made sure Dustin's call was set for eight each morning with his first scene at nine A.M. to take advantage of the morning hours when a child his age is most alert and engaged. That schedule had given their days a structure rarely found on film sets.

After lunch they'd use Dustin's double, Sean Garrity, who at seven years of age could work for four hours and be on set for eight and a half to shoot wide, long, over the shoulder, and any other necessary cover shots of Dustin's character.

Brandon opened the back door of the waiting SUV and helped Dustin into the backseat. Kyra slid in beside him and buckled the straps of his car seat. "Weather looks good all next week and the rebuilt amusement park should be up and running, so you guys rest up and be ready."

He closed the car door and tapped the roof. The car pulled out.

The drive to the compound was blessedly brief. When they arrived at the guard gate, Joan McCreary stepped out and motioned for them to lower the window. Her uniform was crisply pressed, her manner professional. "Sorry to bother you, but you have a guest."

"A guest?" Kyra asked.

"He claims to be a friend, and he didn't have any camera gear or a weapon. But you can never be too careful. I suggested he call you or come back later, but he insisted on waiting."

"Okay." Her mother was in Dallas with Will and she couldn't imagine who else might have known where to find her. "Let's take a look."

The guard nodded crisply then turned toward the guard hut. "You can come out now, sir. But don't make any sudden moves."

Troy Matthews stepped out of the hut, his hands up in prisoner fashion. "Thank God you're back! I think she was trying to decide whether to shoot me."

"I did consider it briefly," Joan said. "But only after he asked me to strip-search him."

Troy shrugged and grinned. "What can I say? There's something about a woman in a uniform that makes me throw caution to the wind."

Joan shook her head, clearly trying not to laugh.

Kyra rolled her eyes. But Dustin was smiling in a way he hadn't all week. "Hello, Broy! Did you come to play with me?"

"I actually came to see if I could take you two to Disney World."

"Disney World? I love Disney World!" Dustin exclaimed joyously although, in truth, he had never been. "Can we go see Mickey Mouse?"

"You should have called first," she said to Troy.

"I would have if I'd thought you'd actually take my call."

"I do have a gun inside, ma'am," Joan said. "If you'd like to borrow it."

"Wanna go to Disney World!" Dustin shouted happily.

Kyra sighed. "I guess you can let him in so we can discuss this."

Troy's grin matched Dustin's as he leaned in the window to give him a high five.

"Will do, ma'am," Joan said. "But don't forget you've got those panic buttons. In case he gets so annoying you need us to come remove him." She smiled. "I'd be more than happy to keep him here in the security hut for a while to teach him a little lesson."

# Twenty-two

The moment they reached the cottage Dustin raced inside to pack. Kyra snapped a leash on Max and "invited" Troy outside to help her walk him.

"I don't appreciate being put on the spot like this," she said as Max squatted. "An adult would have invited us in advance."

"And I would have done that if I'd thought you'd consider the invitation with an open mind."

"That's not the point," she protested as Max pulled her from bush to bush and tree to tree.

"Of course it is." He fell in beside her. "But I've got multi-park passes and a reservation for two rooms at the Grand Floridian. I thought maybe we could just call a truce and go have a good time, and get to know each other better."

"I've known you for three years, Troy. Finding out you're not who you've pretended to be all this time doesn't inspire a whole lot of trust. And I still can't figure out why all of a sudden you're interested in me and want to know me better."

"What can I say? The heart wants what it wants." He shoved his hands in his pockets. "It's not like I haven't tried to talk myself out of you."

"How incredibly flattering." She waited for Max to pick a tree trunk. "And if I ask you to leave?"

"Then I guess I'll have to accept that you'd rather stay here and spend the weekend mooning after 'he who does not deserve you.' After I go you can explain why we're not going to Dustin."

"You do see how wrong this is on pretty much every level. I mean . . ."

"I'm ready!" Dustin appeared in the doorway wheeling his overnight bag. "I packed my pajamas and my bathing suit. Can we go now?"

Troy turned to her and raised an eyebrow, but remained mercifully silent.

"Pleaaaassse?" Dustin ran out to her and looked up at her beseechingly. "Pretty please? With sugar on top? And . . ." He looked so forlorn he might have been the orphan from *Oliver!* begging for "more."

"Fine," she bit out, leading the way back inside. "I'll get my things together. And let's take a look in your suitcase and make sure you've got everything you need." She handed Troy the folder of contact numbers. "You can call your girlfriend at the front gate and find out how we organize pet sitting."

Twenty minutes later they were in Troy's car and headed for the guard gate, where he waved an annoyingly merry good-bye to Joan. The former stuntwoman winked back.

After they exited the compound, Dustin and Troy made plans for their assault on Disney. Then Troy turned the conversation to *The Exchange.* She was shocked by how gently he elicited Dustin's thoughts and reactions. How readily her son answered all the questions she'd been too busy trying to navigate their situation to ask. It was the first time she'd heard him say that his favorite part of acting was being good at it and that his least favorite part was the standing around waiting to "hact."

About midway through the drive her shoulder muscles loosened. A short time later her jaw felt odd. When she reached a hand up, she realized that it had unclenched. When they arrived at the hotel, Troy suggested they send the luggage up to their rooms and get to the Magic Kingdom as soon as possible, because they were "burning daylight."

"Oh, boy! That's exactly what I was hoping!" Dustin said, reaching for both their hands.

"Is that all right with you, Kyra?" Troy asked.

"Sure," she said, somewhat stunned by the lack of sarcasm in his voice. "That's what I was hoping, too."

. . .

Dallas was a blur. Maddie watched it fly by from the backseat of the limo that Aquarian had provided. In it she traveled with Will, from radio station to radio station, and then on to a television morning show, before arriving at the tour kickoff press luncheon put on by the record label. Their PR escort was a leggy blonde named Vicki who was young enough to be Maddie's daughter.

"So, we're not going to make a big deal about you being with Will," Vicki said as they were helped out of the limo. "All you need to do is smile as often and sincerely as possible. If any members of the media ask you a question, you can answer. But, um, we think it might be best not to initiate anything."

"No speaking unless spoken to. Got it." Maddie did not appreciate being treated like a child by someone who actually was one. But she had no problem staying in the background. In fact, it was a relief.

"I didn't mean . . . we just want everyone's attention on Will and the band. You know, not on who he's traveling with."

"I'm happy to go back to the hotel," she began. "I really don't mind if . . ."

"I mind," Will said smoothly. "I appreciate having my 'wingman' here." He turned his back on the blonde and took Maddie's arm. "By the way, you look great. Did you do something different?"

"No." She smiled even as she sent a silent thank-you to Nikki and Bitsy for serving as stylists.

"Just smile and look like you're having fun," he said in her ear. "And if anybody asks, you can tell them I'm your main squeeze. Don't forget to let them know that I'm really great in the sack."

"Oh, no, that's not a good idea . . . ," the young woman began.

"He's just yanking your chain," Lori said, rolling her eyes at the blonde.

"You and I are sitting over there." Lori led Maddie to the record label's table, just one away from where Will and the band were seated with handpicked members of the media. When dessert had been cleared the band posed for photos and a surprising number of reporters' selfies. One-on-ones with the entertainment media followed, the band members moving from table to table as if they were speed dating.

Maddie kept a smile on her face and her attention focused on the band. Though no one in the press spoke to her, more than a few cameras were aimed her way. By the time the event ended and every potential drop of media attention had been squeezed from the day, Maddie could barely form a smile, let alone think.

"We're heading over to the venue for a sound check." Will leaned over and kissed her cheek.

"Oh." Maddie tried to sound enthusiastic. "Great."

Will smiled sympathetically. "You don't have to come for the check. You've been a trooper. I don't remember doing a single interview when we were touring in the seventies." He yawned. "But then there's a lot that happened back then that I don't remember. And even more I wish I didn't." He turned to Lori. "Can you get Maddie back to the hotel?"

"Sure thing."

"But how are you ever going to have the strength to do a two-hour concert tonight?" Maddie asked, thinking of how "on" he'd been all day. Just trailing behind him had worn her out.

"The Majestic's not far, and I should have time to catch a nap at the hotel before we head back." Will paused. "God, I *am* old. That's what amphetamines used to be for."

Maddie fell in love with the Majestic Theatre at first sight. Built in the Beaux Arts style in 1921, just a handful of years before Bella Flora, it took up most of one downtown block. According to the venue liaison who met them that evening, it had spent the twenties as a vaudeville theater, the thirties as the site of Hollywood film premieres, and most of the decades that followed showing movies. Now gorgeously restored and listed on the National Register of Historic Places, it had an opulent baroque lobby with original black-and-white marble floors, decorative molding, egg and dart borders, acanthus leaves, and floor-to-ceiling mirrors in gilt frames. A crystal chandelier shimmered above it all.

The performance hall was equally beautiful, its three levels a riot of Corinthian columns, balustrades, urns, and trellises—all highlighted in gold leaf. Opera-style box seats fanned the walls facing the stage. The carpet was the same wine color as the curtain.

She imagined Avery's excitement over the architecture, how she'd relish the details of the renovation, and wished she were here. The crew had spent the day unloading and setting up. The band's equipment was in place. Dean's drums were positioned on a riser; the backdrop of Hightower's latest album hung between twin scaffolds of lighting. Now they moved around her with a quick efficiency, double-checking the sound, the angle and spill of each light, taping position marks to the stage floor. Everywhere there was movement, purpose, the squawk of communication.

She followed Will into the greenroom, where he offered her a soft drink or bottled water. "Unless you'd like something stronger? I'm sure there's alcohol here somewhere stashed strategically and tactfully out of my sight."

"No, I'm good." She accepted a bottled water, screwed off the top.

"I'm going to sit and go over the set list with the guys, get in the zone." He hesitated. "You can hang in my dressing room. Or, I don't know, I can ask Lori to . . ."

"Don't worry about me. I'll be fine. You just do whatever you need to do to get ready."

His kiss on her cheek was perfunctory, his mind already with Kyle, Robert, and Dean as he went to join them in a corner of the greenroom. Unsure of what to do with herself, she wandered back toward the stage, fingering the laminated all-access pass that hung around her neck. Everywhere she looked, people rushed about their business. Equipment, lighting, and sound were checked yet again. Beefy guys in black T-shirts with *Security* written in white block letters moved to their positions at the doors and corners of the stage as the opening act set up their own equipment.

Aaron Mann appeared at her side. "Great scarf," he said, smiling. "Very rock 'n' roll. How's Will doing?"

"Good," she said. "Focused." He'd fallen asleep the moment he got back to the hotel and had received a wake-up call from Lori exactly thirty minutes before they had to leave for the Majestic. He'd used ten of those minutes to wake up and twenty to shower and dress in wardrobe that mimicked his casual style but wasn't. Both of them now had stylists. "Is there anything I can do? To help, I mean?"

"I think you being here is pretty huge for Will. I thought he came across great today. And I think he was right about letting go of all the visual gimmicks and focusing on the sound. Let me show you where you'll be sitting." He led her to a director's chair carefully placed in the wings, where Will would barely have to turn his head to see her. "They'll be letting the audience in in about fifteen minutes. You be sure and let Lori know if you need anything."

"Thanks." The Aquarian publicist raised a hand in question and Aaron headed over.

Maddie looked at her seat. Adjusted it slightly. Sat. Looked around. Her position within sight of Will's microphone made her think of Kyra on set within sight and sound of Dustin. She stood and shot some backstage photos to send to her daughter. Then she shot photos of the auditorium and sent them to Avery.

She'd just pocketed her phone when Hugh West, the tour manager, stopped to say hi and, presumably, check her off his to-do list. Late forties with a shock of bright red hair, a freckled face, and a high-octane smile, he'd been a teenaged roadie back when Will and the original band were touring. "We're locked and loaded. Ready to rock and roll," he said. "You okay here?"

"I'm good, thanks."

He flashed the smile. "I can't believe how different Will is. Hell, the whole business is different. Rock stars traveling with accountants, and families, and genuinely nice, age-appropriate girlfriends. But, I guess you reach a certain age and you have to get healthy and live right to survive this. I gotta tell you, though, it's starting to feel suspiciously like real life. I was traveling with Alice Cooper back when he traded drink and drugs for golf." He grimaced. "Please tell me Will doesn't golf."

"No, of course not," she said with a smile of her own. "He, um, fishes."

She heard the auditorium doors open and the buzz of excitement as the crowd began to enter. She imagined them finding their seats, settling in, craning their necks in hopes of catching sight of something or someone behind the heavy velvet curtain.

She stayed where she was as the opening band performed. During their last number she felt a presence behind her, smelled the spicy scent of Will's cologne, sensed the heat of him. She rose and turned. He exhaled a great puff of air. His eyes were bright. His excitement was palpable. He slipped an arm around her shoulders and she felt the jolt of it, absorbed its hum. Together they watched Kyle, Robert, and Dean take their places onstage, adjusting a guitar strap, leaning over a keyboard. Dean twirled the drumsticks between his fingers.

As one they turned to Will. When he nodded back, Dean counted the licks off on his drumsticks. The curtain opened.

The crowd was already cheering when Will's hand dropped from her shoulder. He strode out onstage, and the crowd was on its feet. He greeted them. Lifted his guitar from its stand, settled the strap around his neck. When he began to pick out the opening notes of "Mermaid in You," they cheered louder still.

As the familiar melody wrapped around them all, Maddie forgot where she was. Forgot that she had nothing to do. Blue strobes streaked out over the audience. The spotlight bathed Will in its warm glow. She'd seen him play at the Lorelei, at Tampa Theatre, at the concert in North Carolina, but standing this close, watching his eyes flutter closed, seeing the sweat form on his brow, this was something else entirely. His voice was raw and powerful as he disappeared into the music, into the thrall of the crowd.

The audience was equally rapt. They swayed, sang along. Her eyes lingered on the women's avid faces, their eyes telegraphing their interest in more than the music. Any one of them would have given anything to be there with Will. Waiting in the wings for him.

After the first songs, he looked her way and shot her a wink. She grinned back at him, still on her feet, as excited as the crowd. This was the Will who had hung in poster form on her bedroom wall. Glorious and unobtainable. But somehow now hers.

This Will had depths her teenaged self could have never imagined. She saw him now through different eyes, understood his inner demons, knew his strengths and weaknesses, and heard them twisted up inside the music, intimate and true.

Afterward, in the greenroom, she stood back while a crowd

surrounded him. Women postured, radio-station-contest winners stammered, record label people preened, while local celebrities and media folks soaked up the spill from his spotlight. He looked up and scanned the room, his eyes landing on her. Maddie felt a shiver of anticipation as he moved toward her, the crowd parting so he could pass.

"What's a nice girl like you doing in a place like this?" he murmured when he reached her.

"I heard there was a concert," she murmured back, her gaze tangled up in his. "Thought I'd come by and see if the lead singer was as hot as I heard."

"And what did you decide?"

"Definitely hot. Scorching, really."

"I can't tell you how glad I am to hear that." He took the glass of wine out of her hand and set it aside. "Can I give you a ride home?"

"I thought you'd never ask," she breathed back.

"Will? I have someone here who'd like a few minutes." Maddie recognized the PR girl's voice. Got a glimpse of the long legs. But Will was leaning over her. His teeth were nibbling on her earlobe. His breath was warm on her neck.

"Excuse me, Will?"

"Sorry. Gotta go. Early flight tomorrow." Will placed a hand on the small of Maddie's back and gently urged her forward.

"But . . ."

"Please have the car brought around," he said quietly to Lori, who had materialized beside them.

"He's already waiting for you out back," Lori said, elbowing Vicki out of the way. "See you two in the morning."

They moved to the stage door entrance, careful not to catch anyone's eye. In the limo Maddie could feel the adrenaline coursing through Will and, by extension, through her. He kissed her and ran his hands down her back as the car pulled away. His kiss grew hotter, deeper. For a brief moment she imagined the partition going up and her sliding onto his lap. But they were still kissing, their breathing growing ragged when they reached the hotel.

They had the elevator to themselves, and he backed her into the corner and pressed himself against her.

By the time they were inside the suite all she wanted was more. Of him.

He pulled his shirt over his head and dropped it on the floor. She did the same.

Moments later they were naked and in bed.

"Definitely not the seventies," he said as he pulled her underneath him. "According to that clock it's only eleven thirty."

"I hope you're not thinking about stopping to trash the room," she teased even as his mouth began to move on her bare skin. "Or wishing you had some kind of orgy going."

"Nope, not stopping for anything. And all I want is you."

# Twenty-three

Sunday morning dawned bright and crisp and inviting. Gemma and Sofia had slept in, clearly lulled and comforted as much as Nikki was by their father's presence. He filled the cottage, warmed it, turned it into "home" in a way it could only be when they were all together.

Still in their pajamas they sprawled across Joe's chest, as eager to touch and be touched by him as she was.

"You know, we're going to have to decide where we want to be full-time," he said as he grasped a wiggling Gemma and tucked her beneath his arm, pretending to take her prisoner. A giggling Sofia was "imprisoned" next.

"Hmmm?" Nikki turned on her side, her head resting on one hand, the curve of her body serving as an outer wall. Letting her gaze run over Joe's naked chest, his muscled arm, his rugged profile, she dropped a kiss on Gemma's head and added a tickle to Sofia's belly.

"Well, if we're going to stay on St. Pete Beach, I should probably look at renting out the Hibiscus Island house," he said, referring to the house near South Beach that he'd been living in when they first met. "And we might need to consider a bigger place here. Maybe something on Vina del Mar or Bella Vista."

"Oh, but . . ."

"We could keep the cottage—I'm sure my folks would love to spend winters down here near us."

"You'd be willing to do that?" she asked, wondering when she would stop being surprised by his thoughtfulness.

"Umm-hmmm." He plucked Gemma back off his chest, blew a raspberry on her bare arm that set her giggling, then resettled her between them. "My new assignment's going to keep me on the road, and it's important that you and the girls are comfortable and happy. The beach is beautiful and Bella Flora does seem to be the center for all of you. But Maddie could end up spending most of her time with Will, and you said there's going to be a full-court press to sell the units here—it won't be a private Bestie Row anymore if that happens. And Bitsy, well, we'll hear more today about her situation. I'm good either way. But of course, Luvie's here."

She scrunched up her face at the mention of Luvie's name, still irritated at being shooed off and missing Gemma's first real steps.

"Are you sure we can afford to own so many places?"

"Yes. Especially if we rent out the Miami house and maybe include this place in the rental pool when family's not using it."

She stared up at the ceiling, swamped by a swirl of contradictory emotions. He moved so purposefully and cleanly through life while she seemed to blunder along, barely thinking at all. *Completely dependent.*

"What's wrong?"

She continued to stare upward as if the answers to questions she hadn't bothered to ask herself might suddenly appear. "I hate not contributing financially. I've been supporting myself since I was a teenager. I built a business." Things she hadn't even realized she was thinking poured out. "I was . . . *someone.*"

When she looked at him, his eyes were pinned on hers. He turned on his side. Sofia giggled as she slid off his chest. Joe wasn't laughing. "You're still someone, Nikki. A *formidable* someone. Plus, you're a wife and mother. And frankly, taking care of our children, raising them to be happy and secure human beings, is not nothing." He kept his voice even, but she could see the hurt in his eyes. He was so strong, so invincible. And yet she had the power to wound him.

"I know. I do." She sat up against the pillow, drew her knees up to her chest. "Believe me, I've come to understand that all mothers are 'working' mothers. I want to go around and apologize to every stay-at-home mom I pictured watching soaps and eating bonbons. It's just that I feel like I'm not pulling my weight."

"If you keep losing weight like you have been, there won't be anything left to pull," he said more lightly.

"Very funny. Yet flattering," she said. "But not the point."

"I know. And I do hear what you're saying." His eyes met hers, held them. "Your life is completely different than it used to be, and you need a sense of purpose and accomplishment."

She blinked.

"You built a major business and your role in *Do Over* was significant. And I haven't forgotten how instrumental you were in finally bringing your brother to justice. I love you, Nikki. I think it's just a matter of figuring out what else you need to make you feel happier and more fulfilled. Maybe we can take a run down to the Paradise Grille a little later and brainstorm over lunch. I promised to meet with Bitsy and June this afternoon. Do you want to check and see if they'd like to sit down there and talk afterward?"

Her eyes narrowed. "Yes, we could. But I have to say I think you rushed your steps a little there."

"Steps?" he asked innocently. I'm not sure I know what you mean." He added his best *we're in this together* smile.

"Seriously?" she replied. "You don't think I recognize the Behavioral Change Stairway Model? The hostage negotiation model favored by the FBI?" She pulled Gemma back between them. "Step one, active listening? Check. Step two, empathy, including a rephrasing of your understanding of the issues important to the person you're trying to defuse—that would be me—which emphasizes the fact that you listened and understood. Check."

She watched his face, enjoying the surprise that suffused it. "Step three, rapport. Established through your active listening and empathy. And, no doubt, the fact that we're in bed together, and have children together, et cetera, et cetera. Check. Step four . . . hmmm . . ." She flipped over, opened the nightstand drawer, retrieved the printout of the article on BCSM, and read, "'Once rapport has been firmly established, the negotiator is in a position to begin to make suggestions to the other side'—once again me!—'explore potential and realistic solutions to the conflict, and consider the likely alternative available to the other side.' Check." She paused dramatically. "Of course, step five, the actual behavioral change, is a little trickier. And I'm kind of wondering if there's a step six that you can't see unless you've got security clearance? One that advises said negotiator how to defuse the situation when his wife realizes he's using the FBI manual to try to handle her?"

She replaced the printout and flipped back on her side to face him.

"No step six," he said sheepishly. "But I think I'm going to have to suggest they take a look at it. Along with how to negotiate with a woman pumped full of pregnancy hormones. I never figured that out, either."

Sofia watched her father's face adoringly and patted his cheek. Gemma reached up, grasped Nikki's nose, and squeezed it.

"Ouch." She removed Gemma's hand. "The only nose you're allowed to squeeze is your own, missy." She placed Gemma's small hand on her tiny nose. "I'll text Bitsy. But let me explain one thing in the meantime so you can pass it on to the folks at Quantico. Women do not want to be handled. Not even delicately. And definitely not by their husbands. No matter how highly trained they might be." She looked into Joe's eyes. "Clear?"

"Crystal." He kept his face carefully neutral. Nikki did the same. But as they got the girls ready to go out, she realized she felt better. As if a weight had been lifted from her shoulders. It was time to take action, to create the home scenario that felt right for them and to reach for the extra things that mattered to her.

"Ready?" she asked, lifting Sofia into her arms.

"Yep." He picked up Gemma and slung the diaper bag over his other shoulder.

As they took the walkway past the pool and onto the beach, Nikki was careful not to smile too widely. Or whistle. Or betray the new spring she felt in her step. She'd cut out her tongue before she let Joe know that the morning's BCSM had actually worked.

· · ·

Bitsy sat on the bench across the picnic table from Joe and Nikki with June Steding at her side. The twins snoozed in the jogging stroller, a cool salt breeze stirring the fronds of the palm tree that shaded them all from the afternoon sun.

"So, we have confirmation of fraud based on Gary Kaufman's findings," June said as she brought Joe up to date. "Did you get Gary's summary and the copy of the records I sent you?"

"Yes, I read through it and skimmed the records."

"And?" Bitsy asked quietly.

"I have to say that I don't see the FBI committing manpower and resources to getting Bertie back. He did abuse his fiduciary responsibility as trustee, but he didn't go after or defraud others. And the fact that it was a joint account he pillaged makes things a little murkier."

"Oh, but . . ." Bitsy felt her stomach drop. She'd been so certain that the forensic accountant's documentation would be enough to make sure Bertie got punished.

"That leaves us with the Palm Beach state attorney's office then," June said. "This all happened in their jurisdiction and I can see them wanting to take a look at Houghton Whitfield, especially since one of their employees not only had an affair with a client but helped him steal. They could figure out whether the firm participated in or was even aware of what was going on as they should have been, or is only guilty of covering it up." She was looking less and less like June Cleaver and more like an avenging angel. "We want to have a heart-to-heart talk with this former employee."

"I'd rather rip her heart out," Bitsy said truthfully. "Assuming she has one. But Gene Houghton claimed she had a nervous breakdown and that they didn't know where she was."

"Untrue." Joe handed her a piece of paper. "I did a little poking around on my own time. Her name is Susan White. She's still living at her longtime address in West Palm. And there's nothing that shows she spent any time in a hospital of any kind or even had treatment."

"The fact that they didn't even move her shows how sure Houghton Whitfield is that no one's coming after them," June said.

"Well, it has been a year and no one has," Bitsy pointed out. Thanks to her yearlong pity party.

"That's true," June said. "But Susan White was having an affair with Bertie and she helped him steal from you. I'm guessing she had reason to think she was going with him."

"Well, there was a decent-size deposit made into her bank account when she left the company," Joe said. "But nothing crazy and certainly not what one might expect as payment for helping someone steal close to thirty million dollars. Or even enough to look like much more than a severance package."

Bitsy winced. This was why she'd spent that year unable to face the truth. Who allowed someone else to steal that much without having a clue?

"She's probably pretty pissed off at being left behind. That could work to our advantage," June said.

"But even if she is pissed off at Bertie, how does that help us find him and get my money back?" Bitsy asked.

"Finding Bertie isn't the problem," Joe said. "He's not hiding. As Kaufman's report indicates, he set himself up in the Caymans with money from your joint accounts. As far as the Cayman government is concerned, he's an important businessman who keeps a ton of money in their banks, and injects it into their economy."

Fury coursed through Bitsy, hot and corrosive. She was deeply ashamed of what she'd allowed to happen, but she simply couldn't let Bertie get away with what he'd done. Nor would she stay married to him for a minute longer than necessary.

"Can't he be extradited or something?" Nikki asked.

"There is an extradition treaty in place, but Bertie's not a terrorist and he hasn't murdered anyone, so getting him back on US soil through governmental channels would take time," Joe said. "Possibly years, even if the state attorney general agrees there's enough evidence to issue a warrant for his arrest."

Bitsy tried to get her breathing under control. She'd already lost a year, but the idea of waiting for who knew how long for the wheels of justice to turn? No. She wanted results and revenge. And the sooner the better. Preferably before Bertie died of old age while living in the lap of luxury at her expense.

"So how do we get him and the money back?" she asked. "Isn't there something outside regular channels? Something faster?"

Joe looked at her, his dark eyes searching. "There are freelancers with *irregular* rendition skills."

"Irregular rendition skills." She repeated the words. "That sounds way too friendly to me."

"I'm pretty sure that means kidnapping or deceit," June said, nibbling on a French fry.

"It does. And there's nothing friendly about it. But kidnapping can get expensive," Joe said. "And things can go wrong."

"Couldn't you just hack into his Cayman bank account and take the money back?" Nikki asked, pushing the stroller farther into the shade. "Like they do on television?"

"We have guys who do that for us—white hats—but it's not as easy as it sounds. You're generally going in through the target's computer, and the hack has to happen in very specific moments. That would require careful planning and somehow convincing him to transfer money at a specified time."

Bitsy looked at the burger growing cold on her plate. The only thing she had an appetite for at the moment was revenge. Which she hoped did, in fact, taste good cold.

"I can help in an unofficial capacity," Joe said. "I'd like to give this some thought, think about some carrot we might dangle in front of Bertie to get his attention."

"I'd prefer a big stick coming at him from behind," Bitsy said as Sofia and Gemma began to rouse. "But mostly I just hope we can take some kind of action."

"Like I said, we'd need to come up with something that would force him to access the account we're interested in at a specific time so that a white hat hacker could empty the account and transfer the money back to Bitsy," Joe said. "Then once he's penniless, the Cayman government has every incentive to simply put him on a plane and send him back—no formal extradition required. It happens more often than you'd think."

"We'd have to be ready for him," June said. "Have everything in place so that he'd be arrested as soon as he set foot on American soil."

Bitsy nodded and tried to look positive. "All right. I'm willing to go talk to Susan White but you'll have to come with me, June, so I don't tear her limb from limb." She looked into Joe's eyes. "I want that money back, but in case we can't get both, I want Bertie brought to justice even more."

• • •

Dustin slept the whole way back from Disney late that afternoon. But there was a smile on his face as he slept and it was still there when they arrived at the compound.

Kyra watched Troy carry Dustin inside. Her son's head lolled on Troy's shoulder, his silky dark curls awry, his thumb planted firmly in his mouth.

"Where shall I put him?"

"Right there on the couch is good," she said in a whisper. "I don't think he's completely down for the count. I'm pretty sure sleeping will be impossible once the sitter brings Max back."

"Now there's an understatement."

Watching him hold Dustin so gently, Kyra thought about her history with Troy. When the network had first sprung their crew on them that first day at Max Golden's South Beach home and turned what they'd intended as a renovation program into a mean-spirited reality TV show, it was a declaration of war. The cameraman and his audio guy had worked for the enemy.

Troy had not only disapproved of her relationship with Daniel, he made it clear he believed Kyra had only gotten her position on Daniel's film over a friend's because Daniel had taken a fancy to Kyra. He'd seemed to delight in his job of shooting them in the most humiliating and intrusive ways possible and had baited her at every opportunity.

But had he only been doing his job as she'd been trying to do hers? Had his taunts and jabs been an attempt to fuel and film the expected reality TV drama?

She watched him settle Dustin on the couch and carefully drape the afghan over him. He'd bonded with Dustin from the beginning and he had found ways to protect them—shooting video of Tonja's foulmouthed attempt to steal Dustin from her and getting damning video of Lisa Hogan that had gotten the program director who'd threatened them fired. And then there was his rental of Bella Flora, which she'd insisted on seeing only as a hostile act.

Had she misjudged him? Continued to treat him as the enemy long after he'd waved a white flag? Had she focused on his sarcasm to the exclusion of the wit that laced it?

"Kyra?"

"Hmmm?" She blinked back to the present. To the smile on his face. For the first time she saw him without the scrim of baggage that had hidden so much of him from view.

"So, I was saying that I guess I should get on the road. I had a great time. And I'm glad you came." His tone and smile were sincere. She didn't try to question or reframe them.

"Thanks. For everything," she said. "I haven't seen Dustin that excited since the night Max arrived. And he didn't ask to practice his lines. Or melt down. Not once."

"Well, it's kind of hard to be unhappy in the happiest place on earth," Troy teased. "But I'm glad it made him forget about the movie for a while. I . . ." He seemed to think better of what he'd been about to say. "Was it good for you, too?" Two days ago she would have sworn Troy Matthews didn't know how to blush, but his cheeks turned a color that closely resembled pink. "I mean, I can't help wondering what you thought of the experience. You know, at the park. And, um, spending time together."

"Honestly?" she asked as they stepped away from Dustin.

He nodded tentatively.

"Well, this whole getting to know you all over again still feels kind of surreal. I keep expecting the Troy I thought I knew to reappear and tell me we're starring in a revival of *Punk'd*. Or that we're shooting an episode of *Impractical Jokers*."

"Wow. That's not exactly what I was hoping for." He sounded charmingly insecure. "And for what it's worth, the network definitely pitted us against each other. I'm not sure either of us came across as our best selves."

Kyra smiled. Without the old baggage coloring her view, he

was not only easy to be with, he was a great-looking guy. If you liked all-American blond-haired, blue-eyed types who made your child laugh with unbridled glee. As opposed to dark-haired movie stars of Armenian descent who had made you cry.

The blue eyes darkened. Troy leaned closer, and for a moment she thought he was going to kiss her. The thought wasn't completely appalling.

"I really appreciate you going to so much trouble," she said. "And for making Dustin so happy. He had a really great time."

"And you?" Troy teased. "Because every once in a while when you thought I wasn't looking I could have sworn you were enjoying yourself."

"Hmmm," she teased back. As if she hadn't thought about it before he asked. "It wasn't anywhere near as awful as I expected it to be."

"So, you're saying it didn't suck?"

"That's right," she agreed. "It definitely didn't suck."

"Well then," he said, putting a hand on the doorknob. "I'm pretty sure that means we're making progress."

# Twenty-four

Maddie was pretty sure it was Wednesday. Or, possibly, Thursday. Which meant this had to be Chicago. Or St. Louis. Or . . . they weren't even a full week in and already the hotels and cities had begun to blur into each other. She burrowed beneath the covers and felt Will's warm body molded to hers. His chin rested on her shoulder, his breathing even.

Another yawn and her eyes flickered open as she attempted to put the cities in order. After Dallas had been Birmingham, then Atlanta—an in and out so quick there'd been no time for nostalgia and only a couple of hours with her son, Andrew. Greenville had followed, then Nashville. That's right, they'd flown into Indianapolis last night after a performance at Nashville's Bridgestone Arena, and she'd been more than half asleep when they arrived at the hotel. Remembering the detail felt like a victory. The schedule called for greater gaps between performances as they moved west and the distances that the trucks carrying equipment had to cover grew longer.

She yawned again and thought how easy it must be to get jaded. She was not yet immune to the awe of traveling by private plane, the limos that whisked them to and from wherever they went, or the attention lavished on Will and the band and his entourage, of which she was a member. It was a completely artificial existence. But an incredibly comfortable and luxurious one. If you didn't mind living out of a suitcase, or sleeping in a different bed every night.

The thought jarred another. They were in Indianapolis. And this penthouse suite had a fully equipped kitchen. Which meant . . .

There was a soft knock on the front door. Easing out from under Will's arm, she slid out of bed and shrugged into her robe, pulling the bedroom door shut behind her. Lori stood at the door. With her was a rolling kitchen cart piled high with grocery bags, extra cookware, and a blender.

"Okay, so the kitchen staff loaned me the extra blender and casserole dishes and said they'd make room for baking the two extra soufflés down there. We can also place an order for anything you want to serve with them and they'll send it all up with the extra soufflés."

"Perfect. I'm just going to wash my face and brush my teeth. Be right back."

When she returned, the ingredients she'd requested had been unpacked. Two blenders and four casserole dishes sat waiting. Lori handed her a steaming cup of coffee creamed and sugared exactly the way she liked it.

"Wow. Thanks." Maddie took a long sip of the coffee and realized that while she might be getting used to the private air travel and high-end accommodations, someone else serving her coffee in the morning—something she'd done so often for others—was really quite lovely.

"Okay." She set down the cup. "We melt the butter and cheese in the microwave. Each soufflé takes ten slices of white bread cubed." Quickly she grouped together the ingredients for each of the four soufflés. "I'll do the melting and blending. Can you do the cutting and cubing? Crusts come off first."

At Lori's nod, she handed her the bread knife. "How many are we expecting?"

"Ten. Eleven if you count Vicki." Lori made a face when she

mentioned the PR girl. "Except I think I may have forgotten to mention that we were having brunch to her. I'm willing to bet she doesn't eat anyway."

Maddie looked at Lori. Despite the spiky blond hair, biker-chick clothes, and nose ring, she'd proven to be organized, efficient, resilient, loyal, and protective. She was a brilliant gatekeeper and did not suffer fools gladly. Or pushy blond bombshell types intent on climbing the record label ladder.

"I know you told me she's just doing her job," Lori said before Maddie could comment. "But I don't like the way she keeps pushing you into the background as if you're too old to be seen with Will." She winced. "Sorry. But she isn't exactly subtle about it. And I don't like the way she looks at Will. Or the way she started looking at Dean when Will didn't look back. He's got a wife and kids!"

"I can't believe I'm saying this." Maddie poured milk and cracked six eggs into the blender then placed a bowl with cut-up butter, Velveeta, and cheddar into the microwave for melting. "But it seems pretty clear that a lot of things that happen on tour wouldn't stand up to serious scrutiny. No matter how much you'd like to, you can't tell other people how to live their lives. And you're going to have to come to terms with her at some point."

"Not necessarily." Lori slid the first soufflé's bread cubes over to Maddie. "I mean, we only have two more weeks on tour, and after that? It's not like she's going to be hanging out on Mermaid Point." She mumbled something else that sounded a lot like, "Not if I have anything to do with it."

Will arrived in the kitchen as they finished mixing the last soufflé. He was only half awake but already wearing bathing trunks and flip-flops, ready for his morning laps. He greeted Lori and placed a kiss on Maddie's cheek.

"You've got an hour and fifteen minutes," she said. "They're just about to go in the oven."

Which meant she had a whole hour to shower, dress, set the table, and make today's suite feel like home.

• • •

Kyra and Dustin had arrived on set Monday morning rested and relaxed, the "Disney effect" still very much in evidence. They'd spent the morning on the newly completed theme park grounds shooting under a sunlit blue sky that made Rodney Stanfield all but weep with joy.

Kyra watched Dustin's easy delivery as the fictional Roberts family, waiting in line just in front of Christian Sommersby, enacted their first casual encounter with the man who would ultimately kidnap Dustin.

The first three takes went off without a hitch, yet Daniel continued to call for take after take until Tonja, who had watched the replay of and liked each take, finally convinced him to move on.

On Tuesday the Disney effect weakened further, but the weather gods had continued to smile. They'd tackled another setup scene, this time with Derek Hanson, whose rookie security guard character would prove instrumental in finding the abducted child. Dustin delivered his lines perfectly and on cue, as did Derek Hanson. This time it took twelve takes to satisfy Daniel, whose own delivery had, in Kyra's opinion, deteriorated with each take. Tonja had called for a twenty-minute break and then spent every minute of it convincing Daniel that the scene had been adequately covered, an argument that much of the cast and crew hung around pretending not to watch.

"Sorry, champ." Daniel appeared in their trailer after Dustin was released. "You did great today. That . . . that was all on me." He scrubbed at his face with one hand as if he might erase his morning's obstinate indecision. "So, I forgot to ask where you went over the weekend. Joan said you had a visitor?"

"We went to Disney World with Troy!" Dustin said happily.

"He tooked us there. And we spent the whole night and almost two days."

Daniel's eyes fixed on her. They narrowed.

"Is there some reason why we shouldn't go to Disney with a friend?" she asked, watching his dark eyes cloud with a combination of anger and jealousy.

"I don't know. You tell me." His voice had turned oddly seductive and she knew if Dustin hadn't been there he would have been reaching for her, wanting, maybe even needing, to know that she was still his. She told herself to step away. But there was something about him wanting her, even if it was because another man did, that kept her rooted to the spot. "He pretended to be someone he's not."

"Some people pretend they're going to leave their wives. And are so good at pretending that they do it for a living," she'd jabbed back, finally taking that step away, at least temporarily, and wondering as she put space between them whether he'd needed to prove he could have her whenever he wanted her. Or was still that drawn to her.

As it turned out she'd spent a good part of the evening trying to figure it out. And the rest of the evening not watching the phone or wondering why Troy hadn't called.

Now it was Wednesday and it seemed the Disney effect was completely out of juice. In the food tent, she stopped short at the sight of the Deranian-Kay family eating breakfast. Daniel sat at one end of the table, Tonja at the other, and their four children sat two to a side between them. It would have made a great photo op, just as all those shots of Dustin had, but there was not a photographer or entertainment reporter in sight. The children's nannies were not in evidence. This show, if it was one, was for her and her son and the crew. What she didn't know was who had organized it.

"How come we don't get to eat with them?" Dustin asked, staring at Daniel Junior, who was seated next to his father.

Kyra caught the look of triumph Daniel Junior aimed at them. Heard Tonja's tinkle of laughter. It was a masterful scene. Affirmation of the family unit, the connection Daniel and Tonja shared in one living tableau.

"I wanna eat with Dandiel, too!" Dustin cried.

The food tent fell silent. All eyes, including the Deranian-Kays', turned on them.

Dustin tugged hard on her hand and attempted to pull her forward. "Oh, no," she said to Dustin. "You need to calm down right now and stop this behavior."

"I wanna go there!" He stomped his foot. Dropping her hand, he folded his small arms across his chest.

It was Tonja who stood and began to walk toward them, moving like a queen.

Kyra would have given anything to disappear, wished desperately that they'd been delivered to set fifteen minutes later, or simply had a bite in the trailer. But this was not the Magic Kingdom. Or at least it wasn't theirs.

"Good morning," she said, leaning down to address Dustin. "Won't you come join us for breakfast?"

"Do you do this every morning?" The words were out before Kyra could stop them. They'd been here for close to three weeks and this was the first time she'd seen the Deranian-Kay children since the barbecue. Somehow she'd managed to put them, or perhaps she'd shoved them, out of her mind.

"Every morning that we can," Tonja said. "Daniel and I are usually still wrapped up here past dinnertime, but I think it's important to share a family meal every day. At least whenever it's possible. We're usually done earlier than this."

Kyra met Tonja's eyes. They were tired, but she saw no animosity in them. No guile. It was like seeing Darth Vader minus the actors who filled the black suit and James Earl Jones's booming voice. "Thanks, but I don't think Dustin's behavior should be rewarded. We're going to have breakfast in the trailer."

"No! I wanna eat there!" Dustin pointed again at the table where his father still sat. His arm and hand shook with rage.

"I asked your father to stay where he was so that I could invite you myself," Tonja said to Dustin when he stopped shrieking to take a breath. "But I think your mother's right. Next time we'll make sure to save you a place."

Dustin shrieked again and threw himself on the ground. Kyra's heart ached for him. She wanted to pick him up and hold him close and whisper her love. Wanted to tell him that everything would be all right. But the tantrum needed to stop and he needed to learn that this was not the way to get what he wanted. She drew a deep breath and prepared to reach into the mass of wailing, flailing angst to pull him to his feet.

Tonja put a hand on Kyra's arm, and for the first time Kyra didn't shrink away. "I'm sorry. I know what this business and all the attention and special treatment that goes with it can do. We deal with it all the time. Sometimes we're more successful than others."

Kyra watched Tonja glide regally back to the family table. She would have given a lot for a pair of ruby slippers that could spirit them away. Or a magic wand that could erase what had just taken place from the cast and crew's collective memory. She glanced once more at the table, but Daniel had turned back to his plate. Then she leaned over, wrangled her son into her arms as gently as she could, and carried him, still sobbing, to the trailer.

# Twenty-five

Nikki waited until Joe left for work before eating the quarter of a Kind apple, cinnamon, and pecan bar that she'd set aside for breakfast, taking her time to be sure to enjoy the sixty sweet, but not too sweet, calories that would see her through the morning.

It was harder to eat so little with Joe around. In fact, although he'd complimented her on the weight she'd lost, he'd spent a lot of the past week trying to tempt her into eating more and had practically followed her around with water in his attempts to get her to hydrate. On the bright side, his mere presence inspired willpower. And the regular sex had to be burning off quite a few calories. A definite win-win.

When she'd licked both fingers and the inside of the wrapper, she dressed the girls and tidied the cottage, trying to marshal her thoughts. Luvie would be here soon, and Nikki didn't intend to set a foot outside until she'd cut back on the nanny's hours.

She was sitting on the couch, which served as a home base of sorts while the twins used every stationary surface and many that were not as they lunged from place to place with their arms out, their chubby legs churning each time they managed to pull themselves up and balance for takeoff.

At precisely nine A.M. there was a crisp knock on the door—

now that Joe was back Luvie waited to be invited in—that sent them both windmilling drunkenly toward it.

"Come in!"

The key turned in the lock and Luvie's head poked inside. The twins squealed their happiness.

"There my lovelies are!" she exclaimed, stepping in. The twins' last lunge propelled them to her, where they clung as if to a life raft in turbulent seas. "Good morning, Mrs. Giraldi. It's a beautiful day, isn't it? With these two here in my arms I can't think of a single thing that would make it better."

*Great.* Nikki smiled, but it felt as if a warning shot had been fired across her bow.

"In fact, there aren't enough hours in the day when I'm caring for them." She looked around. Took in the straightened living area, the girls' breakfast dishes already sitting in the drainer. "I'll just go tidy their bedroom, shall I?"

"Oh, I've . . ."

Luvie returned, disappointment written on her face. "Someone's already picked it up."

"Yes," Nikki said, determined not to be deterred.

"I'll run some laundry then. Maybe put on fresh sheets. Afterward I thought I might take the girls to the beach to play."

"The cottage is done, Luvie. Everything's clean." If you didn't look too closely. And if drool and spit-up didn't count. She patted the space next to her on the couch. "Come sit down. There's something I've been wanting to talk about."

Luvie came, but she moved slowly, taking in her surroundings as if she might never see them again. She sat carefully, her pocketbook in her lap, her back not touching the sofa cushion. Sofia and Gemma lurched after her.

"It's a small place and I don't have a lot else to do. And this isn't a particularly booming metropolis. Killing time is difficult."

The girls pulled themselves up to their feet using their beloved's knees. Luvie brightened. "Ahhh, but you could volunteer . . . fund-raise for charity. Go to tea." The girls cooed up at her. "That's what all my previous employers have done." Luvie brushed back the girls' hair from their adoring faces. "I don't suppose there's much call for foxhunting here. But you could . . ."

"The girls are, and should be, my number one priority and I *want* to spend time with them. I mean, I'm not as good at it as you. Or Joe. But I did give birth to them, and I think they have to put up with me no matter how inept I might be, right?"

Luvie nodded, swallowed. She met Nikki's eyes. Hers shimmered with tears. "So I'm to be sacked then?"

Nikki opened her mouth. All she had to do now was say yes. Then she could offer praise, add an apology, and offer a bonus of some kind. Not quite as neat or thorough as the BCSM, but the deed would be done. She would have taken the beachhead without firing a shot.

Then the first tears fell. Luvie opened her pocketbook and retrieved a beautifully embroidered handkerchief, the sort every grandmother had once carried. Luvie's hand shook, just as her voice had, as she used it to dab at her eyes. The girls reached up to pat their Luvie's cheeks then laid their heads on her knees in consolation and support. All three of them were now crying.

"I . . . I just don't need so much help," Nikki stammered helplessly, wondering what kind of monster made a sweet old woman and her own babies cry. Frantically, she tried to remember the steps of the BCSM, but the tears and all the eye dabbing made it difficult to focus. The girls' sobs turned to wails and she could barely think at all.

"I . . . I . . . what if we cut back to three afternoons a week and Saturday nights?"

The crying continued.

"And . . . maybe an extra weeknight when Joe's home?" She could hear the desperation in her voice and knew she'd lost any bargaining power she might have possessed.

Luvie's head rose. She sniffed and dabbed at her face with the handkerchief. The tears stopped. "I'm afraid that wouldn't work," the nanny said quite calmly. "I am . . . I must work for my living. I would hate to have to give up this position. I love the girls, and I think they've become quite attached to me as well."

They were attached all right. In fact, they were now clinging desperately to Luvie. For a moment Nikki imagined having to pry their fingers off of the nanny. Then she would stand and point to the door and Luvie would trudge out into the snow, weeping wildly and . . .

In fact, Luvie had recovered more quickly than her employer. She dabbed her eyes one last time then sat quietly, her hands stroking the twins' heads until the sobbing stopped, watching Nikki's face. Assessing her. Both of them knew she wasn't going to throw the nanny out of the house and tell her never to darken their door again. Even if she'd truly wanted to, she couldn't simply fire her. First of all, that would make her the villain in the piece. Second of all, Joe had been understanding about her wanting to cut back Luvie's hours, but if he knew that she had let her go and had no help at all? No, that was not an option. But neither could Nikki leave things as they were. Somehow she needed to prove, at least to herself, that she had what it took to mother her children. Without professional assistance.

"Okay then." Nikki stood. "I'm going to go out for a while. We'll leave things as they stand today and tomorrow. But the girls and I will be going out of town on Monday." She wasn't sure where the lie came from, but she was committed now. There would be no backing off.

"I beg your pardon?" Surprise suffused Luvie's face. "I thought it was Mr. Giraldi who was leaving on Monday."

"Yes, he's leaving on assignment. But I'm. We . . . that is, the girls and I are leaving at the same time—or, rather, an hour later." Lying to Luvie felt kind of like telling tall tales to Bambi.

But Nikki wanted time alone with her daughters and the woman had left her no choice.

"But where are you going?" Luvie asked as the girls wriggled up onto the couch on either side of her.

This, of course, was a good question. "I'm . . ." She hesitated, her brain lurching through possibilities with the same kind of stuttering steps the girls employed. "I'm taking Sofia and Gemma to visit Joe's family."

The twins looked up expectantly at the sound of their names. Nikki hoped like hell they hadn't followed the rest of the sentence.

"Of course, you'll be paid for the time you would have been here while we're gone."

"Oh, thank you." Luvie looked almost as surprised as Nikki felt.

"You're, um, welcome. But . . ." She cleared her throat as the next hole in her explanation hit her. "But, please don't mention this to Joe." She bit back a groan, already anticipating the nanny's next question.

"Mr. Giraldi doesn't know you're taking the girls to visit his parents?" Luvie cocked her head, waiting for an explanation.

"No. I mean I don't want him to know the details because at the end of the visit, I'm going to leave the girls with their grandparents so that I can . . . surprise Joe for a long weekend of . . . a romantic getaway."

"Oh." Luvie sat back on the sofa, her arms encircling both girls. She smiled beatifically. "How lovely."

Nikki smiled in agreement then kissed the girls good-bye. It would have been quite lovely indeed if only it had been true.

• • •

Susan White's home on Sunset Road didn't look like it belonged to someone who had helped steal thirty-some million dollars. It was a one-story mostly brick ranch pockmarked with old jalousie windows. The front yard was an unhappy mix of crabgrass, sand, and unidentifiable foliage too stubborn to die. The cracked narrow driveway arrowed into a one-car garage. An uneven picket fence that had once been white bordered the property.

Bitsy stared out the passenger window of June's car. "Are you sure this is the right house?"

"Yes," June said after double-checking the address against the GPS. "Apparently crime really doesn't pay. No wonder she was so excited when I told her that one of my clients had asked me to deliver something to her."

"I know what I'd like to deliver," Bitsy said as she got out of the car. But the truth was she was sorry she'd come. Righteous indignation had propelled her across the state, but now the last thing she wanted was to meet this woman that Bertie had slept and plotted with.

"Remember, you're the victim here. She's the one who's supposed to feel bad," June said with a bracing smile. "All we're looking for is information at this point and help in going after Bertie."

"Right." Bitsy tried not to drag her feet as she and June walked to the door, tried to remember to breathe as it opened.

Susan White was an attractive brunette in her early forties with wide blue eyes, a peaches-and-cream complexion, over-plumped lips and an impressively large-yet-perky set of breasts, which Bitsy hoped she hadn't paid for.

"Oh!" The woman's eyes went saucer-like when she saw Bitsy. "Oh, shit!"

"I see you recognize my client," June said smoothly. "May we come in?"

"Oh. I . . . ." Susan's inner struggle played out on her face, at least the parts of it that still moved. Let them in? Or close the door in their faces?

Bitsy's internal debate was slightly different. Keep her hands to herself? Or slap this woman silly?

In the end the woman stepped back so they could enter what turned out to be the living room. She motioned them to the sofa, a camel-backed reproduction that was even less comfortable than it looked. "So, I gather no one left me money."

"No," June said. "But Mrs. Baynard *is* my client. And given your affair with her husband and your role in helping him bankrupt her, which the authorities are now going to investigate, we think it would be in your best interest to help bring him back to face charges. Otherwise you could end up taking the fall for the whole thing."

Susan closed her eyes and Bitsy noticed she'd had them done. "I lost my job because of him! He lied to me. He told me he loved me and promised to send for me when he had everything set up. But I'm the one who got set up. It's been a whole year since he left. And you know what he gave me? A couple thousand bucks to tide me over and a burner phone for emergencies. Only he never answered it any of the times I called." She exhaled angrily then sighed. "Did he . . . did he really take someone else with him?"

"Yes. Being abandoned and lied to sucks doesn't it?" Bitsy drew a breath of her own and attempted to dial back her anger. She'd been trained from birth to be polite in all situations, but this was way beyond smiling through veiled insults or cattiness at a cocktail party. "That was my money you stole. And my husband. Disappointing though he's turned out to be, he was mine. Did you even stop for one minute and think about that?"

Once again Susan White seemed to be debating her response. Her eyes narrowed but her forehead and the area around her eyes did not wrinkle. "For about thirty seconds. But a girl's got to look out for herself. You were filthy rich your whole life. Bertie told me all about it. It's not like you earned any of those millions."

"No," Bitsy admitted. "But my family did. And at least I didn't steal it."

"He also told me how you used your money to control him. He said the money at Houghton Whitfield was only a small part of what you had. That you'd never even miss it. What difference does it make? You're still rich."

"No, Susan, I'm not," Bitsy ground out. "Unfortunately, that's just another lie he told you. That was all of it you transferred out of there. Every single penny."

There was silence as Susan White absorbed this. Realized that she had not been the only real victim as she'd believed.

"And your employers?" June asked. "I'm surprised you weren't prosecuted for your part in this. Yet here you are barely ten miles away from the office."

Susan's lips pressed together.

"Did they pay you to keep quiet?" June asked.

Susan turned her head and Bitsy saw the telltale incision lines behind one ear.

"They did, didn't they?" June pressed. "Only not enough to buy a new home. Or travel. Or any of the things you were expecting." She shook her head. "I hate when men don't keep their promises. It makes me want to punish them, you know? Make them realize that they don't have all the power like they think they do."

Susan had gone very still.

"Gene, Mr. Houghton, promised they'd take care of me as long as I didn't say anything. But all I got was one lump payment, then nothing." She swallowed. "I used it to enhance myself. Because I'm all I've got, you know? And because there was supposed to be more."

Bitsy was careful not to groan or wince or ask just how much she'd spent on her "enhancements." All that mattered now was getting her to help them trap Bertie.

"And it's not like I can sue the firm to get it, right?" Susan asked June, her expression hopeful.

"No. Given your role in all of this, you are not going to be filing a suit. But, you could protect yourself and help get back at Bertie."

Bitsy was careful not to look directly at Susan. She made herself as small as possible and kept her face not only averted, but expressionless. In her mind she was shrieking, *Pleeeee-aaaaasssse!*

Finally, when Bitsy didn't think she could take it any longer, Susan said, "What would I have to do?"

"You would give a sworn statement. Tell the state attorney right here in Palm Beach exactly what happened," June said. "Then you would agree to testify in court in exchange for immunity. Meaning they would agree not to prosecute you."

Once again there was a silence that June was careful not to interrupt. Bitsy concentrated on keeping her breathing even and on not distracting Susan White, who had shown no remorse and who had offered no apologies, but was clearly struggling with her decision. Finally, she nodded. "All right. I'll . . . I'll do it."

"Good," June said. "Very good. I'll reach out to their office and get things set up."

All three of them stood. Bitsy wasn't sure what was supposed to happen next, so she left the wrap-up and the discussion of details to June. It seemed clear no hugs or handshakes would be offered or received.

They were at the door when Susan said, "I hope he rots in jail. The only thing I ever saw Bertie care about more than his own skin was showing everybody how smart he was. Pulling off a deal. Making money when nobody thought he could."

Bitsy turned to stare at Susan White. Whom she had discounted and who had so succinctly defined Bertie's motivation. That thing that drove him. His greatest weakness.

Just waiting to be exploited.

# Twenty-six

Within minutes after Dustin finished shooting on Friday, Kyra had packed him and Max into the Jeep for the drive back to the Sunshine. She told herself she wasn't running away, that leaving for the weekend didn't make her a coward. But she felt embarrassed and cowardly. It seemed that when the going got tough, the people who weren't as tough as they thought they were went home.

Just outside of Winter Haven, Dustin's head began to nod. Beside him Max yawned and tucked his nose under his paws. Drained from a week of worry about Dustin and from keeping up her guard, Kyra had to pry her hand from the wheel to even speed-dial her mother's cell phone. She clung to it as it rang, desperate to hear her mother's voice.

"Kyra?" Her mother sounded out of breath. "Are you okay?"

"Yes," she said as firmly as she could. "We've survived another week. Three down, three more to go. Just twenty-one days or five hundred and four hours. But who's counting?"

She heard muffled voices in the background. The squeal of what sounded like feedback from a microphone. The strum of a guitar. "What's going on?"

"Sound check. Then we're going back to the hotel." There was laughter. A chord progression.

"Where are you?"

"I'm not sure," her mother said, sounding spectacularly unconcerned.

"You actually don't know?"

"Oh, it'll come to me." There was a brief silence and then, "Hold on. I've got it. Ha! We're in Kansas City! Denver tomorrow!"

"Is this Madeline Singer? Aka the most organized person on earth?"

"Not anymore," Maddie laughed. "I feel like I'm in that movie, I think it was called, *If It's Tuesday, This Must Be Belgium.* You know, a different day a different city. That's pretty much what being on tour is."

"It sounds like it's agreeing with you. I mean, you sound good." Far better than she did.

"It's the weirdest thing, Kyra. I've always had a huge to-do list. Each day was about checking things off the list, you know? Staying on top of it, being on task. I kind of panicked that week before the tour started, because the list was gone and I didn't know how to function without it."

"I'm thinking you've figured it out?"

"I have absolutely nothing I have to do right now. Nothing except to enjoy being with Will and, I don't know, it's like we're traveling with this weird kind of extended family. Only I'm not in charge of it. I don't have to fix it. Or improve it. Or even feed it. Unless I want to." She paused. "Oh. Hold on a sec."

There was muffled conversation and laughter. Kyra looked at the dashboard clock. It was two o'clock in the afternoon and her mother was enjoying herself, not racing home like her daughter.

This time the laughter was unmuffled. "Will and the guys say hi."

"Hi back," Kyra said.

"I'm going to move into a quieter spot." The background conversation and laughter receded. "So, tell me what's happening with you. Are you still on set? How's Dustin?"

Kyra checked the rearview mirror. Dustin and Max were still out for the count. "We're on the way back to the Sunshine. I . . . we needed to get away at least for the weekend."

"But, I thought Dustin was doing so well."

"He's handling the part unbelievably well. But I think it's getting to be too much for him. He's way too worried about delivering a perfect performance. And he's begun to think he should have whatever he wants the minute he wants it." Kyra exhaled and tried to slow down the rush of words. "It feels like one trial after another. The other morning we got to the food tent earlier than usual and the whole Deranian-Kay family was communing over breakfast together. He lost it."

"Aww, honey."

"And Daniel is, oh I don't know, there's just so much pressure. And I feel as uptight as Dustin. Only I'm trying so hard not to show it; it's . . . exhausting."

The highway blurred and she realized she was crying. "And Tonja is doing a lot of the heavy lifting." The tears slid down her cheeks, but she didn't have a free hand to wipe them away. "There's more to her than I've ever seen before, but I don't know what that means." She sniffed and commanded the tears to stop. "It's everything I was afraid it would be and more. And the worst thing is there's really nothing I can do about it."

There was silence on the other end of the line. She swallowed back her panic at the idea of a lost connection. "Mom? Are you there?"

"I am. I'm just trying to think what I can do to help. And I'm wondering if I should get a flight and meet you at home."

The desire for exactly that flooded through her. The certainty and comfort of her mother's presence would be such a relief, a lifeboat to cling to. Except she was no longer a child. She was a mother. And that wasn't a role you abdicated just because it became difficult. Shame coursed through her. "No," Kyra said. "Just give me a little advice, that's all I need." She attempted a smile and was glad her mother couldn't see how wobbly it was. "Just tell me how you got through all the shit you dealt with after the Ponzi scheme and Dad's breakdown."

"Honestly?" Her mother's voice was soft but resolute. "I just kept putting one foot in front of the other and doing the best I could. Which is exactly what you're doing. I think going home and decompressing for the weekend is a great idea, Kyra. There's no shame in it. And when you get back on set? You can do *any-thing* for three weeks. Dustin's young and resilient and, frankly, so are you. You'll survive, the tour will be over, and we'll all regroup together."

"Right." Kyra stared out the windshield knowing it was time to let her mother go. It took everything she had to say good-bye and relinquish the connection. "Thanks, Mom. I really appreciate it."

"I love you both, Kyra. I'm proud of you. And I think you're doing all the right things. But if you or Dustin need me, all you have to do is call and I promise I'll be on the next plane."

By the time she'd turned onto the Pinellas Bayway she'd dried her tears and resolved to make sure they both enjoyed the weekend. She was not running toward or away from anything. There were no decisions to be made, nothing pressing to take care of. The weekend that stretched in front of them could be whatever she and Dustin decided to make of it. And Troy would help. He knew how to relax and have a good time, and he'd vowed to make sure they did the same. She felt her lips tip up into a smile as she replayed their last phone conversation in her head. It had been filled with laughter and all kinds of extravagant claims that she intended to hold him to. Bottom line, if Troy Matthews said that Dr. Oz believed that a day out on a boat and beach time were medically proven stress busters, who was she to argue?

· · ·

Avery stood on the seawall with Martha Wyatt and her friend Hannah Friedan as Ray snapped photos of Martha's tiny house.

The railed front porch was complete and already held two cane-back rocking chairs. Newly installed windows sparkled in the afternoon sun. As they moved inside, sunshine poured in through those windows dappling the walls and the floor. Wide steps with built-in storage drawers and cupboards led up to the finished loft where the house-shaped bunkhouse bunk bed that Avery and Ray had designed would be built of shiplap and bead board and barn doors that would slide across the upper bunk.

"It feels so bright and airy in here," Hannah said squeezing her friend's arm. "And so much more spacious than I expected."

"It is, isn't it?" Martha's enthusiasm matched Avery's own. "It's all the windows and the skylight. Just wait until you see the finishes we chose for the kitchen and bath."

"It's going to be great," Avery said as Ray snapped photos. "Plumbing and electrical have been roughed in and the appliances have arrived. Cabinets and countertops should be in by the end of next week. Once everything's hooked up and functional we'll finish the rest of the built-ins. And Ray will work on the decorative end." Three weeks had been overly optimistic, but they were making good progress.

"I love what you're doing for Martha," Hannah said as they stepped back out onto the porch. "It's wonderful. I like the idea of something small and manageable like this, but I don't have family with a backyard and I hate to leave the beach. I think I might be able to swing a one-bedroom at the Sunshine if you'd be willing to finish it out for me."

"I'd be glad to," Avery said excited and relieved that she'd have a project waiting when Martha's home was done. But as they discussed setting up a meeting with John Franklin for the following week and sitting down to talk through the design, her thoughts turned to Chase. Who had never seen Martha's tiny home. Whom she hadn't seen or talked to since the morning he'd left her key and let her know the ball was in her court.

Only she was unable to even get off the bench let alone dribble the ball or attempt to shoot.

"Smile, Avery!" Ray took a last shot of her with Martha and Hannah then joined her on the porch as the two women left. "Here, let me get a shot of you for your portfolio. And social media. Maybe we can get Troy to shoot some video after the kitchen and bath go in."

She found a smile but it took several attempts to satisfy Ray.

"You, my girl, are starting to worry me," the designer said. "I think it might be time to put on your big-girl panties and call the man already."

But she had required alcohol the last time she'd done that, and it hadn't ended at all well.

"We both know what Maddie would do in this situation, what she'd tell you to do."

"I know. But I feel kind of like I decided to try skydiving and now I'm in the plane with my pack on and everybody's telling me to go ahead and jump. But I can't make myself do it." She stared out over the water. "And I'm afraid that if I ever work up the nerve, it'll be too late. And he'll be in love with that Riley business."

"I have confidence in you," Ray said, slinging an arm around her shoulders and leading her off the porch and toward her car. "And I'm happy to push you out of the plane anytime."

• • •

Bitsy and June met Joe and Nikki for breakfast the next morning at the Seahorse, a small clapboard restaurant with gaily striped awnings and flower boxes bulging with red geraniums that clung just beneath the run of windows. Across the narrow two-lane Pass-a-Grille Way from the historic Merry Pier, it had held down the northeast corner of Pass-a-Grille's Eighth Avenue since 1938.

From the outside patio they could see boats leaving the pier and fishermen casting their lines from the seawall, while pelicans watched from their pilings and gulls skimmed low over the water searching for their own breakfast options. It was a place known for Southern-style breakfasts and seafood lunches where locals and tourists rubbed shoulders and the service was efficient and no-nonsense.

Bitsy tried not to smile as Joe attempted to talk Nikki into something more than the single scrambled egg and dry piece of toast she ordered, but Nikki held firm and even managed not to groan too loudly when plates of shrimp and cheese grits with bacon bits, omelets with potatoes, sausage gravy and biscuits, and stacks of pecan pancakes arrived. She busied herself cutting up the girls' food and pouring milk into their sippy cups as June caught Joe up on where things stood and the fact that Susan White had agreed to give a sworn statement and testify in exchange for immunity.

"That's huge," Joe said. "Well done. When will she go into the state attorney's office?"

"She has an appointment first thing Tuesday morning," June said. "I've organized for an attorney I know down there to represent her and make sure everything holds up."

"What was she like?" Nikki asked, dragging her eyes from the stack of pancakes Joe had just smothered in syrup.

"I can't say I have any sympathy for that woman," Bitsy said. "She screwed around with my husband, and helped him steal everything I had. Then she blew what little she made out of it on some really unimpressive plastic surgery. But she was still clinging to the hope that Bertie was somehow going to send for her."

"God. I feel worse every time I hear about the things Bertie's done," Nikki said. "I vetted him in every way possible."

"I'm continually shocked by what the approach of middle age can do to perfectly good men," June said. "It's almost stunning when someone *doesn't* go off the rails." She glanced up at Joe. "Sorry. No offense."

"None taken. Though I'd like to believe there are more than a handful of us who have no desire to flee the country to start a new life."

Nikki took a pecan pancake off of Joe's plate. Bitsy thought she might have inhaled its scent briefly before setting it on her plate and cutting it up for the twins, who used their fists to push the food into their mouths.

"I hate having to be away so much," Joe said. "I don't understand how a man could turn his back on his wife or leave his children." He looked at Nikki, reached for her hand. "I don't think I could leave at all if we didn't have Luvie."

Nikki smiled, but shifted uncomfortably in her seat.

"Susan White's testimony should result in charges being filed, which means a warrant for Bertie's arrest would be issued. Did she tell you anything else that might be useful?" Joe asked.

Bitsy looked at June then back at Joe. "She reminded me of just how much Bertie needs to prove himself a winner. How hard it is for him to resist trying to 'win' a deal. Then I remembered you saying that if we could create a reason for him to have to go online to access that primary account at a specific time, a freelance hacker could get in and transfer the money back."

Joe's eyes glimmered with interest. "And?"

"And what if somebody he didn't know approached him with a once-in-a-lifetime opportunity? Something tailor-made for him and way too good to resist?" Bitsy watched Joe's face, barely breathing while she waited for his answer.

"I like it," he said finally. "I've never met Bertie. And I can get in and out of the Caymans in between work travel over the next weeks. I'd be glad to be the one to wave the perfect deal under his nose." He smiled somewhat grimly. "Then, based on his need to 'win,' I'll make sure he has to work damn hard to get in on it."

# Twenty-seven

The prescription for a weekend of R & R might (or might not) have been prescribed by Dr. Oz, but so far it seemed to be working. On the drive in yesterday Kyra had vowed that she would entertain no negative thoughts, that no matter what happened she would see her glass as "half full."

Max had woofed at their first sight of the Don CeSar's mammoth pink facade and Dustin, who'd begun to rouse when they'd turned off 275 on to the Pinellas Bayway, clapped his hands. Even without her mother there to greet them, Kyra had felt the joy of homecoming. Even though her mother wasn't present, her "village" was still intact.

So far Saturday morning had been a lusciously lazy one spent in pajamas eating scrambled egg and cheese sandwiches in front of the television.

"I think I need to practice my lines," Dustin said around a mouthful of egg with one eye trained on the screen where Arthur the Aardvark's episode "That's MY Grandma!" was currently playing.

"We're going to do that tomorrow morning for exactly one hour," Kyra said, pouring him a second glass of juice and setting it within reach on the coffee table. "We're taking today off to relax and go out on the boat with Troy."

"Oh."

"You've got time for about two more episodes after this one," she said, hoping she wouldn't go to mommy hell for using television so blatantly to distract her child. When he sat back on the couch and took another bite of sandwich, she wanted to pump a fist in the air. Instead she all but skipped into her mother's bedroom, where she curled up with the first book in *The Dresden Files*, a series she'd heard about but never found the time to start.

Now it was noon. The three of them stood in front of Bella Flora's front door, Max doing his happy tail while Kyra repeated her weekend mantra in her head—*my glass is half full . . . half full . . . half full*—and tried to prepare herself for once again entering her own home as a guest. Which was bound to feel even worse than ringing her own doorbell. *Half full!*

"Hello." Troy opened the front door. "Glad you could make it." He looked at her face. Winced. "Okay, that was kind of weird, wasn't it?" He motioned to them then back to himself. "Do you think we should swap places and try that again?"

He looked and sounded so earnest that she surprised them both by laughing. "As long as you haven't hurt a hair on Bella Flora's head, I think I can handle it."

"Well then, we're both in luck." He stepped back and bowed at the waist, swirling his hand until it landed palm up like some sort of genie. "Because Bella Flora's hair is totally intact. She had a wash and blowout from a professional yesterday in anticipation of your visit. And she's very happy you're here. She's been missing you guys."

Kyra's eye roll was automatic, but she appreciated his attempt to break the ice. She drew a deep breath as they entered. *Half full, half full, he's trying, he's . . .*

The mantra evaporated as the clean scent of lemon and beeswax tickled her nose. The foyer chandelier gleamed above them, as did the floors beneath their feet. Sunshine streamed through the floor-to-ceiling windows with barely a dust mote in sight.

She sighed in relief and pleasure as Bella Flora wrapped her arms around them.

"You do know I'm prepared to move back into the pool house if you and Dustin would like to stay here, right?"

"Thanks. But we're fine where we are," she said, almost meaning it. "And while I appreciate that you're taking good care of her, I can't really afford to offer a refund right now."

"I'm sure we could work something out." He raised both eyebrows suggestively, but his manner was that of an overgrown puppy that wanted only to play.

"Let's not get ahead of ourselves," she said, even as her lips twisted up into a smile she couldn't have stopped if she'd wanted to. His swim trunks encased muscled thighs, and the faded blue T-shirt skimmed lightly over his broad chest and taut abdomen. As they followed him down the central hallway, she glanced into the living and dining rooms as well as the Casbah Lounge, just to confirm that they, too, were being treated well. But she also noticed Troy's backside and the athletic grace with which he moved. She did her best not to stare at his butt, but bottom line—yes, pun intended—this rakish, easygoing, noncombative version of Troy was compellingly attractive.

In the kitchen her eyes skimmed over the soft green glass-fronted cabinets, reclaimed wood countertops, and Spanish tile floor that Deirdre had designed and that her mother had turned into the heart of this incredible house. *Home.*

"Kyra?"

"Mommy?"

"Hmmm?" Clearly she had missed something.

"Can we go to McDonald's in the boat for lunch then go build a katsle on Shell Island like Troy said?"

"When we get back, I figured we could hang by the pool and maybe grill some steaks?" Troy added.

She looked at both their faces, eager and expectant. Max's tail slapped against her leg like a frantically happy metronome.

"I am at personal plan zero and I'm really enjoying it there," she said truthfully. "I'm up for whatever you guys want to do."

Max woofed. His tail wagged faster.

Troy grinned, all white teeth and polished surfer-guy good looks. "I'd say the vote's unanimous. And I'm glad." His voice dropped and his tone softened. "I know how hard it's been on you these last weeks. Any film has the potential to chew you up and spit you out. But the dynamics on that picture are, well . . . you're carrying a big load, but you don't have to carry it alone. I'm here for you both. I hope you know that."

With his words the weight that she'd been carrying for months grew lighter. So did her step as they walked next door to the Cottage Inn, where Troy's bright blue boat bobbed at its mooring. Troy untied the speedboat, backed out of the slip, then steered them into the pass. Kyra sat beside him, Dustin in her lap, her arms wrapped around his belly. Max stood between them, his face turned up into the cool salt breeze.

They passed Bella Flora, gleaming in the winter sun, and then the jetty. Troy eased forward on the throttle and the boat picked up speed as they moved into the gulf. She breathed the fresh salt air into her lungs and felt her lips stretch into a smile. Bella Flora grew small as they headed north past the low-slung Sunshine Hotel and Beach Club and the bright pink castle-like fortress that was the Don CeSar. She looked up at Troy's strong profile, the blond hair that whipped in the wind, the flutter of the T-shirt that occasionally bared glimpses of lean muscle and tanned skin. And found it even more attractive than Daniel's dark good looks and brooding eyes.

"Lookit!" Dustin pointed off the side of the bow. "It's dolpins!"

She hugged him tighter, watching the adult and two baby dolphins racing just ahead of them, leaping on occasion for what she chose to believe was joy.

She glanced up and felt Troy's eyes on them. With a huge

smile he kicked their speed up a notch. The dolphin family kept pace. Kyra's smile split her face and she laughed aloud. If she'd been a dolphin, she, too, would have leapt for joy.

"Everything okay?" Troy called over the sound of the wind, the hull meeting the water, and the whine of the engine.

She nodded, laughed again simply because it felt so good. She saw no reason to say so, but it was downright shocking how much this man, this day, and this moment did not suck.

. . .

"What time is Luvie due?" Joe stood near the front door of the cottage bright and early Monday morning, his carry-on and briefcase at his feet.

"I asked her to come a little later," Nikki said as he leaned over to pick up and kiss each of the girls. "I'm going to take the girls out for a run. Can we walk you out?"

"Sure."

Nikki opened the front door and wheeled the jogging stroller into place, careful not to make eye contact with her husband as she slipped first Gemma and then Sofia into a seat before buckling them in. She put on her sunglasses, the better to keep him from reading anything in her eyes, and tried to move and react as normally as possible. She hated lying to Joe. And she was not particularly good at it.

They lingered next to the car and she felt his reluctance to leave. "Don't worry," she said. "We'll be fine."

"Just promise me that you won't hesitate to have Luvie however much you need her," he said, watching her face.

"Of course." At least this wasn't a lie. It was, in fact, exactly what she was doing.

"Seriously, Nikki, I'm not worried about paying for extra hours."

She, on the other hand, was a bit worried about paying for all the hours they wouldn't be using, but she kept this to herself.

She could always call Luvie if she had to and simply say that she and the girls had come back early. Something she didn't plan to do unless hell began to freeze over.

She looped her arms around his neck and allowed herself to hold on tightly, a move she regretted when he reached down and slid her sunglasses off her face. "Sorry, but I like to look at the woman I'm kissing."

"Is that right?" she teased, careful not to look away. "I don't know, I think dark glasses add a dash of mystery." She left his sunglasses alone as she brushed her lips across his. He kissed her more fully and crushed her to him. Her heart thudded in her chest. In that moment she detested her dishonesty, but couldn't bring herself to tell him the truth.

"I hate being gone this long. I could have gotten back a bit earlier if I weren't using my free days to see what I can do in the Caymans," he said as he released her.

"It's okay. I'm glad you're trying to help Bitsy." This, at least, was true. "Do you think you can get Bertie to meet?"

"Well, I'm not the fisherman Will is, but I have caught enough bad guys to know how important it is to use the right bait. And I think tempting him with a deal then playing hard to get is exactly right. You have to play to people's natures, appeal to their appetites." One dark eyebrow sketched upward and she felt him studying her. She was very glad she couldn't see his eyes. "And you have to be willing to exploit their weaknesses."

They watched Joe drive off, the girls calling out their good-byes and throwing kisses. Before any of them could tear up at his departure, she turned and pushed the stroller purposefully to the beach and down onto the hard-packed sand. When she'd finished her run and returned to the Sunshine, Bitsy, Renée, and Annelise were waiting to discuss the fashion show at a table under the overhang. Pulling out snacks and juice boxes for Gemma and Sofia, she angled the stroller so they could watch the lounge chairs being set up, the pool being cleaned, and keep track of the brightly colored kite that flew over the beach. They ate and drank and kicked their chubby legs happily. With an equally happy sigh Nikki pulled out the notes she'd made.

"We sold two of the vintage bathing suits and a cover-up," Bitsy said, kicking off the discussion. "I think the vintage/retro thing will make the fashion show unusual enough to get some extra media coverage."

"I've got a handful of friends from the garden club who've agreed to model," Renée said. "And a couple more who offered to create centerpieces. I like the idea of holding the luncheon around the pool."

"Let's do it. If for any reason the weather's a problem, we can always take it inside." Nikki checked the item off.

"And the Pass-a-Grille Women's Club and the Yacht Club have promised some models, too," Renée said.

"I have a couple of volunteers from the Gulf Beaches Historical Museum," Annelise said. "And they're going to run an article I wrote about the history of the Sunshine in the newsletter. Oh, and they and the St. Pete Beach Library are interested in showing Kyra's documentary."

"This is all great stuff." Nikki scribbled notes, jazzed by the opportunity to sink her teeth into the project and elated that she didn't have to prepare for Luvie's arrival or find something that would get her out of the cottage all afternoon. "Let's do a flyer promoting a luncheon discount for anyone who tours the cottages. Do you think someone from Franklin Realty could distribute them?"

"I'm sure we can make that happen," Renée said. "And we're starting to see some interest already. A friend of Martha Wyatt is coming to look at one-bedrooms this week, and she's already spoken to Avery about building it out."

"Yeah, Avery told us," Bitsy said. "And Troy offered to update the Sunshine website and create a promo for the event along with online ticketing and reservations."

"I feel good about the way this is coming together," Nikki said. Actually, she felt good about everything. "I'm thinking Saturday, March fourth. Do you think that gives us enough time to get ready? We could push it back a bit."

"I think early March is perfect," Renée said. "The weather will be gorgeous and snowbirds are still here—they're a prime target for Sunshine cottages."

"I agree," Bitsy said. "Plus Maddie and Kyra will be back and it gives us time to promote and plan."

"Done!" Nikki pounded an imaginary gavel.

As if they'd just been waiting for the meeting to break up, Gem and Sofia began to cry. Nikki glanced at their distressed faces then down at her watch. Yikes. It was almost noon. Her nose wrinkled as she leaned closer to them and realized she hadn't changed their diapers since breakfast? "Oh, my gosh. We've got to go."

"Where's Luvie?" Bitsy asked as Nikki jumped to her feet and gathered up their things. "Isn't she usually here by now?"

"Um, she couldn't come today." Nikki stuffed everything into the diaper bag in too much of a hurry to worry about whether the lie sounded convincing.

"Do you need help?" Renée asked. "Can we do something?"

"No! I mean, no thank you." Nikki turned the stroller. "I'll um, I'll see you later," she called over her shoulder as she pushed the crying Sofia and Gemma toward home as quickly as she could. She was halfway there when she realized that she wasn't sure whether Luvie took them out after their naps. Or whether she'd given them so many snacks that they should skip lunch and have a really early dinner?

By the time she got to the cottage, wrangled the twins out of the stroller, and carried them inside, she was too tired to worry about the finer details of their daily schedule. She changed them and fed them and, despite their protests, put them in their cribs for a nap. Then she sprawled out on her own bed and closed her eyes. If she didn't calm down and get some sleep, Sofia and Gemma might not be the only Giraldis crying.

. . .

It was Tuesday and this was definitely Denver. Maddie knew this because on their flight into the Mile-High City, Will had turned in his seat and casually asked her if she'd ever joined the mile-high club.

"It's not something that came up on our family vacations," she'd replied drily. "Having sex in such a tiny, public, and germy place never made it onto my bucket list."

He laughed. "I don't think the initiation stipulates doing it on a commercial flight, which is a good thing given how much smaller those bathrooms have gotten. But if you wanted to try to stick to tradition, we could visit the bathroom here. It's relatively big and definitely more private."

"True. Hardly anyone would notice if you didn't count Robert, Kyle, Dean, Lori, Vicki, and Aaron." She looked up toward the galley. "Oh, and, the two flight attendants."

Will grinned. "I feel pretty confident they'll pretend they don't know where we're going and that no one will be knocking on that door."

"You're kidding, right?" she'd asked even as she'd started imagining it, some might say warming to it. Just as she always did when he proposed the unexpected so unexpectedly.

"Aw, hell, who am I kidding?" he'd said. "There's a perfectly good bedroom on this plane. I say we go for comfort over tradition. We're still a mile high, so I'm sure we can get you a membership card even if we bend the rules a little."

She'd laughed out loud then. But in truth, the twinkle in his eyes, the private smile on his lips, and the hand that cupped the back of her neck to pull her closer had made her more than ready to follow him anywhere.

Now, hours later, seated just offstage at Denver's Pepsi Center, she felt Will's eyes on her and shivered at the memory of how he'd led her past everyone else without a word and simply closed the bedroom door behind them. She looked up and met his eyes as he picked out the opening notes of "Free Fall," the song he'd written just after they'd renovated his private island for *Do Over*. The first song he'd written in more than a decade.

The crowd began to hoot and applaud. Maddie smiled and fingered the plastic pilot wings Will had pinned to her chest with an intimate wink and even more intimate kiss before they'd deplaned.

She watched him come fully alive onstage, watched him shimmer and shine beneath the spotlight and before the adoring crowd. Sharing this, being a part of this huge public thing with and for him, was proving to be one of the most deeply personal things Maddie had ever experienced.

"God, I'm glad you're here," he said as he came offstage after their final encore.

A roadie handed him a towel, which he slung around his neck and used to wipe his sweaty face and hair. "I'm wiped." He leaned over to brush his lips across hers. "Must have been that high-altitude sex," he whispered, his teeth teasing at her ear.

She smiled and fingered her pilot's wings again. "Thanks for the initiation. Is there paperwork that needs to be filed or am I an official member now?"

He threw back his head and laughed. With his arm slung around her shoulders they walked to the greenroom, where Lori handed him a soft drink as the PR girl stepped up. "Ready, Will?"

"As I'm going to be." He dropped another kiss on the top of Maddie's head, gave her hand a squeeze, then followed Vicki into the throng.

Lori handed Maddie a plate and they helped themselves to food and drink then dropped onto a leather sofa. Silently they watched the willowy blonde lead Will from guest to guest introducing him to members of the press, VIPs, and anyone and everyone who'd scored an opportunity to come backstage.

"I've sort of come to terms with her, but I just can't bring myself to like her." Lori nibbled on a chicken slider as she watched their progress through narrowed eyes. "I mean, it's not like I have to pretend I want to be BFFs, right?"

"Of course not," Maddie said, thinking just how much she would have liked to have her own BFFs there to dish with. "But you're both working for Will and toward a common goal. You want to keep things cordial enough so that you can work smoothly together on his behalf."

"Cordial. Got it," Lori said. At a gesture from Aaron she stood. "Duty calls."

Moments after Lori departed, Dean Adams ambled over and dropped down beside Maddie. He set her empty glass on a side table and handed her a full one. "So," he asked. "Is the doctor in?"

"Well." She took a sip of what turned out to be a very nice Pinot Noir. "I appreciate the refill, and I'm always willing to offer an opinion. What's going on?" She turned to study him and saw his eyes on Vicki. "Ah," she said. "I'm thinking maybe it's not a what, but a who?"

He nodded glumly. "I love my wife and kids. But I'm afraid I'm not turning out to be as good at resisting temptation on the road as Will is." He turned so that his gaze no longer included the PR girl. "You were married for what, twenty-five years? How'd you make it work for so long?"

"Well, to be fair neither my husband nor I were on tour and this cut off from real life," Maddie said carefully. "When you're imagining what this kind of life might be like, you don't really have a clue just how far from reality it is."

"That's the truth," Dean agreed. "I thought about asking Dana to meet me for at least part of the next few weeks, but our kids are in elementary school and it's not that easy to just pick up and go now."

Maddie nodded. "I know. I remember how it was when Kyra and Andrew were small. Everything's about juggling and logistics when you have kids that age. But, I don't know. Maybe if you had family that could keep the kids, Dana could come for a long weekend? Or even bring the kids with her? I'm a pretty experienced babysitter. I could help keep an eye on them if you two wanted some alone time. And I'm sure there are others who would help, too." *Not Vicki, of course*, she thought uncharitably. "I know Lori would be glad to pitch in."

"I . . . I'll ask Dana," Dean said. "It's a good idea. Thanks."

"Next tour maybe you need to have a built-in babysitter or tutor on the crew. Or add it to the venue riders in each city," she suggested.

"Yeah, that's how you know the rockers are getting old when they need to budget for daycare and not hotel room destruction."

They laughed together and she noticed he was too busy thinking about how this might work to follow Miss Tall, Blond, and Available with longing eyes.

"You're a good man, Dean. And the fact that you even wanted to talk about this shows how important your family is to you. I think you've got sufficient willpower to resist doing something you'd regret. Wasn't it Jimmy Carter who admitted to lusting in his heart? Being tempted isn't the same thing as acting on that temptation." She shrugged. "My guess is that even if you can't work out the logistics this time, just trying to talk your wife into joining you will go a long way toward easing the separation."

Dean smiled and nodded. "I don't know how you always manage to put everything so positively, but I really appreciate it. You're the best, Maddie." He offered a hand up then engulfed her in a grateful hug that warmed her from the inside out.

"You've got that right," Will said, coming up beside them.

"She's practically holding the whole crew together. The other day in Chicago I had to wait in line to talk to her." His complaint was infused with a pride in her that reminded her why she was here and just how much she loved him. "If everybody keeps coming to her for advice, we're going to have to put her on the payroll."

# Twenty-eight

The Wednesday morning breakfast with the Deranian-Kay family would go down in Kyra's memory as one of the most uncomfortable and awkward meals ever. Tonja had actually sent a written invitation the evening before, and in view of Dustin's meltdown the previous week when he'd wanted to join them, there was no way she could say no.

A hush fell in the food tent when they arrived. That hush continued as Tonja came to greet them and escort them to their table.

"I'm glad you could join us this morning, Dustin," she said, seating him on Daniel's right directly across from Daniel Junior, who smiled slightly having no doubt been instructed to check his smirk at the door. Tonja returned to her seat next to their youngest and motioned Kyra to the open seat across from Tonja's.

"Did you have a good weekend?" Tonja leaned forward, directing the question to Dustin.

"Yes! We went on Broy's boat!" Dustin beamed. "His boat goes almost as fast as Dandiel's. And *I* got to drive it."

"Right," Daniel Junior said, doubt in his voice. But he did not smirk or sneer.

"I did, too, get to steer. And Troy tole me I did good."

Daniel's scowl at each mention of Troy Matthews was automatic and amazingly similar to the scowl that appeared on Troy's face at any mention of Daniel.

"I'm sure you handled the boat beautifully," Tonja said, shooting a stern look at both Daniels. "That sounds like fun, doesn't it, Marcus?"

The five-year-old nodded and smiled. After that Tonja elicited a comment from each child then introduced another topic. The conversation that ensued was stilted and laborious. Her determination to make the shared meal look like a friendly gathering had Kyra looking around for paparazzi or a hidden film crew. But if this was anything other than an attempt to make Dustin feel included and offer a display of unity to the crew, she could find no sign of it.

Kyra moved the food around on her plate and remained silent. She did not address Daniel in any way and only looked at him when Tonja forced him to join in the conversation and because ignoring him completely might look suspicious.

She'd assumed that seeing him with his family would strengthen her resolve to fight the attraction that still existed between them, but when he poured milk for Dustin or spoke kindly to one of his children, that resolve softened. Resistance felt futile.

Kyra knew she should be grateful to Tonja for the care she took with Dustin, whatever her motives, but it seemed she was far too small a person to simply let go of their years of conflict.

The moment Dustin finished the last of his egg and toast, Kyra stood. "Thank you so much for including us," she said way too brightly. "We're going to go to the trailer now so Dustin can run over his lines and get into wardrobe."

Daniel looked down at his watch. "Time for me to get to work, too." He stood and began dropping kisses on his children's heads.

Tonja's jaw tightened but her smile remained intact. "Of

course. I'm going to get the kids situated then I'll see you all
on set."

Kyra took Dustin's hand. As she led him away, nannies materialized and hurried over to the Deranian-Kay table. Moments
later Tonja strode past them on her way to catch up with her
husband.

As it turned out, breakfast was the high point of the day.
Which began to spiral downward an hour later when they were
delivered to that morning's location where the rest of the cast
and crew were already assembled.

A large batch of extras of all ages had been placed on rides
surrounding the Ferris wheel where the day's first scene was to be
shot. The Second AD positioned others in strategic places to make
the amusement park appear packed from every possible camera
angle. Theme park balloons were tied to some of the children's
wrists. Couples and families were given small bits of action and
choreographed movement to create a convincing backdrop.

Today's first scene would take place largely on the Ferris
wheel itself. Brandon greeted them and escorted them to the set.
Dialogue in this scene would be minimal but the timing of it
crucial as the ride would be moving while it was delivered.

Dustin was excited and, Kyra could see, somewhat nervous
about performing while riding the massive Ferris wheel. The
scene began with Christian Sommersby's character standing in
line directly behind the Roberts family. Mid-scene he would
engineer an introduction and claim to have a son Dustin's age.
He would then get on the Ferris wheel directly behind them
and it would sweep them up into the air. A camera already
mounted on the gondola in front of theirs would shoot the rest
of the scene starting with Daniel, Tonja, and Dustin conversing,
and ultimately widening to include Christian.

"I don't have a good place to put you," Brandon said to Kyra
as primary actors and extras were placed. "You could ride in the

gondola just in front of the camera gondola or a couple behind Christian, but then you'd be an extra and required to stay in place for coverage and editing purposes. It's your call, but I think you might be best staying on the ground and watching on the monitor. We can stop the wheel when it comes back down for you to check on him if you feel the need before we do an additional take."

Kyra hated the idea of being on the ground while Dustin dangled in the air between Tonja and Daniel, but being able to watch Dustin's face and his reaction to what was happening on the monitor seemed like the better idea. "Okay, but if I think there's a problem, you'll bring him down immediately, right?" she said to Tonja and Daniel.

They nodded.

"Are you okay with me being down here?" she asked Dustin.

Dustin nodded solemnly. His eyes telegraphed his determination.

"If anything doesn't feel okay, you look right in the camera and give me the thumbs-down." She demonstrated. "And you tell Daniel and Tonja that you want to come down. Even if it's in the middle of a take, okay?"

He gave her a slightly quivery smile then added a thumbs-up. Reluctantly she stepped back out of the way.

A run-through for the camera operator and the puller, who would shift focus during the shot, followed. Dustin and Tonja delivered their lines without a problem. Christian Sommersby looked suitably normal yet threatening in the gondola directly behind them. Daniel had difficulty focusing. Through multiple takes he flubbed or forgot important lines. The one take he delivered flawlessly was marred by the extra in the gondola behind Christian who pulled out a cell phone she should not have had with her and used it to snap photos of the scene in progress, including a shot aimed directly at the camera.

When their gondola reached the ground, Daniel sprang out

and erupted in a way she'd never seen and hoped to never see again.

"Do you have any idea what your role here is?" he shouted at the young woman while he stormed toward her gondola. "How hard could it possibly be to sit and pretend like you're having a good time on the ride without compromising a take?"

Kyra saw Dustin cowering behind Tonja, who watched with a look of dread on her face.

Daniel stomped away then whirled back again. "Brandon!" he shouted at the First AD. "Weren't these people given directions?"

Brandon stepped forward placing himself in front of the woman who was now cringing in her seat and trying to disappear. "Um, yes, sir, of course. But . . ."

"And still she fucked it up!" He gesticulated wildly in her direction.

Kyra stole a glance at Dustin and saw Tonja climbing quietly out of the gondola. Dustin climbed out behind her.

"I . . . I . . . I'm sorry! I just . . . I wasn't thinking!" the young woman stammered. Tears streamed down her face.

"No shit!" Daniel shouted. "Damn it! Get her off the set right now before I throw her off myself!"

Keeping her eyes on Dustin, Kyra walked around several gaping crew members to snatch him up into her arms. Tonja held tight to Daniel's arm while Brandon helped the blubbering woman out of the gondola. Like everyone else, Kyra watched Daniel finally allow Tonja to lead him away. He continued to shout and gesticulate as they went.

"Somebody's feeling the pressure," a voice said somewhere behind her.

"Yeah." Somebody made the sound of an explosion. "He's like a powder keg with a really short fuse. I don't want to be anywhere near him when he blows."

"Okay, take fifteen, folks," the Second AD yelled when Brandon didn't immediately return. "But don't go far. We'll let you know when we're back in."

Tonja and Daniel returned exactly fifteen minutes later and climbed back into the gondola as if nothing had happened. Brandon took Dustin by the hand. "Are you okay doing a few more takes?"

Kyra opened her mouth to object.

"Sorry," Brandon said. "But I can't put a double in because of the dialogue and the close-ups. I promise you if there's even a whiff of a problem, I'll have him down here faster than you can say supercalifragilisticexpialidocious." The last was aimed at Dustin and accompanied by a wink.

"I can do it, Mommy." He dropped her hand and reached for Brandon's.

They did exactly five takes so there'd be plenty of potential cutaways in editing that would include the replacement extra. Daniel got his dialogue right on every take and the entire crew sagged in relief when Brandon yelled, "Cut!"

Daniel remained silent as he, Tonja, the DP, and the Script Supervisor congregated in front of the video monitor. Kyra knew hers wasn't the only heart pounding. It was Tonja who turned and shouted, "It's a wrap on scene one!" She and Daniel left the set.

"Okay, everybody, we're setting up for two." Brandon raised two fingers in the air. "I want all principals and crew hydrated. And let's get makeup to Christian."

Kyra collapsed into a director's chair beneath a shade tree with Dustin in her lap, too drained to even consider going back to the trailer. She nodded her thanks to the Production Assistant who delivered two cold bottled waters, and made sure Dustin drank. Then she settled back in the chair with Dustin's face buried in her shoulder and rocked gently while crew members tiptoed around them.

• • •

Later that afternoon, Avery paced her cottage. When she tired of the view and needed more square footage, she took her pacing outside and walked the concrete paths that bisected the Sunshine, barely looking at the cottages she'd just viewed with Hannah Friedan or the blooms that lined the walkways and spilled out over cottage courtyard walls.

Her mood would have been better suited to a storm, one with thunder and giant flashes of menacing lightning, but the day was sunny and mild and so she found herself on the beach, where she strode south toward Bella Flora because she didn't know where else to go and because she was fairly sure it didn't count as pacing if you only walked in one direction.

The white sand and blue-green water sparkled in the afternoon sun, just another frickin' day in paradise. For the third time since Hannah and John Franklin had departed, Avery lifted her phone to her ear, set her shoulders, and prepared to call Chase, the one person who would fully understand her excitement over Martha's project and her relief at already having another potential client lined up, and who would want to see her sketches and discuss possible build-outs and even finishes. Each time, she had stopped seconds before hitting speed dial. This time she shoved the phone deep into her jeans pocket and brushed her palms together as if that would be the end of it.

At the jetty, she stood on a rock and stared up at Bella Flora remembering the first time they'd seen her, the push-pull with Chase through the entire renovation. The constant bickering that had led to such sweet kisses.

She blew a bang out of her eyes and wished she could blow away the fear as easily. She'd always seen herself as a survivor, someone who would fight for what she wanted. And God knew, she wanted Chase. Only she was too afraid of getting hurt again to claim him. Soon she'd be pecking at the ground for tiny bits of happiness and clucking out her unhappiness like the chicken that she was. Watching him choose someone else, maybe even that Riley girl. Jeff would probably insist she be invited to their wedding. And she'd have to go. And pretend like it didn't matter. That she preferred being alone. Living in her tiny cottage. Designing and building tiny houses. Settling for a tiny life.

At the fishing pier she leaned on the wooden railing and stared down into the water, but while she could see fish skimming beneath the surface, there were no answers there. They weren't in the blue sky, either. Or in the puffy white clouds.

She missed him. She loved him. On paper it was a no-brainer. And she'd always hated wafflers. She pulled her phone out of her pocket. Her finger hovered over the picture attached to his contact, the one she'd snapped when he was sweet-talking her into bed, the one with the sexy grin and the dark promise in his eyes. But memories didn't travel alone. And suddenly she could taste the bitterness in her mouth, felt the cold, shocking emptiness that had stolen inside her when he'd pushed her out of his life.

Avery swallowed the bitterness, repocketed her phone. But as she began to pace her way back up the beach, she knew she couldn't live in this limbo much longer. Somehow she was going to have to find a way to either let go completely or get out of her own way and get him back. And she'd better choose one of those options soon. Before Riley Hancock wiggled her way into Chase's heart and started picking out her china pattern.

. . .

Dustin was already asleep, wrapped around his living, breathing security blanket, Max, when Kyra heard the soft knock on the front door. Pulling her robe around her, she looked out the peephole. Daniel stared directly into it and offered a self-deprecating smile. He held a bunch of mangled wildflowers in one hand. Some still had roots hanging from them.

When she pulled open the door, he handed them to her. "1-800-Flowers doesn't deliver out here on such short notice."

"Ah." Kyra took them and against her better judgment stepped back to let him in. "And probably Joan would strip-search them if they came at this time of night anyway."

"I had to come and apologize. I'm really sorry for the way I blew up today. I just couldn't seem to rein it in."

There were dark shadows under his eyes and he looked more unkempt than she could remember seeing him. "I'm sorry Dustin's not awake to hear that. Because you really upset him today. That can't happen again."

He nodded. "I know. And I'll apologize to him first thing in the morning."

"I haven't been online, but I hate to think how many cell phones caught that today."

"Yeah," he said quietly. "It's trending. Hashtag newbie director goes apeshit." He closed his eyes, shook his head. "I'm a joke. Going off on an extra like that. God."

As furious as she was with him, he looked so chastened, so vulnerable, her first instinct was to comfort him.

"Oh, Kyra," he said. "What an unbelievable mess I've made of everything." He stepped closer. Put his arms around her and pulled her close, squashing the flowers between them. For a moment she breathed him in, felt her body respond to his, felt it quicken. Just as it always did.

He exhaled slowly against her neck, a letting go. The nuzzle against her skin felt subtle at first, like a child seeking consolation. Only this face had stubble on it, and the body pressing into hers was firm and lean and well muscled.

The erection that nudged between her thighs was the first clue of the kind of comfort he'd come seeking, whether conscious or not. It was the cologne, the fresh hint of spice recently applied, that began to bring her to her senses. Reminded her of all the reasons she could not and should not do this.

"No." She dropped her arms and stepped back, letting go of the flowers that scattered at their feet. He stepped on them in his move toward her and she pushed him away. "No. That's not going to happen." She looked up into his face, saw not only surprise but disbelief. And no wonder. How many times had she said no and then allowed herself to be swept up and carried away? Abdicating control and all sense of responsibility. As if the choice was not up to her.

Because she was watching him so closely, she saw the hint of calculation steal into his eyes. And she knew that this was not a man driven by love and a need only for her. In that blinding moment of clarity she thought of Troy, who had not only declared himself, but applied himself to making her feel better, lighter, happier. Showing her how he felt about her without pushing or even asking for anything in return.

"No. This is a hard no," she said. "I can't seem to stop the attraction, the pull I feel, that makes me want you. But I can control what I do about it."

She straightened and ran her hands down the sides of her robe. "Your family is right across the lake. Your *wife* and your children. I can't believe I'm saying this, but I'm pretty sure Tonja could use a little comfort right now, too. And if you've got half the brains I've always thought you had, and even a quarter of the heart, you'll pick some more flowers on your way and take them to her."

# Twenty-nine

"Sorry. What did you say?" Nikki blinked herself back from the fog bank her mind had been drifting in and refocused on Bitsy, who had come to "help" with dinner and planned to stay for Joe's nightly FaceTime to get an update on what she'd begun to think of as "Operation Bring Back Bertie."

"I said, I think the girls are finished eating."

"Oh!" Nikki checked to make sure that both girls were still strapped into their high chairs. She relaxed when she saw them smiling. Her own smile dimmed when she noticed that they appeared to be wearing most of what she'd put on their plates.

"Have you ever considered letting them eat naked?" Bitsy asked.

"It would cut down on the laundry," she agreed, not ready to admit that she had considered that very idea yesterday as she'd thrown their lunch-stained clothing on top of the mountain of laundry that had grown to rival Kilimanjaro.

"I'm afraid I haven't gotten all that much into their mouths." Bitsy wiped strained carrots from her cheek and hair. "How long does it take to get the hang of it?"

"Oh, I gave up trying to feed them days ago," Nikki said. "The books say they're better off being allowed to feed them-selves." The pediatrician had promised her that the amount of food they ingested was less important than allowing them to gain independence. "All in all I think the increase in laundry and cleanup is worth the decrease in screaming."

"When's Luvie coming back?"

Nikki took a damp washcloth and wiped off Gemma and Sofia's hands and faces then cleaned her own. "I'm not sure. She's still under the weather and, um, was afraid she might be contagious."

"Oh." Fortunately, Bitsy was busy unpacking Ted Peters smoked fish spread and crackers, German potato salad, and all the necessary paper products and not listening closely enough to question the lie. She opened up the containers, filled two small plates, and pushed one toward Nikki. Then she opened the bottle of red wine to let it breathe and retrieved two wineglasses from the cupboard.

Bitsy poured them each a glass of wine then noticed Nikki hadn't made a move toward the food. "Aren't you going to eat something?"

"Thanks for bringing everything. I'm just not really hungry." Especially not when she still needed to get through the call with Joe without letting anything slip, bathe the girls, and get them into their pajamas. After which she'd cuddle and read them a story then put them into their cribs and somehow convince them to go to sleep.

Just thinking about it made her tired. Somehow she'd forgotten just how long twenty-four hours could be—something she'd learned in the weeks she'd spent on bed rest before the girls were born last year. Back then she'd been uncomfortable and lonely and bored to death lying in bed all day and night. Now, only four days into full-time single parenting, she would have sold her soul for half a day in bed. Or even a full night of sleep without one of the twins waking or crying, something else the pediatrician insisted was completely normal now that they were so active and developing so many new skills.

She had asked for this. No, she corrected. She had lied to Joe and to Luvie to get this time alone with Sofia and Gemma to prove that she was a competent mother capable of taking care of her daughters herself. She was not about to give up or complain. And she definitely wasn't going to confess that she was paying Luvie not to come.

"How much weight have you lost?" Bitsy asked. "It looks like the pounds are just falling off you."

"I'm not sure," Nikki said as she piled the girls' plastic dishes and sippy cups in the sink then set the girls on the floor with a few favorite toys. Between finishing details for the fashion show and organizing a more comprehensive vintage and retro section for the gift shop while staying on top of feeding the girls, making sure they had playtime, and attempting to keep them on a schedule, she rarely thought about food. She couldn't remember the last time she'd stepped on the scale.

She startled when the phone rang, then drew a calming breath. She was going to have to control her nerves and put on her game face before she talked to Joe. She also needed to make sure Bitsy didn't give anything away.

"So, I'm going to let the girls FaceTime with their dad and then I'll hand him over to you," she said.

"Great, thanks." Bitsy tipped her wineglass to her lips.

"But please don't mention that Luvie hasn't been here, okay?" Nikki said as casually as she could, given her skittering nerves. "I don't want him to worry. Or feel like he has to come home. I'm sure Luvie will be feeling better soon."

Bitsy looked at her. Nikki looked back.

Bitsy hesitated then nodded. "Okay. Whatever you say. But . . ."

"Hi," Nikki said cheerfully to Joe. "Bitsy's here, and I'm just getting the girls settled so they can talk to you. Where are you?" She put the phone on speaker so they could hear his answer, propped it up on the coffee table, then scooped up both girls. As soon as she had them seated on either side of her on the sofa, she picked up the phone and held it in front of her so that they could all see and hear each other. As the girls broke into gummy smiles,

Nikki slowed her breathing, formed a less gummy smile of her own, and told herself that not mentioning Luvie's absence was only a lie of omission and wasn't hurting anyone.

• • •

Bitsy sipped her glass of wine and nibbled on the food she'd brought while Nikki and the girls chatted with Joe. It was adorable, really, the two babies sitting on either side of their mother, all three of them straining toward their father's face on the screen, the way they broke into smiles at the rise and fall of his voice.

So different from her own childhood during which her parents had left her largely in the care of a succession of nannies who were often as efficient, but rarely as warm or nurturing, as the absent Luvie. Nannies who'd seemed so wonderful in comparison to the boarding schools that had followed. And now she'd never have children, never get the chance to do better than her parents had. The best she could hope for was to regain some of what her husband had stolen, divorce him, and hopefully see him punished so that she could move on.

And what about Bertie? Were he and Delilah parents? Did he dote on their child the way Joe doted on Sofia and Gemma? Bile rose in her throat at the thought. She turned away as Nikki told the twins to say night-night to their daddy, and tried to ignore the stab of jealousy that pierced her at the giggles and exaggerated kissing sounds that accompanied their good-bye to Joe.

"I'm going to get them in the tub. Come on back when you're finished." Nikki handed her the phone with a tired but encouraging smile. "Maybe we'll have good news to toast."

"Hi, Bitsy."

"Hi, Joe." She smiled at Joe's image on the screen, but could feel her pulse racing as she dropped back into the dinette chair. "Anything to report?"

"Yes," he said with a smile of his own. "Things are moving even faster than I'd hoped."

"Really?" She sat up straighter in the chair.

He nodded. "I reached out to a former agent who retired to the Caymans. He knows the players there pretty well and promised to make sure Bertie hears about the investment opportunity we designed for him. He'll be telling him that the principal, that's me, will be in Grand Cayman the middle of next week to take meetings."

Bitsy could barely speak. "I can't believe this is actually happening."

"I'm planning to play hard to get, but I'll meet with him before next weekend to present the deal. And I've got the computer guy I told you about on standby. Timing and precision will be critical."

"Oh, gosh. That's great." She smiled. "I'm so excited my hands are shaking."

Joe smiled back. "There are no guarantees, Bitsy. Things can always go south. But I think we've got a good shot. We have the perfect bait. And I have every intention of setting the hook."

"Thank you so much, Joe." Her voice was almost as wobbly as her hands. "I can't tell you how much I appreciate you getting involved in this."

"It's my pleasure. Bertie has a lot to answer for. I believe in making the bad guys pay. I'll keep you posted." There was a hesitation. "I hope you don't mind my asking you a favor in return?"

"Of course, Joe. Anything."

"Will you keep an eye on Nikki and the girls? And let me know if they need anything?"

"Sure." Bitsy almost choked on the word.

"I told her before I left to have Luvie as many hours as she needs her. I worry about her getting overwhelmed. But she can be so stubborn. Is everything okay there?"

"Um, yeah," Bitsy said nodding. "As far as I can tell everybody's fine."

"Do you know what time Luvie left today?" he asked.

"Um, no." The lie stuck briefly in her throat, but she reminded herself it was only meant to keep Joe from worrying. "She wasn't here when I arrived," she said slightly more truthfully, praying as she smiled that Joe couldn't read her face as easily via a phone screen as he might in person.

"Okay, thanks." He gave her a long look, though she might have been imagining it. "I'll keep you posted."

Joe hung up and Bitsy tidied up the kitchen and wiped down the table, wishing she could wipe away the lie she'd just told. Then she poured two generous glasses of wine and headed back to the girls' bathroom. But when she got there the bathroom was empty. She followed a trail of discarded clothing, damp towels, and a mixture of music and babbling into the pink-and-white-striped nursery. The mobiles, with their dangling stuffed tools and sea creatures, revolved above the cribs, and a selection of children's nighttime music played quietly on an Amazon Echo. The twins stood in their cribs, holding on to the railings, bending and flexing their knees in a bob and weave that might be dancing. Their mother sat in the cushioned glider. Her head lolled to one side. Her eyes were closed; her mouth hung open. She was snoring.

Resisting the urge to take out her cell phone and shoot a few photos, Bitsy picked up the afghan that had slipped to the floor and draped it gently over Nikki. Then she went to Sofia and Gemma, gave them kisses good night and pressed a finger to her lips.

"Go to sleep now, okay? It looks like your mommy needs some zzzzz's."

• • •

It was finally Friday of the week that Kyra had begun to think would never end. Each day the mood on set got tenser. The director grew grimmer. The shooting schedule became more fluid, constantly changing as they tried to make up time, and rumors of budget overruns ran rampant.

Dustin had flubbed his lines twice in today's final scene in the amusement park. Afterward he'd had a complete and utter meltdown that was eerily reminiscent of Daniel's tirade at the extra. Only Dustin's tirade had been aimed at Brandon after the First AD had explained as gently as possible that they didn't have time to do another take and that the mistake would get fixed in editing. That tirade had been full of a four-year-old's version of swear words.

"I wanna go back to my trailer!" Dustin's voice was almost hoarse now from screaming.

"We're not going anywhere until you apologize to Brandon." Kyra tried to keep her voice calm and even despite the fact that she'd repeated these exact words five or six times now.

"Don't wanna 'pologize!" Dustin's chin jutted out in a fair imitation of his father when he didn't get what he wanted.

"Well, you need to. When you yell you hurt people's feelings. We're going to stay right here until you apologize and promise not to ever do that again." Kyra plopped down on the closest director's chair and closed her eyes. The better to hold back tears. Or prevent herself from shouting back at Dustin. She had no idea whether she was handling this properly, but had been unable to think of any other course of action. She had no experience with discipline since Dustin, who'd always been surrounded by adoring adults eager to do whatever he asked, had so rarely needed it. But she was determined not to coddle Dustin the way that Tonja and the rest of the crew seemed to coddle his father. She'd called and texted her mother thirty minutes ago asking for instructions, but so far there'd been no answer.

Dustin threw himself on the grass. He rolled around a couple of times then kicked his arms and legs. Textbook tantrum. The kind you saw in the movies.

Kyra cringed. It took everything she had not to go yank him

off the ground and . . . It was the uncertainty of what would come next that stopped her. That and the number of people watching. She sat frozen, her eyes on her son, trying to maintain at least some semblance of outward calm despite the pounding of her heart and the churning of her stomach.

After what felt like a lifetime later, the tantrum slipped a couple of notches on the Richter scale. Kyra was just starting to think he might finally be winding down to a stop when Daniel appeared. Ignoring her, he squatted down next to Dustin. "What's wrong, little man?" he asked quietly. "Just tell me what you want and it's yours."

"I wanna go to my trailer right now! And I don't wanna apologize!" Dustin spit out with a glance at her out of the corner of his eye.

Daniel rocked up to his feet and stood. He did not look at Kyra. "No problem. Done and done."

Dustin looked surprised. Kyra flushed with anger. Willing herself to ignore their audience, she got up and walked to her son and his father. Quietly she said, "There is a problem and this isn't done. Not until he gets up and apologizes to Brandon."

"That's ridiculous. Everyone's staring. It's better to end this now," Daniel said.

"No, it's not," she said, though her heart was still pounding and she wasn't at all sure what she'd do if Daniel simply ignored her and scooped Dustin up and carried him away. She spoke carefully and quietly so that no one else but Dustin could hear them. "Because then he'll think it's okay to do this anytime he doesn't get his way." She stared into Daniel's eyes and saw him realize that the comment was aimed at him and his behavior. "I can't let you let him off the hook."

"My God, you're serious," Daniel said.

She nodded. Daniel turned and left.

If not for their audience, she might already have fallen back into the director's chair, because her knees felt like Jell-O and she had the beginnings of a killer headache. Instead she took a deep breath and looked down. Dustin was lying on his back staring up at the sky. The clothes he'd worn in the problematic scene and was supposed to wear in the next one were now wrinkled and filthy. His face was streaked with dirt and tears. Twigs and gravel stuck to his curls. Part of her desperately wanted to go pick him up in her arms and rock and comfort him. The other part wanted to disavow having given birth to him.

It was Brandon who walked over to him and offered a hand up. "If you're done now, we need to change your wardrobe and get you cleaned up."

Dustin sighed and accepted his hand, letting the AD pull him to his feet. "I'm sorry, Brandon. I don't really think you're a poopy head."

"Apology accepted," Brandon said drily. "I'm only a poopy head on Tuesdays and Thursdays. I've never been called one on Friday before."

He smiled crookedly at Kyra.

"I'm sorry," she said wearily. "I think the pressure's getting to all of us." She lifted Dustin up in her arms. His head fell against her shoulder and he shuddered out a breath.

"That it is," Brandon said. "And unlike Dustin, some of us are old enough not to give in to it." He gave her another crooked smile. "You, my friend, have nerves of steel. And you have won a day off. I talked to Tonja and she agrees that Dustin doesn't need to work tomorrow. We can shoot around him."

"That's good." Kyra smiled back at Brandon. But at this point a day off was like sticking part of a pinkie finger in a dam.

· · ·

It was late that afternoon before Maddie was able to return Kyra's call. She'd worked herself into a bit of a state imagining all kinds of worst-case scenarios by the time her daughter answered.

"Kyra? I'm so sorry I'm so late in getting back to you. We're in Arizona and it was a free day so we went to Sedona and the Grand Canyon. I just picked up your messages. Are you both okay?"

"Well, I haven't slit my wrists yet and I haven't killed anyone else, either, so I think that's a yes."

"And Dustin?"

"Well, that's a little more complicated. I mean, I knew this wasn't going to be easy, but I spent such a short amount of time on *Halfway Home* and I was so starstruck while I was there that I didn't fully get how far removed from real life a movie set is. Or how you can't escape from the people you're working with."

Maddie heard the catch in Kyra's voice. "Back at you. A concert tour is its own universe, too. And standard rules of behavior don't seem to apply. Sometimes that's truly wonderful," she admitted. "But you get so insulated, so removed from everyday life. And there are all these people swirling around you and running and fetching if you even look like you might want something. I can see how easy it would be to completely fall off the rails. Anyway, what's going on?"

"Oh, God," Kyra said. "Just hearing your voice makes me want to cry. Scratch that. I *am* crying."

"Aww, honey. What's happened?"

"It's not any one thing really," Kyra said. "But we're apparently over budget and behind schedule and Daniel, well, he's not exactly in control of himself or particularly able to make decisions the way he needs to. It's a mess." Her swallow was audible. "He had this big meltdown on set the other day. And Dustin had one today. I've never seen him like that and I didn't know what to do or how to handle it. And everybody was watching. I hope it doesn't end up all over social media like Daniel's did." There was another shaky breath. "I tried not to give in to him, and I did make him apologize to the person he was nasty to, but I don't know, he's not exactly getting lessons from his father in good behavior plus he's still twisting himself up in knots wanting to please him and get attention and . . ."

Kyra's rush of words trailed off, in a huge exhalation of breath. "Sorry. We made it through today. And they've reworked the schedule to give Dustin Saturday and Sunday off even though they're having to shoot around him. Tonja did that. Not Daniel, Tonja!" Kyra presented this as if it were one more insult or tragedy. "What should I do, Mom?"

Maddie would have liked nothing more than to hold her daughter in her arms and smooth her hair off her face like she had when she was a child. Trying to offer comfort long-distance was not particularly effective on either end. "I'm not sure there's anything else to do, Kyra. You're doing what needs to be done. And since you asked, I'm glad you're focusing on Dustin and helping him with his behavior instead of worrying about other people's reactions—or Daniel. It's hard to do, but it's important. And I'm glad that you'll both have the weekend free no matter who organized it. After that you're down to two weeks. You're almost there, sweetheart. And you're not responsible for the movie, or Daniel's behavior or anything but Dustin and yourself."

"I knew I needed to talk to you," Kyra said quietly. "I don't think I even realized how much."

"Do you want me to come, Kyra?" Maddie made the offer without even thinking of Will or his reaction, but this time she was fairly certain it was for the right reasons. And not out of fear.

"No. I . . . I'm sorry my first instinct is to call you when something goes wrong. It's not very grown up, is it? You just happen to be the wisest, most together person I know."

If Maddie had been standing, the burst of love she felt might have knocked her down. "Considering that I'm still grappling with what I want to be when I grow up, I think you've got plenty of time to figure it out, sweetie. And I think you're doing a great job with Dustin."

Emotion clogged Maddie's throat. "I'm very grateful that we're close enough for you to want my advice. And honored that you think I'm 'wise and together.'" A smile twisted her lips. "Guess I fooled you."

"Completely. And here I thought for sure you had all the answers." Kyra's teasing tone turned into a sigh. "I don't even think I have the strength to get us home. But I hate the idea of staying here." She hesitated. "Do you think it would be wrong if I invited Troy to come up here for the weekend?"

"Wrong because?" Maddie asked.

"I don't know," Kyra replied. "Wrong because he seems to be so sure what he wants, but I'm way too hazy on who I am at the moment let alone exactly what kind of relationship I might want with him?"

Maddie smiled once more. "If absolute certainty of who we are, what we want, and what's supposed to come next were requirements for being in a relationship, I'd have to give up Will this minute."

As the words left her mouth she realized just how true they were. She'd been so worried about finally finding a purpose, figuring out what she should *do,* that she'd acted as if her life up until now was somehow less valid than whatever came next. But she'd nurtured her family, raised two children who'd become stellar adults, and she had refused to give up when the life they'd known crumbled.

That was who she was. That was the foundation on which she would continue to build. No matter what path she chose now or whom she chose to travel it with, she would always be a mother and grandmother first. And that was nothing to be ashamed of.

# Thirty

The last thing Avery expected to do that Saturday was have a good time. Especially since the day started with a very loud and persistent pounding on her door. When she threw it open, the completely unapologetic and uninvited Ray Flamingo and Bitsy Baynard marched in, poured coffee down Avery's throat, then practically pushed her into the shower. When she came out clean, but still fuming, a second cup of coffee awaited. So did an outfit that she never would have worn on a normal Saturday. With shoes. Completely accessorized.

"Put it on!" Ray's voice carried from the living room. "Or one of us will come in and dress you!" There was laughter. "Don't make us draw straws!"

She'd come out dressed and grumbling, then whined all the way out of the cottage and into Ray's classic powder blue Cadillac convertible that matched the cashmere V-neck sweater he was wearing.

"Where exactly are you taking me? And why?" she demanded as they "helped" her into the backseat. "You do realize kidnapping is a felony, right? Because I happen to know someone who works for the FBI."

"This is an intervention," Bitsy said. "Because you need to get out."

"We've got a whole day planned for you. It's meant to be fun," Ray added. "So I suggest you try to enjoy it."

"I was enjoying being in my bed," she huffed as Ray turned onto Pass-a-Grille Way. "And I'm not sure if you noticed or not, but I was asleep. And I was really enjoying that, too."

Ray took the Bayway to 275 and she tried again. "Seriously, where are we going?"

"It's a surprise," Ray said.

"A good one," Bitsy added.

The whining slowed as they exited to downtown. It stopped altogether when they were welcomed to the Parkshore Grill and seated at a prime sidewalk table beneath a bright blue umbrella with a view over Straub Park to the yacht basin. Lunch was long and leisurely. Dessert turned out to be a private tour of the nearby Salvador Dalí Museum, which was perched on the waterfront.

Their docent was a cheerful and knowledgeable client of Ray's named Ingrid, who let them linger outside to admire the building, a magnificent thick-walled rectangle that seemed to flow upward into a free-form glass bubble known as the "enigma," which Ingrid informed them was intended as a tribute and reference to the dome atop Dalí's museum in Spain.

Avery could have spent the rest of the day and those to come marveling at the work of art that architect Yann Weymouth had created as well as the spectacular works inside, but she made no protest at all when Ray and Bitsy informed her that it was time to move on. The day had been so unexpectedly spectacular that she didn't even ask, or care, where they were going next.

When they got out of the Caddy she looked across Second Avenue. Her eyes widened to take in the massive building. She clutched Ray's arm as they crossed the street. "I've driven by it a couple of times, but I've never been this close before."

"Didn't I tell you she'd react this way?" Ray said to Bitsy as they crossed the street.

On the sidewalk he turned to Avery. "I knew you'd like it."

"Like it?" She still clutched his arm. "I love it. If it weren't so big I'd hug it!"

"Big" was an understatement. The building took up a large part of Second Avenue South and Fifth Street in an up-and-coming part of downtown. Like the Don CeSar and Bella Flora on St. Pete Beach and The Vinoy in northeast St. Petersburg, it was built in the Mediterranean Revival style with thick plaster walls, arched windows, wreathed columns, iron balconettes, and a multilevel roof and jutting bell tower. Unlike those other properties it had not yet been restored. A No Trespassing sign hung on a locked wire fence that stretched across the main entrance steps. Doors and windows were boarded up; her walls were chipped, pockmarked, and marred by graffiti. Her barrel-tiled roofs were covered in a patchwork of tarps. But all Avery saw were the beautiful bones of the structure. Its potential.

Her first complete thought was, *I'd give anything to get my hands on this building.* Her second, *Chase would absolutely love it.*

"I know what you're thinking right now," Ray said smugly beside her.

"Do not." She continued to study the building. Itched to get inside it. With Chase.

"Do too," Ray said. "You could call him right now, you know. Or text him a shot of the exterior and invite him to come walk through it with us."

Avery tore her eyes from the building. "Walk through it? We get to go inside?"

"I've done work for a Realtor who's a good friend of the current owner. She said she'd let us in."

"Even though we're not buyers."

"Even so." He smiled. "I had to think of something that would cheer you up. Bitsy suggested the Dalí Museum. Maddie suggested maybe touring one of the older neighborhoods. Then I thought this might be even better."

"You were right."

Ray's Realtor friend Justine was a tall, trim, silver-haired woman with genteel good looks and a ready smile, which she flashed when she launched into an enthusiastic and docent-worthy description of the property.

"You are looking at what was originally a YMCA completed in 1927 with the help of $550,000 in community donations. It was designed by Minnesota professor Clarence Brown and local architect Archie G. Parish, who designed many of the original downtown structures. It's approximately 51,000 gross square feet and is four stories tall, with an original basement pool and a fifth-story bell tower. Many of the original Spanish tiles were imported from Seville, and it was designated a historic landmark in 1991."

Justine unlocked the padlock and led them up the concrete front steps to the first-floor entrance. "The building has changed hands quite a few times. There've been plans to turn it into condos, a boutique hotel, a music museum, and a performance venue."

She paused in the tiled lobby and Avery took in the cypress beams, the arched doorways, the ten-light, paired and ribbon steel casement windows with their decorative arches and lintels. The bricked courtyard sat firmly in its center.

"As you can see, a lot of interior demolition has already been done and some restoration work has been started. But things tend to get stalled out. People run out of money and enthusiasm." The Realtor smiled. "In my opinion, it's just waiting for the right person to come along. Someone who recognizes the building's true potential."

"Is it for sale?" Bitsy asked.

"Not at the moment," Justine said. "But I think it could be. For the right price. And the right buyer." She looked around. "My friend really wanted to see this building brought back to life."

"Any idea what the right price might be?" Bitsy asked.

"Well, I can tell you that my friend paid 1.4 million and planned to put another six million into it, but real estate is all about supply and demand. There aren't too many buildings of this ilk. But then not everyone is willing to consider preservation."

Avery closed her eyes and allowed herself to imagine it. It was one of the few times in her life she wished she were wealthy. "I wouldn't mind having seven or eight million disposable dollars to put into this beauty right now."

"Me, either," Bitsy said.

"If things work out, you could," Ray said to Bitsy.

"Well, if that happens and there's actually a serious amount of money left, I'll buy it for you, Avery. It could be a birthday present."

"Why thank you, Bitsy." Avery smiled. "That's very friendly of you, but I think a tiny house would be easier to wrap."

They laughed. But as they moved deeper into the building, Avery looked past the peeling, water-stained plaster, the missing ceilings and windows, the scarred floors and broken tiles to focus on the ornate decorative iron and cast stone panels and carvings, the basement pool, the central courtyards, the fabulous curved walls that led out to the rooftop terrace.

"The way downtown is growing I could see this as a really great mixed-use space," Bitsy said as Justine escorted them out and re-padlocked the gate. "With all the fabulous charm and historical details restored."

After they thanked and said good-bye to the Realtor, Avery stood staring at the building. For a moment she let herself imagine what it would be like to take on this project with Chase. What a dream that would be. Not to mention a restoration worth documenting and maybe even televising.

"Call him." Ray's words yanked her out of the daydream. "This is breaking my heart. *You're* breaking my heart."

"Then I think you need to toughen up a little, Ray," she said, stung.

"No, I don't," he protested. "You just need to locate your backbone. Your mother would not want to see you wussing out like this. It's depressing. Deirdre made some really poor choices and plenty of mistakes. But she didn't waffle."

"Don't bring Deirdre into this," Avery sputtered. "You spent all day forcing me to relax and forget and now you're ruining it. Why did you even bother to get me out of bed?" She turned to Bitsy for help.

"Sorry," Bitsy said. "But Ray's right. It's so hard to find the right person. When the shoe fits you've got to wear it. Or at least put your foot in it." She snorted. "Okay, enough with the shoes. But when you love someone you have to at least try. I had some really great years with Bertie, a good life. Right up until the moment he fled with another woman and everything I owned. I would have hated to miss those good years."

"You can stop helping now," Ray said. "But I think the shoe analogy wasn't bad."

"God, when did everybody get so pushy and philosophical?" Avery cried.

"When you started being afraid of your emotional shadow." This came from Ray, but Bitsy nodded in agreement.

Before Avery could come up with a suitable answer or call an Uber or do something that might halt this conversation, Ray pulled out his phone, scrolled through his contacts, and selected one.

"Oh, no!" she said when she saw Chase's name pop up on the screen. "This is not going to happen. Definitely not now." And yet she stood frozen as he touched the screen again then held the phone out to her. When she refused to take it, he held the ringing phone up to her ear.

Her feet were still rooted to the sidewalk when the ringing stopped. Before she even opened her mouth, a voice she'd hoped to never hear again chirped, "Hi, this is Chase's phone. At the moment, he's too lazy to answer. How can I help you?"

Avery's stomach roiled. She swallowed hard, barely managing to keep down the lovely lunch she'd eaten earlier. With a strangled curse she turned and strode away from Ray and his phone, drawing in great gulps of air as she put distance between herself and the sickeningly cheerful voice that belonged to the relationship-wrecking, boyfriend-stealing Riley Hancock.

• • •

Troy Matthews arrived at the Winter Haven cottage on Saturday with a cocky smile on his face and his arms filled with bags of groceries he apparently intended to cook. He'd barely handed them to Kyra when Max and Dustin jumped all over him. His laugh filled the living room as he tossed Dustin over his shoulder then left him dangling down his back while he pretended not to be able to find him. Which set Dustin to giggling and Max to barking.

"I'm surprised Joan let you in," Kyra said when the hilarity began to die down.

"It must have been the chocolates I brought her. And the fact that I didn't protest too strenuously when she strip-searched me." Troy winked. "At least not the first time."

"Ha!" Kyra rolled her eyes but she couldn't hold back her smile. Already his good humor had brightened and filled the small, silent space. Best of all, he didn't allude to last night's tear-filled invitation or the details he'd wrung out of her.

"Whadda you wanna do, Troy?" Dustin asked eagerly and with a smile that dissipated the tension she'd been living with since the previous morning's public meltdown.

"Well," he said. "We can take the canoe and get a little paddling in. Or we can throw the football for a while. Or maybe play a little corn hole."

"Corn hole?" Dustin chortled. "I love corn hole!"

"I know," Troy said. "I brought you a set. We can play right now if you like, but I don't want you thinking I'm planning to show you any mercy."

"Let's play!" Dustin shouted. "And *then* we can go canoeing. And after that we can throw the football. And . . ."

"Right. Got it. Let's go set up the corn hole and then we'll challenge your mother to a game."

"All right! Let's go!" Dustin grabbed Troy's hand and dragged him to the door. Max went with them hitting everything he passed with a tail too happy to be still.

All of the promised activities followed. And were topped off with steak kabobs on the grill and s'mores for dessert.

"Wow," Kyra said after Troy returned from carrying an exhausted and happy Dustin to bed. "You do know how to pack a lot into half a day."

"I call it intensive action therapy," he said, plopping down on the sofa beside her. "You just keep moving and doing things that are supposed to be fun until they are. It's sort of the whistling in the dark of happiness."

"It certainly worked on Dustin. And just seeing him smiling and happy, well, I can't tell you how huge that is."

"I guess my work here is done then." He smiled but made no move to leave.

Kyra smiled back, looking into his eyes, frighteningly glad that he was there. "I have to say it's kind of hard to imagine someone who comes from your sort of background having to work at finding a way to be happy."

"On the contrary, my dear Watson," he said in an extremely poor British accent, and for the first time she noticed how often he hid the truth inside a joke. "In my experience, rich people aren't necessarily happier than others, they're just better at acting happy. Because nobody really wants to hear some rich asshole complaining about how hard it is to have a ton of money.

There is zero sympathy for poor little rich kids and even less for rich adults. Ask Bitsy sometime."

He softened the truth he'd just shared with another impish smile, offering another glimpse inside the man she'd made the mistake of writing off as uncomplicated, uncharitable, and unthinking.

They sat quietly facing each other. He looked into her eyes in a way that made her think he could see all the way inside her. To a place she'd been careful not to examine too closely.

He leaned forward tentatively. Before she fully grasped his intent, he kissed her, his lips firm and warm and stunningly gentle. "There," he murmured against her lips. "Now we've got that whole first 'official' kiss thing out of the way." She felt his lips smile against hers. "And it only took me three years to work up to it."

She burst out laughing.

"Again, not exactly the reaction I was hoping for. Unless, of course, you believe as I do that laughter is a great natural aphrodisiac."

Kyra laughed. "If you had told me three years ago when you were filming Dustin at every opportunity that I would ever want you to kiss anything but my ass, I would have thought you were on drugs."

"I'd be glad to kiss your ass. Do you want me to turn my head while you bare it?" Again, the teasing tone with a truth wrapped up inside.

For a moment she thought, why not? She was single and over twenty-one. And it seemed laughter was in fact a turn-on. Especially when coupled with kindness. And twinkling blue eyes. And then there was that declaration of long-held feelings for her. Besides, her brain jumped from the man in front of her to the one who had been in her head now for so many years; Daniel was no doubt in bed with his wife this very minute. An image of Daniel and Tonja locked in each other's arms formed before she could stop it.

Troy shook his head. Sat back. His eyes stopped twinkling. "You need to be careful what you wish for, Kyra. I don't think you'd be all that happy if you ever got it."

She sat where she was, speechless.

"All righty then." He sat back, putting more space between them. "Shall we flip a coin for who gets the bed and who gets the sofa?" His tone was once again teasing; his eyes were not.

"No. But I will bring you a blanket and a pillow." She jumped up, unsure whether what she felt was regret or relief, and went to retrieve the bedding. When she returned, his smile and a portion of the twinkle were back in place. "I hope you don't snore too loudly," he said as she left. "It's a very unattractive trait in a woman. One I might be compelled to document and share on social media."

"Ditto!" Kyra teased back, telling herself as she walked to her bedroom that it was better this way, less complicated. She was not disappointed. Not one little bit.

But she left her bedroom door open a crack. Just in case.

. . .

Bitsy knocked quietly on Nikki's door. She'd learned the hard way that ringing the doorbell could spell disaster at this time of evening if Nikki had managed to get the twins to sleep.

The door opened silently. Nikki looked like a bag lady only without a bag. Unless you counted the ones under her eyes.

Yawning, Nikki stepped back so Bitsy could enter. Even in the dim light she looked unkempt and possibly unwashed. Toys littered the floor and almost every other flat surface. Dirty dishes teetered in the sink. The hall closet that held the washer and dryer was open. Dirty laundry spilled all over the floor.

"Have you already talked to Joe tonight?" Bitsy asked.

"Yes. Before I put the girls down. All three of us go a little crazy at the sound of his voice. It's kind of Pavlovian how we react every time the phone rings." Nikki frowned. "I hope we're not setting them up to be emotionally tied to the telephone."

"I think that happens anyway before they become teenagers." Bitsy once again took in her friend's greasy hair and haggard expression. "It doesn't look like you bathed or put on makeup before you FaceTimed."

"Usually I do." She yawned. "But sometimes if I run out of time, I just keep the shot tight on the girls." She swayed slightly on her feet.

"Nikki, this is not good. Tell me what I can do to help! And where is Luvie? Did she get flattened by a bus? Is she lying in a hospital somewhere? Because I can't imagine anything less would keep her away from Sofia and Gemma for so long."

Nikki shrugged, but she didn't make a move to sit down or even offer Bitsy a seat. Which would require clearing away the detritus that seemed to be everywhere. "She's got the flu. A really bad case. She's determined not to infect the girls."

"How are you handling everything you're working on and taking care of the girls alone twenty-four-seven?"

"Obviously I'm not doing it all that well. I just keep going until they finally fall asleep. Women do it all the time." Nikki yawned.

"Nothing personal, but I think a lot of those women are younger. And not necessarily mothers of twins." She peered more closely at Nikki, who had always been so beautifully put together. "I hope Luvie is able to come back to work soon. I don't really want to be around when Joe finds out you've been on your own all week."

"Yeah, we definitely don't want Joe to know that." Nikki emitted another huge yawn. "There's something I . . . oh, yeah." She patted her robe pockets, finally producing a tiny triangle of a page torn from a magazine, which she handed to Bitsy. A phone number was scrawled across it. "He asked me to have you call him at this number. And I'm pretty sure he said he'd already talked to Bertie."

Bitsy recognized the Cayman country code. Gulped. But before she raced back to her own place to make the call, she slid an arm around Nikki's shoulders. "Tell me what I can do to help."

Nikki sighed. "Well, I need two more models for the fashion show—a size ten and a size twelve. And someone to help inventory the new beachwear I ordered. Oh, and when I find it"—her eyes skimmed over the trashed living area—"will you look over my commentary for the show? I think I've got most of the outfit descriptions in but it's pretty rough."

"Of course. And maybe Avery and I could come babysit one evening so you can get out for a couple hours. Neither of us are very experienced, but eleven-year-old girls do it, right? Together we should be able to handle it."

"Sure. Thanks." Nikki yawned again.

"All right." She hugged Nikki good-bye, eager now to speak with Joe. As she left for her own place, she vowed to help pick up the slack and make sure Nikki took some time off. She shoved her unease about Nikki aside as she dialed the number Joe had left.

Joe sounded far away but excited. "So, I sat down with Bertrand this morning. The man's been living high but I guess the more you have, the more you want."

She wanted to ask how Bertie had looked, how he'd sounded, whether he'd come alone, if he'd mentioned Delilah or that he was a father, but Joe didn't offer any of those details and she couldn't bring herself to ask.

Neither could she bring herself to tell him what he'd most want to know—that for some reason Luvie was missing in action and his wife was clearly getting snowed under. Because she was small and selfish. And didn't want him running home before he'd taken care of Bertie.

"I told him I really wasn't sure there was room for him in this deal and that I was only talking to serious players," Joe continued.

"And how did he take that?" Bitsy asked, already imagining the look of irritation that would have shown first in his eyes and then, if he wasn't careful, spread across his face.

"Not well," Joe acknowledged. "Or given our goal, just right. He made a point of letting me know that the investment I was looking for was basically 'chump change.'"

"Yeah." She thought about her husband and how wrapped up he'd become in demonstrating his cleverness and his supposed business acumen. So many things she had either missed or gotten used to.

"If he wants in, he'll have to transfer the money from his account one week from today at exactly eleven A.M. And I made sure it was a big enough amount that he'd have to tap into the primary account and not the smaller ones he's been using for day-to-day living expenses. The freelancer will be standing by and ready to empty that account as soon as Bertie accesses it. Bertie stole this money so it's not as if he'll be able to complain to anyone. But should it ever come up, I will disavow any knowledge of your efforts to reclaim what belongs to you."

Bitsy could hardly breathe as she heard the words she'd thought would never come. When she thanked Joe and hung up, she realized that if all went well, in just one week she'd no longer be broke. Even if she had a few less zeros attached to her bottom line than she had before, she'd finally be herself again.

# Thirty-one

Kyra felt like a runner in a first marathon for which she had not adequately trained. She had run too hard and too fast at the beginning. She had stumbled and encountered unexpected hazards. But the finish line was no longer so far distant as to be unimaginable. She no longer cared whether they reached it at a run, walk, or crawl.

With less than two weeks to go, seven to eight days of shooting left for Dustin, she had traded in her mantra of *half full, half full* for *almost there, almost done*. It echoed in her head when Daniel insisted on take after take, overshooting every scene from every possible angle in an attempt to put decision making off until later. Those looking for immediate answers or action had learned to talk to Tonja.

Morale was low. The early days of perfect takes were far behind them as they limped toward the finish line. But the publicity machine continued at warp speed, churning out photo op after photo op and interview after interview, all of it carefully choreographed to counter the reports of budget overruns and schedule delays that leaked from the set along with the allusions to Daniel's erratic performance in front of the camera and lack of talent behind it.

Today the "friendlies"—the cherry-picked entertainment reporters who could be counted on not to ask the difficult questions—had been invited onto the soundstage for a chance to shoot photos and do brief interviews with the principal actors. Kyra sat in a chair just outside the spill of light where Dustin could see her. There to meet his eyes each time he searched for her. There after each forced smile and every inane question. Even a four-year-old recognized when the same question got asked for the tenth time. And her four-year-old had learned how to deliver the answer like he delivered his lines—as if they came without effort and he sincerely meant them, but she could see the calculation that had begun to sneak into his eyes, the effort it took to appear genuine and enthusiastic when you no longer were. This was a skill that might prove useful later in life, but it wasn't a skill a child should develop. Especially not her child.

"That's great, Dustin. Can you smile up at your dad?" a photographer asked. "Right. Good, that's good. Okay, can we get Chris and Derek and Tonja in the shot, too?"

They rearranged the principals all over the set for stills then opened up to questions. The video team, who were ever present in the same way Troy had always been on *Do Over*, documented the press conference for *The Making of The Exchange*. Only Troy's instructions at the time had been to catch them at their worst while this crew was there to make sure the cast and crew looked good. For a tiny moment she let herself think about Troy and their first "official" kiss.

The whir of motor drives and digital flashes bounced off the hard surfaces of the set. Daniel used his million-dollar smile to good effect and even called the entertainment press by name. His slightly furrowed brow and distracted air were obvious only to those who knew him well.

"So how far over budget are you right now?" The voice came from the darkness not far from where Kyra sat. The reporter stepped into the light, someone she'd never seen before and clearly not a friendly.

There was a buzz of speculation. Daniel continued to smile,

but he was already stepping out of position. At a nod from his wife he left.

"I'll be happy to answer that question. Wouldn't want you reporting rumors." Tonja stood her ground. She leaned down and whispered something in Dustin's ear, and he walked off the set and came to Kyra. Kind of like a mother lion letting the cubs escape before taking on the predator that threatened.

Kyra didn't wait to see how Tonja dealt with the reporter, whether she would kill him with kindness or devour him and pick his bones clean—when someone sacrificed themselves, you didn't linger to watch them get mauled. She and Dustin headed to the trailer.

A short while later someone from wardrobe came to take Dustin for a fitting, and she puttered about repeating her mantra, trying to stay busy so she wouldn't be counting the hours and minutes that remained in the marathon.

When the trailer door opened behind her, she expected it to be Dustin. But when she looked up, Daniel stood just inside the doorway. He looked tired and disheveled, but as she watched he quirked one dark eyebrow upward. "I feel like Tarzan coming home at the end of a long day." His tone turned mock serious, his voice deeper. "Jane, it's a jungle out there."

She laughed but wondered if he, too, had been aware of Tonja the lioness allowing him to scamper off to safety, or whether he'd grown too used to being protected to notice.

The way he looked at her made it clear that his wife was the last person on his mind at the moment.

She felt a quick stab of shame. But even disheveled, he was far and away the most attractive man she'd ever met. Despite the feet of clay she now knew were encased inside the expensive loafers, he approached her with complete confidence born of long experience. Her physical reaction was instantaneous and had also been honed over time.

But for the first time as he leaned over to kiss her, she saw him clearly. Not as a handsome prince from a fairy tale, or even as the mega movie star he was, but simply as a man. A man who had taken on a task for which he was not prepared, and who didn't have the backbone to admit it or ask for help or work harder to master it. He was an outrageously attractive man. But he was not a long-term strategic thinker. And he was not a good director, at least not yet. And he was a truly crappy husband.

He looked at her out of eyes that he'd bequeathed to their son, but this time they looked more "troubled child" than "bedroom." He was the kind of man who could gift a dog without asking, throw a tantrum on set without considering the consequences, have affairs with women then go home to his wife and children. He could be fun and generous, but he wasn't the man she'd turned him into in her mind. He was not a prince and he most definitely wasn't the hero he portrayed so well in movies.

When he slid his arms around her and said, "I can't stand thinking of you with Matthews. It drives me absolutely crazy," she didn't fend him off. But her heart didn't pound like it always had. And his kiss was only a kiss, not the earth moving under her feet. It was not a promise of a bright and beautiful future if only they could figure it out. It was a furtive kiss given by a married man running away from reality.

It held none of the unfiltered emotion that had been packed into Troy's.

She dropped her arms and began to step back as a quick knock sounded on the trailer door, but Daniel either hadn't heard the knock or simply didn't care. Still locked in his arms, Kyra raised her eyes and saw Tonja in the entry.

"Really?" Tonja said to Daniel as Kyra jumped away from him. Her eyes were trained on Daniel as she came toward them. "With all the important and necessary things you could be doing right now to ensure the success of our film—this is what you chose to do?"

The words "it's not what it looks like" rose to Kyra's lips, except of course it was exactly what it looked like. The fact that it had felt so different to her didn't seem particularly relevant to either of the Deranian-Kays.

"Brandon's looking for you to discuss the next setup, and then I promised the reporter you blew off five minutes of your time. I've set him straight and he won't be asking you anything problematic." Tonja spoke with total authority and to Kyra's dismay, Daniel left without a backward glance.

Kyra would have liked to leave, too, but Tonja's eyes were now on her, and she knew if there was a tongue-lashing coming, or even the dropping of a nuclear-strength load of f-bombs Tonja had been holding in check, she deserved it. Because now that she'd finally managed to rip the blinders all the way off, she was deeply ashamed and embarrassed by her behavior, horrified that she had insisted on seeing herself as the victim in all her dealings with Tonja, using the actress's aggressive and foulmouthed vindictiveness as proof that she was the evil one.

If Kyra had been his wife and mother of his children, would she have behaved differently? Chosen her words more carefully? She forced herself to meet Tonja's eyes. Then she braced because she owed Daniel's wife the courtesy of listening to whatever she had to say.

"So." Tonja didn't slump or droop as she leaned against the wall of the trailer, but disappointment and weariness were written across her face. "Honestly, I'm almost too exhausted to care right now. Somehow we have to make it through this movie without losing every penny we've put in, our reputations, and our ability to continue to act for a living. Everything's on the line here and I'm not sure if you've noticed, but Daniel is not pulling his weight."

"I do know. And I'm sorry. I . . . this was not what it looked like," she said hurriedly because apparently clichés were clichés for a reason.

"This is exactly what it looked like," Tonja said matter-of-factly. "And this is exactly what he does when things get difficult." She motioned toward Kyra. "You've lasted longer than most. You've been smarter. You haven't given in completely and, of course, you gave him Dustin." Her smile was ironic and as tired as her voice. "And even I have to admit that against all odds, he's a great kid."

"Seriously, Tonja. It's not . . . I don't want . . ." Kyra's voice trailed off as Tonja shrugged.

"There's nothing else to talk about. As far as I'm concerned, once this film is over, you can have him."

. . .

Nikki set Sofia and Gemma on the Sunshine lobby floor to play and turned her attention to the wall she, Bitsy, Avery, and Renée were contemplating. They'd already walked through the ladies' locker room, where the volunteer models for the upcoming fashion show would dress, to figure out where the clothes racks would go. Maddie had agreed to be in charge of matching models to outfits and keeping things on track on the day of the show while Ray would "zhush" and accessorize before passing each model on to Bitsy, who would make sure they hit the runway, or in this case, the circular route around the pool, on cue with Nikki's narrative. Which would be proofed and tweaked as soon as she could find it in the mess that now threatened to swallow the cottage.

She gestured to a section of wall that divided the lobby from the ladies' locker room. "I've been thinking this would be a great space to put a temporary vintage/retro beachwear display when the Franklin Realty people take over the front desk and part of the gift shop area the day of the fashion show. Showing and selling cottages is a top priority.

"But maybe somewhere down the road we could break

through this part of the wall and steal some space from the ladies' locker room to add a fitting room. What do you think?"

Avery measured the space and rapped on the wall in several spots. "It's not load bearing, and I don't think you'd miss the space in the locker room. And there's no way to expand the gift shop near the entrance because it shares its back wall with the dining room."

"Could you give us a price on that?" Renée asked. "The vintage and retro beachwear is selling well and I think it will sell even better after people see it on models during the fashion show."

"Sure." Avery made a few notes on a yellow pad.

Nikki looked down at her own to-do list, which seemed to be growing each day and possibly reproducing at night. "I've got a call into *the Tampa Bay Times* to see if they can include the fashion show in their local events section. I've also asked them to send a photographer to cover the show." She heard a shriek and turned to see Sofia and Gemma attempting to claim and climb onto the same chair. She blew a limp bang out of her eyes and walked over to her daughters, trying to remember as she pulled them apart, plopped them on the floor, and handed them each a baggie of Goldfish crackers when she'd last washed her hair.

"Sorry," she yawned, reaching for the long-cold cup of coffee she'd brought with her, desperate for the extra shot of caffeine she'd come to need in a way she never had before.

The days were just so long and the nights seemed even longer. Every morning she debated whether to call Luvie and pretend they'd just returned. And every morning after that first shot of coffee she told herself she could make it one more day. And she had.

She hated lying to Joe, but it seemed far too late to admit what she'd done. She looked up and saw a woman passing by the plate glass who looked just like Luvie. Except she was wearing oversize sunglasses and a sunhat with a floppy brim that cast her face into shadow.

"What is it?" Bitsy asked. "You have a strange look on your face. Like you saw a ghost or something."

"No. I'm just tired," Nikki said. And possibly hallucinating. Due to guilt.

"Well, nothing personal," Avery said. "But you look like something the cat dragged in."

Bitsy snorted but didn't disagree.

Nikki took another hit of coffee. "Thanks. Nothing personal about that."

"You do look a bit tired," Renée said more tactfully. "When's Luvie coming back?"

"I don't know. She had some sort of complication and she has to take it easy for a while." Nikki barely held back the groan. The lies just kept on coming.

"Have you been to see her?" Renée asked.

"Um, no." Nikki glanced out the window again, but there was no sign of the woman in the floppy hat.

"Hmmmm," Renée said. "Maybe she needs a little matzo ball soup. They don't call it Jewish penicillin for nothing. Where does she live? I could take some over."

"I don't know," Nikki said, relieved to be telling the truth. "I mean, Joe did a background check, and I know there was an address included, but I've never been there. I think she may be in Gulfport."

There was more shrieking. Nikki downed the last of the coffee and went to separate the girls. Which is what she spent a large part of each day doing. "I'm sure she'll be better soon." She couldn't quite let herself envision how the fiction she'd created and fed to Luvie and Joe was going to go down when both of them were back. She could only hope that by then she'd be able to point to the weeks on her own as proof that she didn't need help for so many hours a week. At which time Luvie was going to have to either settle for less time on the clock or . . .

"Have I mentioned how much I appreciate what Joe's doing for me?" Bitsy asked, mercifully changing the subject.

"Of course you have," Nikki replied. "You're a friend, Bitsy. And that means a lot to both of us. Plus, Joe hates cheaters."

Of course, Joe didn't like liars, either. As Nikki had discovered when she'd slipped away and tried to talk her brother into giving himself up instead of telling Joe where she thought he was hiding. And when she'd neglected to mention that her brother had threatened both of them when Nikki had secretly visited him in prison. And the time she'd kept her pregnancy from him, another not-so-small omission that he hadn't taken at all well. The panic she'd been trying to hold back mushroomed inside her. She beat it back. Nothing would be gained by confessing her transgressions now.

. . .

The night before Bertie's trap was set to be sprung, Bitsy lay in bed staring up at the cottage ceiling, listening to Sherlock's snuffling snores and trying to envision a positive outcome. Because Joe had warned her that although Bertie had committed to the deal and seemed to have no apparent qualms, things could always go wrong, that any plan, no matter how well timed or set up, could fail.

She "woke" before dawn, though she didn't actually remember ever sleeping, and stumbled to the coffeemaker. When the sky finally began to lighten, she pulled on clothes and got out Sherlock's leash. They wandered through small alleyways and up and down the short streets finally settling on a bench that overlooked the bay. Together they watched the sun rise, and although she'd never been especially religious, she offered up a small prayer that Joe's plan would go smoothly and that Bertie would finally pay for what he'd done.

Too antsy to sit still any longer, her stomach roiling too intensely to stop for breakfast, she walked slowly back toward the Sunshine, letting Sherlock stop and sniff every bush, every flower, and what might have been every leaf of grass.

Her thoughts were a jumble of fear and hope and memory. The past year had taught her the hot blaze of anger and the encompassing miasma of hurt and pain. She yearned for the icy cold knife-edge of revenge that would cauterize the wounds Bertie had inflicted.

At nine thirty A.M. she ended up back at the cottage with a panting Sherlock mostly because she couldn't think of anywhere else to go and eleven A.M. seemed a lifetime away. She found Avery and Nikki standing outside watching the girls toddle in the still-damp grass.

"I've got coffee and donuts." Avery held up a box and bag from Dunkin' Donuts.

"And I've got Kahlúa and cream to go in the coffee. Or we can just drink it on its own."

Bitsy felt the sting of tears. "I think I could use a little something to steady my nerves." She swallowed. "And something to drown my sorrows just in case."

"No, we're only thinking positive thoughts today," Avery said. "That's a direct order from Maddie. And she made us promise to text or call her . . . after."

Within minutes the coffee had been poured and doctored, and though relaxation was not in the cards, the Kahlúa and coffee did take a bit of the edge off. Bitsy was grateful for the distraction and the much-needed reminder that whatever happened this morning, she was not alone.

At ten thirty they were huddled on the sofa, making stabs at conversation. At ten forty-five a text dinged in from Joe. Her eyes narrowed, part wince, part fear. She didn't breathe again until she'd read it. *All systems go. White hat standing by.*

Relief washed briefly through her. Then her pulse skittered.

Her heart pounded with the force of a drum. Nikki and Avery scooted closer on either side of her until their shoulders and thighs touched.

When the phone rang at 11:10, her hand was cramped and sweaty around her cell phone. Fear shot through her. She wasn't sure she could answer. Avery pried it from her hand, hit "answer," and gave it back. Bitsy managed to raise it to her ear.

"Hello?" The word was a wobble.

"Hi." Joe didn't identify himself but there was no mistaking his voice. There was a brief silence that made her breath catch in her throat. And then Joe said, "So, I'm thinking you might want to check your bank account. Although he doesn't know it yet, your husband just sent you a little something."

She swallowed. "Th . . . th-thank you."

"My pleasure." Joe hung up.

"What happened?"

"Did it work?"

Nikki and Avery's voices were as shaky as her hands as she nodded and logged on to her account.

She cried when she saw all the zeros. Cried even harder when she thought of Bertie, how much she'd loved him, how much she'd once believed he'd loved her.

Nikki and Avery and ultimately, the twins, cried with her. Because friends didn't let friends cry alone.

Her tears slowed as she realized all the things she'd learned because of Bertie's betrayal. That she was someone in her own right. That she was more than her net worth. That she could survive without wealth.

But she was beyond happy that she didn't have to.

# Thirty-two

That night's concert had just ended as Maddie rearranged the platters of food and straightened the stacks of plates and silver on the buffet table set up in the greenroom. After stepping back and eyeing it in part and as a whole, she added the floral arrangement and fruit basket that she'd taken from Will's dressing room.

"The craft service people are starting to look uncomfortable." Lori materialized at her side. "You could just tell them what you'd like done and let them arrange things."

"Oh, I don't mind," she said. In fact, she was grateful to have something to do besides hanging out once the concert was over. "There's another fruit basket at the hotel that could serve twenty, and Will doesn't really notice the flowers. I hate to see these things get wasted. And this way everybody gets to enjoy it."

"True," Lori conceded.

"And you'll make sure the flowers and leftover fruit go to the children's hospital I found, won't you?"

"Absolutely."

"Thank you." Maddie looked up and saw Griff Monroe, a mountain-size man who'd been on the road with one band or another since the early seventies, approaching.

"Please tell me he's not looking for advice on his love life," Lori said.

Maddie smiled. "That would be privileged information." But in truth the man had a romantic streak wide enough to drive a truck through and a penchant for women who needed saving. He was a surprisingly gentle giant who reminded Maddie of Ferdinand the bull in the children's book she'd read to Kyra and Andrew.

"Have a minute, Maddie?" Griff asked.

"Always." She accepted a friendly fist bump and moved to a quiet corner where they wouldn't be overheard.

A lighting tech named Janis, who had piercings that Maddie was careful not to look at too closely, was next. Lloyd the guitar tech cued up after that. Considering what they did for a living and how much time they spent on the road, their concerns weren't particularly wild or crazy. She'd learned that however people decorated themselves, whatever they had inked or stapled to their skin, they were all looking to make sense of who they were and the world they lived in.

The line evaporated, crew members dispersing like pigeons when a human settled on a nearby bench. The reason was Will. Who now stood where the line had been.

"I couldn't tell if I was supposed to take a number or not," he said drily.

"Oh?" she asked. "Did you have something you needed to discuss?"

"I don't know, what do you charge per hour?"

"I'm willing to settle for 'in kind' services from you," Maddie said, trying not to give in to the smile tugging at her lips.

"So, I'd be trading, say, sexual favors for emotional support?" The post-performance adrenaline poured off him and she felt its pull. He was hot and sweaty. A towel hung around his neck. And she couldn't have cared less.

"Yes. Is that a problem?" Her eyebrow went up.

"Hell, no," he said, closing the gap between them. "But I'm afraid when you've fixed everybody you're going to want to leave. I'll have to hire a whole new band and crew."

"I'm not going anywhere. I told you that." Her lips quirked. "Besides, most of these people have been on the road for a long time. They have deep-rooted problems and issues that they're eager to discuss with pretty much anyone who's willing to listen. We're in the home stretch. No one's working through all that before the tour ends."

"Well, thank God for that," he teased as he slipped an arm around her shoulders and led her past the crowd that surrounded the buffet and bar.

Maddie looked up and saw the PR girl working her way toward them. She had a photographer in tow. "Vicki's headed this way. Aren't you supposed to stay and mingle?"

"Not tonight. Robert, Kyle, and Dean can handle it. Now that Dean's wife's on tour he can't seem to wipe that sloppy grin off his face."

"They do look happy, don't they?" Maddie said, feeling happy herself as they exited the building.

"They do." In the backseat of the limo, he pulled her close and she felt even happier. "Maybe when you've had a chance to decompress after the tour, you could go back to school for an advanced degree. Study psychology or social work or . . . maybe mediation?"

Maddie's smile slipped. Was she willing to go back to school, commit to building something? Open an office? "I don't know. I think I'm looking for more freedom not less." She'd barely thought about the future over the last weeks. She'd been too busy trying to be useful, something more than a hanger-on, to seriously think about what she would do next.

"You're wired to help people. And you are one of the best listeners I've ever known. You need to find a way to use that." Will grinned. "You'd be an excellent bartender. I'd invest in a bar for you, but I suspect there's something deeply wrong with a recovering alcoholic owning one. Although Sam Malone was a former alcoholic and he owned Cheers."

"He was a fictional character." She laughed. "And you're not buying me anything."

She kept her tone light as he continued to throw out wackier and wackier career suggestions, but her earlier good mood had begun to evaporate. No matter how much she loved being with Will, she couldn't see herself living full-time on Mermaid Point away from her friends and family. Nor could she see herself in school, or going to an office every day. She'd spent the last three weeks trying to make the most of being on tour with Will. And while she'd enjoyed being with him, and found ways to feel at least somewhat useful, she had no better idea of what she wanted to do with her life than she had when the tour began.

. . .

"Don't wanna go to sleep! Is too dark in here!" Dustin stood beside his bed, his feet rooted to the floor. Tears glittered in his eyes.

"But the night-light's on," Kyra said gently. "And Max is here. And I'm just in the next room."

"Don't care. Don't wanna get in this bed. And Max doesn't, either."

Kyra picked him up and held him. "Can you tell me why?"

"Is too dark." He buried his face in her neck and she breathed in his little-boy scent. "Wanna sleep with you!"

Last night he'd thrashed and cried out in his sleep, bits of dialogue escaping as he clearly relived the scene they'd shot that day in which Christian Sommersby's character had abducted him and closed him in the trunk of his beat-up car. The cast and crew, his father, and even Tonja, who'd given Kyra a wide berth since finding her in Daniel's arms, had applauded the scene and congratulated him on his acting. But Kyra had heard real panic in his voice. After each take she'd insisted on having time alone with him. Each time he'd vowed he was okay and was ready to do it again.

Today Dustin's character, Tyler, had been carried kicking and screaming into a dark and dingy cabin where he was tied to a rickety chair. Again Kyra had been on the edge of her seat ready to jump up at each cry of alarm. And again Dustin had claimed that he was okay and wanted to keep going as Daniel did take after take until Dustin's sobs turned so heartrending that Kyra, with Tonja's support, had forced Daniel to stop.

Tomorrow afternoon they would shoot a pivotal scene in which Dustin would escape from the cottage. While running from Sommersby he would burst out of the citrus grove where his father and Derek Hanson, who played the amusement park security guard, were tracking him to the kidnapper's remote hiding place. Just when Tyler and his father thought he was safe, the security guard would reveal himself as one of the kidnappers.

Dread and guilt pooled in Kyra's stomach as she looked down into Dustin's tear-streaked face. She should never have let him do this film. Should have trusted her instincts and even gone to court if she'd had to, to prevent this from happening.

"Okay, let's go." She carried Dustin into her room and onto her bed, where he curled up against her. Max settled at the foot of the bed, his head on Dustin's leg. Kyra lay still until Dustin's breathing grew regular. When she was certain he was asleep, she eased out of bed and padded into the living room debating whom to call.

Her mother would come if she asked, but she'd vowed not to ask, and by the time she got here there would be nothing left to do. She'd heard from Troy a couple of times since the night he'd spent on the couch, but he'd kept the conversation impersonal and she sensed he'd decided to keep his distance. But she needed someone to talk to, someone who could understand what a film set was, and what they'd be facing.

"Hi," she said when Troy answered.

"Hello." There was a beat of silence and then, "How's the shoot going?"

"Well, I'd say we were okay except that Dustin's been having nightmares since we started the kidnapping scenes. And tomorrow we shoot his attempted escape and rescue. It's getting to him. Tonight he cried and begged to sleep with me. He and Max are in my bed right now."

She half expected some smartass comment about how he'd had to sleep on the couch, but he'd seen the script and said only, "He should be able to shoot that with a double and do a few cutaway close-ups with Dustin. If there's a problem or something doesn't feel right, it sounds like Tonja's the person to take it to."

"Yeah." Kyra sighed. "She is. Except . . ." She winced and would have given anything to take the word back.

"Except what?"

Kyra closed her eyes but she was too tired and too freaked out to come up with an alternative scenario. "Except . . . that she walked into the trailer and saw Daniel hitting on me and told me I could have him." She still couldn't believe that this could have happened in the moment when she'd finally seen Daniel for who and what he was. Nor could she believe how coolly Tonja had responded. And she really couldn't believe that she'd just told Troy.

"Wow, how convenient. Having the wife's permission and all." Troy's tone was as dry as the Sahara with an undercurrent of anger.

"I don't want him," she said, and for the first time it wasn't an idle protest. "I really don't."

"Could have fooled me," Troy said. "It's only been about ten days since you were kissing me and wishing I was him."

"It's true," she protested, shocked by how much she now cared what Troy thought after all the years of not caring at all.

"I have seen the light and I am over him. I just need to get Dustin through this last week of filming."

"Look. I'm not a Daniel Deranian fan, but I don't think the man would be coming on to you if he didn't think you'd respond."

"And I'm telling you it's not like that," she argued. "He's not thinking at all. He's all knee jerk and neediness and . . . Oh, never mind! I must have been crazy to think you'd understand."

"Oh, I understand," Troy said with a weary certainty. "Way more than I'd like to."

"Frankly, I don't think you understand shit," Kyra countered. And then, because really that covered it, she hung up.

. . .

The next morning was spent out on the dock and playing corn hole and anything else Kyra could think of to distract Dustin and allow him to decompress enough to survive whatever came next. A car picked them up at two that afternoon and drove them out to location on the edge of the citrus grove to the sagging cabin where Dustin's character was imprisoned.

The scene called for Dustin to make a break for it when he was momentarily untied. After leaving the cabin he had to zigzag through rows of citrus trees with Sommersby on his heels. When he came out the other side of the grove, he'd run into his father and Derek Hanson, who was supposed to be helping hunt for Dustin.

The location was humming with activity when they arrived. Brandon and Daniel were in a heated discussion. Kyra had never seen the First Assistant Director, who was known for his calm, unflappable manner, so worked up.

"No. Sorry. I can't sign off on that." Brandon held up his hands, palm out.

"You don't need to sign off on anything, damn it," Daniel insisted.

"Yes, I do," Brandon replied, not backing off. "First Assistant Director is the chief safety representative on set. And I say we aren't switching the car you and Derek arrive in to a boat. I will not allow a four-year-old to swim to it when we don't have the appropriate safety personnel on set."

"We are losing light here, Brandon. And we had already decided to shoot a one-er with the Steadicam and capture the whole attempted escape in one take. The only change will be Dustin racing for the boat and swimming a couple of strokes until I pull him in." Daniel got in Brandon's face, but the volume was loud enough for everyone to hear him. "You can't possibly think I would put my own child at risk? He swims like a fish. He lives on the water for chrissakes. And we need those shots of his face while he's escaping and trying to reach the boat and safety, so I can't put someone else in his place."

"And he will have just run through the grove, shrieking and crying, before he hurls himself into the water," Brandon snapped back. "There's too much room for error. And we don't have a water safety specialist here." He nodded angrily to the medic who was always on-site for liability purposes. Brandon had always been firm but calm. But his fury was full-blown. "Surely you and your investors know about the verdict in the Sarah Jones case in Georgia. The jury handed down a 13.9-million-dollar award to the family of the camera assistant who died on set. And the First AD was deemed liable for eighteen percent of that amount and he will never work in the business again."

"I wouldn't worry about it," Daniel shouted. "Because if you don't shut your mouth and do your job right now, you won't be working in this business again anyway."

Brandon nodded curtly. "I can't shut my mouth, because I am the 'safety officer' here. It is my job to make sure cast and crew are not put in danger without proper safeguards in place." He exhaled loudly and tried another tack. "I can have an aquatics person here tomorrow and we can shoot it then." He shook his head. "You can't do this today."

"Your job is not to tell me what I can and can't do!" Daniel's face was red with anger.

"What's going on?" Kyra asked. She'd looked for Tonja, but hadn't seen her. No one within shouting range was even pretending to work.

Daniel turned his back on Brandon to address her. "We're losing light and we need this shot. It'll make the scene. It's one take with Dustin running from the cabin through the trees over there and into the lake where he swims a couple of strokes to the boat that Derek and I come in on." He placed a hand on her shoulder. "You do know I'd never put Dustin at risk, right?"

She knew he was waiting for her "yes." It was also clear he didn't really think he needed it. She tried to sort through the decision. She'd never seen the First AD so adamant, but was he genuinely worried about Dustin's safety or had it simply spiraled into a pissing match?

Daniel crouched down so that he could look Dustin in the eye. "You're a top-notch swimmer, right?"

Dustin nodded.

"Do you think you can run through the trees and then swim that couple of strokes to the boat?" He pointed to where the speedboat was moving into position not far offshore. The lake was smooth as glass.

Dustin nodded again.

She looked into her son's eyes and saw no fear, only his desire to please. He was comfortable in the water and had practically learned to swim before he could walk.

"Let's do a rehearsal with the Steadicam, but without the water," Daniel said. "Do you understand, Dustin? We start right when you burst out of the cabin and run through the trees with Christian chasing after you. When you get to the water, you stop. We're going to save the swim to the boat for the real take. Got it?"

Dustin nodded again, but his thumb stole into his mouth.

"Brandon?" Daniel stared him down.

"This is a mistake, and I can't sign off on it." Brandon called the Second AD over, said something to him, then handed him his clipboard before leaving.

Kyra watched the first rehearsal still uncertain, the pit of unease in her stomach growing as she waffled. She trusted Brandon, he was a total professional, but the action seemed straightforward. Even the swim to the boat was in shallow water and the boat was anchored. If she were going to refuse to let Dustin do this, it would have to be now. She glanced around, but there was still no sign of Tonja.

She watched the rehearsal on the monitor and saw the heaving chest and the believable terror mixed with determination on Dustin's face as he ran the jagged line that had been laid out through the trees and to the edge of the lake with Christian gaining on him from behind.

Afterward, she sat with Dustin while he caught his breath. "No one is going to make you do this. If we say no, it's no." She smoothed a lock of dark hair off his forehead. "Tell me what you think."

"My Dandiel wants me to do this. And I'm a good swimmer. And you'll be here, right, Mommy?"

She nodded numbly, knowing deep in her heart that she should just say no and live with the fallout.

With a last look in her direction Daniel shouted, "We're burning light. We've got to roll. Everybody in position."

Her nod was small and reluctant, but it was apparently enough for Daniel to put himself in the boat with Derek. Christian and Dustin stood just inside the cabin. On cue Dustin would burst out and begin to run. When he spotted the boat and saw his father, he would run flat out, throw himself into the water, and swim to the boat, where his father would pluck him out of the water only to have Derek pull out a gun and reveal himself as part of the kidnap plan.

"And action!"

Kyra barely breathed as the scene unfolded. Dustin ran as if his life depended on it, his breathing heavy, his small bare feet pounding on the ground, looking over his shoulder fearfully twice at the kidnapper who ran after him. As he ran toward the lake the sun slipped lower and the light turned golden, casting long shadows over the still water, the boat, and the figures in it.

"Hurry! Don't look back! Swim!" Daniel shouted his line.

With the Steadicam still in motion, Dustin ran a few steps into the water then threw himself forward. Kyra stopped breathing altogether as he frantically dog-paddled and swam toward the boat. When he drew near, Daniel shouted encouragement then leaned over to grasp his hand. Somehow he missed. Dustin went under. A ring of bubbles broke the surface and then disappeared. The lake went still and silent. Dustin didn't come back up.

# Thirty-three

Out of the corner of her eye Kyra saw a streak of movement near the edge of the lake. Someone began to scream. As she raced toward the water, her eyes pinned to the spot where Dustin had slipped beneath the surface, Kyra realized that it was her.

Heart pounding, she looked for Daniel, who would be close enough to get to him. Her heart pounded harder when she saw him standing frozen in the bow of the boat, his face etched with shock.

Kyra ran on, her eyes scanning the water where Dustin had gone under, praying for Dustin's head to break the surface, only to get caught in the crush of crew also surging chaotically toward the lake.

"Oh, my God! *Move!*" She pushed and pivoted, straining to see any movement. Her feet went out from under her and she went down. Raw panic spiraled through her. She'd never get there in time, she'd never . . . She struggled to her feet and took staggering steps. Saw a splash of arms not far from the boat, and got a brief glimpse of an adult head—then a flutter kick as someone went back under. Kyra broke out of the crowd and ran faster, but what should have been a sprint was a soul-numbing marathon.

The boat rocked and she saw Derek Hanson slip into the water to help whoever was already there searching. Near the water's edge the medic and Brandon's replacement shouted for people to get out of the way. "No one else goes in! We don't want to stir up the bottom."

Somewhere along the way she'd kicked off her shoes. Her bare feet slapped into the water. The soft bottom sucked at her toes. The medic made a grab for her, but she shrugged him off and took another step. When he managed to wrap his hands around her arm, she turned and clawed at him like the desperate animal she'd turned into, until he let go.

She was knee-deep, cold water swirling around her calves, when a blond head broke the surface a few yards off the bow. Tonja Kay emerged, her clothes clinging to her body, water sluicing off her, like some Amazonian warrior. But the limp body she carried in her arms as she staggered through the shallow water toward land was all Kyra could see.

She and the medic reached Tonja at the same time. The medic drew Dustin out of Tonja's arms and laid him on the grass. Kyra fell down on her knees, her eyes on her child's slack face and closed eyes as the medic tilted Dustin's head back and leaned his head over Dustin's open mouth. Tonja sank down beside her.

"Is he breathing?" Kyra whispered, afraid of the answer.

"Yes," the medic said as he unzipped the front of the wet suit Dustin wore under his clothes and she breathed a full breath for the first time. "But his pulse is erratic." His hands moved gently over Dustin's head. "There's a huge bump back here. He must have hit his head on the boat or a rock on the bottom."

A siren sounded in the distance, drew nearer. Kyra watched Dustin's chest for each movement, each completed breath.

Dustin's eyelids fluttered open, but his eyes were foggy, confused. "Mommy?" His voice was little more than a croak. "Mommy!"

A word she'd been afraid she'd never hear him speak again. Tears of relief blurred her own eyes as he began to cry. She grasped his cold wet hand between hers. "You're all right," she crooned, a prayer and a promise. "You hit your head, but you're going to be fine." She held on to his hand as the paramedics moved him carefully onto a stretcher and carried him to the ambulance for the ride to the hospital. "We'll call en route to make sure they're ready for him."

Daniel wanted to ride in the ambulance with Kyra, but she ignored him. Tonja touched her arm. "We'll meet you at the hospital. He'll have the best possible care. I'm . . . sorry I wasn't there to . . ."

"You were there when it mattered. Thank you," Kyra said. It was the best she could do. Brandon Holloway stepped up and handed her a towel, which she couldn't quite remember what to do with. So she carried it in her free hand, refusing to let go of Dustin's hand even when his stretcher was loaded into the ambulance.

At the hospital, she refused to release his hand until they took him for a CT scan.

"The doctor will come to speak to you as soon as he has the results," the young nurse said, nodding her toward a waiting room.

Daniel and Tonja were already there. Kyra took a seat. Not even wanting to look at them, she stared down at her hands twisting nervously in her lap.

"Don't worry, he'll be fine," Daniel finally said.

The sound of his voice was all it took to turn her fear and panic into fury.

"He better be," she said looking up. "Only it'll be no thanks to you. You changed that scene without even bothering to think it through then pushed everybody to go along." She took a shuddering breath. "And then you made no attempt to save him."

Neither Tonja nor Daniel spoke, and it was a good thing because it was entirely possible that even a single word from either of them might snap the very last thread of her self-control.

"You like to *play* the father, but being a father isn't extravagant gifts and puppies on Christmas Eve. It's being there when it matters. And being willing to put your own life on the line when your child is in danger, for God's sake."

She was more than ready for a fight. She was spoiling for one. But Tonja put a hand on Daniel's arm and neither of them spoke. They wore almost identical looks of relief when the doctor entered.

He was gray haired and middle aged and got right to the point. "Fortunately, the scans show no bleeding or signs of cranial damage. He's got a mild concussion, but should be fine with three or four days' rest. I would like to keep him overnight for observation. You can wait for him in his room. He'll be taken there in just a few minutes."

All three of them sagged with relief. But it was Daniel who pumped the doctor's hand and thanked him profusely. As if he'd been the one to dive in after their son then carry him in his arms through three feet of snow to the hospital. He was extremely convincing in his role as a concerned yet relieved parent, a performance she might have fallen for if she hadn't witnessed his complete lack of parental action at the lake.

"Thank God he's okay," Daniel said when the doctor left.

"Okay?" she said in disbelief. "He has a concussion and is lucky to be alive. And you never even got in the water or told them to stop rolling."

"I'm sorry. I . . . I just couldn't seem to think. I couldn't move." His apology might have been sincere; it was hard to know. "But, luckily, Tonja came in like the cavalry and he's going to be fine."

"Right. We're lucky she was there. She does a first-rate job of stepping in and taking care of things, doesn't she? But then I guess she's had a lot of experience at it."

Unable to look at either of them for another moment, she turned and made her way to Dustin's hospital room, where she took his small hand in hers again and held it through the night, dozing in the chair she'd pulled up close to the bed.

She stirred, her body stiff, as early morning light bled through the window blinds. A new nurse came in as the shift changed. The sounds of activity grew louder.

Dustin's eyelids fluttered open. She saw the sheen of tears. "Wanna go home now. All the way home. To Geema's."

"That's exactly what we're doing," she promised. "As soon as the doctor says you can leave, we're out of here." And if she knew anything about her mother, she'd already be there when they arrived even though when she'd reached her the night before they'd only just landed in Phoenix.

"How come my head hurts?" Dustin looked confused and seemed to have no memory of what had happened.

"You have a headache, because you hit your head while you were swimming."

"Don't memember."

"I know. But the doctor thinks the headache will go away soon." He'd also said that while she should keep an eye out for a rather alarming list of possible symptoms, he'd felt fairly certain that the concussion had been mild and that with rest Dustin's recovery would be rapid.

"And then we'll be able to leave."

. . .

There was a soft knock on the door. When she looked up Tonja walked in with a bouquet of brightly colored balloons, which she carried over and tied to the railing on Dustin's bed. "Hey," she said softly. "How are you feeling?"

"I'm almost better," he said.

"That's good. You were very brave yesterday," Tonja said. "I'm really glad you're okay."

"Where's my Dandiel?"

Even the mention of his father made Kyra's blood boil in her veins.

"He went by the cottage to feed Max and take him out and tell him where you were," Tonja said. "He'll come here as soon as he's done."

"Oh." Dustin yawned and looked up at the balloons. "That's good."

Tonja smiled and unwrapped one of the strings and handed a balloon to Dustin. "Would it be all right if your mommy came out in the hall to talk with me for a minute? She's going to stand right in the doorway where you can see her."

He nodded gravely.

Kyra followed Tonja out of the room, positioning herself where she and Dustin could see each other. Though she now knew that line of sight only went so far.

"I'm so sorry I wasn't there earlier yesterday," Tonja said. "I came as soon as Brandon texted me about the altercation over the water element, but it was almost too late."

She wanted to yell at someone, wanted to make someone pay for what had happened, but she had been there and allowed it to happen. "I hate that I agreed to the scene change. That's the last time I ignore my gut when it comes to my child. If you hadn't been there and gone in the way you did . . ." Tears blurred Kyra's view of the perfect face across from her. "Thank you. Thank you for saving him."

"I once let a doctor tell me my child should be released from the hospital when I could clearly see something was very wrong." Tonja's voice was tight. "We have to look out for our own. That's what mothers do. I'm glad I got there in time."

"His own father didn't go in after him. He just stood there watching." Again anger bubbled hot and furious.

Tonja sighed. "He means well. But like everyone else he's got his weaknesses. I've pushed him too hard, too far. He's a great actor, but I'm not sure he's cut out to be a director. He can't take the pressure. It paralyzes him."

"You can't protect him forever," Kyra said. "His inaction was not your doing. And neither is his behavior."

"No, but I love him." Her smile was rueful. "And it's a hard habit to break."

They were still standing in the doorway when Daniel arrived. "How is he?"

"Better," Tonja said. "I spoke to Brandon earlier. We're pushing call times back a couple hours this morning."

Kyra looked at the two of them. Shook her head. "I still can't believe you not only didn't help rescue Dustin but you never even stopped rolling," she said to Daniel.

"I wasn't trying to film it," he said defensively. "Everything happened so quickly and I just forgot to yell 'cut.' But it's the strangest thing. The footage is incredible." He brightened. "Tonja carrying him out of the water like she did? We can tweak the end and shoot a few more scenes and . . ."

"You've looked at the dailies," Kyra said. It wasn't a question. "Your son almost died yesterday and you took the time to look at rushes last night."

"I had to," Daniel said quickly. "We're behind schedule and we've got to finish. But we can shoot around him for the next few days until he recovers completely. Then we can pick up the shots and scenes we need with him."

"No."

"What?"

"I said no."

"But we need him. We can't finish without him. I promise you the last scenes won't be taxing," Daniel protested.

"And you promised he'd be safe, but then the shot you wanted was more important," Kyra said. "I'm not falling for that again. I doubt I'll ever be able to forgive myself for letting it happen. But I know for a fact that I'll never forgive you for putting your film and your career before our son. If it hadn't been for Tonja, he could be dead right now. You put him at risk and then you stood there and did nothing."

"But the doctors say he'll be good as new in a few days." Daniel's voice was chiding. As if she were overreacting.

"No," she said. "End of conversation. As soon as the doctor releases him we're going home."

"But you signed a contract. You're legally obligated." He said this as if presenting incontrovertible proof that no rational person would argue with.

"Wow. You are really a piece of work." She looked at Tonja, who had been suspiciously quiet. Although she looked slightly uncomfortable, she did not counter her husband's argument. So much for the motherhood sisterhood.

"I guess you're going to have to sue me," she said to Daniel with a cheerful smile that surprised all three of them. "A suit like that could take years to work its way through the courts. Which would put you waaaay behind schedule and allow your fans to let you know how they feel about a man who plays heroes, but risks his own child to get a shot."

The smile slipped from her lips and she took a step closer. "If you make any attempt to force Dustin to appear in so much as another frame of this film, I will move heaven and earth to let the world see exactly who you are.

"Your wife's a smart woman. I'm sure she can figure out how to finish this monstrosity of a film without my child. Even if you can't." She began to head back to Dustin but stopped mid-exit. "I am beyond grateful to you for saving Dustin's life," she said to Tonja. "I'll never forget it. And I promise you'll never have to think of me as a threat of any kind, because I don't intend to be in a room alone with your husband ever again."

She looked into Daniel's handsome face for what she wished could be the last time, and saw only the ugly, self-serving ego-driven coward who dwelled behind it.

"You can have five minutes with Dustin," she said. "Five minutes to tell him how great a kid he is, how well he did in the film, and that he's free to go home now. And then we're done here."

...

Nikki had clearly started hallucinating. Everywhere she went she imagined she saw Luvie. Yesterday at the playground she'd seen an older woman watching from a distant bench. The day before that at the Paradise Grille where she'd taken the girls for breakfast, someone who resembled her had walked by on the beach.

This morning in Publix while she was loading up on cleaning products, which she needed desperately, and food, which she'd run out of days ago, while somehow keeping Gemma and Sofia in separate grocery carts, she'd once again felt eyes on her. But when she looked up all she'd seen was an overweight red-haired woman at the far end of the aisle wearing multiple layers of support hose and a floral muumuu that she couldn't imagine Luvie even being caught dead in.

It took three trips to transport the girls and all the grocery bags from the car to the cottage. After the last trip, she dropped onto the couch with a groan then forced herself to look around. At some point she'd given up on pretty much anything that wasn't absolutely necessary. Dirty clothes still spilled out onto the hall floor. Dirty dishes teetered in the kitchen sink. Toys littered the floor. The cottage resembled a crash site with possessions strewn everywhere and no survivors.

She'd need every minute of the next twenty-four hours before Joe was due back to get it clean. Or at least less like a house of horrors.

"All right, you two." She set the girls on their bottoms in front of the television set, pawed through the stack of DVDs for their favorite Wiggles video, *Here Comes the Big Red Car*, stuck it in, and hit "play." Because that was apparently the kind of mother she was.

"Okay," she warned herself once the girls were occupied. "Don't look at it all. Rome wasn't built in a day. Just pick a couple of things to get started on." This sounded eminently practical and marginally less overwhelming, so she went into the bedroom hall and sorted the mounds of dirty laundry then ripped the sheets off the bed and both girls' cribs. With a flourish of detergent and determination, she started the first load.

At the sink, she rinsed all the dishes and glasses she could fit in the dishwasher, which was nowhere near all of them; she'd switched to paper plates and plastic cups a week ago. Then she put away the groceries that needed to be refrigerated, poured sippy cups of juice for the girls, and wiped down the counter and the dinette table—or at least the parts that weren't still covered with the mail and newspapers she hadn't yet found the time or strength to sort through. In the middle of cleaning the toilets she started to run out of steam. The washing machine and dishwasher were still whirring away, so there was no point thinking about how many loads were left to do. She briefly considered having something to eat now that there was food in the refrigerator, but chewing seemed far too strenuous. In fact, she was too tired to even choose another task.

Sofia and Gemma had conked out on the rug, curled in two identical balls. With a yawn she went to the front door and made sure it was locked then staggered back to her bedroom. Leaving the door open so that she could hear the girls if they needed her, she fell facefirst on the unmade bed for a short and, hopefully, restorative nap.

. . .

"Nikki? Nikki!" A hand grasped her shoulder. Shook her. "Nikki! Are you all right?"

The hand was large. The voice was Joe's. She assumed she

must be dreaming. But when she attempted to burrow back down into that warm, lovely place where she'd been pulled back from, the hand didn't disappear and the shaking didn't stop.

Half awake, she rolled over and sat straight up in bed.

Only this time the hallucination leaning over the bed was too solid to ignore. The person staring down at her was Joe. As she watched in confusion, the expression on his face began to change from one of fear to what could only be called fury. "What the hell is going on here?"

Her thoughts were thick and slow as if her head was stuffed with cotton wool. Her arm shot out for her phone. She brought the screen close to her face. It was four P.M. "But . . . what . . . I don't . . ." She winced. "Oh, my God! Is it tomorrow already?"

He stared down at her. "I was able to get home a day early." He took her phone with its screen of unseen texts. "I've been calling and texting all day. When you didn't answer and then the house looked like it had been tossed and the girls were passed out on the floor I . . ." He swallowed. "My heart almost stopped. I was afraid of what I was going to find in here."

He lowered himself onto the side of the bed with a rough exhale.

Sofia and Gemma toddled into the room, their hair sticking up, their cheeks still red from what she was beginning to remember as their nap on the living room rug. When they spotted Joe, they shrieked with joy. Joe pulled them up onto the bed and they climbed all over him, kissing his face, fighting for a spot in his lap.

She tried to marshal her thoughts, but she was still trying to grasp what had happened. She'd lost the whole day she'd meant to use erasing all evidence of Luvie's absence and her own ineptitude. A whole day in which she'd assumed she would come up with a plausible explanation and a plan for moving forward. Something she'd been far too exhausted being a single mother to even think about.

When the girls were settled, he drew a deep breath and set his shoulders before turning his laser beam brown eyes on her once again. "So, now that you appear to be awake, I need you to tell me what is going on here, how our home got destroyed, and why you look like someone who was just released from a POW camp. I'd also like to know what's happened to Luvie."

The toddler chorus smiled beatific smiles and singsonged, "Luffee!"

"Welllll . . ." It took pretty much everything she had to meet his eyes. She was staring into them when she saw the preternatural calm he used when hunting criminals settle over him. That calm was far more daunting and potentially dangerous than his initial panic-fueled fury.

"It better be good, Nik," he said. "And it better be the truth. Because I'll know. And I am not even remotely in the mood to be lied to again."

# Thirty-four

"Geema!" Dustin buried his face in Maddie's neck as she lifted him into her arms and hugged him tightly. Max's tail did its happiest dance, wagging triple time as he followed his nose to favorite bushes and tree trunks.

Dustin didn't clamor to be put down or relax his hold around her neck as Kyra began to unload the Jeep. She thought her heart might break when he looked up at her with those intent brown eyes and said, "I missed you, Geema. I'm so really glad to be home."

"Me too," she said, trying not to feel disloyal to Will. Who had insisted on sending her home in the record label's plane and shushed her when she'd attempted to apologize for leaving him. "Of course you have to go," he'd said. "I think I'm capable of flying solo these last few stops, although I'm a little afraid our road crew is going to go into Maddie withdrawal. Keep me posted, okay?"

Kyra hauled their things in with a weariness that matched her son's. But both perked up slightly when they stepped into the cottage, which was filled with sunshine and the salt breeze that floated in through the open windows. The fresh flowers on the dinette gave off a softer scent than the egg soufflé that had just come out of the oven. A plate of freshly baked chocolate chip cookies sat beside it on the counter. She poured Dustin a cup of apple juice and offered Kyra a can of sparkling water.

"When did you do all this?" Kyra motioned to the flowers, the drinks now in their hands, and the food that waited. "I know you only got back late last night. It's not even noon."

Maddie smiled. "What can I say? I'm an early riser." And all she'd been able to think about was turning the cottage back into a "home" for the ones she loved to come back to. "It was nice to have a place to putter." She smiled again. "I've always been a nester, but as it turns out the housekeeping staff of most hotels don't really appreciate the guests rearranging the furniture and artwork."

"I saw Joe on his way out with the girls when I went for the last load of stuff," Kyra said. "He had kind of an odd look on his face."

"Really?" Maddie put down a bowl of water for Max, retrieved a Tupperware container of cut fruit from the refrigerator, then sliced the soufflé and filled three plates. "I haven't seen anyone yet. But I spoke with your dad and he'd like to take Dustin out for pizza tomorrow night. He thought Troy might like to go, too. You know, kind of a guys' outing." It was a small trial balloon that Kyra didn't comment on. Dustin had no such qualms. "Oh, boy!" He brightened further.

"I thought we might get everybody together for a sunset toast then," she said as they settled at the table. "Most of my sunsets for the last three weeks have been spent in one performance hall or another, or on the way to one." She had tried not to miss the beach, or the sunset, or her family and friends too much. But she'd begun dreaming about all three several cities ago and wasn't sure how much longer she could wait to dig her toes into the sand. "I was hoping we might go out on the beach after brunch, if everyone's up for it."

"Thas exactly what I was hoping, too, Geema," Dustin said

with a somewhat bigger smile than the one with which he'd arrived. As they sat together and ate, she felt the most exquisite blend of love and relief. She wondered as she dished up more soufflé and refilled drinks and listened to Dustin's exclamations whether anything could make her as happy as taking care of the people she loved.

. . .

A couple of cottages over and a world of domesticity away, Nikki woke. She pulled her face out of the pillow in which it had been buried, and noticed that it had no pillowcase and that the bed was minus sheets. Bright sunlight slanted in through the blinds, but she couldn't tell if it was late morning or early afternoon. Her thoughts floated, sifting through snatches of memory or possibly bits of dreams. Thinking ceased when she became aware of the quiet, which was deafening enough to make her sit up straight in bed. Had she only imagined Joe's early return? No. She could still see the anger on his face and hear the ring of it in his voice. But he wasn't here now. And neither were the girls.

In the master bathroom, where she washed her face and brushed her teeth, it was impossible to ignore just how badly it needed to be cleaned. In the hall her bare feet got tangled in the dirty clothes that still littered the floor. The living area was also exactly as she left it when she'd gone into the bedroom for what she intended as forty winks but had apparently stretched to Rip van Winkle proportions. The only thing that had been "picked up" were Sofia and Gemma, whom she'd left sleeping on the rug like abandoned puppies.

In the midst of the kitchen clutter she found a note propped against the coffeemaker. The lack of even the dregs of coffee was a testament to Joe's anger. So was the message he'd left.

*Took the girls out for breakfast then the playground. Then going to go beg Luvie to come back. Don't pick up anything. She deserves to see how things went without her.*

Shit.

Since he hadn't said anything about leaving herself as he'd found her, Nikki took a long hot shower and washed her hair, which might have sighed with gratitude. Naked, she stood in front of the full-length mirror, shocked at how gaunt she looked after the weeks of running after the twins and being too tired to eat more than the girls' leftovers. Her breasts still sagged and her stomach wasn't exactly flat, but her cheekbones were no longer lost in a too-fleshy face, and the hollow at her throat had reappeared. All the lifting and toting and carrying had toned her upper arms. It seemed that parenting, like hands-on renovation, could replace a trip to the gym.

She pulled her hair into a messy knot at the base of her neck, added eyeliner, mascara, and lipstick—things she once would have never left home without and had somehow forgotten existed—because she thought it might be important to help Joe remember at least one of the reasons he'd originally been attracted to her.

With no clean clothes to wear, she pawed through the closet until she came to a pair of jeans she'd shoved in the back for the day when she might be able to squeeze into them again. They fit. She was sliding her arms into an old *Do Over* T-shirt when she heard the front door open. The girls' happy chatter reached her ears followed closely by Luvie's "May the saints preserve us!" Despite the obvious shock, the nanny's voice could only be described as gleeful.

Joe walked into the bedroom. If he noticed her improved appearance, he gave no indication. "We'll let her enjoy the girls and the tragic mess a little longer. Then we're going to go in so you can apologize and tell her how happy you are to have her back."

"And then will you forgive me?"

"I'm working on it," he said stiffly. "I just don't understand why you couldn't tell me how you felt. Surely there had to be some way to share the burden rather than lying and jeopardizing your health."

"But I tried to tell you how I felt. Then I tried to tell Luvie and get her to cut back her hours. Neither of you would listen." Tears stung her eyes at the unfairness of his accusation.

"And you thought the solution was to take everything on yourself? That's exactly what I was afraid of."

"Well, it might not have been the best possible course of action, but I wanted more time with my children. And I needed to prove that I'm not a total failure in the mother department."

"Awww, Nik." He sat on the unmade bed and shook his head. "You're a great mother. And no one except you thinks you're supposed to be Supermom."

There was a burst of merriment, which was followed by Luvie's "My land, look at all these dirty clothes! And the dishes!" She'd never heard the nanny sound happier.

Nikki dropped down next to Joe. "I'm willing to concede that I need help. And I can handle an apology. But I refuse to go back to how things were."

"She needs us as much as we need her, Nik. More." The anger had begun to dissipate. She saw concern in his eyes. "When I went to the address that's on her driver's license and résumé, she didn't actually live there."

"What?"

"Yeah. You can imagine my surprise given the whole background check and vetting. A few heads are going to roll at the office. And I think I have a whole lot of new gray hairs."

"Are you saying it was a fake address? Is she hiding some sort of criminal past? I mean, she came highly recommended by James Marley and she looks way too old to be a criminal mastermind." Nikki's thoughts swirled with horrible possible scenarios.

"She wouldn't be here right now if that was the case. I can promise you that," Joe said.

"She lived there with her mother until she died. And then

she lost the house to foreclosure." He looked at Nikki. "Her current home is in a neighborhood I don't feel at all good about. I saw someone selling drugs on the corner."

Nikki's stomach dropped.

"She needs and wants the job. And I think we'd be crazy to let her go. But we'd have to pay her enough to allow her to move somewhere safer without coming out and saying so. Her pride may be all she has left." He took her hand and helped her to her feet. "The final decision is up to you."

"Okay." Nikki drew what she hoped would be a calming breath.

"Let's give her a chance to enjoy your apparent ineptitude a little while longer before you get to it, okay?"

They walked back into the living area, where Luvie sat on the sofa with a girl on each side. "I thought it best not to put them on the floor until everything had been thoroughly cleaned. And possibly fumigated."

Nikki looked to Joe. He raised an eyebrow, but she was not prepared to admit that the girls had slept on the rug the nanny didn't even want them to walk on.

"I'll admit my experiment didn't go exactly as planned," Nikki said, not quite ready for a full-on apology and still grappling with what Joe had told her. "I can see now just how much organizational skill is necessary to take good care of the twins and keep the house in the kind of condition you did."

"It can be a bit tricky for those without experience," Luvie conceded with a careful smile. "One must keep to a regular schedule," she said pronouncing it as *shed-ule*. "Children need consistency. In food and in sleep."

Nikki's smile felt a bit tight.

"And, of course, a certain minimal level of cleanliness should go without saying."

*Yes, it should*, Nikki thought. But apparently wasn't going to.

"It's important to set a good example for the girls."

"Of course," Nikki managed. She met Luvie's brilliant green eyes. "But perhaps we should discuss how we might move forward."

"Mr. Giraldi has indicated that you might like me to come back to work for you. And I would quite like that only . . . well, you did lie to me, didn't you? A few times when I just happened to be out, I saw you with the girls and realized you hadn't gone out of town as you'd claimed."

It occurred to Nikki that her hallucinations had been quite real and that Mary Poppins had somehow managed to camouflage the extremely white skin and dark red hair and gone Mata Hari on her.

"It hurt quite a lot," Luvie said. The nanny's voice wavered. As if she were holding back tears.

"Yes, I'm very sorry for misrepresenting the situation. But of course you did get a paid holiday out of it."

Luvie sniffed. "What is money in comparison to trust?"

Nikki sniffed back. "It's my understanding that you haven't been completely truthful yourself."

Luvie's eyes widened. Nikki was careful to keep her face impassive.

"Yes, well. I can truthfully say I fell in love with Sofia and Gemma at first sight." Luvie's face softened and her arms went around the girls. "I love them like a grandmother and I would never put them in harm's way. I would give my life for them."

Luvie's face and voice radiated sincerity.

Nikki drew her first easy breath. "All right then. What happens now?"

"I had thought to be retired by now," Luvie said. "But really, how many games of bingo and pickleball can one person play? I love your girls and I have to work. But I can't live on a part-time salary." Her green eyes were unflinching as she looked at Nikki.

"And I can't live with full-time help, even help as fine as yours," Nikki replied.

"Oh, my. Well then . . ." Luvie's face fell. Her shoulders sagged. "We seem to be at an impasse then, don't we? Perhaps our differences are irreconcilable." She squeezed the girls' shoulders gently and made to rise. "I understand."

Nikki expected Joe to jump in and negotiate a truce of some kind, but he was now wearing his inscrutable face. The choice was, in fact, hers.

"Let's not give up just yet," she said, allowing herself to take in the disaster that was their home and to remember what it had taken to care for the girls completely on her own. "Surely we can work something out." She felt rather than saw Joe's smile. Imagined the girls were listening. "So. What if we give you a well-deserved raise and maintain a full-time salary with the understanding that you will come here as little or as much as we need from week to week—to be discussed and agreed upon each week?"

"You would overpay me *not* to come?" she asked.

"Well, she's already paid you not to come at all," Joe said drily. "It's an unusual business model."

"Quite."

But Nikki was too intent on setting parameters to worry about form. "Maybe hours could accumulate over a thirty-day period. But you couldn't work more hours than I've scheduled in any week." She looked at the nanny, who had a pretty good poker face. "No exceptions. Do we agree?"

Luvie pretended to think, but Nikki was not surprised when she said, "Right then. I'm in."

"And you're good with this, Joe?" Nikki asked.

He cocked his head as if considering, but his eyes and his smile were once again warm. "Yes. Very crafty on your part to overpay someone not to work. Not too dissimilar to the 'buy high, sell low' school of investment." He grinned. "But I couldn't agree more."

Nikki put out her hand. Luvie put her very plump white hand inside it. They shook.

"It might not be a bad idea to put this in writing," the nanny said. "But I do believe we have a deal."

# Thirty-five

"God, it's good to be home." Kyra sat in a beach chair just beyond the Sunshine Hotel's low wall with her mother, Nikki, Bitsy, and Avery watching the sun slip ever lower in the pinkening sky. The gulf glittered with its reflection. Palm fronds swayed and rustled in the gentle salt breeze. Her bare feet were half buried in the cool white sand and she was glad she'd put on a sweatshirt, glad she was finally home, gladder still to be in the center of this group of women. In a place where she could breathe.

With her mother back, the snacks were more plentiful. Bagel Bites and tiny hot dogs in pastry had been added to the requisite Ted Peters smoked fish spread and Avery's bowl of Cheez Doodles. Bitsy had brought the wine.

"So, they were okay releasing Dustin from the movie early?" Avery asked.

"Not exactly. But they did ultimately see that it was in their best interest." Kyra sank lower in her chair and turned her face up to the breeze, thinking about Daniel and Tonja. She raised the glass of wine Bitsy had just poured her. "And I'm claiming being home as my one good thing." She smiled. "This may be the first time I've ever offered without being asked, but here's to being home. And out of Winter Haven. And away from the Deranian-Kays."

They raised their glasses and drank.

"Okay, I'm not even going to try to get fancy here," Maddie said. "I'm toasting Kyra and Dustin's return. And my own. The tour was fascinating and exhilarating, and I'm really glad I went. I do miss Will, but I am also extremely happy and grateful to be home." She raised her glass and they clicked and drank.

The red wine slipped down Kyra's throat in a rush of reassuring warmth.

"I was so sorry to hear what happened to Dustin," Nikki said. "I can't even imagine seeing your child go underwater and not come back up. I go numb even talking about it. How are you both doing?"

"Dustin's doing a little better already, I think. He's as happy as I am to be back and thrilled to be out with 'the guys.' He doesn't remember exactly what happened." Kyra shuddered as the remembered panic and helplessness slammed into her. "And I'm afraid I'll never be able to forget it."

Her mother reached out a hand and laid it gently on her arm. "Even the most awful things begin to fade over time. We don't necessarily forget them, but if we're lucky, they become less painful."

"And what about your disappointment in people?" she asked. She still didn't understand where her mother had found the strength to move past her father's breakdown and abdication of responsibility when their world had fallen apart. "Does that lessen over time, too?"

"I think so, yes," her mother said carefully. "But it varies. Some outcomes feel better than others."

"Personally, I'm a big fan of revenge," Bitsy said. "I think it can promote healing. In fact, every time I check my account balance and see what Joe and June have helped me take back, Bertie's betrayal hurts a little less. I don't even think I'll need a Band-Aid once he's in jail." She raised her glass. "To revenge as a prelude to healing."

They raised their glasses, but all eyes turned to Maddie.

Who might insist she was not the "good enough" police, but so was.

"Too negative?" Bitsy asked. "Because I thought it was more half full than just toasting to 'making Bertie pay.'"

Maddie laughed. "I get it. And truthfully, I'm glad he's finally getting what he deserves. But what if we just drink to 'justice'?"

"To justice!" They clicked their plastic cups and drank.

Bitsy turned to Nikki. "Speaking of your husband, he gave me some serious shit this afternoon for not telling him that Luvie was MIA while he was gone."

"I thought she was sick," Avery said. "I seem to have missed a lot."

Even in the fading light, Kyra could see Nikki squirm. "Well, she's back now and I think we've had a meeting of the minds. She's suffered some serious financial losses so we'll be grossly overpaying her to come less often."

Bitsy smiled. "There's something perfectly logical in there somewhere. And it sounds like we might have to make her a provisional member of the Lost Everything but Still-Standing Sisterhood."

"I'll drink to that." Nikki raised her glass. "And while we're at it, I think we need to devise a secret handshake or password and maybe even a signature cocktail for the Still-Standing Sisterhood."

"It does have a ring to it," Bitsy agreed as they drank.

Avery held out her glass for a refill. "I'm glad you came up with a toast, and I like Luvie just fine. But for the record I am never going to drink tea at sunset."

Bitsy downed her wine then opened another bottle. "I agree," she said as she refilled their glasses. "We will not be toasting the sunset with tea, no matter how 'lovely' or 'restorative.'"

The sun puddled into the water, a subtle, less fiery setting than a summer sunset but every bit as beautiful.

Bitsy turned to Avery. "You know, I heard from Ray's Realtor friend who took us on the tour of the Y."

"You toured a YMCA?" Maddie asked.

"Yes, the historic one downtown," Bitsy replied. "Ray set it up because he thought Avery would enjoy it."

"I did. It's an unbelievable building. It's Mediterranean Revival–style just like Bella Flora and the Don CeSar and it was built right around the same time." The excitement in Avery's voice escalated. "A number of developers and investors have bought it intending to renovate and reuse or repurpose it, but no one's gotten past interior demolition."

"Well, the Realtor confirmed it's not officially for sale. But the current owner isn't willing to put any more money in and she thinks he's stopped worrying about the cheese and just wants out of the trap." Bitsy's smile might have been borrowed from the Mona Lisa. "Meaning he might be interested in selling it at a very reasonable price."

"Seriously?" Avery asked.

"Um-hmmm," Bitsy said. "And I was thinking Downtown St. Pete is booming right now, and it's a large enough space to house retail and restaurants."

"But, now that you have money again and you're about to have your revenge, don't you want to go back to Palm Beach?" Avery asked.

Bitsy fingered her wineglass. "That's all I thought about most of last year. Even while I was down there over New Year's, I was imagining going back in a flash of glory, back on top, showing them they shouldn't have counted me out."

"And now?" Kyra couldn't help asking.

"Now, who cares what they think?" Bitsy said. "I've learned a lot about myself since I came here. And I don't have friends like you-all back there. If they have a Bestie Row in Palm Beach, no one's ever invited me into it. And I'm not sure they'd

understand the Lost Everything but Still-Standing Sisterhood."
She smiled. "I want to continue to help June and her clients, but
I'd like to have something, some kind of business, to sink my
teeth into." She cocked one eyebrow at Avery. "Would you be
interested in handling the architectural end? And maybe over-
see the construction?"

Kyra hooted at the expression on Avery's face. "You look like
someone just told you all the presents under the Christmas tree
were for you."

"Well, that's exactly what getting to bring that building
back to life would feel like. Times one hundred." Avery's smile
faded. "But I don't see how I could undertake a project of that
size alone."

"But couldn't Chase work with you?" Maddie asked.

It was Avery's turn to squirm.

"Clearly I've missed a few details while I've been on the
road," Maddie said, turning to Avery. "Tell me what's going on."

"There's nothing to tell." Avery grabbed a Cheez Doodle and
chewed it as if her life depended on it. "I just haven't been able
to make that full-time forever commitment. And now, even if I
could, he's dating that Riley."

"I'm sure he can't have gotten all that serious about her so
quickly," Maddie said.

"No? Well, she answers his phone. And, well, I don't want to
know what else they're doing together. I couldn't give him what
he wanted so . . . he found someone who could. End of story."

"Only if you want it to be," Maddie said in that calm, im-
placable voice of hers. "Surely you're not going to walk away
from the man you love and who clearly loves you."

"I already have. And he didn't exactly come running after
me," Avery pointed out.

"It's not a matter of who runs after whom," her mother said.

"I'm just so confused and stuck. One minute I'm sure it's too late and I feel like shit. The next I tell myself maybe it isn't, but then I'm afraid that if I commit and trust that he'll never push me away again and he does, that I won't survive it."

The beach had grown quiet. Dusk had turned to darkness. Kyra didn't need to see Avery's face to know that tears had begun to fall.

"You can't let fear dictate your life," Maddie said. "There are no guarantees. But that doesn't mean it's okay to run and hide and never take a chance. You can't refuse to play a game because you might lose. You need to be honest with yourself. And with Chase. And you need to be willing to take a risk to live the life you want with the person you love."

Kyra listened to her mother and wondered yet again how she'd gotten so wise. Where she'd learned how to tell people the truth without hurting their feelings or spiraling into the negative. She'd forced them to search for that one good thing each day when it had seemed an impossible task. And if she could, she'd force them to live their lives to the fullest.

Maddie took the bottle and refilled all their glasses. When she raised hers they all did the same. "To Avery. May she find the courage to have the life she wants and so richly deserves."

"To Avery!"

. . .

As they packed up the chairs and leftovers, Kyra thought about her mother's advice. Was there always a risk attached to reward? They were on the path back to the cottage when Kyra's phone dinged with an incoming text. She recognized Troy's number. They hadn't spoken since his snide comments about her and Daniel. The message read, *Brought Dustin back. We're outside your mom's cottage.*

"There's Mommy and Geema!" Dustin called as they approached. Guess what? We went to Gigi's, and I ate three whole pieces of pepperoni pizza all by myself."

"Wow, you must have really been hungry," Kyra said, pleased at how proud Dustin sounded. It was the most excited she'd heard him since their trip to Disney World.

"He was hungry all right," Troy said. "I told your dad I'd drop him off since it's on my way . . . home."

They all heard his hesitation on the word, but Kyra was watching her son's smiling tomato-sauce-covered face.

"Thank you, Troy." Her mother took Dustin by the hand. "I'm going to get this pizza-eating machine ready for bed." She bent over and whispered something in Dustin's ear.

"Thanks, Troy. I had fun." Dustin looked up and shot Troy a brighter smile than any Kyra had seen since they'd gotten back.

"I guess I need to add my thanks, too," she said as the door closed behind them. "He really likes spending time with you. And he needs every bit of real life he can get right now. We both do."

"Your dad told me what happened." Troy's voice turned gruff. "I didn't like the guy from the get-go, and I've never thought of myself as a particularly violent person, but at the moment I'd like to get my hands on Daniel and mess up that pretty-boy face of his."

"Yeah. Me too," she said truthfully.

"Listen." He took a step toward her. "I'm sorry about what I said on the phone. The idea of him touching you . . . I was jealous and I said stupid things. And when you told me Tonja said you could have him? I didn't hear a word you said after that. I just lost it."

She could see what the admission cost him and she liked him all the more for it. In fact, it occurred to her that she liked him quite a lot.

"Well, for what it's worth, I told Tonja she could keep him. I should have never let Dustin do the film. Pretty much everything I was afraid of happened and then some. Now I just want

Dustin to be himself again and I want to get back to work in some way."

They stared at each other for a long moment. The porch light created a halo on his blond hair, but she knew him too well to cast him in the role of angel. His exhale was loud and fraught with frustration. "I'm really not sure what's supposed to happen next. I want you in my life, Kyra. Both you and Dustin. That's not a question for me." His smile turned sheepish. "But I'm not the guy to wage some long-range romantic campaign. And I don't seem to be that great at dramatic gestures. You're going to have to decide whether you want to have a relationship with me or not."

"So, you're putting this all on me?"

"It did sort of come out that way, didn't it?"

"Uh, yeah," she said. "And frankly, you've kind of strayed back into sucky territory. Because I don't know if you noticed, but I'm hanging on by a thread right now. I'm way too preoccupied to think about a relationship with anybody." She moved to step around him. "So, thanks for bringing Dustin back. Have a good night."

"Wait. That's it?"

She stopped, faced him. "Yeah, I think so."

He ran another hand through his hair. His blue eyes turned intent. "I think you and Dustin should move home. To Bella Flora." He spoke quickly as if afraid she'd go inside the moment he stopped. "I love that house, but it isn't meant for one person. And I can't live there alone while you two are stuffed into the tiny second bedroom here."

"And you'd live in the pool house like you suggested before?" she asked.

"Yes." He nodded and stepped closer. "That way we'd have a chance to spend time together, you know, really get to know each other. No strings. No obligations. Just some time to figure things out."

She'd never heard him quite so earnest. Sincerity looked good on him. But there were some serious flaws in this plan. "I think I told you the last time you suggested this that I can't afford to refund your rent."

"I don't care about the money. I'd spend every penny of it to give you time to fall in love with me."

"And if that doesn't happen?"

"You already admitted that spending time with me didn't suck. And I can do way better than not sucking."

The moon had risen and stars spilled across the night sky. She saw the teasing glint steal into his eyes as he stepped closer. "But just to allay any doubts, I'll promise you this. If you haven't fallen madly in love with me by the time my lease expires in June, I'll move out. No harm, no foul."

"Is that right?" She tilted her head back and stared up into his smiling face.

"Ummm-hmmm." He slipped his arms around her. "But I don't think that's going to happen."

"You don't?" she asked.

"No, I don't." He lowered his mouth to hers and kissed her with a thorough gentleness that surprised her. The tension began to seep out of her. In fact, she felt oddly boneless as if she might melt into a puddle at his feet. The thought made her giggle.

"What's so funny?" he asked when another giggle escaped. "Because I'm kissing my heart out here and laughter wasn't what I was going for."

"Sorry," she said, though she wasn't. She felt lighter than she had in weeks, maybe even light enough to float. "I'll try to give your efforts the serious attention they deserve," she said very seriously. Right before a full laugh bubbled out.

"Fine, go ahead and make fun. I can take it." His lips twisted up into a smile that brushed across hers. Then he arranged them into an exaggerated pucker and applied them to her cheek and made extremely loud kissing noises. When they finally pulled apart they were smiling at each other like goons. "So what do you think of my plan now?"

"Hmmmm. I don't know." She pretended to consider the idea just long enough to keep him from becoming completely cocky. "I think I might be able to live with that plan."

"I can't tell you how glad I am to hear that." He gave an exaggerated sigh of relief then stepped back to take her in his arms. "Because that's all I've got. As far as I'm concerned there is no plan B."

# Thirty-six

It was funny what a little sleep, a grateful nanny, and an attentive husband bent on fattening you up could do. In a matter of days Nikki's memory of the long weeks as the exhausted panic-ridden single parent of twins had already begun to fade.

Now she stood just inside the Sunshine lobby door, surrounded by volunteer models of all ages and sizes, waiting for lunch to be served to the last of the tables arranged around the pool so that the fashion show could officially begin.

The weather was a perfect seventy-five degrees. The sky was a brilliant blue with taffy-pulled white clouds and a crayon yellow sun.

There were twenty tables of eight strategically arranged around the pool deck. Their tablecloths were in the same Flamingo Pink, Blue Mambo, and Banana Leaf as the walls of the cottages that a reassuring percentage of attendees had already toured. The centerpieces, delivered just that morning by Renée's garden club friends, were equally bright with birds-of-paradise at their center and surrounded by every tropical bloom found on the Sunshine grounds and in many Pass-a-Grille gardens, including Bella Flora's.

"Is everybody ready?" she asked as Maddie lined up the models, each wearing retro beachwear or vintage pieces and accessories.

The podium and microphone had been placed midway between the building and the pool.

Bitsy stood nearby prepared to send each model out on cue with Nikki's narration.

"Remember, you want to take your time and make sure you do a turn or a pause at every other table," Nikki said.

"Don't worry, boss," Bitsy replied. "I've got my copy of the script right here, and I'll be listening and reading along. We've been practicing our pacing . . . and all the guests are being served a glass of wine with their meal and a glass of champagne with dessert. So everyone should be in a buying mood."

Ray Flamingo arrived with a tray of champagne flutes. "These are for you, ladies. Just enough to put a little extra glide in your steps." He moved through them handing out drinks along with words of encouragement, then adjusting straps and tilting sunhats to their chicest and most flattering angles.

Avery had been pressed into modeling when one of the volunteers roughly her size had dropped out. She stopped trying to hike the bodice up and the bottom of the two-piece bathing suit down just long enough to throw back the champagne Ray gave her in one long gulp. "I don't understand why I can't wear one of those cover-ups," she complained as she tugged again.

"Because it fits you perfectly and it would be a travesty," Ray replied. "I'll tell you what. Stop fidgeting and I'll get you a second glass of champagne. It'll relax you and maybe give you the courage to call you know who."

"I wouldn't need champagne if I could wear a cover-up over this thing." She yanked at the two-piece again. "Besides," she said, finally giving up on the suit. "If I need alcohol to make a call like that, don't you think it's a sign that maybe I have some legitimate reasons for not making the call in the first place?"

Nikki turned as Luvie came out of the dressing room with Sofia and Gemma in toddler-size bathing suits almost identical to the drum-design bathing suit that Annelise had loved and worn as a child.

"Wherever did you find those?" Renée's sister asked. "They're so adorable and they bring back so many memories." She looked as if she might cry.

"I sent the photo of you in it to a company I found and asked them to copy it," Nikki said as Kyra crouched down to shoot video of the twins.

"Look, Renée!" Annelise brought her sister over to see the girls and their escort, who wore coordinating blue-and-white-striped bathing trunks with a simple white T-shirt and a captain's hat.

"Do you know what you're supposed to do, Dustin?" Nikki asked.

He nodded. "We're the finable. So we go last."

"That's right," Nikki said, turning away to hide her smile.

"I exscort Sof and Gem and hold their hands while we walk all around the tables."

"Exactly right," Nikki said. "And your grandma will be standing by just in case you want her to go with you."

"My God, they're adorable," Renée said as she moved past the three children in a stunning vintage caftan with angel-wing sleeves and pleats in a marvelous fabric covered in pastel lilies. "I predict we're going to sell a ton of those drum bathing suits." She smiled and twirled in a circle that belled the fabric and made the little ones giggle. "This is mine, though. I am never taking it off."

"I knew it would be perfect on you," Nikki said, thrilled to see what she'd imagined coming to life. "I heard that John and Steve have two signed contracts already. Hannah Friedan brought friends, and I saw June Steding taking a tour. I think she's considering a one-bedroom."

"She is," Bitsy said as Joe stepped into the lobby. "And your incredible husband just confirmed that Bertie is being put on a plane to Miami next Friday." She hugged him. "And he's gotten me permission to be there. I can't believe it's almost time to put this whole thing behind me."

"I'm planning to come along as an unofficial observer to make sure he survives the welcome home party," Joe said. "I'm just going to get a quick preshow photo for my folks. I promised them I'd send live video of the girls' modeling debut." Nikki watched him crouch down and saw their daughters squeal with happiness just at the sight of him. She knew the feeling, and as he gave her a peck on the cheek and headed back outside, she wished for the thousandth time that he'd returned to a picture of perfect parenthood and not the frazzled failure he'd found.

*Ah, well.* "What do you say, ladies and gentleman? Are we ready to rock and roll?" Nikki asked.

"Let's do it!" Maddie said.

"Places, everybody!" Bitsy added.

"Les go, Mommy!" one of the twins called out. Dustin beamed beside her.

"Woot, woot, woot!" the models chanted.

"All right," Nikki laughed. "Maestro?" she nodded to Ray, who had put together a playlist of songs for them to strut to. With a nod and a thumbs-up, he pressed "play" and she waited for the opening strains of Stevie Wonder's "You Are the Sunshine of My Life." Then she walked out to the podium and placed her script in front of her. It was definitely time to "rock and roll."

To say that the show went off like clockwork would have been an exaggeration, but there were a satisfying number of oohs and aahs as the amateur models made the most of their concrete catwalk. All of it synchronized to a soundtrack of songs with "sunshine" in their title. Of which it seemed there were many.

The applause was loud and sincere. The finale, which consisted of Dustin's valiant attempts to herd the twins, prompted laughter. When he finally picked Gemma off the ground and carted her the rest of the way, he received a spontaneous standing ovation.

"God, I'm glad we had two cameras on that," Kyra said to Troy. "I was laughing so hard I don't think I got more than a couple of usable seconds."

"Definitely video that can be held over him in his teenage years," Troy agreed. "You know, like on prom night and maybe right before his wedding." He grinned. "In the meantime it'll look great in the Sunshine sales video."

The ovation turned into a group sing-along of the chorus to "Aquarius/Let the Sunshine In" as the models circled one last time.

There was a hugging frenzy at the podium and a rush of attendees offering their congratulations as they moved inside to peruse the clothing up close and make their selections. Nikki smiled for the local press and watched two television reporters do stand-ups with the Sunshine in the background.

"You were great!" Joe said when the crowd around her finally dispersed. "I'd say the show was a success from every point of view."

"Thanks. It did go well, didn't it?" The adrenaline rush had begun to slow but the sense of accomplishment remained.

"I'll say. There's serious buying going on in there," Joe said. "And I know John and Steve are happy with the turnout and attention. They sold at least three cottages and a bunch of beach club memberships."

Nikki drew a deep breath of air into her lungs, and felt a glow of well-being.

"There you two are!"

They turned to see Luvie approaching with Gemma and Sofia already neatly tucked into the jogging stroller.

"Congratulations, Mrs. G. That was a marvelous fashion show," Luvie said.

"Thanks." Nikki smiled at the nanny. "I thought Dustin

and the girls were fabulous and totally stole the show." She grinned down at her daughters, her heart filling with love.

"Would you like me to take them home for their nap?" Luvie hesitated. "Or would you prefer to do the honors?"

Nikki met the older woman's eyes, saw the goodwill in them. "I'd really appreciate you putting them down for a nap." She smiled. "But thank you for asking."

"Not at all." The nanny smiled back. "Off we go then." She turned the stroller and off they went, the twins jabbering in their own private language and not even looking back. This time Nikki saw it as the good thing that it was.

"Well done, Nik," Joe said with an approving smile. "I know you were too busy to eat. Why don't I take you somewhere for lunch?"

"Hmmmm, I guess I could eat," she said. "But do you mind if we just go up to the rooftop grill? I'm too tired to even walk to the car."

They made it up the Plexiglas stairs and took a table overlooking the beach. Joe ordered them cheeseburgers and fries.

"So, one fashion show and luncheon down," Joe said. "What do you see happening next?"

She looked at her husband's handsome face, with the kind eyes and their web of smile lines, and thought how lucky she was to have found this man, who was even more attractive on the inside. "I haven't thought this all the way through, but I believe the vintage is going to continue to sell well. I'll be interested to see what I can make happen with an expanded showroom in the lobby. Then if Bitsy actually buys the downtown Y and it's renovated for mixed use . . . I don't know . . . maybe we could add a second location."

"You want to run two retail stores?" he asked, his surprise evident.

She was a little surprised herself, but it felt good.

"Well, nothing's going to happen tomorrow. But I really enjoy the research and buying, and it felt great to have something to sink my teeth into. We did *Do Over* out of necessity. This is the first work-related thing that's felt like *me* since I lost Heart, Inc. And now that we're paying Luvie for all those hours . . ."

"Touché." Joe smiled. "I wondered how long it would take you to get to that."

"Oh, I plan to give you shit about it for the next twenty years or so," she teased. "But you were right that having help, especially with twins, isn't necessarily a sign of weakness." She toyed with the glass of water that had arrived, and forced herself to meet his eyes. "Do you forgive me? It just seemed so important to prove that I could take care of the girls on my own, but I'm sorry I lied."

He reached across the table and took her hand. "I'd like to believe we can talk things out better in the future. But you were right, too—I didn't really consider where you were coming from. And I didn't listen the way I should have." He exhaled. "But in the future I'd rather yell it out than hide things from each other."

"Agreed," she said, squeezing his hand. "Are you really okay if we stay here?"

"Yes." He looked out over the beach and the gulf that it bounded. The Don CeSar stood tall just to the north. "I think this beach suits us. And it's a quieter, gentler place to raise children than South Beach."

She sighed in relief and felt a renewed sense of peace at his answer. This was the closest thing to home she could remember since her own childhood.

The burgers and fries arrived and Joe handed her the ketchup. "I expect you to eat every morsel on your plate. And then we're going to order an exceedingly fattening dessert."

"Is that right?" She went for a challenging tone, but for the first time in a long time she felt an odd stirring in her belly that she thought might be hunger.

"It is. I don't want you to lose another ounce. I can't let the mother of my children waste away."

Nikki smiled as she doused the fries and added a dollop to the burger. Her stomach rumbled, but she was starting to think it wasn't a rumble of hunger but of happiness. With Joe's dark eyes pinned on her face, she picked up the burger and took a huge bite. He watched her chew. At his smile of encouragement, she took another bite. Then she had a fry. And another.

With a nod he picked up his own burger and began to eat.

Briefly, she considered giving him a hard time. But the burger was delicious and she wasn't sure she'd ever had fries that tasted as good as these. There might, in fact, be such a thing as "too thin," but at the moment she was very glad there was no such thing as too happy.

. . .

The last of the guests and models had left and cleanup was done, when Maddie felt eyes on her. She looked up from the rack of clothes she'd been straightening.

"Hello, Maddie-fan." Will walked toward her, his craggy face lit with a mischievous smile.

"Will? Oh, my God! What . . . how . . ." She laughed and shook her head. "You've got me stuttering again. Why didn't you tell me you were coming? When did you get here?" Not waiting for an answer she rushed into his arms and looped hers around his neck. His lips were warm as they kissed through their smiles. She breathed in his spicy, masculine scent, felt the hard planes and angles of his body.

"I wasn't totally sure I was going to make it, so I thought I'd take a chance and surprise you. I got in too late for the fashion show, but I did stop to check in at the Don."

"You're staying at a hotel?"

"I'm kind of hoping we both are," he said, his smile growing wider. "Your place is a little small for four, plus the dog and I've only got a couple of days. I've missed you. I figured this way we could, um, make the most of them."

She felt a ripple of what she'd learned to recognize as lust, but also a tremor of trepidation. Now that the artificial existence that was life on tour was over, would he expect to discuss what would come next?"

"Of course, I'm happy to feed you first, you know, to build up your strength," he teased.

"That's very generous of you. But I've already eaten."

"Hmmmm . . . maybe a walk on the beach then? I wouldn't mind stretching my legs."

"Sounds good." She stuffed her phone in her pocket. At the low wall she took off her shoes and stepped onto the beach, her bare feet sinking into the cool, soft sand. Will took her hand in his and led her down toward the water.

"How were the last gigs?" she asked when they hit the hard-packed sand and turned toward the Don CeSar, its huge pink castle-like walls and white-trimmed windows in stark contrast to the brilliant blue sky.

"Really good," Will said. "Except I swear the whole damned crew was in Maddie withdrawal. Everybody sends their best." He smiled and though she couldn't see his eyes through the dark sunglasses, she knew that they turned the color of whiskey when he smiled, and could imagine the crinkles around them. His dark hair with its gray threads brushed his shoulders and stirred in the breeze as he turned his face up toward the sun. He slung his arm across her shoulders as they passed the Don and continued their walk.

A windsurfer cut across a low swell. In the sky a small plane towed its banner for an all-you-can-eat shrimp dinner at a local restaurant. She saw people recognize Will as they passed and was relieved when no one approached them.

"How are Kyra and Dustin doing?" Will asked as they walked through the shallow water.

"Better," she said. I think they're as glad to be home as . . ." Her voice trailed off.

"As you are?" he asked quietly.

"Oh. I . . . I hope you don't think . . . I . . . I . . . didn't mean . . ."

He stopped and removed his sunglasses. A small smile played at the corners of his lips as his eyes met hers. "You think I don't know that this is *home* to you?"

"Well, of course you do. I . . . I . . . just didn't want you to think that that meant that I . . . don't um, didn't want . . ." This was what came of being taken by surprise. She hadn't stuttered this badly since the day they'd met.

"It's okay, Maddie." His smile turned rueful. "That's how I feel about Mermaid Point. It meant a lot to me that you came on tour with me. Hell, everything's better when we're together." He grinned. "With the possible exception of fly fishing. No offense intended."

"I feel the same way." She laughed. "And no offense taken. Although I'm sure the fish population of the Keys is missing the entertainment I typically provide."

"I think you might be right about that." He bent down and kissed her, his lips moving on hers until she could feel the blood whooshing through her veins. "But I brought something I want to give you. And there's something I've been wanting to ask."

She looked up into his face, but her heart was thumping and she didn't hear what he said next, because her thoughts were pinging off each other and she was hearing what she'd said to Avery about how she shouldn't be afraid to make a commitment to the man she loved and who loved her. About telling the truth. And what was that logical next step for two people who loved each other but marriage?

Will reached into his pocket and pulled out a small jewelry box. Air rushed out of her lungs. She fell back a step. Panic flooded through her.

"What's wrong?" he asked. "What's . . ."

But she was shaking her head, putting out a hand to stop him. "I love you, Will. And I love being with you. I do. It's just . . . I can't . . ." She looked into his eyes but saw only confusion. Well, who could blame him? She needed to head him off at the pass here, explain what she was only now just fully realizing, before he asked a question she'd have to say no to. "I just . . . I was . . . The thing is I was married for twenty-five years. I gave Steve and Kyra and Andrew all of me. I revolved around them. I can't . . . I don't want . . . I can't do that again." She swallowed, aghast at the words that had come pouring out of her. All of it true, but still not what someone about to propose would want to hear. "I'm so sorry, but I just can't marry you."

She exhaled. Braced for anger or disappointment.

Will blinked in what could only be surprise. "Whoa. Whoa. What?"

"And if that means you'd be happier with someone who can make that kind of commitment, make you the center of their universe, I'll hate it, but I'll understand."

He blinked again. Straightened. Opened the jewelry box.

It was her turn to blink. Because the piece that now glittered in his hand was not a ring, but a truly beautiful reproduction of his Gibson acoustic guitar complete with strings made of gold and diamonds on the frets.

For a brief moment she was afraid he was going to laugh.

"I had this made especially for you by an artist I know as a memento of the tour and a thank-you for helping me find my way back to everything I was running away from when we met," he said as heat flooded her cheeks, and she prayed for the sand to open up and swallow her or a wave to come and pull her out to sea. "I didn't mean to scare you with it."

"Oh, my God!" She couldn't face him. She'd never be able to look him in the eye again. She made to turn, but he reached out and grabbed her arm before she could take a step.

"No, don't run. Don't go. And don't you dare be embarrassed." His voice was quiet but urgent as he turned her so that their backs were to the beach and no one could see their faces. "Because I love you, Maddie. I am all in. And if you wanted to marry me, or even thought you might, I would happily drop down on one knee right this second and ask you."

She closed her eyes tight, willing this to be a dream, but the wet sand between her toes and the salt breeze teasing at her skin were real. And so was the man holding her against him.

"We're lucky as hell to have found each other. We're great together, Maddie. But we don't have to be married unless we decide one day we want to be. Or even live in the same place unless at some point we decide to. The only people we need to please or answer to are ourselves."

He turned her in his arms. "Are you listening to me, Maddie? Do you understand what I'm saying?"

She forced herself to look up into his eyes and saw only love and admiration shining out of them. She'd been telling herself all this time that she could do anything, be anything, choose anything. But deep inside she had only considered traditional choices. Will was right. "Can it really be that simple?"

"I don't see why not," he said. "You're more than I ever dreamed of, Maddie." He leaned down and kissed her. "I like us just the way we are," he murmured. "And if it ain't broke, there's absolutely no need to fix it."

He kissed her again, his mouth insistent on hers, until she forgot where they were and most of her embarrassment and everything else but the feel of his lips and the words of love he kept whispering.

# Thirty-seven

Bertrand Baynard walked out of the Jetway at Miami International Airport looking a little the worse for wear. He glanced down at his phone then up at the departure board, no doubt checking the status of his connecting flight to Buenos Aires. Which he would not be on.

It had been almost fourteen months since Bitsy had last seen her husband. Fourteen months since he'd disappeared without a word of warning or apology to start a shiny new life without her. Her heartbeat sped up and she could feel her pulse skittering in her veins.

Joe Giraldi stepped forward. "Hello, Bertie."

Bertie's eyes widened. "You? You ripped me off!" He said this with an odd mix of shock and anger. "You stole everything I had and you have the nerve to show up here?"

"It sucks, doesn't it?" Bitsy stepped out of the shadows, her eyes on his face. Her legs wobbled as she took her place next to Joe, but she kept her head up and her gaze steady. So she got to watch his face fall. Saw him look from her to Joe and back again. Had the pleasure of seeing him put two and two together.

"You?" he asked, and the shock on his face would have been

comical if it hadn't confirmed what she'd suspected. He'd barely given her a thought since he'd left her. It had never occurred to him that she might come after him.

"Afraid so," she said. "Poor, stupid, little old trusting me." She stared into the eyes that she'd once thought beautiful and intelligent and now just looked shifty. He glanced down at his watch, the antique Rolex that had been her grandfather's and that she'd given him as a wedding gift. When she had been so stupidly in love.

"I was willing to share it all, but it wasn't enough for you. You stole everything, Bertie. Everything. You made me a pariah and a laughingstock. Not to mention homeless."

"I'm sorry." He threw out the apology with all the panicked sincerity of a child caught with his hand in a candy jar. But she heard not even a tinge of remorse. "Is that what you came to hear?" He shrugged. "Things went south and I couldn't recover."

"And so you ran and took what was left with you."

He checked his watch again.

"Where's Delilah? Or are you running out on her, too?"

"She's not in the picture anymore."

"Did she leave before or after you lost all your, I mean, my money?"

"Does it matter?" He glanced around as if looking for a way out. But the only way was through Joe.

"And your child?" She'd tortured herself all this time with images of him doting on Delilah and their baby. Lavishing them with attention and everything her money could buy.

"There was no child. It turned out she was never pregnant." He said this as if it hardly mattered, and she knew once and for all that there had been no extenuating circumstances. No compelling reason for his betrayal. There'd been only greed and self-interest. If he'd ever loved her at all, it had been far too weak an emotion to weather the smallest storm.

"But of course she could have been." Just as Susan White could have been and maybe a whole host of others.

"Is there something you want?" he asked. "A point of some kind? Apparently you and your friend here got almost everything back. But I've got a plane to catch, so I don't really have time to play twenty questions."

"I'm entitled to answers, Bertie. And a divorce." She motioned to the waiting process server June Steding had sent and whom Joe had brought in with them.

The server took advantage of Bertie's surprise to step up and put the divorce papers in his hand. "You have been served." He held up a clipboard and a pen. "Please sign here."

"Seriously?" Bertie smirked as he signed the papers. "You staged all this to get a divorce?"

"Not exactly. But you have cured me of marriage." She drew a deep breath. Beside her, Joe turned his head and nodded.

"Right then. So, if you're finished with me, I've got a flight to catch." Bertie took a step forward. Before he could take a second, a Department of Homeland Security agent and a uniformed deputy from the Palm Beach County Sheriff's Office stepped into position next to Joe. "Bertrand Baynard?"

"Yes?"

"Mr. Baynard," the DHS agent said. "You are under arrest for multiple counts of fraud and grand theft. And will now be escorted back to Palm Beach to await trial."

Bertie's smirk disappeared. His face flushed with shock and disbelief. "What the hell? What are you talking about?"

The deputy stepped forward. Joe looked on silently, but Bitsy saw the smile of satisfaction on his lips.

"This is bullshit!" Bertie protested as the deputy handcuffed him. "You can't do this! I want an attorney!"

"Good luck with that," Bitsy said. "They're not so responsive when you don't have money to pay them. But I'm sure the court will appoint one for you."

"This is total bullshit!" Bertie hissed.

Bitsy watched him struggle against the handcuffs as reality began to set in.

"You ready?" Joe asked quietly.

"Almost." She squared her shoulders and looked at her soon-to-be ex-husband. "For the record, you really shouldn't use women and discard them the way you do. It really pisses us off. Hell hath no fury and all that."

Bertie's eyes narrowed.

"Take Susan White, for instance. This might not even be happening if you'd taken her with you like you'd promised. She's agreed to testify against you in exchange for immunity."

"God," Bertie said. "You've turned into a real bitch."

Beside her, Joe took a menacing step forward. Bitsy put a hand out to stop him.

"But I didn't start out that way. You, on the other hand, have apparently always been a cheat, a thief, and a liar."

She stood watching as the deputy led him away, only slumping when he'd disappeared from view. She'd gotten revenge and struck a small blow for womankind. It was time to make the triumphant exit she'd imagined.

Only the gate and the waiting passengers blurred in a kaleidoscope of color. There was a sucking silence in her ears. And she seemed to be having trouble catching her breath and moving her feet. Her hand shook as she lifted it to her cheek. It was wet.

She turned toward the blur that was Joe. "Am I crying?"

"You are. And you have good reason." He put an arm around her shoulders and drew her close. She squeezed her eyes shut and buried her face in his chest.

"But I'm supposed to be happy," she cried into his jacket. "I thought I'd be . . . so happy."

He simply stood and let her cry what felt like a flood of tears.

Telling her it would be all right, that she'd done what she had to do, in the same voice she'd heard him use to calm the twins.

Finally, the flood began to recede. She lifted her head, swiped at her cheeks. "This is what I wanted. But I feel like shit. I'm completely pathetic."

"No," he said with complete assurance. "You are strong and smart. And you didn't roll over and let him get away with what he did. You can be proud of that. You will be once the adrenaline is out of your system."

She looked at the sodden mess she'd made of his clothes. "I think I owe you a new shirt."

"Not necessary. I kind of enjoyed myself." His lips quirked upward. "In fact, while he was spouting all that shit and I was reminding myself that even though I was here in an unofficial capacity, I really couldn't punch his lights out, I started thinking maybe you should ask Nikki for a refund on this match."

She snorted. "Yeah, well, I'm gonna want you to be there when I ask her and she finds out it was your idea."

He threw back his head and laughed. "Listen, Bitsy. Bottom line, you got a good chunk of your money back and you handled yourself beautifully today. Plus, we caught the bad guy. In my line of work that calls for a celebration."

"It does?" she asked skeptically. She'd begun to breathe more normally, but she wasn't entirely certain the waterworks were over.

"It does. How long do you have until your flight back?"

She pulled out her phone, roused it. Her first normal act in a completely abnormal day. "About an hour and a half."

"Perfect." He slung a friendly arm around her shoulders. "Come on. There's a bar right over there. I'll buy you a drink."

"Thanks, Joe. For everything." She sniffed, swiped at her cheeks, then reached over to pat his tear-soaked shirt. "All things considered, the drinks are on me. If we drink them fast, I should have time for at least two."

• • •

It seemed to Avery that everyone but her had somehow managed to get their shit together. Kyra and Troy were clearly "a thing," and Kyra and Dustin might even move back into Bella Flora. Maddie and Will had found a way to continue their relationship without having to move or get married. Nikki had tamed Mary Poppins and she was already starting to kick ass with the vintage and retro beachwear. Even Bitsy had stopped being a victim and not only gotten a lot of her money back, but had the satisfaction of being there to watch Bertie carted off to jail.

They were all moving forward with their lives. Only she seemed stuck in a limbo of her own making, unable to step all the way back or move all the way in. And seriously unable to concentrate.

"Good grief!" Ray Flamingo waved both hands in front of her face to get her attention, which should have been focused on the floor plan in front of them. "Please. I beg you. Call him. Work something out. Even a booty call might improve things."

"Not funny," she snapped.

"Not joking."

She repositioned the floor plan and huffed at him in irritation, but it was more of a sigh than a huff.

Ray grimaced. "Boy, that was weak."

Normally she would have huffed back at him with both barrels, but she just didn't have the strength. Her jaw was tight from gritting her teeth and holding back tears. Her body was exhausted from the dead weight of unhappiness that had wrapped itself around her. And her chest . . . yesterday the dull ache she'd grown used to had become so sharp that she thought she might be having a heart attack. And wasn't sure she cared.

"Come with me." Ray took her by the shoulders and gently, for him, propelled her out of Hannah Friedan's cottage and down the walkway to Maddie's.

He knocked lightly. "It's Ray. Is the doctor in? I brought a patient."

Maddie pulled open the door.

"This woman needs fixing. Or possibly a cattle prod."

"How about grilled cheese?" Maddie asked.

A warm melted cheese smell wafted out. And it might as well have been broccoli.

"I told you it was bad," Ray said when Avery didn't react. He pushed her through the door then closed it behind him.

"Come sit down." Maddie wiped off Dustin's face and hands then sent him and Max into the bedroom to play. Moments later she set a plate that contained a grilled cheese sandwich and a mound of Cheez Doodles in front of Avery. A glass of milk followed.

"Thank you."

"You're welcome. There's more if you want it."

She picked up a Cheez Doodle because she might be grossly unhappy, but she was still breathing. She bit into it, but its normal cheesy wonderfulness was missing. She set it back on the plate.

Maddie's eyes brimmed with sympathy. "Tell me where it hurts."

"It's my chest. I feel like someone punched a hole in it and everything's leaking out." She looked up into Maddie's eyes. "And all these great things are happening work-wise and Chase is the only person who would really understand. He would love the Y even more than I do and I can't even show it to him."

"Why not?"

"Because basically he told me not to bother him unless I'm ready to get married."

"He actually said that?" Maddie asked.

"Pretty much."

"Avery, honey, all relationships require compromise—by both parties. You two are going to have to talk this through."

"But how?"

"I'm not sure. But you're going to have to be in the same place." She thought for a moment. "Why don't you ask him to come see the Y—I'm sure Bitsy can arrange it. Then just show him around and talk about the building. See how it feels. Maybe it will propel you forward. Or maybe it'll confirm that he's not someone you want to spend your life with. Or maybe you two will find something in the middle that will work. All I know is that you can't keep torturing yourself like this. Sometimes it's better to make a decision, even if it's not a perfect one, than to do nothing at all."

Now here she stood three days later on the sidewalk in front of the Y watching Chase walk toward her. She was dry mouthed and sweaty palmed while he moved as if he didn't have a care in the world and might start whistling at any moment.

Dark stubble covered his face, his bright blue eyes were clear and direct, his smile was . . . friendly-ish. More appropriate for discussing a renovation than coming to grips with a joint future.

"So Bitsy's thinking of buying the building?" he asked, turning to take in the facade.

"Yes." She tried to gather her thoughts, but she was so aware of him it was hard to think. "The plan is to restore it as closely as possible to original while turning it multiuse. A lot of interior demo has already been completed."

She removed the padlock and he helped shove the temporary fencing that stretched across the front stairs out of the way. As they walked up to the front door, she watched him take in the chipped plaster and cracked stonework. Neither of them spoke until they'd stepped inside and closed the heavy arched wooden door behind them.

Chase did a 360 in the center of the tiled lobby, emitting a low whistle as he turned, taking in the ten-light windows, the stair's decorative iron railing. "Even all beat up she's a beauty."

He ran a hand over a pockmarked wall and it was a caress. "I swear I can hear her crying out for help."

And there it was. "I know. It's the weirdest thing. But from the first I felt like she'd been waiting. There've been multiple owners, all kinds of people promising her things and pulling at her and taking her apart piece by piece. Only to let her down. Somehow she's been hanging on and waiting for the right person. For me." She swallowed, gathered her courage. She'd vowed that whatever happened today, she would at least be honest. "Or maybe for us."

He looked at her closely, and she looked back, careful to mask her neediness even as she felt the pull of him, true north on her internal compass. She showed him through the space, but while his eyes moved from detail to detail, her eyes remained on him. She saw the way he held himself. Saw him run a hand gently over an expanse of hand-painted tile, saw him fall in love just like she had.

"The original barrel tiles are in here." She took him to one of the rooms in which row after row of roof tiles had been laid out on the floor. They crouched down together as she pointed out the doves that had been stamped on the ends of the terracotta tiles. "Enrico would go crazy over this building. He's the only person I'd trust to do this roof."

"I wouldn't mind having the whole Dante family here," Chase agreed.

It was Chase who had first introduced her to the family of artisans whose ancestors had first been brought over from Italy by Addison Mizner to work on the Mediterranean Revival–style homes and estates he'd built all over Palm Beach. Members of the family had spread throughout Florida and had worked on Bella Flora and the Millicent in South Beach as well as Mermaid Point and even the Sunshine.

"Why don't we send them some shots of the building? I don't

think it would take much more than that to get them to sign on."

She heard the "we" and knew that she had him. Like her, he was already imagining the restoration, thinking about what could be taken back to original, what would have to change. But could they manage a professional partnership if their personal relationship fell apart? Would she even want to?

"Do you have sketches?" he asked.

"A few. Nothing formal. But Bitsy asked me to draw the plans."

He leaned back against a wall. "How long until construction might start?"

"Well, first Bitsy has to actually buy it. I'm sure that's not going to happen overnight. And I do have other work. Martha Wyatt loves her tiny home. Before it was even finished she referred me to a friend who bought a cottage at the Sunshine; quite a few sold as a result of the fashion show. I have the opportunity to finish them out. And I will but . . ."

"This would be a once-in-a-lifetime opportunity." He completed her sentence. And all she wanted was to throw her arms around him and never let go.

She managed to resist by turning and leading him up the stairs. On the third floor they stepped out onto a sawdust-strewn patio and leaned over the concrete balustrade to take in the view of Tropicana Field and a slice of downtown. She knew the time had come to get to the heart of the matter but instead heard herself asking, "How's your dad?"

Then she asked about Josh and about Jason, all of whom seemed to be doing great. She watched his face as he talked, but what she was listening to was her own internal debate. Her litany of fears. Her candy-assed worries that it wouldn't work out. As if she hadn't survived her mother's desertion, her father's death, a divorce, the loss of two television shows, and Malcolm Dyer's Ponzi scheme.

What was the point of being careful? She'd known Chase since childhood and loved him long before she'd even realized it. She was completely miserable without him. What exactly was she waiting for? And what was the use of being safe if you were only living half a life?

"Avery?"

"Hmmm?"

"Are you all right?"

"Of course." She attempted a reassuring smile but it felt kind of quivery. Before she could dissemble or chicken out she said, "I was just thinking how much I'd like for us to work on this project together."

He cocked his head and looked at her in a way that made her fear he could see all the way inside. She wasn't sure what he was looking for.

"Even if we're, you know, just . . . together professionally." She hesitated then forced herself on. "Would it bother Riley if we worked together?"

"Riley who?"

"You're not seeing her anymore?" She tried not to sound too hopeful.

"I barely saw her in the first place."

"But you brought her to Bella Flora. She answered your phone."

His shrug was sheepish.

"You just *pretended* to date her?"

"Well, no. I took her out a few times. But mostly because I hoped it would finally make you see the light."

For a moment she considered pushing him over the side of the balcony. It wasn't that far. He might even survive.

"I have been absolutely miserable and it was just a ploy?"

He brightened. "How miserable were you?"

She slugged him in the arm. It hurt. "I don't believe this!"

"Hey, desperate times call for desperate measures," he said.

But seconds later the smile flickered out. His tone turned serious. "Aw, hell, Avery. I love you, and I've been miserable, too. More than miserable. I've missed you so much it hurts."

She froze for a moment as his words sank in. Her own heart leapt as his lips quirked. "And desperate measures call for . . ."

"Truth!" She automatically shouted the name of the game their families had played together when they were children. On the count of three each person had to say something true.

"All right," he said. "Category?"

"About the building," she said. "One, two . . .

"You're the only one I want to work on this building with," she said at the same time he said, "There's no way I'm going to let anyone besides me work on this building with you."

They laughed. Okay. It was a start.

"Category?" he asked.

"Riley Hancock."

He counted them down.

On three she shouted, "I bet she couldn't even drive in a nail!" While he shouted, "She couldn't spell 'construction'!"

They both laughed. A laugh that unclogged her throat and began to mend the hole in her heart. "Category?" she called out.

He looked her in the eye and said, "Marriage."

She held his gaze, swallowed. "All right. One, two . . ." On three she closed her eyes and said, "I love you and I'm ready to get married." He said, "I love you and we don't have to get married."

She opened her eyes. "Did you mean that?"

"Did you?"

She snorted. "This is unbelievable. I finally agree and you don't want to get married anymore?"

"That's not exactly what I said," he countered. "And I'm starting to remember why I always hated this game." He grinned.

"This isn't funny."

"Actually, it is."

"All right," she conceded. "It's a little funny." All she knew was she could breathe again. And they were not only talking to each other, they were laughing.

"So, I think I have an idea," he said. "A compromise."

"I'm listening."

"*You* agree to marry me at some mutually agreed-upon time in the future before we require walkers and still have our teeth. And *I* give you this." He pulled a small jeweler's box out of his pocket and opened it. The emerald-cut diamond glittered in the afternoon light.

"But . . . that was your mother's."

"Yeah." Chase smiled. "She would have wanted you to have it. And Dad insisted."

Her vision blurred as he lifted it out of the box. Elaine Hardin had mothered her when her own mother had not.

The first tears fell as Chase sank down on one knee and reached for her hand. "Are you good with this?"

She nodded. "Are you?" Tears of happiness slid down her cheeks and dropped into the sawdust-strewn concrete as he slid the ring on her finger.

"Hell, yes," he said beaming. Rising to his feet, he took her into his arms. "I can't wait to get started here. In the meantime, you know how I react to the smell of sawdust."

She smiled as he nuzzled her ear, bent to kiss his way down her neck to the sensitive hollow at her throat. It was a smell that never failed to stir her.

"The only thing that could turn me on more right now is if you had a hammer in your hand," he murmured. "Or you weren't wearing anything except your tool belt."

She laughed even as she continued to cry, but he wasn't the only one who couldn't seem to hold on tight enough. His kiss was deep and drugging.

"You're going to have to stop crying, though," he said, finally lifting his mouth from hers.

"I know." She nodded and sniffed, but the tears continued to flow. When she smiled she could taste their sweet saltiness.

"After all," he said, tucking her under one arm and pulling her against him. "We're going to be working on this place soon. And everybody knows there's no crying in construction."

# Epilogue

It was almost April. The sky was a bold and beautiful blue decorated with wisps of white clouds. It was their first sunset at Bella Flora since Kyra and Dustin had moved back in, and they intended to make the most of it.

"Do you think she missed us as much as we've missed her?" Maddie asked as she followed her daughter down the central hallway and into the kitchen.

"Are you kidding?" Kyra asked. "I'm pretty sure I heard her sigh with relief when Dustin and I carried our stuff in. Now I just feel her smiling."

"Well, it was nice of Troy to move into the pool house," Maddie said as she unpacked the Ted Peters smoked fish spread and began to spread it on crackers. "And she doesn't look any the worse for wear or a lack of female occupants."

Kyra smiled. "Shocking, isn't it?"

Nikki and Bitsy arrived with the ingredients for strawberry daiquiris. Soon the whir of the blender drifted across the hall from the Casbah Lounge. Avery joined them in the kitchen with the requisite family-size bag of Cheez Doodles and a bag from a local gourmet shop. The engagement ring Chase had given her sparkled on her finger.

Soon the food was plated and the daiquiris blended. They carried their sunset snacks and drinks out to the loggia and settled around the wrought iron dining table. The breeze off the water was gentle and cool. Boats moved slowly through the pass. Above and beyond it birds rode unseen jets of air, the caw of gulls mingling with the low whine of boat motors.

"Wow," Nikki said as she began to fill everyone's glasses. "Where did the caviar and toast points come from?"

"I brought them in Deirdre's honor," Avery said. "I hope wherever she is she knows about Chase and me."

"I'm betting yes," Maddie said as they began to fill small plates. "And I'm equally sure she's thrilled about it."

Avery reached for a Cheez Doodle. "Jeff said that he and my dad always thought we'd be a good match. I did have a brief crush on him as a teenager, you know, before he became such a pain in the ass."

Kyra laughed. "Funny how sometimes the biggest pains in the ass can turn out to have such nice stuff hidden inside."

"That's for sure," Nikki agreed. "If you'd told me when special agent Joe Giraldi was using me to try to catch my brother that he'd end up being the father of my children, I would have said you were out of your mind."

"Ditto," Maddie said. "Remember how obnoxious Will was when we landed on Mermaid Point?"

"And then there was Bertie, who looked so good and turned out to have a rotten center," Bitsy said.

"Almost nothing has turned out the way I would have written it," Maddie said. "You know, if we were in a novel and I was the author."

"There've been a lot of plot twists and things we didn't see coming, all right," Kyra said. "I remember the first time I saw Bella Flora. When I was pregnant with Dustin and still thought Daniel was going to come and carry me off on his white horse."

"Yes, well, that would have been a shorter story," Nikki said. "More like a fairy tale."

"Speaking of the dark prince, what have you heard about the film?" Bitsy asked, taking a sip of her daiquiri.

"They managed to finish without Dustin," Kyra said. "And honestly, at the moment that's all I care about. I don't think Dustin will be hearing much from his dad until they at least get through the first cut."

"Do you remember the first time we saw Bella Flora?" Nikki asked. "She smelled like a locker room full of moldy bathing suits. And she didn't look much better."

"She was in horrible shape," Maddie said. "But Avery fell in love with her at first sight, and John Franklin kept trying to get us to see beyond the dirt and grime."

"If we'd had the muscle or the money to tear her down, we wouldn't be sitting here right now," Nikki said quietly. "I was so furious at the time I considered pulling her down with my bare hands."

"And if she hadn't been so horrible, we would have sold her." Maddie smiled and raised her glass. "I think that's tonight's first good thing. To Bella Flora. If we'd been able to tear her down or sell her, our lives would have been completely different. We probably never would have even gotten to know each other."

"To Bella Flora!" They clinked and drank.

Maddie felt Bella Flora's thick plaster walls hunched protectively behind them, sensed her approval. They had brought her back to life and she had done the same for them. No matter what came next she would forever be a part of their story.

"I have a good thing to toast," Bitsy said. "I've reached an agreement with the current owner of the former Y and I've already retained a company to design and renovate. Half that company is sitting here right now." She nodded and raised her glass to Avery. Once again they toasted and drank.

"Which brings me to my good thing," Avery said as Nikki refilled glasses all around. "Chase and I were approached by

Netflix. They were looking for a husband-and-wife team to do an original renovation show. We convinced them to go with an engaged couple and their merry band of friends who renovate a historic YMCA."

"I'm taking it that we're the merry band?" Nikki asked.

"I sure hope so," Kyra said. "Because Troy and I already had an initial conversation with them to pitch the newly formed Singer Matthews Productions as shooter/producers, and we assured them that the former cast of *Do Over* was going to be a part of it."

Kyra raised her glass. "To Netflix, the Y, and the merry band. My good thing is that we're finally going to get to do the *Do Over* we originally intended."

They clinked and drank as the sun hovered over the gulf, its reflected brilliance shimmering beneath it.

"If we toast too much more, someone's going to have to carry me inside," Kyra said.

"Tell me about it." Avery slathered caviar on a toast point and popped it into her mouth. "I'm starting to think Deirdre might have known what she was talking about. This caviar business isn't half bad."

Maddie joined in the laughter and sighed with contentment. The temperature had begun to drop but the warmth of friendship was better than any blanket. They had Bella Flora and each other to guard their backs. And one more good thing to toast. "I think it's your turn, Nikki. Do you want to tell them or should I?" Maddie looked at the woman who had evolved so dramatically since the day they'd all first pulled up in front of the neglected house that had become home in all the ways that mattered.

"All right," Nikki said. "I'm happy to announce that Maddie and I have already reserved space in Bitsy's building for a vintage clothing and designer consignment shop. I'm going to handle the buying and she's going to focus on organization and staffing. That way I'll have time for Joe and the girls and she can travel when she wants." She raised her glass. "To good things!"

"To good things and great people to share them with!" Maddie added as the puddle of red sun oozed into the gulf and leached the last bits of color from the sky. "Most of all, to our friendship. And to getting to live right here on the best beach ever!"

They sat and talked in the gathering dusk, their faces alight with excitement over all that lay ahead. If this were, in fact, a novel, the author might be tempted to type "the end."

But Maddie knew that the journey they'd so unexpectedly begun together was far from over. It was just time to turn the page, so a new chapter could begin.

# BEST BEACH EVER

## WENDY WAX

# DISCUSSION QUESTIONS

1. At the beginning of the book, Madeline Singer, Avery Lawford, Nicole Grant, Kyra Singer, and Bitsy Baynard are living at the Sunshine Hotel and Beach Club. How do they each feel about the fact that Kyra has been forced to rent out Bella Flora? Is it harder on some of the women than others?

2. Madeline is an amazing mother and tends to nurture everyone around her. Is there a Madeline figure in your life? Maybe your own mother or someone you met later in life who offers you sage advice in difficult situations? Madeline often struggles to put her own needs before the needs of others. Do you identify with her feelings of being torn between her loved ones and finding a career path of her own? Do you agree with the choices Madeline makes in the novel?

3. Avery wonders if she can trust Chase again after his emotional betrayals in the past. Do you understand her reluctance to enter into a relationship with him again? Do you believe people deserve a second chance? Is love between two people enough to overcome any relationship difficulty?

4. Do you agree with Kyra's decision to let her son Dustin act in his father's movie? What does Kyra learn about Daniel Deranian's and Tonja's parenting skills while she and Dustin live on the movie set? How does Kyra change as a mother throughout the novel? How do her feelings toward Daniel and Tonja change?

5. Nicole is struggling with motherhood. Why do you think she wants to prove she can look after the twins on her own? Does society put pressure on women to be perfect mothers? Do you think Nicole is a perfectionist? What does she learn about mothering in the book? How is it similar to or different from what Kyra discovers about being a parent?

6. Nicole's body changes after giving birth. Do you understand why she struggles to come to terms with her new shape? Can you identify with her insecurities?

7. Bitsy has the opportunity to get revenge on her husband, who stole her fortune and ran away with another woman. Do you agree with how she punishes him? In the course of the book, Bitsy learns how hard divorce and abandonment can be on women and children. How has Bitsy changed since she lost her fortune?

8. Maddie, Avery, Kyra, Nikki, and Bitsy are a close group of friends who offer each other enormous support throughout the book. Do you have a similar circle of friends or one friend you can always count on? What makes your friendship so strong?

9. Which woman's challenges—Avery's, Kyra's, Maddie's, Nikki's, or Bitsy's—resonate most with you? Why?

Photo by Beth Kelly

**Wendy Wax**, a former broadcaster, is the author of thirteen novels, including *Sunshine Beach*, *A Week at the Lake*, *While We Were Watching Downton Abbey*, *The House on Mermaid Point*, *Ocean Beach*, and *Ten Beach Road*. The mother of two grown sons, she lives in the Atlanta suburbs with her husband and is doing her best to adjust to the quiet of her recently emptied nest. Visit her online at authorwendywax.com and on Facebook at facebook.com/authorwendywax, and follow her on Twitter @Wendy_Wax.